A PROMISE ALSO RINGS

BY R.C. PILLERT

MIGRAINE PUBLISHING
Published October 2017
Copyright © 2014 by R.C. Pillert
Cover designed by R.C. Pillert
Cover illustrations by R.C. Pillert
This book is a work of fiction.
All rights reserved.
ISBN 9780999278512

Acknowledgements

I want to thank my wife for her support and especially her invaluable second set of eyes on this project.

It is said that a woman is more than happy to point out a man's flaws. It is also said that a man is more than happy that she did not find them all, lest she not marry him.

ONE

For love can be etched round a star.
So placed beyond the heavens can its spirit be.
But temporal do these things ring...

As he sat on the bed, he thought about the unfinished poem of his youth and smiled wryly at the folly of youth. With its beautiful fresh faced, naïve belief in the promises we made to the ones we love, or have loved, and especially to ourselves. He turned to the meandering floral pattern in the nap of the carpet. As he drove his mind through its deep pile he felt the ache, the one that called him back to his shipwreck of youth and promises. The night would be long now and he hoped the woman he was about to meet could get him through at least part of it.

His mind surfaced when he heard a soft knock. He was about to get up, then remembered what the email stated and relaxed. When the door opened, his irises dilated to capture the glow of a woman, who was about to bring splendor into his night. He muttered loudly "Oh, God," when his splendor stepped into the room. He flinched wildly as anguish rapped what was left of his spirit. She waved her hands frantically, almost dropping her evening purse, when she saw his grimacing body language, and the repugnant twist to his mouth. "Oh, God, it's ok, it's ok, shhh, I'll leave, I'll leave. Please don't get upset. I'll leave."

Tranquility you knock on so few doors, he thought, as peace settled over him. Peace he had not felt in over a decade. He thought, oh heavenly Father what you've willed against me limits my claim against you if she be your recompense. Oh, grief chased soul of yesteryear, come; fragrant your thoughts in her fields of lavender and blue iris. Brief is this moment to steal in the shadow of his back, so stiff is his neck.

He felt paralyzed. Something deep inside was circling him. He wanted to gasp loudly as if he were in the clutches of a predator. He felt burning in his chest as he quivered in ecstasy from its crushing talons. He thought with deep reverence, my God, my pen. He stared into her eyes and thought do you bring my pen?

She was of average height and about his age, early thirties. Her blonde hair, demure frame, and prominent soft facial features found themselves competing like a middle child with her alarming blue and lavender eyes. She had a remarkable rare gene that took color to a place on the spectrum that a painter would not feel confident to palette.

He felt the winds of his past pick up, bringing with it a single stanza from one of the many incomplete poems of his past. As he stared into her eyes, he thought, so blue are you, so blue am I, and so blue was my yesteryear.

Confused by his unruly spectacle, she solicited for clarity. "I'm so sorry. Did you not read the email? I'm the fill in." She followed up with a formal scripted statement after he nodded. "If you would like, I'll leave, and we can reschedule you with someone more pleasing than I at your convenience. I don't want you to be upset with the service or me. We will make it right for you."

When she felt her client composed, she lowered her arms, which caused her three thin white bracelets on her left arm to tinkle as they fell to her wrist.

She felt as if she were apologizing again. "We shouldn't take these things personally that things aren't working out. It's nobody's fault that my appearance has fallen far short your expectations. I'm getting older."

She paused to torch the next apology that had formed in her mind. She now felt she was apologizing to herself for the assaults upon her youth. Her past blew her back to the bayou when she was a little girl watching the disinterested still waters, the jaded blue skies, and the unconcerned cypress, all going about their day as she trembled while listening to her mother's instructions. 'It always feels like rain Momma.'

Her past then placed her at the point when she was leaving adolescence. She felt tears pushing their way through as she thought, my mistakes of youth have punished me like the pedestrian girl next door. Neither one of us to have a date, know a kiss, nor hold a term of endearment close to our heart, because of the birthmark of circumstance the world has stamped upon us. She felt her grief trodden soul of her yesteryear reminding her. Our mistakes no matter how young we were or short lived they were... She paused in her thoughts to search her feelings for anything that might have changed, but finished with, our hounds will always be at our heels.

She narrowed her mind's eye and focused on the shortcomings of men, and said with a pitch in her voice as she glared at him, "A man uses his eye as an index of appearance to value, like some sort of credit scoring, when judging a woman's worth. An eye I don't understand."

She stiffened, then quickly flicked a tear with her middle finger that had seeped through, and said angrily, "A banal eye. An eye that all men possess and most prefer, while denying the other permission to capture the joy that lies on the other side. I don't understand that kind of mind or hear-" She stopped abruptly to chide herself for breaking.

He put his hands in his lap and listened as a stoic, intently, mind emptied of judgment or affirmation.

She collected herself, and cleared her throat in an attempt to regain professional control, but faltered, bitterly.

"Though your index has arbitrarily diminished my score, truly, there's so much more to me on the other side of all this, and that cannot be indexed. Walk in the shoes before judging crooked feet."

She forced a smile and moved confidently to salvage the remaining pieces of this demoralizing encounter by putting her heels together, straightening up, and clutching her evening purse firmly as the final proof of composure, which was the end of her apologizing. And now with a completely restored elegant posture, she cocked her head, and said with an unapologetic sharp edge, "Should I leave? Too old? Low score? Past any possibility?"

She suspended her rant when she noticed a light flickering in his eyes, caressing her. She questioned the veracity of her arguments, as she watched the flickering. Yet, her feelings were still hurting from the bruising his spectacle inflicted.

She thought, perhaps I misunderstood, and found her professional voice. "My name is Gwen if you're still interested."

The stoic stiffened. His eyes widened slightly, but he remained reserved as he thought, oh Father, your recompense has now revealed her full symmetry. I see that she yields far more than a blessing, surly not a cruel hoax. I've thought You many things, but not that.

He turned to her makeup stains his spectacle caused, and said with tenderness, "You misinterpret my reaction. It comes from a part of me that is in a long standing battle over conscience. You're very beautiful and I believe you have a deep emotional range unmatched by any woman."

He pondered her challenge to her value. "And that eye you speak of belongs to a man who knows nothing of the treasures that lie in the glow of a woman."

The stoic, genuine in his remarks, straightened up and continued. "And the other side is the better part of you and of all women. It holds a spiritual dowry most men will never appreciate, nor understand as sacred. Inside are many possessions she longs to give, but they don't tolerate contingencies or consider anything as conditional. She won't give them easily, but when she does, she will hand them over completely and with great joy."

The stoic paused for the tender eye she held. "But there's one possession that presides over all the others and belongs at a man's side and is his greatest asset."

He concluded his elevation of women. "No woman is lesser man in the eyes of the Creator."

She lowered her eyes and thought such deep sensitivity, and then her phone buzzed in her purse. "I'm sorry. I really need to take this."

She slipped off her dress, folded it neatly, and placed it on the chair at the writing desk across the room. She took a tissue from the box on the desk and dabbed the makeup smudges under her eyes. She placed the phone on the desk, bent over, and placed her elbows on the desk. She tapped the screen and craned her head around. "Bear with me. It won't take long, and it won't interfere with your time." He came up behind her and tactilely examined the bony prominences of her spine. She stopped tapping for a moment and sighed. "Mmm, that feels nice, you must be a chiropractor," then returned to tapping. After a few text words she noticed he stopped. She craned her head around again, and found him sitting on the bed. "Are you all right?"

He gazed deeply into her eyes and thought, Father you've given her such a beautiful glow. "I'm unsure."

"Your first time?"

She abandoned her phone and sat next to him. He listened intently as her voice instinctively transitioned back to its professional tone. "It's ok. Fantasies aren't what they seem sometimes. You may have had an idea before you came and now somehow it completely changed in your mind and that's ok. Sometimes fantasies have to ferment in the mind for long periods and practiced often."

"We had a client one time that just couldn't get it right. After several tries, he found that what he really wanted was to be with another man, and the service was happy to refer him. So don't feel bad if it doesn't happen right away." She blinked, looked away, and thought, why does he stare into my eyes like that? She returned to her phone. "Not much longer."

He came up to the desk, bent over right next to her, and pressed his shoulder and hip to hers. She covered her phone with her hand discreetly, and gave him a polite smiled. He stared into her eyes and became pensive, while studying their anatomy. She felt anxiety swimming in her mind, and thought, why am I so nervous? Men have never made me this nervous before. Charles was right. I should have stayed in the office, and let him rotate Kim through. I've just been out of the loop too long.

During his studies he noticed her pupils dilating and thought, this is so damn confusing. Is this right? So close and those beautiful blue rings. Should I attempt a second life? I'm so unsure.

He leaned over to kiss her cheek and she flinched with great exaggeration. The stoic returned to his studies and thought, she doesn't belong here, too nervous. "I'm sorry. Is that not permitted?"

She blushed. "Well, it's just that tenderness is usually reserved... well, you know." She felt her blush deepen, and travel, mottling her neck. She turned to the wall quickly and thought, I feel so self-conscious. There's no lust for footing. God, it's so warm in here. I've got to leave. I don't understand this. I'm so lost. Just handle me and get it over with. Where's the man in you?

He dropped the stoicism, grinned, then said, "Well, at the bottom of the email there was a kissing coupon. I thought I would redeem it before it expires." He continued to grin, while watching her cheeks rise and the corners of her mouth turn up slightly forming a smile, and said, "You know when heaven created redemption, hell offered coupons." He chuckled lightly when sparkles appeared in her eyes.

"Coupons," she said, and then released a bound up chuckle.

The party clown brought more sparkles to her eyes. "It's true. A brilliant business model hell knew heaven couldn't compete with."

She contained herself long enough to ask, "Ok, how so?"

"Could you imagine being stuck in heaven as a known discount? All that gossip." He exaggerated a frown, pursed his lips like a sour old woman. "I can just hear the Crank sisters now. A couple of cloud squatting old biddies, one would say to the other 'Oh hell, I guess they'll let anybody in.'" He grinned, then said, "The other would say 'Amen to that sister.'" He animated back to the original. "'Hell, I wouldn't have worked so damn hard if I thought it was going to be this damn easy to get in, the gall. I think I'll go to group after shuffleboard and sing Kumbaya. My nerves are shot.'"

"'Amen to that sister, and watch the cookies. I know for a fact that they were dragged over from bingo. All broken and beat up...Damn, why does the sun feel the need to shine all the time. There's something to be said for a little creepy Goth. Shit, love and happiness my ass. Where's that lazy Heathcliff?'"

As she burst into laughter, he bumped her hip with his, and added, before he sat down, "Stay away from the cherubs. We're watching you, Ms. Discount."

She thought he is something else and that sweet laugh. She turned her phone over, turned to him, and crossed her arms like a suspicious spouse. "The pseudonym you chose is rare and something tells me it's your real name."

He straightened up and said playfully, "Why yes, it is."

She chuckled. "I'm sorry. I'm not laughing at you. It's just that you're so funny. The service strongly recommends the use of pseudonyms for security reasons. Why did you use your real name?"

"Well I thought about it, and then thought better of it. What if I like the pseudonym better and found that we were compatible and wanted to date. You have no idea how jealous my real name is. It already has issues with my first name. We have to wait for that bastard to fall asleep whenever we feel a date night coming on. Damn, all the accusations and demanding. You have no idea what it's like living with a real name, Oh, Lord, not to mention all the harassing phone calls at work that you would not believe."

He moved down the bed slightly. "Oh honey, throw your purse down and scoot in." He tickled her again. "Besides, I can't get my first name to do a three way with a pseudonym. He says it sounds too much like a meth ingredient."

She burst into laughter again and grabbed another tissue from the box. "Aniel, you have got to stop. You are too funny."

He glanced furtively at the ceiling, and thought, an unmistakable laugh. She's so pleasing, but I'm unsure if I should. Father what do you think? My pen, I feel you circling again. He mused upon his promise, Gwen, and his illusive pen. Poesies clustered around me, but I cannot scribe any. He was paralyzed again as his estranged pen of many years wrote a fresh new line in his mind. He thought, beautiful Gwen, I know now you bring my pen.

A lull appeared which allowed tension to reclaim the room. She blushed a light rosé and fidgeted as he poured into her eyes. She thought, I want my dress. I'm too old. He's not even looking me up and down. I don't have it anymore. I should have listened to Charles. I'm like a dancer past her prime. Once you're out of your twenties..., damn. God, it's so warm in here.

The stoic in him returned. He stood, and kissed the palm of her hand. "Is this permitted?" Her labored breathing returned. She felt her rosé turn burgundy and thought, what does he want? This is so confusing. She felt the blush travel to her neck, then her back moistened.

He released her hand, captured her face with both his hands, brushed his thumbs across her cheekbones, and tenderly kissed the corner of her mouth. "All I've ever wanted is to step into the glow of a woman's beauty, and pass through," he asked, "Is that permitted?"

As he kissed her face, she closed her eyes, and added more questions to her thoughts. She raised her arms and placed her hands on his wrists. Her bracelets tinkled as they slid down her arm. He felt her hands and kissed her fingers. Her eyes remained closed as he released her face and placed his hand on top of her head. He ran his fingers through her hair, clenched his fist gently, and pulled her head back slowly. He placed her chin on his chest, and cinched her tight with his other arm, triggering her to wrap her arms around him unconsciously.

She thought, Aniel I don't know what you want and I don't understand men. I just understand what they want to do, but you... He blew gently into her face and this time petitioned. "Gwen, please give me permission."

She opened her eyes. Her pupils were fully dilated and her face was ablaze.

He whispered, "I've denied the banal. Now permit the capture."

Her tender eye returned as her face cooled. As she poured into his eyes for the first time, she became pale and anxious when she saw the flicker turn to light in his eyes. She panicked when she realized this light was for her. A possessive light, and now a storm was blowing through a life that sought only reclusion and a heart devoted to poverty. She thought, Aniel, please, no tenderness, it frightens me.

He released his grip, recaptured her face, and kissed her hard and deep. He abruptly ceased kissing and reengaged her eyes. "There's a glow deep down inside a woman and is given at her creation. It's not the glow of pageant beauty that flees when age glares in contempt. That beauty is under lease. No, this glow is immovable and immortal."

He caressed her face with the back of his hand, blew gently again, and whispered while kissing her face, "When the heavens strike their lamps, turn your heels to their milky river, and gaze far off into a field of resplendent solitary stars. When you peer between them you'll see a faint glimmer, God's window. That's where heaven places the immortal glow of a woman as she passes through to Him."

She was ablaze again. He picked her up, laid her gently on the bed, undressed her completely, and sat on the edge of the bed. He stared into her eyes for quite a while before his gaze traveled her curves. As she lay still, she felt the bayou intruding until the light in his eyes returned to hers.

The pedestrian girl timidly caressed the dream of being a woman with standing until she reminded herself of her birthmark. And now, with the added burden of age, she felt compelled to apologize again and whispered, "I know I've lost my schoolgirl..."

He placed his fingertips to her lips and matched her whispering now that the room's ambience had transitioned to spiritual tenderness. He took his fingertips and caressed her curves.

As the light in his eyes danced, he whispered, "Tis the glow of a woman round God's window, blessed be He."

He undressed and engaged her and felt his ache intruding and thought, it has been so long. Is this right? She feels so good, but my feelings are hurting me. Should I leave? I'm so unsure.

She did something that she had only dreamt of since leaving adolescence. She initiated a single kiss of her own free will, a brief, almost imperceptible, brush upon his cheek. She thought, Aniel, please. I don't know what I'm supposed to do for you. All I know is that men only want the rote from me, and she began to mechanically move her hips.

He quickly placed his hand on her hip, squeezed gently, and whispered, "No, no. Shh no movement, please, no movement." He nuzzled her lips with his nose, while whispering, "I pray that the mint on your breath finds its way through your lungs and into your bloodstream, and perhaps with intervention from above finds its way to your glow, passes through, and returns to me. Truly, to pass through the glow of a woman's pageant beauty, and capture her on the other side, is a man's greatest joy."

He thought oh, Father above, should I pursue? Is it right? If I do, all I have to offer is this shell, if she's even attainable.

As he kissed her again hard and deep, the muscles in her back tightened, and her lower back came to a full arch. She panicked and thought, something's pushing past me. Oh, God, I can't stop it. I don't know what you want, but I don't think it's this, not the body. When it was over, a quick, but slight, rigor traveled across her chest leaving goose bumps in its wake, which she thought felt strange as if a ghost had just past between them.

"Are you cold?" he asked. Her burgundy blush

returned as she looked away, shyly, and shook her head. He sat up on the side of the bed and picked up where he left off on his drive through the carpet's nap.

She came to a kneeling position behind him, placed her hand on his shoulder, and thought, I don't have what you're searching for, and I'm so sorry. I didn't mean for that to happen and I feel so ashamed. I don't know why it happened.

She rested her head on his back and whispered, "Aniel." He remained fixated on the carpet. She picked her head up, called his name again, and cleared her throat. "Aniel, I don't feel that I've helped you."

He kissed her deep and smile brightly. "Gwen I'm perfectly pleased."

"I'm glad."

He glanced at the clock. "I'm sorry. I've taken up too much of your time."

When they finished dressing he sat back on the bed. She stood in the middle of the room, put her heels together, clasped her evening purse with both hands, cocked her head, and smiled warmly. "Are you going to be alright?"

He nodded while admiring her elegant posture.

She turned and was about to leave when he called her name. She felt her neck flush and thought, Aniel please, my name. Why is it when you call my name, it feels like you've been searching for me. Calling and calling, but I can't get to you. Like a dream, but I don't even know you, so confusing.

She turned to him and he gestured to the money. She

shook her head, and he stepped towards her. Startled, she inched back. He stopped dead in his tracks.

"I'm sorry. Am I frightening you?"

She relaxed. As he captured her face, she dropped her purse and unconsciously wrapped her arms around him. He searched her eyes for quite awhile and whispered, "So blue are you."

He pressed her against the wall, held her face, and kissed her several times. As his eyes glassed and his voice cracked, he said, "Gwendolyn, first kiss will be forever lost, then all the rest turn to wallflowers in the domestic space between a man and woman," he tenderly kissed the corner of her mouth, "but for this man...," and stopped abruptly when tears pooled, and his diaphragm was about to spasm.

He released her, retrieved her purse, walked to the writing table, and faced the wall. She turned to leave, hesitated for a moment, but left when the winds in her mind picked up.

As she skipped down the hall she knew Charles would be all over her with questions. She thought, what just happened? I want to go home, crawl into my tub, and cry. She was about to burst into tears and desperately needed to get past his suspicions.

As she rounded the corner she nearly plowed into him. Normally, he wouldn't approach her or the girls out in the open, but since they were alone he said in a hushed voiced, "Shit, Winnie you took too long to ping. I had to text. You know I don't trust new clients. God, I was sweating bullets. I kept turning the card key over and over in my pocket."

She cleared her throat. "Charles, please, everything's fine. I just want to go home."

His suspicions escalated. "Winnie, look at me." She panicked at first and thought, please don't badger me. I just want to go home and cry. She quickly constructed a stiff, but passable smile. "Everything's fine. I just want to go home. I'm tired."

She rested her hand on his massive shoulder. "You were right. I've been out of the loop far too long," then she turned her head and gazed down the hall.

He nodded. "Yeah, sometimes we just have to, or kick ourselves later for not trying." He paused briefly to admire his wisdom, and turned back to his duties. "Let me text the girls..."

She turned quickly and cut him off. "Could you take me home first, and come back for them. I know it's inconvenient, but I would really appreciate it."

He looked at her suspiciously. "Ok I'll text them to stay put."

As she headed towards the stairs, he frowned at her strange behavior and now had to strain his hushed voice to compensate for the distance between them. "Damn it, where're you going? Take the elevator. You're supposed to appear as a guest."

"No, you take the elevator, it's faster. By the time I reach the lobby you should already have the car pulled up."

He was about to engage her when the elevator opened. He smiled and nodded as guests exited. She made it down one flight before bursting into tears, and thought, Aniel, I don't understand. What do you want from me? She began to shake while fumbling through her evening purse for a tissue.

Charles walked briskly through the bar towards a back corridor, which read, "EMPLOYEES ONLY" and slipped out a back door that led to the alley. He glanced around suspiciously as he took off his hotel jacket. He trotted down the alley to a parking deck, found his car, placed the jacket in the trunk, and changed his shirt. She was waiting out in front as he pulled up.

He was about to get out and open the door for her, but she waved him off and got in, quickly. She latched her belt, and stared out the door window. His suspicion welled up again. "Are you sure you're all right?"

She didn't answer and bit her nails. When her condo was in sight, she turned to him. "I'm fine. I just want to take a hot bath and go to bed."

As he pulled up, she turned to him again. "Charles I'm fine. We'll talk tomorrow, ok."

He nodded, but was still bloated with suspicion. "Ok Winnie," then studied her face. "Why are your eyes red?"

"Allergies."

She crossed the street and let herself in. He waited for her text. When his phone buzzed, he looked up to her windows and saw the lights pop on. He turned to his phone, read the text, "thx xo." He thought for a moment, then drove off.

She dropped her purse, ran into the bathroom, turned the faucets on full, and threw in bubble bath. She rushed to get her clothes off. She tore her hose and ripped her dress fighting the jammed zipper. She had a deep appreciation for her clothing and always took immaculate care of them, but now she didn't care. Her only goal was to sink into her tub before bursting into tears again.

She just stepped into the tub when her diaphragm, quivered, and released a spasm. She sunk down into the bubbles, grabbed a washcloth, quickly pressed it to her face, and burst into tears. She turned the water off, stared at the bubbles at her feet, gazed up a few inches from them, and suspended primal engagement there. In her thoughts she clustered the brutal rape, the fantasies of men, and Aniel around it. She tried to untangle the confusion and burst into tears again.

She soaked her washcloth, wrung it out, wiped the snot from her nose, and returned to her menagerie of confusion. No one understands violence she thought, violence has no goal. It's an evolutionary remnant of something savage left over since the beginning and forever embedded in our stem. A parasite claiming legitimacy and demanding full citizenship in human behavior and views its brutalizing as natural as love.

She turned to the fantasies of men and thought men view primal engagement as a single sensation, like an itch, that has the same experience every time. We're so far apart. Men just want to go from one to the other, always scratching, whereas women try to be one and the other for them. Don't scratch, it hurts us both.

Lastly, she settled on Aniel, pushed engagement aside, and saw a man come up and kiss her, look deeply into her eyes, and in the reflection of his, she saw all her empty spaces. Everyone has empty spaces, she thought, that will never be filled or can't. But that's not what caused her to cry. She thought, tenderness has a spiritual mass that doesn't belong in the empty spaces of a woman without standing, but here is a man... She burst into tears again.

The water had lost all intimacy. It was just cool tap water now. The bubbles had dissipated except for a few tiny clusters. She stepped out, dried off, put on pajamas, and stood by the window. She drank wine until she was sleepy enough to get through the night.

Charles texted the next morning. "On the way." She was waiting at the curb when he pulled up. He got out of the car, came around to open the door, and said, "You ok?"

"Yes, much better."

As they drove off, he felt she was unusually quiet, but didn't press.

They made their way up to the office. It was two adjoining rooms on the fifth floor, which had a conference table in the middle of the room, big enough to seat five or six. To the left was the door that led to his office, and to the right, at the end of the table, was her desk. Windows lined the wall opposite the door and went the full length of the room.

She sat behind her desk. He pulled a chair from the conference table and sat in front of her desk. He thought, shit something's eating her alive. I wonder what the hell happened in there.

Her silence compelled him to probe gently. "Well, Winnie, do you think we have a permanent client?"

She jumped straight up, which caused the back of her knees to sling the chair against the wall making a loud bang and giving it a large bruise. She moved quickly to the window, looked down at the busy street, and bit her nails.

He had lanced a nerve and thought, Goddamn, she's a vibrating rod, and said, "Shit, what the hell is wrong with you." She paced anxiously without speaking.

"Goddamn it, did he hurt you somehow?"

She turned quickly and put her hands out in a calming gesture. "Oh no, no, nothing like that." She knew how agitated he would get if he thought she or one of the girls had been hurt.

"Then what the fuck is wrong?"

She walked back to her original spot and turned to him. "Charles, you're a man, you wouldn't understand." He softened his tone. "Ok, so I'm a man and probably won't understand, but I'm your friend and you can tell me anything, you know that."

She blushed, turned back to the window quickly, and said timidly, "I climaxed."

She had never climaxed with a man before, only as an adolescent during self-exploration.

He was about to laugh, but caught himself instinctive, it was Winnie. He cleared his throat. "Well, that's wonderful," then realized he had very little instinct for women.

He watched her shaking, and thought, oh shit, the teakettle is about to blow. Damn, if I had a dictionary, opened it to a random page, closed my eyes, and put my finger down, it would land on the exact wrong damn word, and wonderful would be the bull's eye. Damn I just stepped into a big pile of dog shit.

There's the shaking all over, the distended neck veins, flushed face, gritted teeth, the flared nostrils, and now it's going to blow, wham. She stomped back to her desk, glared a hole straight through him, slammed her hand down, opened palmed on the desk, which broke one her bracelets. "Goddamn it. In this business that's an illicit response."

He sat straight up and said hotly, "Ok, Winnie you're right. I'm a man and I don't understand. I think it's great, but what the hell do I know."

She pulled her chair back to the desk, brushed down the back of her skirt, sat quickly, and apologized to her close friend. "I'm sorry. I'm so wound up. I don't know what to do."

"It's ok."

She looked down and saw one of her heirloom

bracelets lying in pieces on the desk. "Oh, God, my bracelet."

He gathered the pieces. "It's ok, I'll take care of it," and placed them in his jacket pocket. He probed gently again in an attempt to remove the anxiety from his good friend. "Let's try and figure this out." She folded her arms, and placed them on the desk.

"Ok, do you think you have feelings for him?"

She checked her feelings quickly and covered them with a glare. "Good God, you're as useless as computer support. I've already gone through the obvious a thousand times."

"Yeah, I guess you checked the plug." They both fell silent and he sat back, gazed up at the ceiling, and became lost in deep thought. She dropped her head down as she fidgeted, trying to suppress the emerging feelings, and glanced up on occasion, counting on his preoccupation of the moment to keep his suspicions dozing, while she wrestled for control.

He sighed, left the ceiling, and focused on her. "Ok, why don't we work the problem from the other end. Let's push you aside and look at him." She felt warm around her neck and her pupils dilated slightly when she felt him in her mind.

He sat up sharply, intent on problem solving. "What's his fantasy like?"

She sat up anxiously and placed her hands in her lap. "What do you mean?"

"His fantasy, what's it like?"

She appeared confused. "Fantasy, I..., I don't think he has one."

Puzzled he said, "What? All men have them. What did he do?" She crossed her arms and glared.

"Ok, forget I went there."

He leaned back in his chair, sighed, and pondered. After a moment he sat up and felt as confident as a stumping politician. "Do you remember that play we went to when the curtain got stuck and everything came to a dead stop. It lost its magic when the stagehands came out. It felt like a play the rest of the night, even the actors sensed it and the whole thing felt awkward."

"I felt so embarrassed for them."

"That's it, Winnie. You see, the client is like the actor on stage and the girls are stagehands. They're too busy handling the backstage and don't have time to think. He didn't have a fantasy and your curtain got stuck and it was just damn awkward after that."

She thought yes, just an awkward situation, that's all it was. She rang that bell to distract her heart and convince herself, then nodded in concurrence. "Charles, that's the only intelligent thing you've said today."

"Shit, I don't know what all the fuss is about anyway. It doesn't matter. You'll never see him again. We told him you were just a fill in, and I'm going to punt him to Kim, if there is a next time." He narrowed his eyes slightly and pointed his finger at her. "And you can stay in the office where I think you should have been in the first place."

She jumped straight up again. The chair hit the wall enlarging its bruise. She moved quickly to the window and bit her nails, and thought, oh next time, what do I do...and what will you demand, if next time. Spring shivers saliently now. Don't remove my winter bedding and disturb my frozen peace. Please don't wake me. I'm beginning to feel my burning buds bursting in new summer flames. Oh, next time, blow them out and don't come back, no next time. Cease your summer drive and pass me by this time, and perhaps wait until some other time... Oh how the lily drips, for the enigma on my lips.

He frowned and thought, Goddamn what hell is up her ass. She's vibrating again. She took her other hand, pressed the glass, and stared out into the street below. He watched her nail biting for a while, and felt compelled from her past complaints to say something. "Winnie. Nails."

She whipped her hand down quickly as if she just saluted, turned, and glared.

He put his hand up. "Hey, you asked for an elbow whenever you bite your nails. You get pissed when you wreck your manicure, and then elbow the shit out of me for not saying anything."

"I'm sorry," she said, then she clasped her right hand over the left to check her biting, and gazed far off into the sky.

"Winnie, how 'bout instead of bringing sandwiches back; I take you to lunch, treat's on me." He tapped his pocket. "I need to drop this off anyway."

"I would really like that Charles, thank you, but I don't want you feel like you have to take care of me or fix me."

"We're friends and that is exactly what friends do." She stared into his eyes, then nodded feeling empty.

He went to his office and thought, maybe this shit will settle down in a couple of days. He took off his jacket, put it around the back of his chair, and booted up his computer. Charles worked the security side of their service. A big black man, Ex-Marine, two hundred thirty pounds with massive shoulders, he worked out hard to keep his Marine build, and kept his Marine haircut. He said he was a Marine and will always be a Marine and his bushy mustache was his token transition to civilian life.

He had a very good arrangement with the Sweeny Hotel two blocks down where they provided their service. He insisted on a master card key and said he didn't want to have to fumble with a bunch of fucking cards if there was trouble. He rented the same rooms on third and fourth floors next to the fire escape. When business was brisk he would pace on the landing of the stairwell evenly splitting the distance. He called it lurking patrol.

His phone was always fully charged and changed out whenever the battery became too old and discharged quickly. The girls must ping within a certain amount of time upon entering the room, and ping after they count the money, and again when they were safely on the elevator. The ping was a simple one or two letter text.

Payment was always in cash and clients were to stay in their room for an hour afterward. He never solicited for new clients. They all came from recommendations from the few original clients he had left. New clients always made him anxious. He would walk the hallway frequently until suspicion pushed him into the stairwell. He didn't trust them until they were established at least a year and used the service frequently.

He rotated his email accounts frequently, and when a client asked for services, he would give them a specific date, time, room number, and a last name to give to the reservation desk. He paid cash for the room so there was no card transaction. They were to come up with a first name pseudonym to go with the last name he gave them and encouraged them to change it frequently. Before rendering services, clients would be scheduled for lab work. He used the same lab. One he trusted, and when the lab faxed over the results he would email the client to set up a date. He deferred lab with original clients.

He wanted to know as little as possible about them, though he knew his original clients well. The less you know the less there was to tell. That was his business credo. He didn't even know what they looked like and didn't care.

He wore a Sweeny security jacket around the hotel. When the work night was over he headed to the bar and went through the "EMPLOYEES ONLY" door, and out into the alley. He moved quickly down the alley, while taking off his jacket. When he arrived in the office parking lot, he put his jacket into the trunk of his car and changed shirts. He would pull up to the curb in front of the hotel, and insisted on opening the doors for the women so it gave the impression of a shuttle service. He always changed up the pick up routine and sometimes used the alley.

The service closed on Thursdays which meant Wednesday night was pub night for him. He would head down to his little neighborhood bar, the Blue Diamond. Everyone knew him as "LT," short for lieutenant, and he would meet up with his Ex-Marine gunny sergeant buddies, Odell and Danny, where they drank and played cards. The object of which was to lose. The winner had to buy drinks.

He was a creature of habit in the bar. He felt it was the best way to relax his mind and untangle the knots from work. The first thing he did when he entered the bar was to have a shot of whisky. The bartender asked him one time why he did it. He said to him, "Because I need a stiff drink, before I have to look at those two ugly, card cheating sons' of bitches." The three were inseparable.

The Sweeny was a four star Hotel with traditional lay out. It had a typical revolving door, with a large marble-floored atrium. Down a few paces to the right was the registration desk, to the left was a large open lounge area, and on the other side of the lounge was the bar.

Sweeny management was very happy. They received a free impressive security guard and steady room rental. In return, they gave him a small room in the bar area for the girls to change and to stay out of sight. They all called it the snug. It was through the "EMPLOYEES ONLY" entrance and right before the exit to the alley. The room was small with a closet for costumes and a small rectangular table with six fold down chairs. It had a full bathroom with a large shower. The girls dressed business casual and appeared as guest's, pulling a light carry on for costumes.

Gwen worked the business side. She kept the books, tended to the girls, and did payroll in the snug every Wednesday night after the last client. She kept the costumes repaired and cleaned. If the girls were to see a new client and he was unsure of a fantasy, she dressed them and lectured them on proper appearance. It was all about impression.

When the girl walked into a room and a man looked up, the first word that should come into his mind was elegant. Dress length was crucial, too high would appear adolescent, too low, old. The length of a dress for their age should cut right above the knee. The knee was the fulcrum of a man's vision. What was covered up, and what was not. Balance drew him in.

She spent a lot of money on clothing, which irritated Charles. He would say "I can't tell if it's a hundred dollar dress or five." She would grin, and say, "That's why a grunt like you can't afford this service."

There were three girls in their early twenties, Kim, Sasha, and Abigail. Kim was confrontational and assertive, redheaded, tall, with blue green eyes. Charles didn't like her, thought she was disrespectful. Gwen tolerated her because her clients seem to enjoy her aggressiveness. Sasha was at the other end of the spectrum. She was a black woman with a light chocolate complexion, and was of average height. She read a lot and wore big glasses when she was not working.

She was frugal and was always lending money to the other two, who went through money like drunken sailors. She was Charles's and Gwen's favorite because she had a business head about her. She was saving her money and planned to quit the service when she had enough to pay for college.

She always sat by Gwen in the snug during payroll. Gwen would grab her chin on occasion and point to the other two, and say "You two ought to be more like her and save your money. The service is like dance or a sport. When you're out of your twenties no one wants you." Charles backed her up by chiding them harshly. Sasha would say she didn't mind because they were her friends, which irritated him because she would not charge them interest to teach them a lesson.

Abigail was somewhere in the middle. She had dark hair with dark eyes and a little above average in height. She would go on a savings miser, followed by a spending binge. She was a big prankster and loved to pick on Charles. She enjoyed busting him out in front of the hotel guests, especially on the elevator, because he couldn't escape.

Once when she saw him on a crowded elevator, a

shit-eating grin filled her face, and she said, "Hey, security guard? You know I think they're cooking meth down in the kitchen. You really ought to check it out."

He cringed and said, "Yes ma'am, I'll check into it," and planned to exit the next floor to take the stairwell. He knew that she was not going to stop, which really irritated him.

When all the shocked guests exited on the same floor, leaving them alone, he said, "Stop fucking around, you're going to get us caught."

She was incorrigible and said, "You ever consider pet therapy?" After he cracked a smile, she said, "One good spit in the face from a llama and you'll forget all about your drug addiction."

They both laughed. "God, you're just like that damn Odell."

He was extremely fond of her, just wished she would save more, and think about the future, but he would remind himself that she was in her early twenties and no different than him at that age. He knew counseling a twenty year old was a waste of time. They were never going to be permanently ill or die.

It was mid July, six weeks had passed since their first encounter, and Aniel remained deeply embedded in her mind. Her behavior was unchanged. Charles' level of concern rose, but she continued to say she was fine. He came out of his office quietly sometimes to check on his friend, and found her staring out of the window with her hand on the glass and sometimes both. He wanted to press her, but was unsure if it would do any good.

Payday rolled up and all were in the snug, seated around the table. Gwen shook her head at Sasha, and said, as she did every payday, "Now how much do they owe you before I start writing checks?"

Charles sat quietly reading his criminal psychology magazines. Gwen considered them cheesy tabloids of imaginary murders to feed the insipid mind.

He agreed. "Yeah, that's true, but the imagination is where the deviant mind frees itself from the moral compass, and plots a way into the street."

After she settled the pay, she held a brief staff meeting. They understood how important it was to keep the client happy and coming back.

Kim spoke up. "I don't know if this new guy is happy. I don't think I was right for him."

Gwen sat up placed her arms on the table, clasped her hands together, and looked at her intently. "How so?"

Kim frowned, put her elbow on the table and palmed her chin, then slumped. "I don't know. I like a little more action. All he wanted to do was blow poetry. I think I bored him."

She turned to Sasha and added. "I think the little book worm would have been a better choice. Shit, it was like talking to a damn Chinaman. I couldn't understand a damn thing he said. It was glow this, beauty that. Hell, all I did was smile, nod, and think damn, I don't know what the hell you're talking about. Damn, it was miserable. It got creepy when he asked 'how is she before I...'"

Gwen cut her off sharply by popping the table with her hand, which startled everybody out of the quiet evening ambiance. "What?" She glared at Charles and fidgeted wildly. "He asked for her? He asked for her?"

Her face went up in flames as she slammed her hand down on the table again, this time dismissing their ambience for the night. "Damn it, Charles, talk to me. Did he ask for her?" Baffled, she muttered, "How did I miss his name? He would never have used another name." She became more agitated and started to huff. She glared at Kim and raised her voice. "Did he kiss you?"

She set Kim off when she said sharply, "Answer me." They squared off. Kim popped her chin out quickly, leaned forward. "Ewww Gwen, clients don't want that. You know that. We just sat on the bed while he blew poetry."

Charles hid his face behind his magazine, while his bouncing shoulders gave away his chuckling.

Her huffing escalated. She pushed her chair back, aggressively, and stood straight up wrestling for composure. "Charles, I want to go home now."

She turned to Kim, quickly, still huffing and glared hard. "Is that all you did?"

Kim stood straight up, matched her glare. "I did?" Their fur was fully puffed now.

He stood with a big grin on his face, then said, "Ok, Winnie, let's all calm down. I made him change his name. I don't let them punch a used ticket. You know that."

He looked over at the girls, with Kim still fuming, and offered a peace settlement. "Ok, who wants pizza, treat's on me." They all nodded.

Kim, still locked into glaring match with Gwen, said "And I hope they have plenty of cold beer, because I'm burning up."

He tried to deescalate the tension by turning to pizza. "I know this great little pizza place. The most wonderful pies and they have my favorite topping," but felt mischievous and turned to Gwen, "ego."

She clinched her jaw. "Take me home."

He pulled the car up to the front of the hotel, got out, and opened the back door for the girls, and the front for Gwen. She glared at him the whole time, while he bit his lip. The girls pulled out their phones. Gwen huffed and fidgeted, while Charles grinned. Dead silence filled the space between them.

When he pulled the car up to her condo, she flew out and slammed the door, which interrupted the girl's phone love. Charles chuckled, and Kim said, "What the hell is up her ass?" He waited for the usual text, but got something extra, "in u pos," which made him bust into laughter. He read the litany of texts that followed, and said aloud, "Shit, I don't know what that means. Damn, I don't think I know that one either." His eyes became huge. "I haven't been called that in a long time, gotta remember that one." He texted, "Driving, check u later."

They all gathered around the table eating pizza and drinking beer. He was sipping his second, when his phone went off. He picked it up and muttered. "Oh shit, now I have been called that." Another text came in. He stopped, abruptly, and muttered, "Shit, I think that one's made up." He went totally silent as he tried to make sense of it and shook his head when he couldn't. "Gotta be that Cajun shit. Her French roots always show when she's really pissed" He looked at Sasha with tears in his eyes. "Baby girl, hand me a napkin." He wiped his eyes, looked at his phone, then said, "Now, I like that one. That's clearly American. I doubt she calming down, though."

As he placed his phone on the table it buzzed again. He laughed, touched it with his finger, and pretended it was a hot ember and made a sizzling sound. "It's gonna to burn all night folks."

They all looked up from their phones and Sasha said, "Why are you laughing so hard?"

He wiped his eyes again. "I have this friend who was set up on a blind date, but got stood up for the second, and now is mad at the world, and stomping up and down the room cursing me."

Kim caught on and grinned broadly, then said, "Hey

Charles, is this friend pacing up and down, biting her finger nails, and kicking the dog." He was red faced and could hardly speak, then took a deep breath. "And the cat, too."

It was early morning when he pulled up to her condo. She was already waiting. When she got in, he gave her a big grin, and a sporting tease. "The old gray mare ain't what she used to be."

She turned to him, with a tear in her eye. "Can we just go to the office?"

His heart plunged towards shame. "Oh, Winnie, I'm so sorry. Please forgive me. I've stepped over the line." He continued his litany of apologies until she had enough and said irritably, "Charles, please."

She made her way around to her desk, placed her purse in the bottom drawer, brushed down the back of her skirt, and sat quickly. He came to the front of her desk and stood. "Winnie, I'm truly sorry."

"I know," she placed her arms on the desk and clasped her hands together and said, "Charles, please sit down. I want to ask you something."

He pulled up a conference chair, sat down, and leaned forward. "Ok, what is it?"

She glanced at him briefly, looked down, and cleared her throat. "Next time he emails you, could you please let me know? I think it would be in the best interest of the service if I interviewed him to see if he's dissatisfied with me or the service somehow." She blushed, as she reinforced their business logo. "You know it's important to keep the client happy and coming back."

He tried to hold back a snicker best he could, and thought, I'll be Goddamned. You're so prideful. Shit, I know we'll loose a client for sure after you get a hold of him, poor bastard. He sat on his snicker, while applying a straight face. "Ok, I'll make a note of it." He stood. "I need to check the emails." He headed towards his office, and bit his lip.

She went to the window and gazed down into the street. Her eye caught a young girl who appeared mesmerized by a window display of a clothing boutique. She shook her head like a wise adult and thought, he's just a mannequin, sweetie, and the light in his eyes is just that. It's not yours. If you had a birthmark you would understand about dreams of standing.

She wanted to burst into tears, but she had done enough of that last night.

Her behavior remained unchanged. He continued to come out of his office and check on her and most times she had both hands pressing the glass, which rang his bells of concern and he felt that confrontation was imminent if she didn't settle down to her old self soon.

Some days, as he sat in his office, he listened to her heels make a rhythmic cadence as she paced. It reminded him of marching and old stories. He would sit back and reminisce. The marching halted at intervals and he knew she was pressing the glass.

He came out at noon as he always did, placed the night's schedule in front of her, and asked what she wanted for lunch. She never paid much attention to it until he came back with lunch, but now she made furtive glances at it every time he plopped it on her desk. He thought, shit I wish that fuck would email me, so she can ream your ass out, and I can delete you from the system. Then she can she get back to her old self. Damn, she's prideful.

It was mid September and a little before lunch. She got up from her desk pressed one hand against the glass and thought, oh, God, Aniel please. Charles came in, but she was unaware. He dropped the schedule on her desk which drew her from the window. She turned and saw him grinning like a wily pickpocket.

She cocked her head. "What?"

 He didn't say anything.

She said impatiently, "What is it Charles?"

"He insists on you this time."

She blushed and turned back to the window, quickly.

"Well, Winnie, what do you want to do?" He thought, poor bastard she's going to eat you alive. She bit her nails and continued to gaze out the window.

"I'm so unsure."

Irritated he said, "What? This guy has been eating you

alive and now you have the opportunity to confront him and you're fucking unsure. Shit, I don't understand. I thought you wanted to interview him." He paused for feedback, but she was silent. "Do you want me to punt him?"

She shut her eyes tight and rang her bell vigorously. "Wait. I need to walk and think."

"Walk, shit you've already taken the finish off the floor for the last two months. Damn it Winnie, I wouldn't get into your business, but what gives, are you afraid of his answer?"

She sighed, but kept her back to him. "You're right. I'm sorry. Please set it up."

He put his hand on her shoulder, spun her around, and encouraged. "You're nervous. Interview him, and get your ass back in the office where it belongs, ok."

She nodded. "Ok."

He closed his eyes when he heard the soft knock, and the sliding of the card key. He turned down the volume on the clock radio and sat on the bed.

She walked to the middle of the room as she did before wearing the same blue dress. She thought, God, he's so beautiful. How the light dances. Nothing has changed. She felt the pedestrian girl deep down and stared at both birthmarks, and thought, we're two marked girls who can only dream about our mannequins.

The dancing light in his eyes came to a dead stop to allow capture. She tensed up slightly and thought oh, next time where are you? I need your wind. My burning buds.

Blow them out. Take what's inside of me, and go away.

As she held her captured light she thought, Aniel. I know the world will neither understand nor believe that some buds do bloom their first season, late, so it repudiates them. I just know that for me I'm full of blooms for you. But your tenderness has that spiritual mass and it frightens me, because these burning blooms only have standing in my private thoughts. Your tenderness, Aniel, can't thrive in my empty spaces, because that spirit turns in shame and I'm forever denied an indulgence. I implore you, take your mass and leave me be, under my winter bedding, and allow only my private thoughts to stoke these burning blooms.

His smile started off slight, and then grew rapidly to full warmth when he captured the glow surrounding the splendor of his night. "Oh, God, Gwen I've missed you."

She furrowed her brow a little and crossed her arms. "Why did you not ask for me?"

He felt joy spring up at her apparent concern. "Am I being dragged on the carpet?"

She chuckled as she put her hand to her mouth, and cleared her throat. "I would just like to know."

"I think about you far too much and I feel it's not right. I had to go to the other to get you off my mind, but all I thought about was you," then he thought, pursuit is demanding an answer.

She blushed, turned, and placed her phone on the writing table after she pinged. The pedestrian girl kept her back to him, and closed her eyes for a moment to cover her birthmark. She turned back to her mannequin and dreamt of a kiss.

He engaged her eyes for the first time. "You are so beautiful." He felt his ache return and thought, I'm still so unsure, God, the dreams.

As she shot her eyes down in response from another blush, he glanced at the ceiling briefly and thought, what do You think I should do? He rested his eyes on her. "You have such beautiful glow."

She thought, pretty words mannequin, but do they come from the froth of dreams or lust.

He didn't say anything for quite awhile, just remained engaged. She fidgeted as she felt anxiety wash over her and thought I want to leave, but I want to stay. I've got my answer. I need to leave. Oh, God, Charles is right it's just ego. What did he say? Oh yes my curtain. I've got to keep my mind working and think about other things. As she stared into his eyes she added to her thoughts, maybe the play will keep its magic.

He turned up the volume on the radio in an attempt to bridle her fidgeting frame in order to soothe it. She put her heels together, and cocked her head, slightly. "That's pretty, what is it?"

"If The Light In Your Eyes."

"If the light in your eyes, what?"

He stood and inched towards her. She inched back in response to his advance. He stopped abruptly. "Am I frightening you?"

"No, no I'm frightening myself."

He took both of her hands and kissed them. "It's a Jazz ballad. A ballad runs along a simple truth, and it neither understands complexity, nor does it tolerate it, because it only knows one simple truth."

She thought, Aniel I have my answer and I'm so pleased with it. Please don't make me pay for my answer, don't kiss me. Take from me only what men want and let me run away, but just don't kiss me. I get so dizzy.

He held her face in both of his hands and thought I'm so confused again and that feeling, the tidal forces that exist right now. The gravity pulsating inside the glow of a woman compels all men, but yours is so unforgiving, should I? I so hoped this rencounter would give me full resolution, but I'm still so unsure. I sometimes think that our morals were smelted in the blazes of hell, and once driven apart, its demons feast on our confusion.

He paused in his thoughts to enjoy the eagerness in her kiss, and then returned to his thoughts, oh pursuit bear with me through this smelting. I feel my pen the victor. She placed her hands on his wrists as she did before, and her two remaining bracelets tinkled together as they slid down her arm.

He slipped her dress off and draped it carefully over the chair back at the writing table. She believed his tenderness was not implied as she thought, as you lay me down, I know that I'll receive my garment's treatment.

Anxiety seeped into her mind as she felt the wind from next time, and thought, oh, next time, you're here. Please return me to my frozen peace, and go away.

She felt moisture flow and flexed her pelvic muscles in a futile attempt to halt its progression. She thought, oh, next time, I've pleaded with Aniel, now must I plead with you? Is this what you've planned for me this time? To torment me by drowning the lily in my blossoms' flames. If you must, please wait for the time when I can have standing, but we both know that will never be, because my mark freezes me when I feel the spirit and I'm left with nothing but your wind as I turn my back on you. All you can do is pass me by. Is that all you'll ever be for me, scores of missed opportunities?

He held her face in his hands again, kissed her deep, blew gently, and whispered, "If the light in your eyes ever sought another I will always love you." He blew again. "You see, Gwen, ballads understand only one thing, simple truth, but we marble it with doubt all our life."

He picked her up, laid her gently on the bed, and as he engaged her, he whispered again, "If the light in your eyes ever found another I will always love you." He kissed her hard and deep and looked deeply into her eyes. "And when the light in your eyes dims and you find yourself at the end of your road, your cane by your side, and all are gone, turn to the inside and you'll find me. Simple truth" He kissed her hard and deep again. "You see, simple truth accompanies us throughout our journey, and it's only at the end of our road when we're finally reckoned to it, but then it's too late."

Her back tightened followed by the full arching of her lower back as before. She shouted out in her mind. I'm so sorry it's stronger than me and shoves me out of the way. Forgive me. I know you don't want this. I'm so ashamed. She whispered in a low husky voice, "Oh, God," and shivered.

He released her quickly when he felt the ache calling him back. He sat up on the side of the bed, and drove the carpet as before.

She cried, sat straight up, and wrapped the top sheet around her. She hopped off the bed, stood in front of him, and wiped the tears from her cheeks with the sheet. "Aniel. I'm so sorry that I don't have what you're looking for."

He stared deeply into her eyes, and said softly, "Gwen, I'm perfectly pleased," then thought, I am pleased, but the aching draws me back to my ship and my smelted morals paralyze my heart whenever I move towards you. Oh Father I don't know what to do.

She straightened up, cocked her head one way then the other, dropped the sheet, and straddled his lap. She placed his chin between her breasts, stared into his eyes, and caressed his face with her fingertips. After the long tactile exam, she held his face and kissed him hard and deep several times, before returning to the exam, first his orbits, then the bridge of his nose, then his lips. Her tactile joy was interrupted when he whispered, "Please permit me."

She searched his eyes for a moment, kissed him, and

resumed the exam. After several more kisses she wrapped her arms around his head, pressed her cheek to the top of his head, and thought, while nuzzling, oh, next time, as the lily drips, she's ignoring standing's flailing contempt, for the moment anyway.

Her mind was at peace during the rapture of larping as his spouse.

He closed his eyes, placed his hands on her soft back, pressed her tight, and examined her soft prominences as he listened to her heartbeat. Her rate was up slightly, elevated not from anxiety, but an elevation of anticipation that was cool, patient, and confident. It was a rate that was eager to please, and was now ready to enjoy volleys of provocations again. She was ready to lie back down, but when he whispered, "Gwen, make us sure," her eyes flew open like a young mother whose toddler's intimacy and desire were now awake and very hungry.

Frightened, she hopped off. "I'm so sorry."

"Don't be."

They dressed and he sat as before. She walked over to the writing table, tore off a piece of a memo pad, and wrote something down. She took two of the twenties lying on the table, and tucked the paper under the rest of money. She held up the twenties, and said playfully, "Cab fare."

He stood, and moved towards her, just as he did at the end of their first encounter. She froze. He felt her freeze, which prompted him to slow his pace. Her rate picked up, not from fear, but from her winds of next time. She said softly, "I'm not frightened."

He captured her face and searched her blue rings. "Gwendolyn, the spirit is a world replete with hope and the heart but a fragile vessel where it dwells," he paused in a futile attempt to control his pooling tears, "but when the spirit is crushed, it releases what's left of its world into that vessel, then the spirit withers and dies, and the heart is left alone clinging to the fidelity of its promise, while the rest of the world..." He stopped abruptly, released her quickly, as his diaphragm tightened, and returned to the wall as before.

She felt her vessel whirling in the opportunity of next time and was about to burst into tears as her mark pushed her through the door, letting it pass her by.

She ran to the stairwell directly across from the room, grabbed the railing, and sat on the first step. She put her face in her hands, and cried for a moment. She craned her head up, and peered into the narrow rectangular shaft the railings created, and cried out. "Aniel, please. Why not just give me my answer, and let me go. Please don't hold me down. I don't have what you're looking for. God, why me? I'm just a businesswoman."

She remembered she wrote down her phone number and thought, oh, no, what have I done? I'm so sorry, that was a mistake. I don't know why I did that. I've never done that before, God, that's such a breach. I'm so sorry. I won't answer. I can't. I'll change my number. She tore her last tissue in half and pressed the two pieces to each eye. She dried them as best she could with such little to work with.

She whispered, "Aniel, I was born to poor shrimpers on a boat in a bayou and when Daddy left us..." She stopped abruptly, and became somewhat detached as tears ran their rivers.

She stiffened as she searched for her proofed composure, but only found the child inside tugging at her sleeve, apologizing. "I know Momma did the best she could. She had to lend me out. We were so hungry. 'Remember child, there's no shame when you're hungry.'"

She soaked her fingers in the raging rivers on both cheeks and whispered, "So I would just shut my eyes, and lay as still as the bayou and feel the rain inside, but with you. I can't explain it. My eyes won't stay closed and I can't be still."

"Aniel I know I'm marked as trash, and standing can't survive in my empty spaces, but when I'm with you I truly believe there is more to me on the other side and I don't see my mark. Do you?"

She recovered quickly, and swabbed her make up stains with the two tissue balls she rolled up, and thought, I've got to get past Charles, and texted. "Resolved. Tired. Home. Out front."

He pulled the car to the curb and opened the passenger door. "Ok?" She nodded.

"I'm glad. I'll drop you off, and go after the girls." He watched as she buzzed herself in and waited for the lights and her text. His phone buzzed and it read her standard "thx. xo."

She didn't bother with the foot race this time. She knew she wasn't going to make it. Tears streamed down her face as she filled the tub and undressed. She hung up her dress, came back to the filling tub, laid her head on its rim, stared into her empty spaces, and grabbed her washcloth when she felt her diaphragm spasm. She wiped the snot from her nose, turned the faucets off, and slipped in.

She looked at the space above her feet as before and saw Aniel. She pushed him away, but he kept coming back until he finally settled in and refused to leave. She held her breath and sank under the water. She came up and dipped several times, but couldn't wash him out of her mind.

She stepped out of the tub, adjusted the towel on her wet head, cinched the tie on her bathrobe, and stared down at the street below. A malfunctioning street light flickered and came on as a man passed under. She thought, a man only sees a woman when he needs to fill a desire.

A moth flew into the now righted lamp's light and bounced off its glass. She thought, please find another lamp. I'm just a businesswoman trying to run my business. I don't have what you're looking for. I'm too old for the heart and have left it long ago, it belongs to the young. I'm going to retire in a few years, live modestly, and be as still as the bayou. The moth flew off and she thought, thank you, Aniel... Oh no, please come back. The moth circled the lamp several times, settled on one spot, clung to the glass, and focused. It stilled its wings and appeared to whisper into the light.

Her thoughts drifted to her mother's mental illness and then to Paul, whom she hadn't thought about in years. He was her high school sweetheart. When they graduated they planned to marry and attend college together, but he decided to join the military and send for her later, once settled. But as he climbed onto the bus, he told her he wasn't going to send for her, and that he wasn't ready for all this.

Both broke, they parted. One left home, while the other left a woman with standing, because the bayou convinced her that that was all she knew. And there was no shame when you were hungry.

She thought about lying with Paul, but couldn't remember much, kissing, remembered some. But Aniel, kissing, she thought, it's not so much the kiss, but the residue it leaves behind, which the heart reconstitutes and atomizes. The heart dances in the spiritual mist until it realizes it's only mist. I haven't kissed in over twelve years and I don't even know if I'm doing it right. She apologized.

As she stared down at the empty street, she looked towards the boutique and thought about the mesmerized girl. She shook her head as the wise adult again, while tears pooled and thought, irony you mock me. Here is a beautiful man in the real world who doesn't care about birthmarks only the affections of this pedestrian girl, but she's only been schooled in dreams.

It was mid December and the cold weather had finally made its way to the bone. There weren't enough layers to be had, or coats that could be donned to hold back the cold now in full bloom. The holidays were the slow period for the service. Business travel gave way to family travel and reunions. Every year for the last four, Gwen and Charles took some of the profits from the service and treated themselves and the girls to a week's vacation on the island.

Her behavior drifted, and seemed to mimic an autistic state at times, especially while pressing the glass. Charles worried and noted a slight dilapidation in her appearance. She didn't high polish anymore. It was something only the eye of a close friend would notice. He didn't push her, but thought vacation's coming up and that's exactly what she needs. He kept telling himself that at every encounter with her odd behavior. She didn't look at the schedule anymore and left her phone at home, telling him she was just forgetting it. He didn't buy it, but didn't know what else to do, and thought vacation.

It was the payday before vacation and he looked forward to pub night. He plopped down the schedule, and asked her what she wanted for lunch. She turned from the window. "Oh get what you want. I'm not hungry."

He furrowed his brow. "Come on, Winnie, you need to

eat."

"Maybe later, you go ahead."

"Alright, I'll wait too."

"I know what you're thinking. Charles, I'm fine. I'm just not hungry right now," then she added after a grin, "Besides, at 230 pounds, you won't wait long."

She turned her thoughts to vacation and sighed, then said, "I'm really looking forward to vacation."

"Me too, I think we all need to relax."

She chuckled, then said, "Charles, relaxation is only a concept for someone like you, until the grave, but I'll make sure you're cremated. You're body needs to rest."

"See there, that's my little Louisiana hot pepper. You're laughing again, now give the world hell."

She refreshed her sigh, then said, "Vacation," and he headed to lunch.

She pressed her hand to the glass and thought, oh, God, Aniel please don't call. I feel like it's coming soon and I don't want to answer, but I need to hear your voice and dream.

Charles changed clothes, locked his apartment door, and headed down the street to the Blue Diamond. It was a diverse mix and vibrant. He walked in and the bartender said, "Hey, LT, ready for your whiskey?"

"Where have you ever heard a man tell fuck and liquor, 'I'm having second thoughts', and don't try to pour that cheap shit Wayne tries to push off on the customers. I know he's pouring shit in the good bottles."

The bartender winked. "Don't worry. I know where he keeps the good stuff and if I get caught, I'll say take it up with LT."

"Where are my redneck grunts?"

The bartender grinned, then said, "Oh, Odell called and said that he and Danny are working on the truck." The bartender winked. "Odell told me not to let you spend too much, because you are his honey hole tonight."

LT grinned, and felt that deep love for his friends he always felt when he entered the bar, his bar, his home, and said, "That bastard is in for a surprise tonight. I think I got those cheating sons of bitches figured out." He pointed his finger with love and respect for the bartender, his bartender, his friend. "I'm the one who's going to lose tonight and not a dime will come out of my pocket."

Two women came up and sat at the bar. They were friends who worked in the same state office. Brenda was heavy set with blonde hair, dark eyes, and in her late twenties. Keisha was not quite as heavy, but the same age. They were best friends and habituated the same bar stools a couple of nights a week, especially payday, and occasionally they would get lit, and trash their men.

The bartender came up. "Hello ladies, the usual?" They smiled and nodded. He brought back two glasses of red wine. "I just opened a new bottle."

Keisha said derisively, "Oh, bottles now, what

happened to the fifty five gallon drum of left over piss Wayne usually tries to pass off?"

LT slapped the bar. "Shit, you got to watch that bastard."

The bartender explained. "He forgot to order it and had to run out buy a couple of cases retail."

Brenda giggled, then said, "We'll pinch his wholesale and watch him squeal retail." They all laughed.

When the chuckling subsided, Keisha straightened her crooked glasses caused by her chuckling, and admired all the colors of the cheaper liqueurs and spirits cast to the lower shelf in the usual tavern feudal system behind the bartender, which triggered a memory.

She beamed. "Hey Posey, make me a Gwen."

Brenda perked up. "Yeah, you haven't made one in a while."

"Can't. Wayne has a fit, says it's a waste of good liquor."

Keisha sarcastically. "I don't see how that's possible. You have to have it first."

Brenda chuckled and pushed her, while LT shook his head.

"Ok," she said, "so how much would it cost if it was a drink you could drink?"

LT furrowed his brow, puzzled. "What do you mean if you could drink it?"

The bartender replied, quickly, like an enthusiastic shopkeeper, proud of his merchandise. "It's toxic. I have to use chemicals to make it glow."

LT furrowed his brow with greater confusion. "Shit, Aniel why make a drink you can't drink?"

Keisha jumped in pitching. "Because it's so cool, especially when he drops the pearl in," she turned to Aniel, "so how much?"

He thought for a minute. "Oh, about seven bucks."

"I've got an extra three to spare," she glared at LT, like a dominant older sibling, "give me four."

He straightened up and put both hands on the bar. "I'm a grunt not stupid, save that for the civilians."

Brenda pitched. "Come on LT, it's cooler humping cool and their baby's going to be the coolest."

He thought about it." Ok, but it better hump like no other or I'll take it out of your hide."

"Disappointment can't afford this ride."

He handed over the four bucks and a voice behind him said, "Shit, I don't know LT, I don't think she's worth four bucks, maybe a little change."

Brenda looked over his shoulder at the voice. "Look, disappointment thinks he's going to ride."

LT whirled around and grinned like a boy meeting up with friends, and said, "Are you two bastards ready to win?"

Odell was hardcore. He didn't believe in transition and believed that if you had served in the Corps you would always be a Marine. He characterized himself as an Alabama redneck Marine. He kept his shirt tucked and his shoes shined, and said LT and Danny were sissies for negotiating with civilian transition. It made them weak and when the big one came and the Corps needed a real gunny, not this sissy shit they have today, they'd look for him to whip the Corps back into shape, and he'd be ready.

Danny was quiet and softhearted. He had big feet, which made him clumsy. He grew his hair out long, kept it braided, and said he did it to piss off Odell.

Aniel looked around and said cautiously, "Better wait until the crowd settles down, it takes awhile to make."

LT turned to Brenda. "Don't start without me." The three went to their table and played cards.

Aniel wiped down the bar as customers left and washed the glasses that Rosy brought from their tables and said, on one of her return trips, "Have the tips been good."

"Not bad," and returned to her tables.

He closed his eyes while washing, and thought about how pleasing Gwen's kisses were, and pondered her scent. His eyes flew open when he heard Rosy clear her throat. "What cha thinking about tiger."

He blushed, but recovered quickly. "I think this ought to be a titty bar."

"Not with these saggers."

He noticed LT coming up to the bar frequently. "Damn LT, when are you going to pull out the big surprise?"

LT staggered a little, and belched. "Don't worry, got um on the ropes." Aniel shook his head as he poured the drinks.

When the bar mellowed, Brenda shouted towards

Aniel. He nodded and went to the stock room. He came back with a box full of bottles. Brenda put two fingers in her mouth and whistled towards the grunts' table, and waved them in.

They all gathered around while he mixed the liquor and chemicals. He added the last chemical and the liquid began to glow. LT, wide eyed, looked over at Brenda. "Shit, this is worth it."

She grinned and said to Aniel, "Now she can't step out without her pearl."

The grunts were amazed, they got low on the bar, and stared into the glass. Some strays behind them were sipping and muttering in amazement. Wayne came up, grimaced. "Goddamn it Posey. I thought I told you not to waste liquor."

Keisha snapped her head up. "Shut the fuck up, Wayne. We bought it."

Brenda chimed in. "Fuck ditto Wayne," and suppressed a belch.

Everybody laughed and Aniel chuckled, then said, "How do you fuck a ditto?"

"Six glasses stumbling over the moment. It can be done."

He got down low with the others and placed a glowing bead on the surface of the drink. LT beamed like a child in the midst of a discovery. "Is it phosphorescent?"

He nodded. "Now watch."

As the bead sank slowly, he whispered, "Hear me

Gwen. Let me feel your beautiful glow again."

LT chuckled, then said, "I didn't know you have to talk to it." Aniel blushed as the bead found its specific gravity, which was dead center, and remained motionless in the liquid, like a lazy Koi, and glowed brightly.

He stood and smiled as if he were a blue ribbon winner. "The Gwen."

Keisha rocked on her stool about to bust. "Tell her story again. The grunts haven't heard it."

"I'm sorry sweetheart. You only paid for the drink."

"Damn it, Posey, if I buy a Gwen I get her story."

He rang the tip bell. "Let it be known throughout the land if you buy a Gwen, you're entitled to her story."

"You're damn right. Now go on."

He bent over and rested his elbows on the bar, leaned in close to them. "All women have a glow deep down inside, it's the glow of their love."

Keisha broke in. "Shit, I'm taking you home."

"Oh no, I've seen Otis."

"Oh, he's just a big teddy bear."

"Yeah, on that side of gender, I think I'll stay on this side of the bar."

He continued. "You see, Gwen is a woman trapped behind her glow of beauty. She comes from a conceited clan, who are blinded by their vanity, which has convinced them that the glow beauty is love, but she doesn't believe it." He looked at LT. "Have you ever had that feeling that something wasn't right, but you couldn't prove it. That sense that you

57

know something's wrong, but can't prove it scientifically, and you don't care because you know you're right."

LT shouted for Odell and looked around frantically. Everybody laughed when Odell said, "Damn LT, I'm standing right next to you." He turned quickly and they were nose to nose.

LT stammered excitedly. "You remember when we were on that roof in that little shit hole village in the sand box and I said I had a bad feeling about it and I went against orders and we got the hell off."

Odell nodded. "You saved our asses that day."

Danny tuned in. "Yeah, and I said I was going to marry you for saving our asses." He finished his drink, and added, "Now, I'm still available."

"Shit, you're too pretty you might cheat on me."

Keisha broke in. "Posey, finish the story."

"So she sits chained behind her glow cradling her love in her hands. Her clan has told her all her life that what's in her hands is only a reflection of her glow. She tells them that she doesn't believe it and that it's not a reflection, it's her love, but she's unsure. She decides to go on a quest to find a man that can see past her glow, to her love. Her clan scoffs and says you'll come back humiliated."

"She sets off and goes to all the villages looking for a man who can see past her glow to her love in her hands, even the average man can't get passed her glow. A man comes to her."

He stopped and looked around at all the intent faces. "Have you ever had your world turned upside down?"

They all nodded and Keisha said, "Everyday honey." The group chuckled, lightly, and he continued. "I came, I mean a man came and turned her world upside down. She fell, and while she was free falling he said, I will catch you, but she became frightened, and thought he was going to hold her down and only see her glow of beauty. So she ran back to her clan humiliated and remains chained behind her glow holding her love."

Brenda puzzled. "Let me see if I have this straight. I was too drunk last time I heard it. So she sits behind her glow and wants desperately for men to see her love, but they can't, because they're mesmerized by her glow of beauty. But if she has never seen her love either, how does she know it exists?" Brenda pondered for a moment, snapped her fingers, and said excitedly, "She goes back humiliated because she has lost faith in her love, and thinks they're right, it's only a reflection."

Aniel pointed his finger at her, and said, "Precisely. She's been taught all her life that beauty is love, but she still feels her love, and it never goes away. She just can't see it and that feeling never leaves. She can't get to it to believe in it, because her glow and clan has confused her all her life, so she sits behind her glow chained to her love, both tormented by her glow. Gwen will never experience love. She will always be chained behind her glow holding her love and wondering if it is only a reflection."

Keisha's lower eyelids pooled. She blinked several times and turned to Brenda. "Girl, is my mascara running?"

"Eww, better start thinking tax shelter, because the restroom is about to be your second home."

Keisha glared at Aniel. "Thanks a lot, Posey." She headed off to the restroom with Brenda in tow.

Brenda craned her head around before slipping through the door, and found Aniel. "Was love an in-law in your childhood home?"

Danny became glassy eyed, slammed a twenty dollar bill down on the bar. "Here's twenty, now change the fucking story and let her have her man."

LT watched the twenty flounder for a moment and snatched it up. "Hey, that's the twenty you owe me." Danny stood slack jawed, while O'Dell pounded the bar with his fist and laughed like hell, which triggered LT to hoot.

He pressed his hand against the window as he read her text. He dropped his hand down to his side clutching the phone, which felt like a bar of ice. He gazed up into a field of resplendent stars and thought, what makes a man so completely? Not his laurels, his honor, or his good deeds. He paused to collect his thoughts... but a woman's kiss, which also has the power to repair. As tears pooled he thought, my ache and I desperately need your handiwork. Don't deny us your kiss.

He rubbed the memo note bearing her number

between his thumb and index finger and thought, though my morals have ceased their smelting, and resolution has routed all doubt, and pursuit bugles, I'm now basting in her scalding contradiction. And I believed you were to bring my pen.

He jiggled the latch of the locked window as he looked down at the street four flights below, and thought despair you are but an open window for most. His diaphragm gave a short spasm as tears streamed. He thought, but for me you are locked. Father, am I so inglorious in your eyes that you deny me courage for the window? You've already taken my will to write. Father, please grant me one or the other.

He heard a faint click and felt heat deep in his chest. He looked over his left shoulder at the lifeless, flat, dingy wallpaper covering the refrigerator, it had not cycled on. He turned around, scanned his drab apartment, and heard nothing.

He turned back to the window and felt his chest becoming hotter. A kiln lit. Its gas jets opened and flooded the orifices, and row after row of burners ignited, and were now ablaze, giving it life. He believed He had returned it.

As it pushed through, he closed his eyes to catalog the second most important event of his young life, and marveled at what had been missing for so many years and now refused to be ignored. The mystery of creativity took control. He sat at his computer and felt his pen seated in his hand. He revisited an old file, stared at it stone cold for a moment, and deleted it. That was that.

The writer was now ready to step off the porch of his self incarceration a free man, and head off, emboldened, clutching his pen. He glowed brightly with confidence now that his ice age was over. The bubbling mud pots and geysers were now percolating under the frozen caldera in his mind, pushing up creativity, and ready for the explosive surge that was to come.

As the writer settled in for a long night with his active caldera, he thought I shall write a collection of romantic poesies and dedicate them to the one who brought my pen, beautiful Gwen... Thank you Father.

Charles grinned as he, Gwen, and the trailing girls strolled towards the security checkpoint. He gazed out the airport window at all the mounds of snow and said to his companions, "Ahh yes, Christmas in the sand."

Gwen smiled and nodded. Abigail was behind him and winked at the other two behind Gwen. They giggled as she quickly flanked him, put her arm through his, and said loudly, "Oh, darling, did you remember to pack the revolver."

The two in the back burst into hearty laugher, which ignited Gwen. Charles now flushed and wide eyed reeled wildly. "Goddamn it, airport security has no sense of humor."

She giggled and said, "Oh, now darling, just tell them you're reformed, and I'm sure they'll over look your prison record and warrants. By the way, all those warrants were just unpaid parking tickets, right?"

He shook his head. "I swear to God, you're just like that damn Odell."

He looked over at Gwen who was still smiling and pointed to her. "See, I like that. Vacation's working on you already."

She sighed. "I think you're right." She turned to a window to say good-bye to the snow, and turned back quickly. Windows always provoked thoughts of Aniel.

They were well into the air when the captain turned off the seatbelt sign and delivered his scripted welcome, and added, "Folks, the cold city is now in the rearview mirror. Enjoy your stay on the island."

Charles turned to Gwen with enchanted thoughts of the island. "Maybe we won't ever go back."

She fumbled frantically with her seatbelt buckle until it opened and jumped straight up with a wild look in her eye. "I need to use the restroom."

He thought damn, I hope she's not going off again.

She closed and locked the door, grabbed a tissue from the vanity and pressed it to her eyes, and whispered to her reflection, "Aniel, I have to go back. I need to find you and ask you to please release me, as I think I would you. To capture the other side of a woman and not release her, God, it's more than anyone can take."

She grabbed another tissue and thought, I want to go back to the city so bad. I want to apologize for my birthmark, and kiss you one last time and have you tell me I'm released. Please don't fill my empty spaces. I'm unworthy. Let's just be friends and please don't speak of things we feel we won't ever have.

As she grabbed another tissue there was a soft knock at the door and a voice said, "Ma'am is everything alright?"

She cleared her throat, opened the door, and said as she recovered, "Oh, yes, I'm fine."

Charles whispered as she sat down, "Damn, are you alright?"

She patted her stomach. "It must have been the chicken last night."

Wide eyed he said, "Whoa, I know what you mean. You know Odell won't eat chicken to this day. We were hunkered down near this little shit hole village during our tour in the sand box, when I noticed him eating a ration that had green chicken. I said, damn, gunny you think you ought to be eating that?" Charles laughed and said, "That damn Odell said, 'LT if it's American, by God I don't care what color it is. I'm damn proud to eat it, and shit it later.'"

As he tooted, she glanced around horrified, and whispered with harsh dissonance, "Charles, please, we're in close quarters and tuning you out is an art they don't have time to acquire."

He put his hand up. "Ok, ok, it's a damn funny story. I'll tell you when you're feeling better." She stared in disbelief for a moment. "Art has its limitations. Thank you anyway."

A young man with a Marine crew cut directly across the aisle said, "Sir, I would like to hear it."

Charles looked around her and grinned big, then said, "What's your rank Marine?"

The young man said with pride, "Just made Corporal, sir."

He elbowed her. "Trade places." She looked at the window and thought, oh no, not the window.

The chatter was brisk between the two men. She looked out over the wing into the vast space of the sky and thought, please don't fill my empty spaces, release me. She pulled the shade down, closed her eyes, and did her best to tune out the Marines' chatter.

The small cab was cramped. Charles sat in the front, while Gwen and the girls were in the back, piled on one another, but all smiling. He craned his head around and announced with excitement as if he were starting a new tour of duty. "It'll be damn nice to drip sweat again."

They looked at each other oddly, searched each other's face for concurrence as to the absurdity they all thought they had just heard, and all looked to Gwen to give their unanimous retort. She obliged. "Must have been the mortar shells."

The hotel came into view. It was a split-level. The reservation desk occupied the center of the lobby with a set of steps to the left that led to the rooms. To the right was a large lounge with the dining room towards the back and furnished cliché island decor. Behind the desk was a large open bar. French doors were in the back of the dining room leading to a large balcony overlooking the ocean.

He had reserved two sets of adjoining rooms facing the ocean. They all went to their rooms to freshen up to meet at the bar later. Gwen and his room adjoined, while the girls spread out across their two adjoining rooms.

She didn't bother unpacking and went immediately out onto the balcony, placed her hands on the railing, looked out over the ocean towards the northwest, and thought, I've given myself a week to forget you, please help me. God, it seems like there's someone behind me, fighting me. Damn, I'm the one who owns my mind, but sometimes I feel like I'm losing it. Please believe me. I'm not the one for you. I don't usc my hcart. I'm a businesswoman. I wouldn't know what to do with it.

I don't know why I filled in. The schedule was in front of me, I saw your beautiful name. A simple feeling came over me, and I felt like I was pushed from behind. This feeling refuses to leave now that I've captured... something. And it's so simple in texture not like the fatiguing complexity of Braille. It has this overwhelming fullness that I can't empty or explain. Just a simple feeling and now it has become like Braille ever since the light in your eyes. Now let's just be good friends and not speak of things we'll never have.

Mid morning the next day they all met in the bar as planned for a shopping excursion. The downtown area was a half mile from the hotel. Kim and Abigail pulled up the rear hung over, but fresh, and snickered at Gwen's and Charles's clothing. She was in all white, from her bathing suite and cover up, even down to her flip-flops and hat. Charles snickered,then said, "Damn, you must have an allergy to color."

She retorted quickly. "I don't know what you're laughing at. You look like hotel security."

Kim nodded. "She's got a point."

He was dressed in a dark jacket and slacks with a white shirt open at the collar.

Abigail sarcastically. "Yeah, that or there's a cartel close by."

Gwen defended her style. "I prefer white, it's cooler." She turned to him. "God, Charles are you ever going to relax? You're screaming for help."

"Winnie, relaxation is a state of mind."

She shook her head. "Charles, relaxation for you will be the aftereffect of a toe tag."

He gave his close friend a warm smile, and said with affection, "There's my Louisiana pepper sauce."

Downtown was slight and had one main street, where most of the shops and activity were concentrated. During the tourist season commerce takes its natural course and expands, spilling out into the streets and sidewalks under awnings and tents. The buildings were single story, brightly painted, and in various degrees of dilapidation from the assaults of sea, salt, and weather.

The small street appeared as a busy painter's palette

by the myriad of tourists wearing brightly colored clothing as they arrived. Gwen and the girls were thumbing through racks of dresses spread out along the sidewalk, and bargaining with each other for the extra space in Charles's bag. Sasha wandered over to a jewelry vendor across the street when Charles came up holding a box of cigars.

She stared at the box. "Surely not."

"Oh no, no, Odell and Danny." He looked around. "Where are the others?"

"Doing what they've done for the last four years, fighting over the extra space in your bag."

"Damn, I should charge."

He weaved through the crowd and came up to the three. Gwen inquired innocently. "Uh, do you think you have extra space in your bag?"

"I'm wise to you Winnie, now how much you want buy."

"Charles. A grunt like you has no real use for space." She looked down at his cigar box. "Everything you need could fit in that."

As they chuckled, they heard scuffling behind them on the other side of the street. All four were now scanning through the crowd looking for the action. Charles caught a glimpse of an older adolescent trying to pull the handbag out of Sasha's hands. He had already turned over two dress racks and was plowing through the crowd like a ball player in full sprint when he caught the pickpocket.

He grabbed him, picked him up, slammed him down, supine on the sidewalk, and buried his knee in his chest.

Gwen tripped in her flip-flops a few times and bloodied her knee by the time she made it over to them, winded. Louisiana flooded her mind when he drew his arm back like an archer drawing the string of his long bow.

He pointed his index and middle fingers like the boy scout pledge and was about to plunge it into adolescent's trachea. She shook violently and shouted. "Charles, stop. He's just a pickpocket."

He was now dripping the sweat he had asked for.

She cried when he didn't respond, but collected herself quickly when she saw the adolescent close his eyes in anticipation to his end, like her in Louisiana.

She shouted. "Lieutenant. Stop."

He looked around with brisk movements. He was in combat.

She lowered her voice. "Charles, stop. You're flashing. It's me, Winnie, we're on vacation. Please let him go. He's just a pickpocket. No one's hurt."

He stood and the adolescent fled clenching a limp shoulder. He was now soaked in sweat, nostrils flaring like a winded thoroughbred and appeared dazed. He shook it off quickly. "Back to the hotel." He glared at the shocked women and shouted. "Move out."

Gwen gazed at the trembling women, gestured towards the hotel, and said, "Just go."

He was in the rear marching them briskly and

pressing them hard with Gwen between him and the girls. They were close to the hotel when Abigail craned her head around to Gwen, with tears in her eyes. "I need to slow down."

Gwen gritted her teeth, whirled around, put her hand on his huge soaked chest. "Goddamn it, slow down. We don't have a soldier's stamina. We're women in flip-flops, now slow down." They locked glares for a moment. When they reached the lobby, Charles took an immediate left and went to his room.

Gwen looked over the field-punished women. They had never seen him flash. She reassured them, and said, "Let's chill on the hotel beach today and have plenty of drinks." She gazed down the hall leading to the rooms. "God knows we need them."

The girls headed to the bar while she left to console Charles.

The three women sat down and ordered drinks. Sasha ordered tea but caught the waiter as he was about to leave. "Shit, give me what ever they're having, what ever it is. I don't think ice tea going to make it this time." The waiter smiled and the other two laughed. Abigail pondered his behavior and turned to the others. "Ooh, the way he handled that kid makes you look at him kinda of different."

Kim stared in disbelief. "The only thing I see is a grenade about to go off and the only thing different now is more distance."

Sasha chuckled, then said, "You know he gives job security a renewed appreciation."

They relaxed and sipped their drinks. After a long lull, while over looking the ocean, Abigail turned to the other two. "Damn, could you imagine if he had a teenage daughter? God, I don't think a boy would ever come around."

Kim concurred. "You better start taking up women, because I don't see a pair boxers in that future."

Sasha, now a little lit, chimed in, "Or get used to a life of selfies in the convent."

They all busted out laughing and Kim said, "Damn, I don't think Jesus could pass his field tests."

As the drinks flowed the Charles jokes grew in absurdity, but funny.

She cleaned her skinned knee and knocked softly on the door separating their rooms. She waited until she heard "Come." She opened the door slowly and stepped in. She heard his voice from the bathroom.

"I'll be out in a minute." She sat on the long wicker bench at the end of the king size bed, placed her hands in her lap, and waited.

He was bent over with his hands on the sink staring into the mirror. He thought, talk to me. Where are my grunts? Come on Odell, Danny? Damn, I fucked up today, talk to me.

He reminisced about the day he decided to resign his commission. The colonel asked him to meet him in the enlisted barracks. Odell and Danny were there when he stepped in holding a manila folder and asked, "Have you seen Colonel Sky?" Odell came up to him and punched him hard in the gut. He fell to his knees and puked. He looked up at Odell with anger in his eyes. "I ought to have you court-martialled gunny."

Odell sighed, disappointed. "I don't think that's possible civilian. Maybe take me to civilian court on assault." He paused, crossed his arms, and looked at Danny. "I'll just tell the judge that you were bad mouthing the Corps and attacked me. Shit, you're the one quitting; who do you think the judge is going to believe?" He turned back to him. "You know the Corps has a lot invested in you. Not to mention me and Danny busting our asses and risking our lives to groom a leader."

He came to his feet, gritted his teeth, and stood. "You have no idea. I fucked up. I panicked, and now two of my men are dead. I don't have it. I don't have leadership. All I can see are the pieces of private Wilson and Abrams. Don't talk to me about leadership. You don't have a clue."

Danny straightened up. "Attention on deck." They all came to attention when an older man with thin gray hair and pale blue eyes walked in from the back. He put his hand up. "At ease, gentlemen."

Charles always had deep respect for Colonel Sky, even before he knew him. He heard a lot of stories about him. He didn't pay much attention to what the officers thought. He

was their competitor for rank and felt anything they had to
say was biased. He listened to the boots, especially out in the
field when they thought he wasn't listening. He listened to a
young gunny's story about when Sky took his cap off and
bitch whipped a young lieutenant with it.

They were out in the field at a command post and a
request came in for ordinance at the front line. The whole
area was getting beat to shit and all the carriers were out. An
old gunny was helping the corpsman bag and tag the dead,
when the young lieutenant shouted. "Hey you, old gunny, get
your ass over to ordinance and do something useful."

Sky, a major then, cap whipped the shit out of that
punk and said, "You fucking maggot. Show respect and call
the man by his name before you potentially make a patriot of
him." He didn't understand that part of the story. He figured
it got fucked up as it was passed around.

The Colonel looked intently at the young lieutenant
holding his belly. "You don't understand what the Corps is
all about. Yeah, you fucked up and lost two men. When I
was young man with my first command I lost all, but two,
because I panicked. The only two left were a young gunny
and a private who was alive, but brain dead. I curled up next
to a tree, felt sorry for myself and blubbered that I was unfit
and was going to quit."

He glared at the lieutenant and pointed to a small
bump on the bridge of his nose. "That gunny gave me that.
He planted his hand in my face and told me what the Corps
was all about." He paused to gaze with deep appreciation at

Odell and Danny, and turned back. "Do you know what a patriot is?" He frown at the bellyaching lieutenant. "That gunny taught me it's not that warmth in your chest or that feeling of hubris pride while waving your little flag during a parade, watching patriotic soldiers march in pressed uniforms, and when it's over you feral up your little flag for next time and pick the confetti out of your hair. It's not sitting in fold out chairs on the deck of a ship, listening to long winded speeches, while old women fan themselves. That's patriotism. The patriot takes the bullet."

He looked up at the flag on the wall and continued. "You know there're just a few patriots left, most are dead, and the oncs still alive are in love with her. You see, the time will come when she'll whisper, 'I need you to take a bullet for me.' The patriot will gaze upon her one last time, empty himself of hope, and when he's on the beach, and the bullet flies through him, and he drops to his knees, he'll know at that moment he's been given the privilege to court her."

"She'll whisper her vows, 'The patriotic will soon forget you after they furl their little flags, but I will always love you and never forget your love for me, and I will engrave your name in the ramparts of liberty.'" He narrowed his eyes. "You see, you'll never really know if you're in love with her, until you've been given the privilege to take the bullet. The Corps is all about her."

He paused reflectively. "I loved that gunny, lost him on an ordinance run." He looked at all three of them as patriots.

"Carry on gentlemen," and left out the back.

Odell came up to him, took the folder. "You know what a soldier's fire is?" He took him out behind the barracks where Danny was starting a fire in a burn barrel. Odell looked at him intently and pointed to the blazing fire. "That's a soldier's fire. They've been burning long before the Greek and Roman armies, far into antiquity, but they're all the same. Soldiers sit by them mourn, celebrate, plan, and they comfort. It's been going on for thousands of years."

Odell tossed the folder into the fire. "A soldier's fire, let's honor the fallen." The lieutenant shook his head, looked at the two gunnies, and said, "No, gunny, you're wrong." The two looked at him confused. "It's a patriot's fire." He watched as the folder turned to ash.

"Carry on gentlemen," he said and left.

He washed his face, looked intently back into the mirror, and thought, thanks gunnies. He stepped out of the bathroom. Gwen looked up. "Are you alright?"

He sat down heavily beside her. "Am I the only man in America that can fuck up a vacation?"

"Yes, Charles you are, that and relaxation." He chuckled and she reached up kissed his cheek. "Come on you ole grunt. Let's start over."

He rested his elbows on his thighs, and clasped his hands together smartly. "I love the Corps," he paused out of respect for his PTSD, "but it gets me into trouble sometimes." He sighed, then said, "I never had the privilege to take a bullet for her, but she knows I would. God, I'm in love with her." He stood invigorated. "Come on, Winnie, let's head to the beach. We look like old people hanging around the room."

They stood on the dining room balcony and waved to the girls.

She turned to him. "Let's go to this little cabana I saw down the beach on the way from the airport."

He looked at her and then the girls. "I'll walk you there and check it out."

She rolled her eyes. "Good God, it's just not going to happen for you is it?"

"Now, Winnie, it's not over yet. There's still hope."

When the cabana was in sight, she sensed the stares from vacationing families. She came to a dead stop and frowned while critiquing his cartel suit. "Damn it Charles. I feel like I'm being escorted off the property."

He chuckled, took off his shoes and socks, rolled his pants legs up to mid calf. "There, that's best I can do, and next time stay off the property." As they approached the cabana, she nodded. "I really like this."

He looked around, excitedly. "Winnie, you found a good one. It's all families, nice and safe. I like it a lot." He looked over his shoulder when he felt a tug from patrol. "I better get back. The redhead is starting to kick in her stall."

She rolled her eyes again and raised her hands,

exasperated. "Go, there's no hope." He winked and headed back. She sat on a stool over looking the ocean, placed her white hat and bag on the bar, and fluffed her hair back to its natural position.

A short portly man with gray-blue eyes, tightly curled graying hair, came up, smiled warmly, and said in a light Irish accent, "How may I serve you, my dear?" Smitten by her all white attire, he thought ahh the symbol of purity, but it could also be some sort of personal symbol. Now it lures me with its teasing speculation.

"White wine please."

Indeed, my mouth waters, he thought.

When he returned, some beach meat had just pulled up and eyed her. She fidgeted in her seat, and when he was about to leave, she squeezed his wrist. "There'll be a really nice tip if I don't get hit on."

He looked over his shoulder and turned back. "My dear you have rare blue eyes, it is only natural that young men take notice."

"They're a curse."

He pointed his finger straight up to emphasize his point. "The caretaker's burden."

She glanced up occasionally as he chatted with the men. They all turned their attention to the ocean and sports talk when he left. She relaxed when she heard sports talk.

When he returned, she said in relief, "I owe you. What did you say for them to give up so easily? A man could be served a restraining order and consider it foreplay."

He chuckled, then said, "I told them that you are a lesbian on a bad break up."

She laughed loudly and covered her mouth, briefly to suppress the adolescent burst, then said, "You are a very clever man."

He felt the water swirling in his mouth, and circled his speculation. He nibbled for clues. "The island has only one shot at you, and wants to give you the experience you are looking for."

Paul, then Aniel flashed in her mind. She dropped the jovial banter and said hopeful in a stranger, "What if you had an experience once long ago and you don't want another, but you keep coming back?"

He thought, the answer is now somewhere in my mouth. He put his elbows on the bar, came close, and smiled warmly, then said, "That is the island's favorite customer."

She put her elbows on the bar, interlaced her fingers and balanced her chin, cocked her head, and glowered, insulted, now that she felt him pitching for future hotel business by humoring guests. "How so?"

Insulted, he obliged her challenge, and straightened up, placing his hands on the bar. "Because they are troubled." He glanced over at the families splashing in the surf. "The happy do not need the island. You see, some come to the island in search of an experience that does not exist, and convince themselves its acquisition is buried somewhere in the next visit, a loop of illusion, but most come to sever ties." He paused to punctuate his last statement with a glower of equal value. "To that other experience you keep coming back to."

She popped her chin off her fingers, fidgeted, sat back, and placed her hands in her lap. She was out matched.

Indeed, he thought, I taste its flesh now and it is flush with love. But what has happened for her to be this distraught and what about him? Oh speculation you tease with only your flesh. How I need your bone. Your sinews cannot carry the finale alone.

He gave her warm reassuring smile, then took his index and middle finger, and animated them like scissors. "She begins to cut ties moving methodically. When she reaches the end and thinks all are cut, she turns back to check for anything that might have been overlooked. She is surprised to see that someone behind her has been mending all those ties. Now, this cutting and mending can go on for a quite some time, but eventually there is going to be a tipping point and someone is going to win."

She placed her arms back on the bar and said timidly, "Who wins?"

Dominating, he placed his elbows back on the bar, leaned in, and said dead cold, "The one behind you. She is stronger and keeps coming back, dragging you with her."

She sat up straight, and wrestled out from under her subordinate position, and said hotly, "This island is blowing its only shot."

He forfeited the match now that she was smarting, and

looked deeply into the eyes of the little woman who was in love, and of whom he was growing very fond of. "This island is willing to risk it." She kept her aggressive posture. "May I please see a menu?" He nodded with a fond expression. "Certainly, my dear."

When he returned with the menu a fresh batch of beach meat pulled up. He placed the menu in front of her. "I will be right back." She relaxed when she heard sports talk again. He poured them drinks and tended to the other guests.

Her posture had not budged when he made it back.

"Now, I am middle aged and sometimes I do not always recall exactly what I have said. Now, did I say you were coming off a bad break up or a hard break up?" She turned red faced when she saw that he was afoot again. "What's the difference?"

He rested on his elbows, leaned in, and glared intently. "Now, with a bad break up things are still connected and there is hope." He straightened up, swung his hand down on the menu, sharply, like a butcher cleaving. "With a hard breakup you have killed him in your mind and he is never coming back, because now there is no possibility of mending. Everything is completely severed with no hope."

She put the palms of her hands on the edge of the bar and squirmed on her stool. He thought, indeed, as he craned his head around and shouted. "It is a bad breakup gents."

She flared her nostrils, clenched her jaw, snatched the

menu up quickly, and huffed. "What's the most fattening thing on this menu?"

He gave her a warm smile, came close, and said, "Patience, my dear."

She slammed the menu down. "Then I'll have the salad."

He took the menu and nodded. "Very well."

She stabbed at her salad while watching him chat with guests. When she saw a vegetable that resembled a potato, she harpooned it with passion.

When she finished he came down and smiled, then said, "Are you still angry?"

She smiled, and shook her head. "Angry enough."

He nodded. "Fair enough." She stared into his eyes. "Do you blister all costumers equally?" He shook his head. "My dear, only those whom I care about." As he observed her eyes glassing over, he reached for her hand. "Patience and resolution sometimes never find each other, but once I find a friend, I cherish them." He kissed her hand, then waved to a young man walking up the beach. "Ah, my relief is here. Have a pleasant day, my dear." She nodded, then reached for her napkin as he left and felt hopeful in a stranger.

She turned her attention to the ocean and mused on its beauty, until she saw a young man headed her way. She panicked and thought, oh, surely to God, that's not you. Please, Aniel, that can't be you. She was about to hop off her stool and run back to her hotel. As the young man came closer she slid off her stool, stood beside it, and was about bolt, when she heard a woman's voice call out "Victor." She sat back down shaking and thought that could have been your double. I didn't hear his voice, but that could have been you. Unnerved she settled up and left.

Late night settled in and Charles was sitting up in his bed reading through his magazines by the glow of the nightstand lamp. He had the balcony door open to a moonless night. The breeze was light and the scents and sounds were sedating. There was a soft knock coming from the adjoining door. Puzzled, he laid his magazine on the nightstand, and straightened up. "Winnie?"

"May I come in?"

"Of course."

She came to the foot of the bed. "Would you mind if I bunk with you tonight?"

He sighed heavily as sadness came over his face. She fidgeted slightly and he knew that anxiety well, the memory of the rape, which is triggered by violence. "I'm sorry Winnie. My morning fuck up has got you thinking about Louisiana."

"A little."

He grabbed the sheets on the other side, and whipped them back, sharply. "Hop aboard sailor." She smiled, placed her robe on the long bench at the foot of the bed, climbed in, fluffed the pillow, and laid on her side with her back to him. He returned to his magazine, read for a while, then popped her hip with it. "You awake?"

She sighed. "I am now."

"Good. I've got a funny story. It'll cheer you up."

She sighed again. "Great, now I'm awake, captive, and the jailer's full of himself."

"Oh, you'll like this one."

She put her hand up, cut him off. "No chicken."

"Oh, no, this one's funnier."

He began. "We were in the sandbox and that damn Odell..."

She cut him off again. "Why do all your stories come out of the Middle East? I thought you were deployed all over the world?"

"Yeah, we were, but the most fun was in the sandbox playing with the sand fleas. Shit, how much fun can you have in the Artic, or bobbing in the South Pacific? Shit, you're too damn scared that something's either going to freeze off or get chewed off. Damn, I much prefer the safety of the Middle East."

Her shoulders bounced as she chuckled. "God, Charles."

"What?"

He continued "We were on patrol and came up to this little burned out house in a quiet village, and if it's quiet when Americans are about don't blink, because there will be trouble."

"So, I sent Odell and Danny in to sweep the house. They gave the signal and we all piled in. We were standing in a small living room with no door and blown out windows. It had a little open kitchen towards the back with a small eating bar separating the two rooms and the side door next to the kitchen was blown. Out the side door was a long four-foot high rock wall blown out in various places."

"I don't like staying in those houses long. One grenade and the whole thing will implode." He paused to ponder an observation, and mumbled "Building codes, damn." He continued. "I looked at Danny and was about to give the order to move out. He was red faced and laughing so hard he wasn't making any noise. I said, 'what the fuck's wrong with you gunny.' He pointed towards the kitchen. I looked..."

Charles stopped abruptly and began laughing uncontrollably. He put his index finger and thumb to his eyes and wiped the tears, which triggered her to chuckle. He collected himself. "Odell was in some old black burka, looking through that little screen they have for the eyes, he put his hands on his hips, and looked at me. 'Darling, how would you like your goat?'"

"Everybody busted up, then shit hit the fan. A firestorm of bullets came flying through. We all dropped and I looked at Danny and shouted. 'Get them out along the wall.' I was hunkered down by the bar waving my men through the door barking orders. When they were all spread out and dug in..."

He stopped to wipe his eyes and popped her hip. "That damn Odell laughed like hell and said, 'Darling, I know you're busy with your conflict and all, but could you please get this fucking shower curtain off of me so I can retrieve my weapon.' Damn, I started laughing so hard and said 'damn, gunny, I'd court-martial you right now if you weren't so fucking funny.'"

"We made it to the wall with Odell tripping at almost every step. I looked at Danny and he was so bad laughing I didn't think he was breathing. I watched Odell fighting to get out of the burka. It looked like he was in a bag with an alligator. Shit, I could hardly breathe myself. He finally came out with a wild look, and said, 'God, I look dreadful in black. You don't think anybody saw do you?'"

"Shit, all hell broke loose. They were giving us everything they had, while we were laughing our asses off. Odell put the burka on a long rod, held it up, and waved it. I had tears streaming down and said 'what the fuck are you doing?' He said, 'Giving them the burka sir.' A corporal next to Danny spoke up. 'Sir I know a little of their language and I think they're insulted.' Shit, that just set everybody off again. I said 'Corporal the intentions of the US Marine Corps are not to insult anyone, that's not in our nature. We are only here to kill sand fleas, and tailgate.'"

Her shoulders bounced to the joy she felt in the warmth of her friend's laugher.

She rose up on her elbow and craned her head around. "Damn. Charles, I don't understand how you can laugh when someone could have been seriously injured or killed."

He wiped his eyes again. "Oh come on, shit, you could

be in a hand basket half way to hell, and you know damn well someone's going to cut up. And you better pray to God you're not stuck in one with Odell."

"Good God, Charles, the whole point of prayer is to avoid the basket in the first place."

"Oh, come on, Winnie, don't be so stiff, now say something funny." She lay her head back down, and sighed. He popped her hip again. "Hey, I got another one." He paused to analyze the complete story. "Oh better not, need to edit that one, might be a little vulgar."

"Edit? I'd settle for an occasional filter. I'm going to sleep."

He tossed his magazine on the nightstand, wiped his eyes as he chuckled, and turned the light off. She looked towards the balcony, lit only by starlight, and watched the rhythm of the breeze work the curtain like a stage play about to begin. Past the curtain, Jupiter looked like a masthead light of a ship far out on the ocean.

As he snored lightly, she closed her eyes and thought about what the little Irishman said. She felt the one behind her come up and say, "I want him."

Her eyes flew open and she thought, oh, please.

She spoke again, this time through gritted teeth. "And I want to lay with him a lot and most of all to be held down. I'm in love with him."

She sat up quickly and was about to go out on to the balcony, but Louisiana pushed her back in bed, forcing her to remain still and awake and running from the one behind her most of the night.

Dawn light finally arrived, lashed to the breeze that had been busy luffing the curtains of the deserted stage all night when she woke from a light doze. She grabbed her robe, went back to her room, and closed the adjoining door.

She cleaned up and dressed, and waited for dining room to open. She found an empty table out on the balcony among the seniors who bed down early and rise early, and thought, I'm not far behind all of you. Aniel, can you not see that? Please release me. You're young and beautiful. I'm too old inside. You need to find a young woman to hold down, one who's complete, not this old woman who's empty and has nothing to offer.

My empty spaces hold me up and allow me to hide. If you understood empty spaces you would realize they're not meant to be filled. The owner designed them to keep things out, because she's a failure. You only get one chance at the heart and I couldn't hold him. I didn't even know he didn't want me.

So you see I failed two. Paul and my heart, because I wasn't adequate enough to keep either. Aniel, you would be the third. I would fail you. I can't even have children, too many infections. No standing, total inadequacy, I'm so sorry I saw the light in your eyes and now have failed you. Please, now let's just be very good friends and not speak of things that aren't for us.

She was on her third cup of coffee when Charles pulled up a chair. He ordered coffee and said, "Better?" He noticed dark circles under her eyes and she said, "I couldn't sleep." Last night's sadness returned to his face and heart. "I'm sorry. Maybe we can find something to do today and take your mind off of it."

She shook her head. "I've been over Louisiana. God, Charles your snoring sounds like a thunderstorm. I would have been better off in a Kansas City train yard."

"Well, I'm glad you're better."

They all spent the next few days shopping, tanning, swimming, and putting on weight, except Charles. He was in the gym every morning and on guard duty thereafter.

At noon on the second to last day of their vacation, Charles, Gwen, and Sasha were waiting in the dining room for the other two to shake off their hangovers and join them for lunch. When they arrived the two looked beat to shit. Charles grinned, while Gwen chuckled, and Sasha giggled. The two laid their heads on the table.

Kim said, "Just chop it off and make it quick."

Abigail qualified. "No, lethal injection. Charles might use a spoon."

"Nah, too quick. I'm thinking elbow."

Sasha was thumbing through snorkeling brochures and said, "I think I'll snorkel."

Charles furrowed his brow. "Hell no, there's shit in there that'll sting, bite, or kill."

"Well, you'll just have to go with me."

Abigail perked up. "I'll go. I need to soak my head."

Kim rose up. "I don't know. Your pounding head might attract a shark."

"Good. I'll stick my head in its mouth and skip the spoon."

Kim laughed, then put her hands on sides if her head. "I'll pay you if you don't make me laugh."

They finished lunch, then the happy, the disgruntled, and the hung over headed to the docks. Gwen thought about the Irishman and headed back to the cabana. She acquired her original seat, enjoyed the ocean, while waiting to be served.

An older adolescent came up and took her order. She looked at his nametag, smiled, and said, "Tonto. I really like that." She glanced around and saw a middle aged man with dark hair and with a cluster of keys hanging from his belt, counting money in the cash register.

She said to adolescent, "Where's the little Irishman?" Tonto became wide-eyed shook his head slightly and mouthed no, no.

The older man looked up with a scowl on his face, glared at the adolescent. "Has O'Shea been hanging around again? Damn it, what did I tell you?"

Gwen looked around the adolescent and returned the scowl. "Do you have an issue with my husband?"

Embarrassed, he stammered for a moment. "Oh, I'm so sorry Mrs. O'Shea. I was thinking about another O'Shea. Please, we here at the Blue Crab want all our customers to be happy. I'm so sorry."

He stood in front of the adolescent still red faced and said sternly, "Tonto, Mrs. O'Shea is to have all her drinks on the house today." He looked at her and apologized again as he left.

Tonto waited until he was out of sight, turned to her, astonished. "That was so sweet. Wow, you think fast."

"Where is he?"

He came closer. "George doesn't like him, says he harasses the customers."

Some beach meat pulled up and eyed her. She whispered, "Would you do me a favor?"

He nodded.

"Would you tell those men that I'm a lesbian, because I'm about to get hit on."

He gave a hearty laugh, than said, "You are so funny, sure."

He was about to leave when she grabbed his arm. She hesitated for a moment. "Tell them I'm coming off a bad break up." She relaxed when she heard sports talk.

He tended to the dry customers, and came back to her. "He's weird in a cool sort of way. I like him. He talks to me like you're talking to me now, not like Pop. He always talks down at me."

"What does he do?"

He looked up and unconsciously followed a young girl with his eyes. She thought, God, adolescence.

He said, while following the girl, "Oh, he's a writer. He doesn't write anymore, though. He works my shift when George isn't here. I feel bad sometimes, because he won't take any money for working it. He says he's not interested in money, and that talking to the tourists lets him go off island and that's far more valuable."

"Why does he not leave?"

Still fixated, he said, "I asked him that once and he said he made a promise that he wouldn't."

The girl was now out of sight and he looked back, and she said, "Do you know where he is now?"

"No, but I can show you where he lives."

He came back with a drink napkin and drew out the directions. She finished her wine and handed him a large tip. His eyes widened and he stammered. "Ma'am that's too much."

"That's for letting him go off the island."

She went back to her room freshened up, changed into white shorts and a white blouse, and rented a scooter. She followed the narrow winding road up a large hill and came to small house that sat far back from the road. It had a tin roof with a narrow covered porch large enough for two wicker chairs with a small table between them.

She could see him sitting in one of the chairs. He

stood and squinted as she remover her ponytail band. She shook her head briskly, and combed back her wind blown hair with her hands and reapplied the band. As she walked towards him, he smiled broadly, then said, "How is my little cabana lady?"

She stopped a few paces from him. "I'm not barging in am I?"

He shook his hands gently. "Absolutely not, my dear, please come, sit." He thought, I shall have your bone. I am reignited. She stepped onto the porch and they introduced themselves.

"Let me get you something to drink."

She stared at the table supporting the half empty bottle of scotch. "I'm afraid that's a little too strong."

"Tea then?"

"Now don't go to any trouble, water's fine."

"Nonsense, have a seat, I will put the kettle on."

He came back and handed her a bottle of water. "Until tea." He sat. "Now what brings you to the top of the hill?"

She looked out over the stunning view of the ocean. "It's beautiful," then turned back. "I went back to the cabana looking for you." He said playfully, "Now you are not hitting on me are you?"

"I assure you my intentions are honorable."

"Good, because you have me at a disadvantage, I have given you all the tricks in my bag."

She chuckled, then said, "I've been quizzing Tonto

about you."

"Yes, a fine lad, but you know there could be an issue with accuracy when using an adolescent for reference."

"True, but he did have some interesting things to say." She paused when she felt a growing fondness for him. "May I ask you a question?"

"Certainly, my dear, if I can ask you something before you leave."

Nervously, she said, "Do writers always keep their readers anxious until the end?"

He leaned towards her looked at her intently. "Why else would you read them?" She wanted to transcend fondness to friendship, but that would require some measure of intimacy.

The wicker chair felt like an easy chair and she relaxed. "Tonto says you're weird in a cool sort of way, but the scooter shop owner says you're crazy as hell."

"Well, you have quite a problem on your hands. Do you believe an adolescent fresh out of innocence with accuracy issues, or a middle-aged man with his nose buried deep into his business and accepts common village opinion for convenience, since the truth is too time consuming to acquire, and will probably be of little value once rendered anyway?"

"I'll go with weird in a cool sort of way."

Pleased. "I am neither, actually. I am merely lost in fantasy."

She shook her head. "Fantasy, God, how ironic."

He jumped to his feet put both of his hands on the arms of her chair and leaned in close. She became wide-eyed, and pressed herself farther back into the chair cushion, which transitioned back to plain wicker.

"Do not be frightened, my dear. I am just intense." He sat back down. "You see, irony is my mistress. I believe she was sent her to help you or me, or both," he and added," and I hope it is the latter."

She relaxed. "You almost blew 'in a cool sort of way.'" He laughed and slapped his knee.

He reclined back deep in his chair, then quickly sat up. "Oh, yes, tell me of your encounters with fantasy."

She was hesitant at first, but felt the easy chair back and an evolving friendship, and told him all about the service.

When she finished, he laid his head back and said with the wonder of a child, "Oh, my dear, what an amazing life. You are a treasure of stories." The teakettle in the kitchen whistled. He leaned forward. "Ah, the train is in the station. I will be right back."

He returned with a large glass of iced sweet tea and set it on the table beside her.

"You shouldn't have gone to all that trouble, water was enough."

"Nonsense. I consider you my friend." The hope in a stranger gave her a friend to cherish. "As I do you." He held up his glass, and said, "Friendship till death then." She raised her glass. They shared a toast and a warm smile.

As they sat and sipped, a thought crossed his mind. "From the way you describe your business partner, he appears to be a bit of a contradiction to easy island life."

She covered her mouth, briefly, when she giggled like a schoolgirl, and said, "He's the standard everyone uses to measure the absence of relaxation."

They paused and gazed out over the ocean at the afternoon sky. She looked at him intently. "Why did you stop writing?"

"Ah, yes that would be your question. My dear, I write all the time. I do not publish."

"But Tonto-" She stopped abruptly, then shook her head, "Accuracy issues."

"Now I hope 'cool sort of way' remains in good standing."

"Oh, yes, it's intact."

He stood, scanned the ocean for a moment, and turned to her. "We all write my dear. Our minds are writing even as we sleep. Your service has hundreds of amazing stories, but to put them to paper is a tedious and time consuming proposition that most can not afford."

She sat up. "Perhaps I need to repackage. Why do you not publish?"

He sighed. "When you publish you are asking the reader for something very precious, something that can only be given once, because once it is given it is gone forever." He was about to speak when she shouted out, almost unconsciously, "Your heart."

He turned slowly, gazed at her all white attire. He thought, indeed, you have handed over your bone, and my speculation is at rest. His eyes glassed over as he thought, she has lost her love to once long ago. She now feels jilted, and forever wears bride's white as punishment. Such a romantic creature whose heart has been steeped in the fairytale of once. One heart, one chance, one failure..., and now all are gone. Oh, bone, you have punctured my throat.

The heart is a failure more than once, he thought, but a fast learner and does not understand just once. She is a failure at love, but not the heart. No, she is not a failure at love, it is all around her. Love keeps her close. She loves her friends. She is a failure of the heart; or perhaps she feels the heart has failed her somehow. Who failed whom? She does not understand it and has applied it only once, but something will not let her just discard it. Ah he has rekindled it, but is it enough to set her fairytale of once, aflame?

He came up to her and put his hands on the arms of her chair, as he did before, and leaned in real close. She backed into her cushion again. "Are we revisiting?"

He glared hard. "You are not a failure. You never have been. The heart is like a child, it learns as it grows, and it fails often. The heart must practice. My dear, you have used your heart only once and you think you have failed at everything. You cannot hold it back, it wants to love. The one behind you is you wanting to love. You are not a failure of the heart."

He watched as tears pooled in her lower lids. He went into the house and brought her a tissue. She thanked him and he walked to the other side of the porch to give her space. He leaned up against the porch post and stared out over the ocean. The sunlight was starting to pour into the porch as the sun approached for its setting. He kept his eyes to the horizon. "Their time. You see, when a reader gives you their time that is a precious gift, and a covenant forms. I felt like I was disappointing them. The reads were stale and I was disappointed for them, but the reviews were good and the stories sold. But it was time to stay the pen and spare them. So I abdicated for the sake of the covenant."

He glanced over and noticed she had the tissue crumpled in her hand with no place to hide it.

She planned to keep it and discard it later.

He reclaimed his seat, and held out his hand. "My dear there is no shame between friends. I have never told anyone what I have just told you." She held up her tea and handed him the tissue. "To friends till death."

"You know, I think she came for the latter."

She gave a diminished chuckled. "I think you're right." She sighed as she reclined and felt the easy chair of their friendship, but was provoked by her friend's assumptions and challenged. "You can't possibly know with any certainty that your readers would find you stale."

"Why, of course I can."

She leaned in to her friend and challenged again. "Ok, how so?"

"Because I am a reader, too." They chuckled as they turned towards the ocean.

She felt their measure of intimacy full now and asked her good friend. "Why did you promise not to leave the island?"

He sighed. "I did it for my wife."

She sat straight up, bright eyed, and tapped her feet excitedly. "I would love to meet her."

He looked down and assessed the wood porch planks. "She is not with us anymore."

Her posture stiffened awkwardly, then she lowered her eyes, and they remained frozen on the planks for a long, uncomfortable, moment. "I'm so sorry. I wish I would have never brought it up. I'm so sorry."

"My dear, there is no reason to be sorry. We had many good times."

He scanned the ocean searching for a way to satisfy his friend's question without divulging his true reason for remaining on the island and prodding her to dig deeper.

"The reason I acquired my reputation as crazy by most of the island population is because of her mental illness." She leaned forward and tried to get closer as a gesture of comfort, while he remained fixed on the ocean.

"You see as she became worse the twist in her mind convinced her it was me that was ill." He paused. "With mental illness, insight does not stand a chance. It is always the one you love and not you. So, I took advantage of her absence of insight and I took up the burden of bazaar behavior because it had a sedating effect on her. She remained calm for long periods as long as she could console her disturbed husband, but as you can see it had consequences" He paused filled with joy. "But what a generous bargain."

Tears returned to her lower lids. He handed her the crumpled tissue. "It was not all psychosis, pills, and screams throughout the night. We had wonderful times. Oh, how she loved to walk." He rubbed his portly belly. "As you can see, I have been a bit neglectful."

Her slight smile rose and fell, quickly, like a shallow respiration. "God, it's still so sad."

He pointed his index finger straight up. "Ah, but it was happy, too."

She watched as the sun took its seat now that her friend and her easy chair were back. She sighed. "It's so beautiful." He leaned back out of her peripheral. He was a master of the sunset like most islanders, who've spent most of their lives on islands observing sunsets and rises. He knew exactly what to say to release the heart from the jailer. The mind holds a tight grip on the heart, but even it has a weakness, aesthetics. He knew to stay behind her peripheral vision and not disturb the mind as the heart escaped.

When the time was right he said in a low soothing tone, "It is beautiful." He paced his timing of evocations to allow the mind to immerse itself fully in the aesthetic of the moment, which would allow the heart to tell everything it knows. He said again in that same soothing tone, "Sometimes it makes me think of the one I love." He paced himself, leaned forward slightly, and saw what he was looking for, and thought, indeed. She was smiling. He continued, "Sometimes I do not want the one I love to say anything. I just want to smile at the smile that is given just for me."

As Aniel called out to her, she ran towards her empty spaces, but when she arrived, the one behind her had beaten her there and wouldn't let her in. He called out to her again. She whirled around, and he was right in front of her.

The one behind her came up, pulled her hair, extending her neck, and pushed her chin onto his chest, and whispered, "I know your secret."

He said, softly, "Sometimes I walk up to the one I love and ask, please not to speak, just kiss me." He was holding her face, and blew. She fidgeted and murmured loudly. "Oh, God," then stood quickly and bit her nails.

He raised his eyes, briefly, and thought, madly indeed, once of long ago is an ash. She whirled around and he kept gazing at the ocean, then looked up, and smirked.

The teakettle flared her nostrils, and said hotly, "I thought your bag was empty?"

He raised his hands and shrugged. "An Irishman has many bags."

As she narrowed her eyes and pursed her lips, he said, "Are you angry with me?"

She grinned, and said, "Angry enough."

"Fair enough."

"It's getting late. I need to return the scooter."

He jumped up. "Oh, let me have your email."

He dashed into the house, and came back with pen and paper. "Now, my dear, I want to hear all your stories, leave nothing out. Now, I tend to be a bit long winded, so bear with me if you find my writing a tad long."

After they exchanged emails, she crossed her arms. "I'm braced now. You said that you wanted to ask me something before I left."

He glanced at the setting sun. "I believe it has slipped my mind."

She said teary eyed, "I'm going to miss you."

He looked, deeply into her eyes. "Now, my dear, you will be back next year and I hope perhaps one will be added to the entourage."

She crossed her arms and glared. "The island's blowing it."

He hugged her and whispered in her ear, "The island is all about risk."

She kissed his cheek and left.

Early morning, the dining room just opened, and she sat at a table joining her seniors on the balcony for coffee. It was overcast and the cool breeze convinced her to walk the beach one last time before heading to the airport. She thought about the Irishman and what a deep affection she had for him, but complained, I can do with out all the trickery, though.

She heard a voice behind her say, "May I join you?"

She turned and smiled, then said, "Why, of course," then cast her eyes towards the French doors. "Where's Charles?"

"Oh, he's up."

She chuckled. "Oh, I bet."

Sasha sat and ordered coffee. "He banged on our door and said, 'Get moving we leave at 1200 hours.'"

They both giggled like schoolgirls , then Sasha went on. "Kim shouted, 'Shut the fuck up, and learn to tell time. If you mean noon just say that.' Abigail said, 'We have plenty of time. What are you worried about? 1200 hours puts us somewhere into next month. Relax. Go back to sleep.'"

She put her hand to her mouth, briefly, then continued. "He said, 'I don't want any shit out of you, just be ready to move out'. He laughed after that and said, 'you damn little Odell. I'll be checking on you two at 0900 hours, which will be nine o'clock for the illiterate and in two hours for the smart ass.'"

Gwen wiped her eyes with a napkin. "God, he's back in the city already."

After they finished their coffee, Gwen stood. "I'm going to walk the beach one last time," then grinned, and said, "before the grunt stows me like field equipment."

"May I join you? I need to tell you something."

She looked down a little anxious. "I feel like even the wrapping paper it comes with has concern all over it."

They walked slowly in the surf, staring straight ahead, holding flip-flops, and their tongues, contemplating ideas to circumvent the dead silence that had just joined them. They both knew that she would be leaving soon and Sasha was anxious about her reaction. Gwen glanced at Sasha's profile and thought about the streets where she lived at her age, before she fled with Charles after he killed the two rapists and then the ghetto streets where Sasha was raised. Her concluding thought was both streets share a singularity, the emptiness of family.

As with the Irishman she considered Sasha her friend and broke from the silence like the stilted planks. "Tell me."

Relieved that her reaction was one of apparent acceptance, Sasha beamed and said flush with love, "Peter. I've been meeting him in the park every Thursday. I never planed for things to move in this direction. I just wanted some place quiet to read."

They both sat in the sand and watched the surf wash over wrecked pedicures from a week of beach walking. Sasha watched as children played in the surf, then burst into tears. Gwen, shocked, scooted closer, put her arm around her. "What in the world is wrong?"

She collected herself easily now that Gwen was wrapped around her. "Ever since Peter, I've realized what I really want. I do want him, but there's something behind him, just as important."

She burst into tears again and Gwen held her tighter. "Tell me."

She wrapped her other arm around her and rocked her until she appeared settled, then she released her, put her hand under her wet chin, and looked into her soppy face. She waited with the patience and wisdom of an older sister. Sasha collected herself again. "To be a mother and have a family."

Gwen burst into tears, released her, and buried her face in her hands. Sasha laid her head on her shoulder. "You too?"

She nodded but kept her face covered. She felt the shrike impale her through her chest with a thorn and leaving her to hang from its bush. The shrike was truth. Though she had Charles and the girls to love as a family, they all could have children and family, but for her the shrike was perched on the end of the bloody thorn pecking at her birthmark and infection scars.

When the sobbing and sniffling came to an end, they both sat side by side staring at their wet hands.

Sasha sniffed. "I want to tell him the truth. I don't think it's right to let him assume that I'm just a little bookworm. I'm so scared I'll lose him." As they looked into each other's swollen eyes, Gwen shook off her self-pity, turned her attention to her distressed little sister, and said with the genuine concern for a family member, "Quit the service and tell him the truth. I will lend you the money for school."

"I'm so afraid he won't understand."

The older sister said sternly, "He may not and there's nothing you can do about it, but finish school, and when you've graduated, start over. By then, enough time will have passed to make the service irrelevant. Your brief stay will bury easily." They paused and both stared out over the ocean as if to plan strategies for Sasha's future. They both rummaged through their thoughts as if it were a box of fixes, but Gwen found something bitter in her box and thought you have no birthmark of consequence, college partier. She quickly dropped her jealousy and thought, but I'm really glad for you.

As they continued to stare out over the water for strategies, the bitterness Gwen found in her box led her to her empty spaces. "Motherhood for some will only be a vicarious proposition as the cool spinster aunt."

The optimism of the ghetto child turned and kissed her cheek, and said, brightly, "But there's a child in your life nonetheless." She felt tears pool when she saw Gwen's birthmark, something she never thought about before, though they have had many intimate conversations of which she felt privileged to hear. She shot her eyes back to the ocean and blinked rapidly. She realized that she was nothing but a selfish whiny child, whose future had always been held in trust. She cleared her throat and continued to blink, but more rapidly and wanted to share her trust with big sister, but that impossibility only brought her closer to tears.

They watched the surf surround them. As it retreated, one of Sasha's flip-flops drifted out quickly. When she reached out to snatch it, her big sister grabbed her arm just as quick. "Let it go. It's the service. Now pursue what you really want."

They both looked up when they heard a woman shouting and saw a young mother chasing a toddler down the beach towards the water.

Gwen nudged her. "There you are," she gazed out over the water again and added, "and that's the greatest, but last joy in life." She paused as if to find something more to add, but lowered her head and stared at her feet. She turned to Sasha, noticed her wet eyes, and said coolly, "Don't worry about me or pity me," then she gave her a grand smile, and said with jubilation in her voice, "Just bring Auntie your babies to spoil." Sasha hugged her and whispered, "You'll always be family."

They sat quietly in the peaceful lull the waves brought, then Sasha chortled exuberantly. Gwen, captivated, thought, beautiful bride, and said, "What?"

"I would sit on the same bench every Thursday and Peter would walk by and make a comment on the book I was reading." She giggled, then said, "One time I was reading 'Empty Spaces' when he came up and said something silly. I giggled and said, you've never read this book have you?"

Gwen cut her off. "That's an interesting name for a book."

"Oh it's one of his older ones."

"Who wrote it?"

"Frances O'Shea. Some say it's his best work."

Slightly pale, Gwen said, "What's it about?"

She said with excitement, "Oh, it's really cool. It's about a young married couple. The husband is a shopkeeper. He's a very gentle soul who talks to everyone. He says that it better be in a shopkeeper's nature, or else he won't be in business for long. He has trouble with his wife. She begins to slowly spiral into mental illness, and his life becomes complicated by a young woman who keeps frequenting his shop. Her husband comes to confront him, because he believes they're having an affair. Well, the man's wife shows up and they both deny it. He doesn't believe them and pulls a gun. When he's about to shoot the shopkeeper, she steps in front of him and takes the bullet."

"He goes to prison and the gentle shopkeeper comes to visit every week. The husband tells him every visit that he's going to kill him when he gets out. Well, the poor little shopkeeper has dual burdens. His wife is becoming worse and the husband's time is getting shorter. The shopkeeper continues to console him religiously. During a visit the husband says you're just trying to change my mind with all these visits, but it won't work. The gentle shopkeeper becomes exasperated and says you want to know the reason why your wife kept coming to my shop? The shopkeeper glares hard at him and says she came to my shop because she said that she never met a man who wasn't always angry, or a man who shared a meal and didn't take the better portion. A man that she hadn't laid with that wasn't all about him, or be told that her opinions are of no value. I was the only gentleman she ever knew."

"The shopkeeper's wife becomes worse, but she says there is nothing wrong with her, it is him. He learns that if he acts crazy it soothes her, and she is calm for long periods under the illusion of being his caregiver. But it has its consequences. The town's people stop coming to his shop. He eventually loses his wife and the husband gets out, and pities him when he hears that he's crazy and thinks he drove him to it, and hangs himself. In the end the shopkeeper says an empty space is where we begin, and then we're born in another."

Gwen looked over her shoulder at the large hill, approximated the porch, and whispered, "And books are left to walk the beach alone."

Early spring, coats were off and sweaters welcomed. Her behavior reverted back. Charles sat in his office, listened to her pacing, and knew when she was pressing the glass. His concern was coming to a point where confrontation was imminent. She didn't polish anymore. Her hair was a quick brush through and her manicure looked like a preadolescent girl's, chipped from the boredom of tedious high maintenance.

It was payday. She shook her head, then sighed at Sasha and said, as she always did, "Alright, how much do they owe you?" After writing checks, she closed up her ledger. Sasha critiqued her hair and her hands. "I've never known you to let yourself go." She thought about their intimacy on the beach and felt that it somehow triggered depression, and wished she had never opened her mouth, but she was now determined to get closer to her sister.

Gwen glanced at Charles. His eyes were locked and loaded, waiting, as they hovered over the top of his magazine. After a conspicuous delay, he looked back down, slowly. She looked down shyly and blushed. "Oh I'll take care of that first thing tomorrow morning." His eyes hovered again. She knew that meant he would be following up on that statement.

Sasha put a large bag on her lap, pulled items out, and placed them on the table. She placed a new book first and a D battery next. The battery caught his attention.

"Damn, baby girl what's up with the battery?" Abigail giggled, and said, "You must be saving that for the convent." Kim pushed her.

Charles joined in. "Shit, I've been to scary places around the world, but there's no way in hell that I would ever spelunk in that bag."

Sasha giggled, then said, "I'm trying to find my wallet."

"Cut your losses and reinvest."

The jovial table banter ignited Gwen. "I hate to admit it, but the grunt's right. How in the world do you manage a piece of luggage like that?"

The laughter settled down when she said, "Found it." As she began to reload her bag, Charles noticed her book. "Hey let me see that." He picked it up and inspected it. "I'll be damned."

"It just came out and has excellent reviews."

They all looked up and watched intently as a grin grew to match his pride in his friend. "I didn't know Aniel was a writer. I've known him for years. You see that?" He held it up, pointed to the cover like an instructor. "That's the Gwen. It's really a cool drink."

Sasha said excitedly, "Would you get him to autograph it?" She bounced in her seat like a child out of control. "Can I meet him? Can I meet him?"

Chuckling at her antics, he said, "I'll trade him for your battery." He turned to Gwen still pointing. "Hey Winnie, look your namesake." Her mouth gaped slightly as she turned pale. Concerned, he said, "Damn, girl, what's wrong?"

She flared her nostrils, pounded the table with both fists, and shouted. "Goddamn it. Take me home." She pushed her chair back violently, and fell out. She jumped to her feet, pounded the table, and kept saying over and over, "Take me home. Take me home."

He looked at her and the book, and said baffled, "Is this just a story?" Grappling, he said, "Winnie?"

She pounded harder and shouted. "Goddamn it, take me home." The girls became anxious. They had never seen her this agitated before.

She ran to the door and fumbled wildly with the handle. He jumped up, wide eyed and then turned wild-eyed and said, "Shit... I'll take you home, but control yourself." He raised his voice. "Goddamn it we're at work." He dropped the book and pushed the table aside violently when the door flew open.

The girls scrambled to retrieve flying purses and phones. He managed to grab her before she passed through. He squeezed her arm, gritted his teeth, and whispered through adrenalin heaving breath, "I'll take you home, but in an orderly manner, ok?" He released her and they slipped out into the back alley.

He gritted his teeth and rhythmically squeezed the steering wheel, while she was fidgeting wildly in her seat and biting her nails frantically. Neither spoke.

When he pulled up, he whirled around and ripped through the silence to aide his distraught friend. "Damn it, I didn't know he was your Aniel. I never gave much thought to the pseudonym. I don't pay any attention to all names coming across the computer." The teakettle exploded and he thought, oh shit.

She made a fist, and swung her small mallet on the dash, breaking another bracelet. "Goddamn it. He's not my Aniel."

He huffed. "I see why you can't drink it now." He glared hard and said angrily, "Because it is toxic." As she fumbled with the door handle, he softened his voice. "Damn it, Winnie, he's in love with you. Love at first sight, who the hell knows where that comes from." He reestablished his anger as he thought about his good friend from the bar. "And, Goddamn it, that is wonderful."

"Leave me alone."

He softened again. "There's nothing wrong with someone else loving you besides me and the girls." He furrowed his brow slightly and said firmly, "He's a damn fine man. He's in my circle."

"Let me out."

"You should be so lucky." He punched the door lock and she flew out. He leaned over and buried his elbow in the seat. "Get on the fucking computer and read it online." He paused when bar memories flooded his mind. "Give the man a fucking chance."

"Leave me alone." She stared at him for a moment with tears in her eyes, and then slammed the door.

He lowered his window and shouted as she ran across the street. "At least read his book before you turn him down."

He raised his hand, made a fist, as she buzzed herself in, then swung his huge maul, and buried it in the dash, and thought, oh shit, my poor car. God, this is going to be so expensive. She texted "In." He looked up to the third floor, saw her light come on, and texted "read it."

She sat at her computer desk behind the couch and booted it up. Tears spilled as she thought, Aniel, I thought we had this worked out. You were going to release me. She grabbed a tissue folded it neatly, dried her eyes, stared at it for a moment, then crumpled it, and thought, oh Frances, I wish you were here.

The computer was up and she kept the tissue in her hand as she typed. She queried several combinations and came up empty. She sat staring at the screen with her hands in her lap. Her last query brought up "The Gwen." It was an image of a cabana on a beach.

She smiled as she felt him forming in her mind, then stood abruptly and thought, Aniel we had an agreement, remember? We weren't going to think about each other in that way anymore. I know we didn't make any promises, but I believe we need to work harder. Now let's not make promises we feel we may not believe, but let's do agree to work harder, ok? Now, let's be the best of friends and not talk of love.

She sat back down and thought about what Charles had said. She typed in her name, but this time she associated it with stories instead of drinks. At the top of the page was "Gwen's story." She stared at the entry, then put her hands back in her lap, and rolled the crumpled tissue into a ball. She continued to stare and roll and thought, Aniel I'm so frightened, what if I see you and if I hear your voice?

Charles was almost at the girls' condo, with his squeezing and gritting carried over from the trip with Gwen.

Kim and Abigail were in the back immersed in phone love with Sasha between them. Sasha caught his eye in the rearview mirror. He could see the concern on her face. She said, "Is she going to be alright?" He gave her a warm fatherly smile.

"Oh, don't worry baby girl. She's hot headed, just needs a little time to cool off. Everything's fine." He chuckled, then added, "You'll see, by Friday, we'll all say what crazy ass woman who fell out of her chair."

The phone lovers snickered, while Sasha glared, "I'm still worried."

He pulled up and turned in his seat. "Seriously, she'll bc finc."

She shook her head. Little sister smiled as she pieced together all of Gwen's erratic behavior ending with her downturn in appearance and formed a simple truth. "No, you just haven't figured it out yet."

He smiled patronizingly as they filed out. He waited for their text, and then drove off.

They all gathered in the kitchen. The phone lovers were popping corks and gossiping the latest phone trash, when Sasha said simply, "She's in love with him." The phone gossip then paused for the local gossip.

Kim, skeptically. "Charles?"

Abigail busted out laughing, then said, "Could you imagine him trying to run her through his field tests?" Kim added her opinion. "She would kick his ass if he tried to pull any shit like that."

Sasha giggled, then said, "Now that's a love you can't give away, and his poor mother will be stuck mopping that lame shit up."

The Charles jokes escalated as she reached into her bag and held up the book. "Him."

Kim lit up when she read the title. "Hey, that looks like something glow boy would write."

Sasha nodded.

Kim drew contemplative, briefly, as her perspective concerning Aniel, Gwen and her years in the service were evolving. As the shrike was about to impale her, she said simply, "Yeah."

Abigail flushed the shrike out when she said, "Now staple Charles to them."

Kim humored her way from the thorn. "You know, I think I'll read it."

Sasha giggled and said, "Do you remember how?"

"Yeah, you're right. I'll just wait for the audio book."

As their banter waned, Abigail stared at the book for a moment. "I think I'll read it."

Sasha narrowed her eyes and said in a serious voice, "It'll frighten you."

"It's a romance. How can it be frightening?"

Sasha held fast to her serious demeanor. "Because reading takes your mind." They both looked at her oddly.

She continued. "When you watch a screen of any sort

it doesn't have your mind. You're still conscious of
everything around you. If you go to a movie your mind is still
conscious of its surroundings and is easily distracted. We're
always thinking of other things, while screens are running.
Even here when the TV's on, you watch it, but it'll never have
your mind, because you're doing other things, both
physically and mentally. A book is frightening because it
reminds you that you're finite and are going to die."

She went on. "The writer, Frances O'Shea once said
that people don't read like they used to, because unlike the
screen, when you look up after an hour or two of reading,
you realize you've lost something very valuable and will never
get it back. Books remind us of our mortality and we become
very sensitive to the movement of time, and it frightens
most."

"Being lost in a book and then looking up to realize
you've lost time, and you're a little older and closer to death
is frightening," she grinned mischievously at two anxious
women, "but the few who read know of the great power it
gives us." She pulled out her phone and looked at the time.
"See, I held you captive for three minutes," she chuckled,
"and took ten minutes off your lives." Kim glared at her. "You
scared the shit out of me. I'm never going to read again."

"You don't read."

"Damn right and that's why."

Abigail broke in. "You ought to be a writer. That was
good and creepy."

Charles locked his door and headed to the Blue Diamond like every pub night, but was irritable and grumbled to himself over her unreasonable behavior. He turned his attention to Aniel as the bar came into view and thought about the time he consoled Danny.

Danny was out in the field with his squad. It was at the end of the day. The watch was set and the rest were sitting and eating. He got up to sit with Odell when his clumsy feet tripped him and he kicked Corporal Miller's weapon. It discharged and shot Miller right through the head. He had struggled with it ever since. It was ruled an accident due to an improperly secured weapon.

Danny ignored promotions and wouldn't apply the new rank strip on his uniform. Colonel Sky had a deep appreciation for his suffering and tolerated his strip refusal, but increased his rank in his record.

When Sky came into range of retirement he came to the barracks and asked Danny to walk with him. As they walked he said, "Gunny, everybody knows I'm a short timer, and I would like you to retire with me." Danny looked at him oddly. Sky went on. "The new skipper doesn't understand the patriot. I know him well. I'm afraid if you don't strip up you'll be busted back, and I don't want to see you coming out as a private."

Colonel Sky died on the anniversary of Miller's death and Danny took it as request denied for forgiveness. The day before the funeral, he was in the bar drinking, cursing himself, while being consoled by Odell and Charles. He threw chairs forcing the two men to pin him occasionally. Aniel came around the bar, in a dash, to console him, when Wayne looked at the winded grunts piled on Danny and said, "Goddamn it, another broken chair, I'll make the call."

Aniel whirled around, spat in his direction, pointed his finger, and shouted. "You fucking piece of shit, this man's loosing his battle, and all you can think of is a stick of fucking wood, shit." He spat again. "Take it out of my check," and headed to the grunts table.

The two now had him calm and sitting in a chair. He squatted down, put his hands on his knees, and said softly, "Hey grunt, I wouldn't insult you by pretending to understand how you feel. But I do understand torment. Torment doesn't care about you. It lives its own life and if you happen to get in its way don't think it'll look back with pride at its quality work. That wouldn't make any sense to it."

"Linking the coincidence of the accident and Colonel Sky's death in your mind doesn't help it or strength it, because it doesn't care. It only hurts you. Danny, torment is timeless, it cares for nothing. If we were timeless, would we care for anything? Sometimes I think that's why God allows us to die, so we won't turn into torment. I almost pity torment and that in of itself doesn't make sense."

"It wanders and we will never understand it, because it can't be understood. It's as old as God. Go to his funeral and salute him and Miller, then come home to the ones who love you, because torment doesn't care in any way. Torment will always dwell around us and sometimes in us, but we don't have to dwell on it."

Danny stared at him for quite a while. At last he said, "Could you spare a cup of coffee for a vet? I need to sober up."

He tapped his knee. "Done."

Odell said, "Shit," as he looked at LT, "looks like movement Lieutenant."

LT grinned, and said, "Well, gunny, looks like you're going to pony up some gas money."

"Why the hell do you think I said shit?"

LT headed to the bar for the coffee and waited for him to finish. When he turned with the tray, LT had tears in his eyes. "I want to thank you for helping my grunt."

He looked at him puzzled. "LT, he's my grunt too."

She continued to stare at the entry and thought, Aniel, I don't think I can do this. God, I know if I see your image, or hear your voice, it will remind me of your kiss. A kiss by itself is not so important, but yours accuses me of something. But what frightens me the most is not so much the accusation. We've all been accused of something. Aniel, it's what your kiss leaves behind, I'm afraid it moves far beyond accusation, and a futile argument will be given by me when it presents the damaging evidence that I can't let you go, but I have to.

Please don't love me, because I would fail you. I'm nothing but trash, and when I press enter, and you begin your play, then my story will fail all three and confirm me. Smite my chest with truth, then let it splay my ribs and you will cry, because an empty space is all that's inside.

She pressed enter, then panicked as she fumbled for the speaker volume, and thought, oh no, I can't hear your voice, especially if you call my name.

As the video panned she saw people she didn't know, then it settled on Charles grinning and inebriated. She frowned and thought, bastard. The panning finally rested on the drink at which point she stopped the video. She put her hands in her lap and mused.

Charles stormed into the bar, pointed at Aniel, but quickly frowned at the thoughts of Gwen, then said, "You."

Aniel chuckled. "Ok, LT, we've established me, now what can I do for you?"

Charles made the ok sign pointing the three extended fingers at him. "I want three."

Aniel raised his eyebrows. "Ooh, somebody's really pissed you off."

"A friend of mine loves this woman at work, but she just pisses on him." He pounded the bar. "Shit, she doesn't deserve him."

Brenda glared and said with an irritated intuition, "She's too kind if it's just piss."

Keisha backed her up. "Yeah, she knows he's just looking for a steady tap, please."

LT straightened up and pointed his finger at the two pessimists. "No, not this guy."

Intuition rolled her eyes. "She's uh walkin while the wood keeps on uh talkin."

He pointed directly to Aniel. "He's just like him."

The two looked at one another, shocked, and Brenda said, "Damn. Dump that hump, she ain't worth a bump."

He smiled at Aniel, then said, "Can't, she's like a story book to him." Aniel blushed as he poured three whiskeys.

LT exploded into fit agitation again and pointed at each drink. "The bitch, the witch," then shook his upper body and arms and said, "and just damn." The three were amused by his exasperation. He downed the first drink and stared down at the bar. He sipped the second quickly, and put it down. He picked up the third one, held it to his forehead, and thought, what the hell is wrong with her. He glanced up at Aniel then back down and focused on Gwen.

What the hell's wrong with you Winnie? Shit, you should be so lucky. He looked up again, then back down, and thought, here's a man who loves you. Shit, he wrote a book about you, dedicated a drink for Christ sake. God, if that's not love. But you, shit all you do is have outbursts, pace incessantly, and bite your nails. What gives, outbursts, pacing.

He thought, ok, LT, let's analyze this from the beginning. She jumps up, becomes irrational. She paces, bites her nails, and her appearance has turned to shit. He sighed heavily and thought, ok, irrational, pacing, nails, and appearance. Damn let me think, ok first day, jump, pace, nails. He sighed again and thought, come on grunt, damn. What have I left out? He thought for a while and started over. Ok, jumping up, pacing, nail biting, climaxing. He paused and then a big grin dominated his face as he thought... that's it.

He slapped the bar, then shook his head, and thought I'll be Goddamned. She's madly in love with him, you stupid grunt. He shouted. "Damn."

Aniel chuckled. "LT I believe damn is in your hand." He looked at the whiskey in his hand and shouted again. "I've figured it out."

A voice behind him said, "Figured what out you drunken grunt?" He became self-conscious as he turned and saw Odell and Danny. He said quickly, "The key to the universe."

Odell shook his head. "Shit, now I know you're drunk and a perfect time to play cards."

Danny had a look of disappointment on his face. "Damn, LT, I just quit my job. I thought you were going to make us rich."

Aniel jumped in. "Well, LT what is it?"

"How the hell should I know? It's somewhere out in the universe." The grunts headed to their table, while he gathered up LT's glasses.

She remained still and thought I have to get through this. Afterwards, we'll talk and settle this misunderstanding. She turned the video back on, and hesitated before she switched the volume on. She heard his voice and thought, oh, God, your beautiful voice. She was about to turn it off, but stopped herself and thought, I need to get through this, and later straighten everything out, yes. I will call him and tell him I'm not the one. That he's mistaken and that we just got our feelings confused.

It was all just fantasy and somehow it was accidentally pushed into the real world. It's ok. It's nobody's fault. He'll understand that, surely. Of course, that's it, how foolish of me. Damn, women have fantasies, too. Oh that's all it is, just a mix up, how ironic. I've been with fantasy for so long and now it turned and bit me. Frances, you would love this story. I'll call it fantasy's bite. I just had a brief fantasy and it confused me. I feel so much better now.

She listened to the rest of the story and convinced herself that it was a beautiful story, but nothing more than a fantasy.

The video panned up to Aniel and he smiled warmly. She chirped loudly, covered her mouth, and thought, oh, God, the light in your eyes.

As tears spilled, she knew at that moment Aniel Posey was no fantasy.

Charles staggered to the bathroom and thought I've

got those bums on the ropes now, cheating bastards. He thought about Gwen. He pulled out his phone, and strained his eyes to pop the double phones back together. He held his focus long enough to text about the video, when the twins returned. He blinked, and thought damn, you two again. He chuckled and peed.

He was surprised at the quick response. He zipped up, integrated the two long enough to extract the response, saw something a little extra and laughed out loud. "Now, I have been called that and recently by a hotheaded Cajun."

She put her phone down, poured wine, sat back down in front of the computer and stared into his eyes. She drank and talked to his image. "Aniel, all I've ever wanted is to retire soon, shut my eyes, and have the bayou and the world go away. All you ever wanted is to step into the glow of a woman's beauty. You see we want different things. I know I live in a box, but that's ok. And I know I'm drab and uninteresting and that's ok, too."

She turned the computer off, turned the radio on, emptied the bottle, walked up to the window, and pressed the glass. A deep and soothing voice filled the room. The radio voice said, "Let's step off the high energy highway, and let me throw a speed bump at you, slow it down, and let's take the back road. Here's one I found hiding under the dust, a ballad, it's old but classic. See if you recognize it."

As she gazed at her reflection in the window, a

woman's voice filled the room:

"I see it's still on your mind.
Oh Darling, that was so long ago and once upon a time.
How many times have you promised to place it on a train?
Or put it on a plane and just let it go by?
Darling forgiveness can't ask, if you can't say good-bye.
Don't let what you've found about the things I've hidden, remain.
Darling, lies and alibis, are the cobbles that pave lovers' lane.
Now let tomorrow start with kisses, as we let it all go by."

She felt the one behind her in her reflection and braced for her grit, but she wasn't angry. She didn't say anything. They both just stared into each other's eyes and listened to the ballad.

When it was over, the one behind her burst into tears. "How long are you going to hate me for Paul?" She burst into tears again. "Why did you wake me and now won't release me." She now felt angry, "I know your secret."

Gwen turned from the window, opened a new bottle, ignored her heart, and drank heavily. When she had sufficiently drowned herself and felt sleepy enough to pass across the threshold into the world we can't control, she hoped it would deliver a respite from Aniel.

The sunlight was pouring through the windows when

she returned from the bookstore. Her phone chimed and she frowned when she saw the number, then pinged.

She sat on the couch, stared at the book on the coffee table for a moment. She picked it up, and rubbed the raised lettering of the title with her fingers. She cried when she caught sight of her wrecked manicure, which was her reminder that she was on a journey.

She was placed on a piece of sheet ice, that was ripped from the wreckage of her frozen peace, and set adrift by her burning buds, to be blown towards a man, by her winds of next time and this book was his shoreline.

She rubbed the letters of his name and smiled unconsciously. She caught herself and thought, ok, I'm going to read this, call him, wish him well and get back to my business. She picked up the book and read the title.

TWO

Odes To Love

A voice from behind a swinging kitchen door said, "Honey, don't leave yet. I haven't finished making your lunch." A young man with light brown eyes, brown hair, a little above average in height, sitting in a chair in the formal dinning room, separated from the voice by the swinging door, whirled around to a middle-aged man sitting at the end of the table busy inspecting a new phone fresh out of its box. "Shit, Dad, help me out. I don't want to hurt Mom's feelings, but I'm too damn old for lunch packing."

The older man held the phone up, and turned it over and over. "What's it worth to you?" He inspected the back. "Son, how do you turn this damn thing on?"

The young man grinned, then said, "No, the question is, what's it worth to you?" He added mischievously, "Lunchboxes and phones are my life. We're all on the playground of life, and you haven't been going to class. Now, if you want my protection from the bullies, you help me out with Mom, then I'll explain one feature, and we'll negotiate the rest." They both chuckled and the young man suggested playfully, "You really ought to go to class."

The older man looked over his readers, and said, "I've taught you well. Never give something for nothing and always make them go first. Who needs class? I've never had any class, so why go to class?"

He shouted towards the swinging door. "Marilyn, stop packing his lunches. He's a sophomore in college now and too damn old for his mommy to be packing his lunch." He winked. "How the hell is he supposed to pick up chicks if he's carrying a bag that screams I'm a momma's boy?"

The voice in the kitchen struck a low somber tone, as if reading a memorial inscription. "Honey, do you feel you're too old for Momma to pack you a lunch? I'm so sorry if I've embarrassed you." The older man snickered, then whispered, "Get out of that one slick"

The younger man beamed, and said smugly, "Watch a pro, there won't be a single hurt feeling spill out of the kitchen." He craned his head towards the kitchen. "The alpha male is right about the chick part, they keeping asking me when I'm going to upgrade my lunch box. But I don't care though, because the way you pack puts the Chinese to shame. Besides it supplements my crack habit. My dealer can't get enough of your chicken." She chuckled and the older man smiled with pride, then said, "Taught you well Son," and went back to his phone.

When her chuckling subsided she said, "Honey, do you have enough money for lunch?" He looked at his father and beamed smugly again. "It's ok, Mom. I think I have enough for a snack. I can wait until supper."

"Oh goodness that's not enough." She paused as if to calculate future lunches. "Honey, how much do you need?" He looked at his father, who was preoccupied inspecting the phone, and though it all too easy, and said, "Oh, I don't know with inflation and all."

"Will ten be enough? I know college cafeterias are expensive." He leaned into his father, who was still preoccupied. "Ten will get me a bag of chips and a soda, but that's all I need until supper."

"Goodness," then in a stern voice, she said, "Dale, give him twenty."

Dale looked up surprised. "What?"

The young man grinned, then said, "Keep up old man, I just played you."

Dale laughed slapped the table. "You little shit."

Marilyn swung the open door forcefully, stepped through quickly, and glared at her husband. "Are you cursing Henry again?"

Henry jumped in. "Oh, no Mom. I saw the whole thing. He definitely cursed you."

Dale slapped the table again. "That's my son, always out smarting them."

She pointed her finger at her son. "You've been mischievous all your life."

She went back into the kitchen and Dale said perplexed, "Now how do you turn this damn thing on?"

Henry felt like the king of the hill. "Pony up old man."

"You know what. When I'm gone, I'll look down from heaven, slap ole Gabe on the back, point to you, and say you see that little shit taking everyone to cleaners, well, he belongs to me. I know when he sees that, you'll get prime property on any cloud of your choice," then he smirked at the king, "so long as it's right next to your Momma."

Lately, Henry had felt as if something was growing deep inside, trying to awakcn, whenever their game of quips spontaneously erupted. "I think I'll claim adoption and hope for the best. By the way, heaven is an assumption for you, for Mom it's apparent."

Dale handed him twenty and Henry took his father's finger, ran it along the top of the phone. "You feel that little recess?"

Dale beamed like a child with a new discovery. "I'll be damned, never noticed."

"If that excites you wait till you get a hold of a toaster."

"Funny."

"Now, put the phone up to your mouth like a microphone, press the button, and say, 'On', then let up and there you have it." The childlike grin reappeared on Dale's face as he practiced with the phone held like a microphone.

While the phone was on, he produced a puzzled expression. "Son, what the hell are all these little colored squares?"

Henry slapped him on the back. "Those are very expensive features, homey, that are really going to cost you. I want your lunch money every day."

He stood behind his father and pointed at the top row of apps. "That first one is when you want to talk to a Chinaman." He pointed to the next one, grinned, and said, "Now, that one's for a hooker." His father chuckled. He pointed to the third one. "Now, don't press that one, that's for last rites." Dale laughed, which drew a chuckle from his son, then he continued. "You see that red one in the center, that's if you want to launch missiles at said Chinaman above."

Dale burst into laughter, then collected himself. "Son, I've got no beef with the Chinese. Now which one do I press for the Russians?"

"Sorry, homey, but the phone was made in Russia so it's disabled."

"Now I know you're lying, because there are only two things the Russians are any good at."

"And what would that be."

"Vodka and wreaking havoc."

"I gotta go. I'm going to be late." He turned, stepped into the foyer by the front door, and reached for his backpack hanging on the banister of the staircase.

Marilyn popped back through and stroked him.

"Honey, be careful," then she grabbed his chin, "now, if you're bullied promise you'll tell us."

He gave his mother his mom eye roll. "Mom, fifth grade passed away with lunch boxes. Besides, ole super hero over there will come in a flash as soon as he figures out his new equipment, then he'll launch his said missiles."

She chuckled and kissed his cheek. "Call me if you need anything."

As he was about to pass through the door, she said sternly, "Henry, don't jump off the porch. Last time you almost broke your ankle."

He gave her another mom eye roll. "Mom. You're stuck in fifth grade. I'd make you my girlfriend, but I gotta go."

When he closed the door, she rolled in into an old memory from the second love of her life.

He ran across the eight foot wooden porch, leapt over the steps, and rolled his ankle. He stood, grimaced, and thought, shit, she jinxed me as he hobbled to his car.

She finished her memory with a smile, then turned to her husband, to share. But was perplexed by him addressing his phone like a microphone. "What on earth are you doing?"

"I'm turning my phone on like Henry showed me." She grabbed a paper napkin off the table, dabbed the moisture from the corners of her eyes, in pursuant of the absurdity. "Mercy. I can't wait for you to do that in public. Henry, Henry."

Annoyed, he said with confidence, "I'll have this bad

boy mastered by noon."

"I don't think so. Dale. You crawled out from under a rock yesterday holding a rotary phone. Even the best laid plans don't happen by noon."

She shook her head and he narrowed his eyes and said dead serious, "They were damn reliable."

"I've got to go to work," she said, as she left to retrieve her purse, then added, "and don't forget to mow the grass and don't plow up my flower beds."

He pulled into the last student parking spot, patted the dashboard, and thought, you did fine my little ghetto sled and no belching when I turned you off and no complaining. My, what a fine spot you found. Someone's in a good mood. He got out grabbed his backpack, closed the door, and observed the many rust spots all over the mismatched paint, and thought good, no one stole them. He quipped, again, before he left. If anybody tries to steal you, blow your horn rainbow.

He was on the sidewalk that led to the Science building. When he arrived he'd planned on taking the pig trail that led to the English department. As he came closer, he noticed a young woman with blonde hair. She had her heels together and her head cocked, standing in front of the building with a printout in her hand. He thought, damsel in distress. Maybe, I'll call for homey superhero who talks into phones like a ham radio; then again maybe not, he might launch missiles.

He came up behind her. "Ma'am, I'm sorry but it's not for sale." She turned around and laughed. He thought, God, those beautiful blue eyes, so deep and so blue. What a lucky man who ever has you. Something like that, how proud would you be to have that draped on your arm? Well it'll be someone better than me.

"I'm learning the campus. I was going in to find this room." She pointed to a room number on the printout.

He gazed down at her beautifully manicured nails and thought, what a beauty, then looked at his hand, helping to hold the paper straight in the breeze, and thought, what a beast.

"I tell you what," he said as he pointed to a side door. "Take that door, go up one flight, and it should be just to the right."

He felt what was deep inside, again, which felt like a fetus trying to be born to the world. "Now don't forget to pay the troll under the staircase."

She noticed a twinkle in his eye. "You are so funny." He pointed to the main entrance. "Now, you don't want to go through there, because in this heat you'll be floating in a pipeline of b.o. Now, I'd rather pay the troll."

She burst into the joy of laugher, while he felt the joy of her company. He pulled his short sleeve up slightly. "You know, I think I'll get a tat with the letters TOBO."

She giggled and said, "I know the first letter must be troll."

"Yeah, over bo." There was a pause in laughter. She cocked her head and nibbled her bottom lip while studying his face. Her pupils dilated revealing two blue rings. He thought, she's seeing too much troll, gotta go. "Gotta go, going to be late."

He made it home, parked in front, patted the dash, thought, good girl, and went in. Dale was in the kitchen, sweating profusely, and drinking a beer when he walked in. "Damn, Dad, I thought the idea was to stay hydrated."

"Not when you consider all your options."

Henry shook his head, then glanced around the unfinished lawn. "You want me to finish."

"No, Son, I got this. Hey, how did school go?"

He nodded. "Not bad, gotta little homework."

"Meet any chicks."

He thought about blue eyes, her manicure, and the troll. "Oh, no Dad, I figured you and I would join the monastery."

"Nah, too much praying, don't want to irritate Him."

"I'm outta of here."

He made his way upstairs, opened his door, and dropped his backpack at the foot of his bed. He had placed his computer desk right in front of his window, so when he wrote he could gaze out into the world. He booted it up, sat on the end of the bed, and gazed out the window. The air conditioner cycled on and the vent began to luff the window's shear as blue eyes entered his mind and searched his face.

The machine finally unfurled and waited patiently for a user.
He stared at the patient curser for a moment, then he came
up and typed.

Query To Blue Eyes

He sat back down and mused. His eye found its full
potential and now what was inside was born.
He typed.

Would you ever consider brown eyes, blue eyes?
Oh no, too strong, like whiskey, maybe wine.
Ah, a gaze only then, for brown eyes, blue eyes?
If you mind the cabinet and keep it locked when we dine.
Then it'll only be wine for brown eyes, blue eyes?
Pour, be content with the cork you have, plenty and fine.

He deleted it and thought come on, homeboy, you're
stalling, get to work.

He slumped down in his chair, observing the frog in
the jar, on the lab table, and thought, shit, why the hell do I
have to take this miserable course every Thursday. What the
hell does this have to do with writing? Damn. He stared at
the frog for a while longer and thought, you must have been
the slow one. He thumped the jar with his finger, you know
frog legs all this whining isn't going to get you back in the
pond. Suck it up and get through it, shit it's only one
semester, by the way, I think that formaldehyde gives your

coat a nice sheen.

He was musing far off when someone dropped a large stack of books right next to him. He furrowed his brow, gritted his teeth, and thought, God, just when I thought it couldn't get any worse, some rude fuck shows up. He snapped his head up, and planned to eye down the rude piece of shit, then set the boundaries for rest of this miserable semester of biology lab.

She smiled as her face lit up face lit up, and said, "You."

He dropped his frown, quickly. "Ma'am, that's my last name. My first name is Hey."

She burst into laughter but stopped herself when she attracted the instructor's attention. She sat down quickly, giggled, and said, "You're going to get me into trouble," then apologized, "I'm sorry I dropped my books. That was rude." She stuck her hand out. "I'm Gwendolyn."

He shook her hand and thought, God, I already knew how beautiful and now so soft. He looked down at their hands clasped and thought I hope who ever has you blue eyes... He quickly cauterized the maligned thought from oozing further. "Hey You is my birth name, but you can call me Henry."

She released his hand. "Henry, you have a twinkle in your eye and I think it's going to get me into trouble all semester." He thought, how I love to hear you say my name, but what would I give to hear you call my name? She studied his face and thought, such a beautiful name, then broke off and reshuffled her books. He did the same.

Class was about to begin when he noticed a somewhat sad look on her face while staring at the book on top of her stack. He got low on the table, looked up into her eyes. "What wrong blue eyes?"

Her face lit up followed by a bright smile. She thought, what a beautiful man I never noticed before. I was so busy learning the campus. The way the light dances in his eyes. "It's this book. I have a test coming up next week, and it troubles me."

She handed it to him. "Oh, Gwen's 'The Glow of a Woman,' good read."

She became pale, fidgeted, and wrung her hands in her lap. He straightened up quickly in response to her odd reaction and said with deep concern, "Are you ok?"

She relaxed. "I'm ok. It's just a little warm in here."

"What about the book?"

"I don't understand what she means when she says 'She sits behind her glow holding a torment she won't let go.'"

"Oh, that's her love. She can't have it, but she can't let go either." He saw she was still puzzled. "Let's start over. The protagonist comes from a very attractive clan." He paused and searched her eyes. "You're an attractive woman. You see you didn't flinch or even blush, because you've heard it all your life. The mirror has jaded you, so you've never noticed. The protagonist is the same way, but she feels something.

Something so slight, like a flash in your peripheral vision, that's so quick you can't identify it, but nonetheless it's there and it's real. She becomes unsure, because..."

He stopped and searched her eyes, while she was staring into his. He cauterized again. "Because it's only wine and that's all you'll ever get." He blinked, blushed, and turned quickly to the frog. "Hey, if you have time after frog gigging we can pay the troll a visit on our way out the side door, and sit under the sycamore to go over it."

She giggled, while watching the instructor, and whispered, "Henry you're going to get me into trouble," then accepted his invitation. "Hey You, I would love to."

She observed an ambience around them that seemed to be planning something. She turned pale as she thought you, it's you. I know it's you. It can only be you. It has to be you. Beautiful Henry. Oh God above, my promise can't be foolish pride now that you've sent Henry. I know he'll see me, because... it's as if you blew him in on the wind for me.

She broke off and placed the book back on top, with her arms on either side of the stack, and stared at it. He shook his head, and placed his hand on her wrist. "Gwendolyn, it's just a book."

She sighed, and looked down at his hand. He retracted it quickly and blushed. "Sorry, personal space." She turned quickly in her chair, put his hand back. "Henry, I was just thinking about the book," then reassured him with a smile, and said, "That's all." She gazed into his eyes and thought, and hope too.

Refreshed by her tactile acceptance, he said, "Does he come with a death certificate? Hey do frogs have assets, and would we need an amphibian conversion table of fair market value?"

She giggled loudly and then took his hand in both of hers, squeezed it lightly, and said, "Henry, you have to stop. I'm giggling like a schoolgirl."

She rubbed her thumbs across his knuckles unconsciously. He engaged her eyes and thought, blue eyes would you ever consider brown eyes. He watched as her pupils began to dilate. He'll be a better man than me, he thought. Probably has one already.

IIe observed a small gold band on her finger with etched stars all around, and thought oh, there he is. She moved, quickly, to explain, when she saw the obvious expression on his face, questioning. "It's not that. It's a promise ring." She grinned while reading his follow up expression. "It's a reminder of a promise I made to myself."

The instructor began to address the class and they both straightened up and opened books.

The late August sun was brutal as they stood in front of the tree, which had a full compliment of students under its skirt. He looked at her and grinned. She pointed her finger. "Henry, you have that twinkle in your eye."

"Gwendolyn, have you ever been on a road trip and noticed all the cows under trees mid day." She grinned and he said, "Come on Elsie let's moo our way to a piece of shade." She burst into the joy of laugher ignited by the young man in front of her.

They found a spot on the outer edge towards the backside of the tree. He sat with his legs crossed. He was surprised when she sat right in front of him, cross-legged, with their knees touching. He thought, why is she sitting so close, a woman this beautiful? This is so confusing. I don't understand.

Gwendolyn sat holding the troubling book, while Henry felt himself stepping into the glow of a woman's beauty.

Gwen checked the page number, closed the book, and placed it on the coffee table. She walked up to the window and pressed the glass. The sunlight had already migrated to the other side of her building. She looked down at the busy street and thought, this is confusing and I'm so sorry. I don't have what you need and if I led you to believe something that can't be, I do apologize.

The one behind her laid her head on her shoulder and whispered, "It can be, just give me another chance. Please, I want him."

She pulled away from the glass quickly, went to the kitchen, made tea, sat on the couch, and continued to read.

"Henry, are you ok?" He thought, she's new here, probably needs a friend until she finds her feet. Shit, I need to relax, and be a friend, and help her out, until she finds someone better than me. He looked into the crowd and back at her, grinned, and was about to say something when she put her fingertips to his lips. "Henry, I know you're going to say something funny." She removed her hand and rubbed her thumb across her fingertips. "Explain the story before I'm too giggly to remember."

The sycamore shaded and listened patiently as it had for seventy years, while she continued to rub her fingertips. He came to the end of the story. "So she comes back humiliated and sits behind her glow holding her love tightly in her hands. Now her love's small but very strong. Don't think that just because something is small that it's not strong, because it's very strong."

He gazed into her eyes, then up into the blue sky between the branches, then back into her eyes. "Her love is like your beautiful blue eyes." She blushed and her pupil's dilated. He watched the dilatation and followed the peaks and valleys in her irises for a moment, and said, "Blue is recessive you know, and at your creation little blue chained herself to the judge and said 'I want to see. I want to be Gwendolyn's eye color.' She never quit and kept pestering the judge 'I'll never let her go. I belong to her.'"

"The judge dragged her everywhere and she never quit. When it was time for your eye color the judge reached for dominant traits. When he had laid the boggy, uncured foundation of the dominant reed beds, little blue wrapped her arms around his legs and said, 'No, it will be me. I've worked hard and never quit. So it will be me.' The judge looked down at little blue with her chin set like stone, clinging to his robe, and felt jurisprudence filling his chest and was reminded that it's not all about practice, principle, and precedent. Those are the cornerstones. Jurisprudence emanates from under those stones in the soil of compassion which holds those stones up. He picked little blue up, removed her chain, and carried her to the dominant reed beds of dark amber and burnt sienna that he had begun. He gazed upon her, and said, 'It will be you,' then took a deep breath."

Henry paused as they both were staring deeply into each other's eyes. He whispered inaudibly, "The wind in the reeds, 'tis rooted." He blinked and continued. "He blew parting the reeds and drying the boggy beds. When he felt they were sufficiently dry, he placed little blue in the parted reeds, while maintaining a gentle breeze until she could take root. When he stayed the winds, the reed beds were now a field of lavender and blue iris."

He searched the small rings of blue around her fully dilated pupils. "And now you're..." he paused for quite a while, "so blue."

Henry realized that discoveries were rooted in the wind, which seemed to come from nowhere, and some had heartache attached.

She thought, Henry, am I as beautiful to you as you are to me? Henry, do you see me? I'm right here past the lavender and blue iris. Please see me Henry. Sometimes I think God created my hope in a storm to make it stronger, but I'm frightened now, because I realize now that the storm is you, and you may pass me by.

He came through the front door, hung his backpack on the banister in the foyer, and took an immediate left through the formal dining room and into the kitchen. His father looked up from the breakfast table. "How did school go, Son?"

"I met this drop dead to die for."

Dale clenched his jaw and shifted in his chair. He looked at his phone on the table and thumped it with his finger. "Top tier, huh?"

Perplexed by his father's agitation, he said, "What's wrong, Dad?"

Dale readjusted himself in his seat and stared at his son for a moment. "Son, I'm going to hit you hard and fast."

Henry sat nimbly, puzzled by his father's agitation.

"Son, if you're at the point of hope with this woman, you're a loser."

Still puzzled, "What do you mean?"

Dale looked into his son's puzzled face and loosened his agitation. "Women that are rich in beauty eventually seek the wealthy. She probably already has a boyfriend, because top tier is never left alone for very long. A wealthy man will find her and she will live in opulence. It's ordained as expected."

He stared coolly at his son. "Your mother's not attractive." Henry furrowed his brow and postured. Dale smiled, then said, "Relax, Son, your mother is beautiful." Henry grappled with his father's seemingly unrelated puzzle pieces.

"Your mother and I are punchbowl, but you're a handsome fella maybe not top tier but right under."

Henry shook his head, bewildered.

"You'll understand that later, but when I met your mother I knew I had a chance, a damn good one. Hope is on the bottom and a slim chance is a mountain top above. Hope flounders on the bottom, and tells itself that all it needs to do is build a ladder up to a slim chance and then it'll have a damn good one."

He paused, to let the latticework of perplexity he had created in his son's mind resolve. "Son, all hope will ever build is a gerbil wheel and run it all its life, constantly building ladders in its mind, so it doesn't have to face itself in the mirror, and be reminded that it's only hope."

He searched his son's face. "Son, she's not for you. I would rather you be stung now than crushed later. A rich woman like that will be picked up by the wealthy, and if not by graduation, she'll sit in the bullpen of social circles and wait. The rich and wealthy think differently. They're not for us and don't want us."

Henry watched his father search the wall with his eyes, then turn to him. "Rich women like that are few in number, and the rest of the feminine world squirms from body shaming."

Dale continued with sadness in his eyes. "We in the West look down our noses at those in the Middle East and chide them on how badly they treat their women. We say they torture them culturally, and livestock is treated better, but it's hypocrisy. The West just uses a different rack of diet and image. Some will practically shave their bones and try to press themselves into a frame that was never meant for them."

He stared into his son's eyes. "I don't think most men want to hurt them though, but they do have something men deeply desire."

Henry grinned and his father reciprocated. "Besides that Son, there's something deep down inside of them we want, but can't seem to get to."

Henry said smugly, "You mean like a glow."

Dale slapped the table and said with excitement, "Damn, that's it, Son. I see college is paying off already. Yeah, I like it."

"Damn, Dad, when did father son bonding became so Goth. Shit, now all I want to do is become a funeral director."

"Oh good, discount."

"I've got homework."

He sat on the end of his bed as before and booted up. He stared at the patient curser for a moment and again typed:

Second Query To Blue Eyes

Is it only hope then for brown eyes, blue eyes?
My silence should answer your rhetorical tongue.
Deny then, all brown eyes, blue eyes?
Only those who hope for rungs.

Friday, mid morning and an abundance of sunshine was pouring through the cafeteria windows. He found a table towards the front by the tray line, dropped his backpack, and began pulling books out when he heard an excited voice call his name.

He turned towards the voice and saw her holding up a paper and shaking it. "Look, Henry, I got a B+."

A big muscular jock standing beside her came up and put his hand around his neck squeezed gently, clenched his jaw, and gave a forced smile, then said reluctantly, "I want to thank you for helping her out."

Henry glared at him and pulled his hand off. "Dude. Space. Don't try and hump me. I'm not after your chick. She was in a jam and I helped her out."

The young man blushed from the surprise spanking and straightened up.

Henry turned to Gwendolyn and held his crushed heart in check. "See, I told you. I knew you could do it. Sometimes books are hard, but if you stick with..."

The young man cut him off. "Yeah, sometimes when

I'm lying on my bed and I'm thinking about the game, I look over at all those books getting me down and think damn those-"

Henry cut him off and said sarcastically, "Oh, that's seasonal book depression or SBD as we in academia like to call it."

The puzzled young man said slowly, "Wwwhat?"

"Yeah, imagine you wake up tomorrow in the library and are told you and the entire team have to spend the season there."

The dazed young man had a far off look, and said, "God, that would be so depressing, just sitting there with nothing to do."

"That's why they get depressed." Gwendolyn burst into laugher and the young man chuckled, and said, "That was funny."

Henry replied, stone faced, "Indubitably."

The young man saw a friend across the room, waved, and said, "Come on Gwenie I need to talk to T."

Henry jumped straight up, inflamed, and said, "That's not her name. That is not her name."

The young man curled his lip, annoyed. "Dude, it's just a name."

Henry squared off with him and said, "That's not her name."

The alpha male towered over him and was now spanking him. "Dude, it's just a name."

Henry forced a smile, then said, "You're right. What's in a name?"

The young man looked at Gwendolyn. "Let's go."

Henry sat back down and continued where he left off. When they came to the cafeteria doors, the young man walked briskly to catch up with his friend leaving her behind.

She came back and sat down. "Henry don't be angry. I'll fix it. I'll talk to him."

He put his hand up and cut her off. "Oh no, it's my fault and I apologize. It's none of my business what your boyfriend calls you."

She sighed. "Henry, he's not my boyfriend. We just had a couple dates, that's all."

Odious. "It's none of my business Gwenie."

She narrowed her eyes, then pursed her lips, and left quickly.

Later, as he was closing his books a middle aged man, with dark greasy hair and wearing a white apron came from behind the tray line holding a small cup. He pulled up a chair in front of him and said, "Try this."

Henry looked up. "Hey, Willie, what cha got."

"This is going to make me millions." Henry looked at him skeptically. "What is it?"

"Yogurt."

He nodded and took a bite. He grimaced and forcefully spit it back into the cup. "Damn, Willie, it tastes like raw fish."

"Yeah, it's great."

"Yeah, when bulimics are on the run and can't find a spoon. Shit, what's wrong with you?"

"Dude, I'm telling you, fish yogurt is the next big thing."

"Willie your mind is frightening."

"Dude, I'm serious. You know all those health morons who think they'll add a couple of extra minutes to their life if they roll in granola and lick the slime off a frog? They'll eat this shit up. We'll talk up fish oil, it's hot right now."

Henry put his hand up to cut him off. "Willie, there's no we here."

Willie scooted closer. "Dude, I'm letting you in on the ground floor, besides sardines have gotten a bad rap."

"What the hell are you talking about?"

He straightened up and narrowed his eyes. "Have you not ever noticed most people's attitude towards the sardine?"

Henry cut him off again. "Willie, I gotta go. I'm going to be late."

"We'll discuss our business venture later."

"Shit. Willie you need to hide your crazy."

He remembered his observation. "That chick's into you."

Henry produced a flat affect. "Oh no, she's not for me, besides she has a boyfriend."

"I don't know, after the field meat left her in the dust, her eyes were all over you. Even after she left you, she stood by the doors for a long time and poured into you. She only left when I came up."

Henry said skeptically, "Dude, something that fine doesn't see something like this, please."

Willie cocked his head puzzled, while grappling with his friend's perspective, and he shook it off. "Maybe she's slumming, lucky you."

Henry held his skepticism in check, while obliging him with generous ear.

"She probably gets bored and slums occasionally. Hey, people slum all the time."

He hung his backpack on the banister and headed to the kitchen when he heard his father there. He pushed the swinging door open, slowly. "She's got a boyfriend."

His father looked up from the table. "Sorry, Son, but I think you kinda knew that."

He sat down and slumped. "You know it stung, but what's funny, the whole time I was looking for a honey bee and then a fat red wasp came up behind me." He sighed. "Willie said she might be slumming."

His father turned down the corners of his mouth and nodded. "Yeah, I can see that. Like I said, the rich think differently. Insightful man."

Henry waved his hands. "Oh no, no Dad, seriously, Willie could never pass for insightful. There's no way in hell he could ever afford the ticket."

"Ok, let's say experienced." Dale observed sadness

emerging in his son's eyes. "Hey, Son, it's Labor Day weekend. How about you and I go fishing."

Henry beamed at the thought of distraction from Gwendolyn. "Yeah, that'd be sweet."

Dale beamed at the thought of spending time with his son. "Ok, let me get the rods and tackle in order and plenty of beer and we'll be off."

"What about Mom?"

Dale grinned and felt their time together had already begun. "Son, I'm going to give you a life lesson. When a woman wakes up in middle age, and before her feet ever hit the floor, all she can see are stars floating around her head."

Henry chuckled and already felt better. "What the hell are you talking about?"

"Son, if the threshold of any hotel doesn't have at least four stars above it, her happy ass won't even give a thought."

"Damn, Dad, what about food then?"

"When your momma finds out you're going, we'll eat like kings."

They heard the front door open and Dale said, "Speaking of happy asses."

She pushed the swinging door open, quickly, and glared at her husband, suspiciously. "Are you cursing Henry again?"

Henry jumped in before he could speak. "Oh no, Mom, that was definitely for you."

She chuckled, placed her purse on the table, put her

readers on, and sorted mail.

Dale winked, "Hey, you little hottie. How about we head to ole cabin number 5 and do a little fishing."

She came to a dead stop, looked over her readers. "Heavens, Dale, sometimes I think you need cognition testing."

"Mom, I've been telling you for years he needs to be committed." Henry stood and put his arm around her. "Now, Marilyn, I know this is a difficult decision, but it's for the good of the family and the neighborhood, because once he's out, the neighborhood will return to its former glory and we can hold our heads up again."

She burst into laugher, grabbed a napkin from the table, and dabbed under her eyes. She stroked her son then returned to sorting.

Dale winked again. "Well, I guess it's just me and homeboy then."

She stopped, looked up, and tabulated. "Goodness, I need to go to the store." She looked towards Henry. "Honey, what would you like Momma to get?"

After the snickers, Henry turned to his father. "Damn, Dad, is there anything you don't know?"

Dale fell somber for a moment. "Son there's a lot of things I don't know. I just know a lot about the things that are important to me."

Henry smiled, then said, "Well, homey, I think I'll finish up this homework so I won't have to fool with it when we get back."

He dropped his backpack, looked out into the world, booted up, and waited for the curser that had now turned impatient. He typed:

Final Query To Blue Eyes

Friends only then blue eyes?
If hope minds the rung.
Forget you blue eyes.
Shame, such bitter tongue.

Tears pooled as he counted the curser blinks. He blinked, cleared his throat, and thought, nonsense, then typed:
Adieux.

He woke abruptly, fumbled for his phone, and saw it was early morning. He sat on the end of his bed and watched as the full moon poured its warm light through the sheer which felt cold filtered on the other side. Tree branch shadows formed on the sheer and danced like shadow puppets when the air conditioner cycled on.

He watched the shadow show for a while, and thought, blue eyes, I shouldn't have been so harsh. Forgive me. Could you help me interpret this dream? You were crying on my shoulder saying 'Henry I'm not for you'.

It didn't seem to come from the tier, but from the

heart. Help me. What happened to your heart? Has it been crushed? Ah, someone else has it; I remember now, but still why would you slum if your heart is with him? Perhaps I'm asking a rich question and maybe I'll never understand the rich heart.

Sometimes I wish you weren't so blue, then you might see me. He chortled softly, then thought, damn, I need to oil my gerbil wheel. I thought I heard hope. He sighed and thought, oh blue eyes, if the heart would only leave us alone, so we could return to being still, but it's awake now and very hungry and I have nothing to feed it.

Gwen checked the page number and set the book on the coffee table. She went to the window and pressed the glass. It was late afternoon and the sidewalks and streets were swollen with post workday office souls moving briskly. She thought about what she had just read.

The one behind her laid her head on her shoulder and whispered, "I'm so hungry."

She pulled her hand away from the glass and sat back down.

The one behind her laid her head in her lap and whispered, "So hungry."

She picked the book up quickly and continued.

The car was loaded and Marilyn was fussing over Henry. Dale closed the trunk and opened the driver door. He put his arm on the roof, smirked, then said, "Damn, Son, I think your momma's got single child affective disorder."

She whirled around and pointed her finger. "And don't drink too much."

As they approached the lake, Henry felt a lump by his left hip. He reached down, picked up a cracked phone, and quipped. "I see the super hero has been hard at work."

"Shit, I was completely torched, sweating bullets, and had a down mower. The breeze kept closing the damn side door to the garage whenever I raised the window to get a breeze."

Henry cut him off. "Ok, Dad, with that information I'm going to apply Dalc logic and solve this mystery. Knowing you, the best thing to wedge into a door jamb to hold it open is a 300-dollar phone." Dale nodded, then Henry said, "I have no further questions for this witness." He opened the glove box and held the phone up. "This isn't happening is it?"

"No, Son, it's not."

Henry tossed it into the glove box. "Damn, why does Mom bother trying to groom and culture you. Shit, it's not like you have any shot at an office."

"Son, I'm going to give you another life lesson. A woman's mind is sometimes like the ancient Egyptians who built the sphinx. We don't know what the hell they were thinking when they built the damn thing. It's something that makes no sense and sits out in the middle of desert where nobody can get to it even if were useful."

They followed the narrow gravel road that ran the edge of the lake. Small docks came into view on the left and to the right were some small cabins recessed back into the tree line. Dale pointed. "Ole number 5." He sighed flush with fond thoughts. "Your momma and I had some damn good times in that cabin."

Henry shocked. "Oh, God, Dad you didn't violate my mother in there did you?"

"Son, fishing with a woman comes in two parts and we did the other part."

"You're telling me more than I want to know, oh, God, my poor mother."

The cabin was very small, one room, with a fireplace to the left. Its mantel charred and discolored from years of use. A single bunk bed was flush against the back wall. To the left of the bunk's headboard was a kitchenette, and to the right of the footboard was the bathroom. There was a modest round wooden table in the middle of the room with four mismatched chairs.

Henry followed his father in, both loaded with supplies. They stacked them on the table.

Henry looked around. "Damn, it'll never be the same. I never thought about why you always rented this one all these years. That's why secrets were created to protect the innocent."

Dale laughed and Henry looked down at the table. "Surely, not the table?"

"No, Son, this one's new. We broke the other one."

Henry looked over at the bunk beds, then at his father, horrified. "Please, tell me it ain't so."

He beamed more full of love and life, than of himself at that moment, enjoying his time with his son. "Not to worry, couldn't get her on the top bunk. She was afraid it would fall through."

Henry shook his head. "My poor mother."

Dale was flush with joy, again, tormenting his son. "Shit, Son, this is where you were conceived."

Henry sat heavily in a chair. "Damn Dad, do you have no shame?"

Dale sat down and opened a bottle of beer, while Henry headed to the kitchenette to put away the food. He watched his father open another beer. "I thought we were going to fish?"

Dale craned his head around. "Oh, yeah, we are, but we have to develop our strategy to out smart them."

He quit stocking, abruptly, and shook his head at the absurdity. "I believe evolution has us covered."

Henry decided to make a sandwich, while his father drank. He placed it on a paper plate, grabbed a jar of pickles, and sat down. Dale put his elbow on the table, palmed his chin while observing him open the jar, and said, "Nice."

Henry sighed. "Do you want it?"

Dale looked away. "Oh no, no I can do without."

"Shit, do you want it or not?"

He turned back. "You didn't put too much mayonnaise

on it did you?"

"Damn, I'll make another one."

He pushed the plate over to his father and got up. Dale took a bite and frowned, disappointed. "Son, there's no pickle."

"They're right in front of you."

Dale craned his head around, and said playfully, "You wouldn't make a very good wife."

"You're an impossible man."

"Now your mother would have already anticipated my pickle needs and put one on my plate."

"The only reason she would pickle your needs is to shut you up. Damn, my poor mother."

Their boat was backed into a cove like a kitten in a paper bag, which hid them from distraction and produced solitary thoughts. Dale smiled warmly at his son. He returned the smile, but was puzzled by the unsolicited affection.

"Son. Do you still want to be a writer?"

He beamed, then said, "Oh, yeah."

"You know if you're going to be a writer you need experiences." He leaned over, patted his son's knee, and grinned. "But we all know you don't have any."

Henry blushed. "Yeah, I know, but you know what, I plan on listing you as a reference, but thought shit he's not an experience. He's a trip."

Dale laughed, then turned dead serious and belayed

down wisdom to his son "Son, I hope you have amazing experiences and can write them for the world to enjoy. Art belongs to the world not to the artist and I think they know that. I think they were given this amazing gift to produce works and then give them to us." He looked deeply into his son's eyes. "Son, I truly believe you'll be one."

He searched his son's face. "You still think about that girl?"

He blushed and shot his eyes down. "Yeah."

Dale felt the fullness of fatherhood as he played only two of its notes simultaneously: the ability to spend the necessary time to impart life lessons, and the shear joy of that time. "You need experiences, so treat her as material. Observe her as a journalist would. Be objective. Study her, and maybe you'll bring to the world, some day, insight into the rich. That would be a wonderful piece."

Henry beamed. "Thanks Dad. That's what I'll do. That's exactly what a writer would do. She's just a project. I don't care what Mom thinks. I don't think you crawled out from under a rock yesterday. Shit with that kind of wisdom you had to be out at least a week."

Dale slapped him on the knee. "Steady the boat. I need to pee." He stood and tripped over his pole and fell in. Henry burst into laughter and when he surfaced Henry said, "I didn't know the parks department kept urinals down there."

"Well, I just found one."

Late night and Henry was sitting at the table. Dale was on the bed behind him. "We didn't catch anything; maybe we'll have better luck tomorrow."

Henry craned his head and grinned. "I don't know about you, but I pulled in a large middle aged white man." He and his father shared a good laugh. When the laughter simmered to an occasional chuckle, Dale said somberly, "Are you having a good time?"

Henry sensed that these times would end soon. He'd be forced to turn the page and confirm that his father didn't know everything. "Yeah, Dad, I am."

"Son, there's an old Chinese proverb that says 'If your world takes a notion to take a spin, then it's time to pay the bed a visit before the floor comes a callin.'"

They said good night. Henry went to the mantel, grabbed an oil lamp, lit it, and placed it on the table before he turned out the ceiling light. As he sat by the glow of the lamp, he pushed out an empty chair gently with his foot, and interviewed Gwendolyn, while the freight train rumbled in the lower bunk.

He gazed through the window by the door and watched the moonlight trying to arouse the sleepy lake. As Gwendolyn formed in his mind, he followed the light to its source and thought, blue eyes as you travel the tier, I give you a wish. I've stepped off the wheel and ignored the rung. So, I know it doesn't come from the useless, psychotic, bottom of wistfulness that wants to be a mountaintop above. I know this to be true, because this wish is selfless and is wished for you alone. I hope that when you find your wealthy man you don't feel compelled to slum anymore. I know its rich and I'll never fully understand it, but somehow whenever I apply the gaze you've allowed me, I think I feel something that doesn't want slumming. And that is my wish for you.

What was born deep inside of him was now growing rapidly and his acute eyesight seemed to grasp more of the spectrum and could almost see around corners, the artist's gift.

Dale pulled off the highway into their residential neighborhood and glanced at his son texting. "Texting that girl?"

"Oh, no, my other girl. She wants to know when we'll be home."

They pulled into the driveway and noticed Marilyn standing on the porch with her hands on her hips and a scowl on her face. "Homey, I think that's for you."

Dale snickered full of love and life. "Now, counselor. I don't believe you have any evidence. It's pure speculation."

"Well, counselor, I don't believe evidence is of any value in this case, because I'm a single child disorder and we know I can do no wrong, despite all the fresh mounds in the backyard."

Dale shoulders bounced as he chucked. "Glad we don't have a dog; you're way too pretty to be in prison."

She flew down the wooden steps took an immediate

right and walked briskly down the sidewalk. Henry stepped out and greeted his mother as she approached. When she arrived she hugged him tight. "Sweetie, did you get enough to eat?"

He looked over the roof of the car at his father. "Oh, no Mom, Dad hocked all the food and blew it on a strip club and left me all alone in a dark spooky cabin." She covered her mouth and laughed.

Dale narrowed his eyes at her, and said irritably, "I don't know why the hell you're laughing. I believe I know my way around a strip club."

"You're too cheap to pay the cover." She reapplied her scowl, when her frightful issue returned. "You told me you killed that roof rat. I was awake all night listening to him in the attic. I thought he got in a couple of times."

He put his hands up, waved them gently. "Now, Peaches, I didn't say I killed him. I said I baited him. There's a difference."

"The only difference is he's not dead. Now, kill him this time."

He chuckled and looked at Henry. "Son, I feel another life lesson." He laughed full of himself. "You want it? I found it on the side of the road."

"No thanks I'm still working on the hitchhiking sphinx." He kissed his mother's cheek. "I'm going to wash the lake off," then looked at his grin bloated father. "I'll help you unload after."

Thursday's lab rolled up and he sat at the table proofing an English essay when he felt her next to him. His pulse quickened. She didn't sit down at first, but stood beside him holding her books. She watched him read for quite a while. She cocked her head, put her heels together, and filled herself with possibilities. She finally sat down, pushed her books aside, got low on the table, and gazed up into his eyes, flush with love. "Don't be angry with blue eyes, brown eyes. I fixed it." He unconsciously smiled as she straightened up.

He gazed into her eyes and thought, so blue. He then remembered the lake and thought, oh yeah, the project, thanks Dad. He continued to gaze into her eyes and thought, how can I extract the reasons for her slumming behavior without her knowing? I need a blind of some sort, but what? He smiled flush as well, then said, "I'm not angry. I'm just funny about proper names."

She frowned, put her hand on his wrist. "Henry, I still feel like there's tension."

He grinned and she raised her eyebrows. "Henry, you're twinkling."

He glanced at the terrarium of live frogs, turned to their splayed ones in their trays, and said excitedly, "Gwendolyn, don't say tension. That's frog for croak. Damn, now they'll be jumpy all day"

She fell into a spasm of laugh which caught the attention of the professor. He glared at her. "High school, really."

She blushed. "I'm so sorry."

She put her arm around his bicep, when the professor turned back to the board; she came close to his ear. "Henry, you have got to stop. You just got me into trouble." He thought, oh Gwendolyn you feel so good. Your soft hands and the scent of your hair. He pulled himself out of the sedation, reached for his cauterizing gun, and thought, get it together homeboy, this is just one project of many you'll have.

She straightened up and turned towards the instructor, but kept her hand on his bicep and unconsciously squeezed. He thought, ah let the slumming begin. I understand the journalist's credo of who, what, when, and where. Those are the bindings and pages of a book, but the why, that's the type. The journey into mind, that's truly what journalism is all about, the why. So why me? I'm just an average dude. Why did she pick me? As I observe her, I do notice she giggles and laughs a lot, so perhaps she finds me amusing, like a circus chimp. She's a little girl entertained by her circus chimp and maybe the jock is her humping chimp. He looked down at her beautiful manicure and thought, God, what a zookeeper. He chuckled to himself, damn so many chumps.

He thought about Heather. She was pretty, but not drop dead. He fell contemplative as he continued to observe her manicure and thought about their break up, how mutual it was, with no fighting, no pangs, or long walks late into the night. They just somehow came to an intersection, shrugged, and waved goodbye.

Why do I have this churning in my pit whenever I look at Gwendolyn? It's an unforgiving churning laced with anxiety and uncertainty. I've never been in love, but I know this couldn't be it. Love must have its own distinct beauty and feeling of joy, not anxiety, doubt, and waking in the night, but still....

She retracted her hand quickly, blushed when she realized her errant hand didn't want to leave. To ease her embarrassment, he said, "Don't worry. I was born without a personal space. I'm the family shame. My mother hasn't come out of her room in twenty years."

She put her hand to her mouth, squeezed his wrist and with the other. "Henry."

They were well into dissection when he observed the frog's heart and all its vessels. As his eyes drove the vascular highways, he was lost in thought and just stared. She assessed his frog. Puzzled by his pause, she said, "What are you thinking about?" He didn't say anything.

She put her instruments down, squeezed his hand, which pulled him out of his trance. He thought, God, your hand, the way it feels...

He looked deeply into her eyes as she continued to hold his hand and said, "The heart." He watched in amazement as her pupils began to dilate, and fill her fields of lavender and blue iris in response to two simple words. He felt himself standing in her fields, while what was inside, grew exponentially.

He whispered softly, "When the mystery of life flickers and the heart, perched upon its fetal pole, begins to beat and start its journey, it's unaware a simple question will be asked of it, but can never be answered."

She released his hand and searched his face. She thought, you're so beautiful. Henry, I want you. Find me Henry. I hope you want me as much as I want you. Can you step past and join me?

"What question?" she asked, as he continued to stand in her fields, but remained silent. She unconsciously reached up, stroked his cheek, and whispered softly, "Henry." Conscious of her stroke, she discreetly pulled her hand back.

He blinked. "What is love?"

At that moment the wind in the reeds picked up and he found a poet rooted, inside him, and still growing, who would be obsessed by that simple question all his life, driven by the catharsis staring into his eyes.

He slowly turned back to his dissecting. She thought, no Henry, it's not what, but when, and I feel now. She turned to him at the end of class. "Henry, would you sit under the sycamore with me and lets discuss the book?"

Puzzled, he said, "Why, you got a B+?"

"I want to understand it better."

The old sycamore shaded and listened to them all September as they discussed the book, but only heard two hearts trying to answer a simple question, one, who unequivocally knew, the other driven.

The early October frost insisted on sweaters in the morning, but relented by mid afternoon and allowed them around the waist. She was sitting in her lab seat when class started. She was frantic when he didn't appear. She fidgeted and glanced at the door frequently. She was about to leave when a woman with a large upper body and a heavily pierced face, said, "Hey Blondie." She turned towards the voice. The big girl held up her hands revealing grease stains. "Don't worry, he'll be here. I had to fix his wreck."

Henry slipped in, came up to the pierced faced woman, wrapped his knuckles lightly on her table, and pointed at her. "Dude, I owe you one."

She looked at Gwendolyn. "If you weren't here I'd miss the show." Henry looked at her oddly and she waved him off.

He sat down, and observed Gwendolyn's pale cheek as she stared straight ahead, then he cast his eyes down to her wringing hands. He got down low, gazed up into her eyes. "What wrong blue eyes?"

She turned to him and narrowed her eyes slightly. "You're never late. I was afraid something might have happened."

His eyes twinkled. "Oh, yeah, I was over at the chemistry lab fighting evil elements along side the noble metals in the house of periodic. It was nearly over taken by a band of cheesy zinc." He whispered in her ear, "My queen, I bet you a nickel, no pun intended, but I suspect lead foot is behind it all."

She pursed her lips, tight, to suppress the joy of laughter, love, and Henry, but in abject failure, the only visible course left was to cross her arms and move her lips from pursed to pout. "Henry it's not funny. I was worried."

Her arms remained crossed in protest. He put his hands on the table, and drummed it lightly with his fingertips. "Ok, let's have a moment of silence while were in the morgue." Her shoulders bounced as she tried to fight her laughter. He gazed at the pickled frog. "Shit, were in one anyway."

She covered her mouth quickly trying to salvage what was left of her crumbling concern. His antics took over. "You know bussing at this eating establishment is awful. Pickled frog has limited shelf life. I'm thinking health department."

She constructed a serious voice. "Henry, do you not ever worry about things?"

"Oh now, Rainbow, my sweet little ghetto sled just had a moment and needed little consoling."

"Henry, I don't think I've ever seen you quite so full of yourself."

He engaged her eyes, glanced at her pink sweater, back to her eyes. "You're pink in deep blue. I like it."

She blushed and thought, Henry I'll wear it everyday if it pleases you. She put her phone in her lap and began tapping.

He looked over and said playfully, "Wow, so many buildings. You must have changed your major from architecture to something that makes money."

The corners of her mouth rose to the occasion, then she said, "I don't need them anymore." She fell into a pensive state and thought, now that I might have you, but you have to find me. Sometimes I feel so far away. All my hope, in this storm, I place.

"Hey, I got solid B on my poem."

She looked up quickly. "May I read it?"

"You know I was really sweating this assignment."

Puzzled. "Why?"

"Because it's not writing, writers are gabby. They love to yack. It's their nature, but a poet despises words. I don't even think they like to talk."

He turned in his chair to face her. "Gwendolyn, poetry comes from the heart and inside the heart of a poet lies a kiln. He constructs his art from the thing he hates most because that's all he has. He constructs his words carefully then fires them in his kiln. When he feels they're well polished and all the edges are softened he removes it quickly from his heart and places in ours, but there's always something lost in transfer and that saddens him."

He animated his hands as if he were holding a small bowl, transferring from his chest to hers and came close to her breast, blushed, and pulled his hands back, quickly, and continued. "Words are inadequate, but that's all we have with which to communicate what is in the heart."

She turned completely in her seat to face him and thought they're yours Henry. Everything I have is yours. She looked deeply into his eyes and smiled slowly. When her smile was in full bloom he cocked his head, puzzled, and returned the blossom. "What?"

She said with surprise in her voice, "Henry. There's something that doesn't need a kiln, something that's never lost in transfer. Something that has been around long before words filled the mouth. Something that is well satisfied for its first, but hungers for the second and the day will never be long enough for them all."

He cocked his head the other way and remained puzzled. She drew silent for a moment to restrain what she longed to give him. She leaned forward slightly. "A kiss."

She straightened up, and narrowed her eyes almost to a glare. "Henry, when a woman kisses a man," she leaned forward again, "and says 'I love you'" She smiled unconsciously when she saw his flushed face and fully dilated pupils. "She's giving him a sacred gift." She paused, searched his face, and spun her promise ring around. She leaned in close to his face and blew gently. "Her loyalty. A woman will always love you and never leave you. She hands it over completely and with great joy and will be at your side until the end."

She stopped spinning her ring and straightened up. His jaw dropped slightly. "Damn, I have no retort. I'm speechless."

She chuckled, and said, "It won't last long." Her mood quickly segued to pensive as she thought, are the virtues of women slag in a man's kiln?

She dismissed the morbid thought as she gazed into her Henry's twinkling eyes, and said, "Let me see."

He reached into his backpack and handed it over. "Gwen gave me the inspiration. I thought about the average man in her travels."

She turned pale, fidgeted and shook, while wringing her hands. Visibly concerned, he squeezed her wrist. "God, Gwendolyn, are you ok?"

She squeezed his hand. "Yeah, it's just a little warm in here." He removed his hand and she gazed down at the paper and whispered the words.

"Is the least thought of less, when all tossed aside?
At best then, a spectacle, your least while at your side?
When mused back on all, am I just a shame to hide?
I suspect the glow of a woman has a beast inside."

She slammed the paper down on the table glared at him. "These words are ugly and untrue. Love has nothing to do with looks." His question to Blue Eyes was answered, as he pulled out another paper with a B marked at the top. She pointed her finger at him. "You're so mischievous, your poor mother."

"That's odd I don't think I've ever been characterized

like that before."

"Henry, you're fibbing."

He chuckled loudly, catching the attention of the professor. He blushed and said, "Sorry." After grappling for control of his volume, he whispered, "Now, you're getting me into trouble."

"Good, you deserve it. Now may I please see the paper?"

He put his elbow on the table, palmed his chin, and handed it over. "How do you know when I'm fibbing?"

A mischievous grin appeared on her face. "If I told you that, then I wouldn't know when you were, now would I?" Proud of her quip, she turned to the poem and whispered as before.

"What I found between us
Was born on the heels of hind goose.
But when he arcs his neck to follow back his path,
What is between us will now lie behind us.
It is then I will take its sacred impression and carry it
always.
And I will grieve not for my loss.
For I know it ever flourishes in the glow of a woman."

As an emerging poet, young Henry believed he had found through Gwendolyn that love was a spirit, and falling in love was only the journey seeking to possess that spirit, which he believed had always dwelled in the glow of a woman. Women would always be the sole stewards of love's spirit. He had convinced himself that they would never complete the journey together and possess that spirit, and for the rest of his life he would only carry its sacred impression in his heart, and never see it again or have it, because she was the only woman he would ever love, but he would grieve not, because he had witnessed that spirit in her and was comforted to know that it would forever flourish in the care of a woman.

Gwendolyn wasn't burdened by the obsessions of a poet, she simply wanted Henry.

As tears pooled in her eyes, he squeezed her wrist, and said, "Gwendolyn, it's just a poem."

She blinked several times. "No, Henry, it's not." She thought, a poet leaves his birth life in search of the other, but does he leave all the world behind? Poet, don't leave me behind.

He listened sincerely as she said, "It's true. Everything happens so fast and then some of us could be gone in one migration and some of us may never have the opportunity to explore what could be between any of us." He glanced at her damp eyes and thought, the only thing that's true is that I love you and I won't see you next semester when the goose returns. He picked up his instruments and returned to his frog. His eyes glassed, as he thought; God, is this love for me, anxiety, churning, and when she's gone, emptiness?

He cleared his throat as tears pooled, and thought, I'm

in love with her, and I'm stranded, with only hope to make me crazy with the squeak of its wheel, and when the storm of permanence screams in, the wheel will whirl violently, screeching like a turbine with molten bearings, because this wind will never stop, driving me mad. He cleared his throat again. What the hell is wrong with me? Shit, homeboy, dude, wake up. She's not for you. She's just a project, nothing more. Dry it up. There'll be another next semester.

She asked "Would you sit under the sycamore with me and let's just be still and not read the book?"

He sat and leaned back against the trunk of the tree. The cool October air had pushed most of the sycamore's flock out from under her wing to warmer spaces. Gwendolyn sat right next to him, by hip and shoulder. He was accustomed to her sycamore spacing and thought that perhaps under trees she perceived personal spaces as somewhat modified and casual. Maybe sitting under trees brings her the greatest delight and happiness, and when one's happy one does tend to pin inhibition, while keeping a steady hand on the latch.

She craned her head up, faced him, and said, "Henry it's all so short." He thought, Gwendolyn you are so beautiful and hope wants to be top tier so bad. How then is a kiss without loyalty defined? I guess a slum kiss, arousal without love, damn the rich.

He grinned, then said,"I'm not. I'm almost six foot."

She chuckled and pushed him. "Henry, be serious.

You're so incorrigible."

"Ok, I'll be serious if you stop being so morgie."

She laughed, covered her mouth quickly in an effort to discipline herself, then removed her hand, and applied reserve. "What's morgie?"

He pointed to the lab. "You've been around too much dead shit. It's not all about body parts you know."

She fell into a state of uncontrollable laughter. He thought, you're like a little girl being licked by a litter of puppies. I love you, and so want to hold you down and kiss your giggling face all over, but you're not for me.

She collected herself, looked at his smiling face. "Henry I love" She paused before she finished, "the way you make me laugh."

He felt something between her pause, but ignored it. "Damn homegirl, I think a dog turd rolling across the sidewalk would make you laugh."

"Henry, only you. You make me so happy."

He blushed and thought, Gwendolyn I love you so much, and if you just consider my arm... He quickly admonished himself, stop homeboy. I need to leave.

He glanced at his phone. "Homegirl, I need to head out to English." He felt mischievous. "I need to put you in the nunnery."

They stood and she looked up into his eyes. "Oh no, you're twinkling again." She willingly took the bait, crossed her arms, and said with a straight face, "Ok, why do I need to be put in the nunnery?"

His countenance fell to melancholy, which filled the space under the sycamore with hope, cauterizing his mischievousness. "So, the One better than all of us will have you always." He handed her his poems. "See you Thursday, homegirl."

Oh, God above please give me Henry. My heart is swollen from laughter, but my soul hurts, and I don't want hopelessness to take me to rooftops anymore. The parapet is a mile high whenever I have him under our sycamore. Momma always said hold out your hand when you hurt, and Jesus will be there, but I don't think Jesus will make Henry love me.

She wadded up the poem of average man and threw it in the trashcan beside her desk. She sat on her dorm bed, gazed out the window, read the goose poem several times, and thought, oh goose, does loyalty not have standing in your travels. Is it not enough? I would never leave him, never. Oh goose, please stay between us always, never migrate, and let me have him for a lifetime, oh Jesus, if not for a lifetime, a while then.

Late October and the cool air was the dominant driver of the weather now and sweaters were now permanently fixed. Henry was at the kitchen table loading his backpack. Dale sat irritably observing him, but said innocuously, "Son, how's the project going?"

He looked up, nervously. "Good."

Dale searched his son's face. "I'm not talking about school. What have you written about her?"

Henry shifted in his chair, shot his eyes down, and cleared his throat. "Well, I haven't had time to write anything. School keeps me busy."

Dale sighed. "Son, look at me." Henry blushed and looked up shyly, because it was now Father lecturing. Dale narrowed his eyes. "I'm not talking pen and paper, or computers." He pointed to his own heart. "What have you written in here?" He gazed deeply into his son's glassy eyes, then gazed out the window into the backyard at his wife for a moment, turned back, and said stone cold, "You're in love with her."

Henry stood abruptly. "Dad, I really need to go. I'm going to be late."

Dale put his hand up and said softly, "Please sit down." Henry sat, but avoided eye contact.

"Son, I'm glad."

Henry looked up to his father, puzzled. "She's not for me."

"I know, but what is for you is the experience."

"I didn't think it would hurt this bad. I thought it would make me wiser like you."

Dale watched the tears pool in his son's lower lids. He came around the table, quickly, and picked his son up. Henry's diaphragm gave a short spasm. Dale kissed his son's neck and rocked him. "Son, you're already wiser than me." He gazed over his shoulder at his wife again. "I'll never suffer your experience. I was spared, but I think you have to have these experiences to bring us art."

He sat at the lab table thinking about what his father had said when Gwendolyn walked in the room. He thought, oh heaven above, your greatest creation, the glow of a woman. She sat close beside him and he seemed distant. "Henry, you seem blue."

He looked at his brown jacket. "Ma'am I'm sorry. They don't make blue Henry's anymore, only brown."

"I see. I was mistaken."

He pinched the sleeve of his jacket. "Sorry ma'am, but you don't want this color." He was expecting to bandy quips, but she glared coolly into his eyes and said stone cold, unmistakably. "I know what color I want."

Their unnatural conversation was still ringing in their ears as they began dissection. When she reached over his arm for an instrument her breast pressed his arm. He thought, I can't take this anymore. Gwendolyn will you please start your slumming, so we can get it over with, and I can write about it.

He stood and massaged his thigh vigorously.

"You ok?"

"Leg's going to sleep."

As she turned her attention back to dissection, he scooted his chair a few inches from her. She turned her head quickly. Tears pooled as she perceived a great chasm between them, each side groaning under the strain as it shifted.

She thought, he's tired of me. He doesn't want me anymore. He kept his head down and buried himself in his work. She sniffed and cleared her throat. When class was over she collected her books and left quickly.

A week rolled by. She lay on her bed facing the wall in the fetal position. Her roommate bounced in, a chubby girl with dark hair and eyes. She tossed her backpack on her bed and booted her computer. She looked at her roommate, puzzled. "Gwendolyn, arc you sick?" She didn't say anything. Her roommate came over, sat on her bed, and rubbed her arm. "Are you ok?"

She craned her head around. "I'm ok"

"This is your lab day."

"I don't feel like going."

Her roommate turned her attention to her computer, and said, "Oh, by the way, some guy came looking for you."

She sprang out of bed. "Henry?"

"He didn't give his name. He was a big football looking jock."

She sat heavily on her bed and frowned. "Jordan."

"You really like this Henry?"

She stared out the window. "Molly, I don't know if he sees me."

"What? Are you joking with those peepers?"

She turned to her with tears in her eyes. "Yeah, but does he see me?"

Molly turned from the computer, puzzled. "What do you mean?"

"You see me because you're a woman, but men, once they look into my eyes; it turns into this or that."

"This or that?"

She sighed. "All my life, all I've ever heard was 'check this out', or 'I'd like some of that'. I'm just this or that. I have no identity past the eyes." She paused to align her closing thoughts, while staring at her ring. "A promise of folly."

Molly sat by her and put her arm around her. "I've always assumed-"

Gwendolyn cut her off to spare herself from the rest of the sentence, and said stoically, "And I have nothing to complain about, I know."

Molly grabbed a couple of tissues from her desk, handed one to her, and wiped her own eyes and said, "You know, when I was a young girl I remember crying to my mother 'why am I not pretty.'" She paused long enough to refresh the memory. "My mother was something else. She was so quick witted. She looked down at my wet face and said, 'Sweetie if everybody was pretty, then we'd all have to search for ugly to make us feel pretty, and that would be pretty ugly.'"

Molly rubbed her back. "I hope this Henry loves you like Rodger loves me." She felt a tug from the human condition, as she stared into Gwendolyn's eyes.

Gwendolyn puzzled said, "What?"

"Medusa was the only Gorgon who Ovid felt compelled to create mortal." She paused when she felt that tug flash a glimpse of insight. "I think because we all need someone to persecute." She studied the anatomy of her eyes. "I sometimes think that's why the tragedies were created, because the civilized world deems it illicit now for us to torment her in the street."

She went back to her computer while Gwendolyn balled up and returned to the wall. Molly looked out the window to relax and find the mood into which to settle, when she saw a frantic young man approaching every woman on the walkway. She thought, God, he's agitated. She smiled when he came running towards the dorm, and thought, you don't have to be a psychology major to figure this out. She turned to Gwendolyn. "Prince Henry is uh comin and he's uh plowing everybody over."

She jumped out of bed and looked out her window, beamed, and shouted. "Henry."

He jumped three steps at a time, landed on the second floor, and frantically pounded on every door shouting her name. She ran out into the hallway and shouted. "Here, Henry, I'm here." He ran up hugged her briefly and she thought, oh your scent, press me Henry, press me.

He put his hands on her shoulders and said winded, "Gwendolyn, are you all right? I was so worried and panicked. I bolted from the lab as soon as class was over."

Tears pooled in her lower lids. "Henry, I thought you had grown tired of me."

He dropped his arms, hung his head, and looked as flaccid as a stringed puppet just released by the puppet master. He collected himself and held her face for the first time. She placed her hands on his wrists which caused her bracelets to tinkle when they slid down her arm. He engaged her eyes in a way he'd never done before. "Gwendolyn, God couldn't make me grow tired of you." He released her. "And I can prove it, but first let me tell God I just needed to borrow him for a little poetic license."

Her burst of laughter brought her back, and he said, "You've missed a lot of work. Let's get you where you need to be."

She said with full exuberance, "Here, Henry, I need to be here with you."

Molly chuckled loudly and thought, it doesn't get anymore in love than that. I've got to meet the Prince.

Gwendolyn searched her face nervously, then she winked with assurance that their conversation would remain private, and said to Henry, "Your voice sounded familiar. I thought you were a friend of mine."

After they introduced themselves, she gave Gwendolyn a confident nod that she believed Henry sees her for who she is, and said, "Yeah, my friend sees me everyday."

They collected her books and headed to the cafeteria to spread out. They found a table close to the tray line. He pulled her books out and sat down. She sat on the other side of the table opposite him.

He furrowed his brow. "Why are you over there?"

She looked down shyly. "Henry, I'm unsure."

He reached across the table put his hand under her chin lifted it, engaged her as he did in the hallway. "Well, I'm damn sure." She beamed, bolted around table, and sat next to him sycamore style, hip by shoulder.

She wrapped her arms around his bicep and laid her head on his shoulder. "God, Henry I've missed you."

He closed his eyes for a moment, sat under the sycamore of August, and felt the glow of the woman he loved. He opened the books quickly when slapped by the cruelty of her impending slum.

"Henry, have you ever felt like you were fading away."

He looked at her oddly. "I'm not sure I know what you mean."

"I can't explain it, it's like you're disappearing."

He struggled with the concept, but had nothing to offer. "You mean like disintegrating."

"It's like all your life you're crashing parties of strangers and you never know anyone. You keep going from party to party and no one knows you and you feel like you don't know yourself and disintegrate in front of everyone, but they don't even notice you disintegrating." She concluded. "I wonder if people disintegrate all the time and maybe I'm just in line checking out." She checked her spilling, and said apolitically, "Henry I don't mean to talk a bunch of smack."

He narrowed his eyes, disappointed. "Gwendolyn you're pouring out from your heart and I feel like you're trying to explain an experience that perhaps I'll never fully understand, but it's not smack. Don't ever think that."

"Henry, sometimes when I'm alone and looking out a window I see myself flying."

"Well, you know flying can be an interpretation of art, or a release of some sort."

She turned somber. "I think it's more of a release."

"What kind of release."

"From disintegration."

He walked her to her dorm room. She unlocked the door, turned, and said, "Thanks for the catch up."

"Ma'am, I prefer mustard."

She didn't laugh. She just gave a slight smile that wasn't from anywhere. A disintegrating smile from all the parties he will never fully understand. She kissed his cheek. "Thanks again." He nodded and headed down the hall. She closed the door, and paused when saw that Molly was gone. She fell back against the door, slid down it like a blob of mud, and sat on the floor. She craned her head up to the ceiling, and thought, Henry you have to find a way. She gazed up to the heavens and whispered, "Oh, God, please help him find a way. I love him so much."

He sat on the first step of the dimly lit stairwell, wiped his eyes, gazed up, and thought, she's starting her slum what does hope do. I love her so much. Dad, it hurts so bad and I don't think experience will ever understand that the heart is finite. He stood, berated himself, and finished his thought with pull it together homeboy. The project doesn't care.

She remained sitting on the floor staring at the wall. The corners of her mouth turned down and her diaphragm gave a short spasm. She stood quickly and impulsively headed to the roof with her ring in her hand. As she gazed over the edge, she thrust out her fist clutching her ring, and was about to let it go and disintegrate, but she drew it back and thought, not here, not now. My Henry will find a way. Oh, God above if he doesn't find a way and I disintegrate, please chide me lightly, because I can't help being this or that. Sometimes I feel bullied by the glow of a woman.

He spread his books out on a table near the tray line, and studied. He gazed up to ponder when he saw Willie coming towards him looking around nervously, and carrying a cup with a spoon buried in its center like a flagpole. He thought shit he must think it's Lent with all this fish.

Willie sat down quickly, glanced around again, as if he were monitoring the movements of authority. He slouched down slightly, appearing to hide from their suspicions, and whispered, "Henry."

Henry chuckled, then said, "Damn. Willie this is a

college cafeteria not prison dining. We can skip the prison code."

Willie furrowed his brow. "Henry, this is some serious shit." He put the cup on the table. "You gotta try this."

Henry shook his head and put his hand up to stop the ruse from unfolding. "I'm not doing sardines. I don't care if they come with a signature series bulimic spoon."

Willie straightened up insulted. "You've already let it be known how you feel about the noble sardine. It's yogurt."

He searched him suspiciously, took a bite, and nodded. "Not bad."

"By the way that chick's into you. I know you don't think she is, but I don't know Henry. I think she is."

He put the spoon back into its hole and glared. "Dude, do we need to revisit this and that again."

Willie put his elbow on the table, palmed his chin, and pondered for a moment. "I don't know Henry. I've changed my mind. I saw you and her the other night and she was all over you. I mean bad over you."

Henry stabbed at the hole with the spoon.

"Is she slumming you yet?"

He blushed looked into the cup, cleared his throat, and gave a short "No."

"Yeah she's into you alright" He paused to load his wisdom. "Because slummers get bored pretty quick. It's been long enough that she would be looking for more strange to pork her by now, and knock yours in the dirt."

Henry set the spade deep, with one quick thrust, and

said curtly, "Maybe she is. How would I know?"

Willie pulled his hand out of his palm quickly, narrowed his eyes slightly, and gave a confident, but short-tempered response. "No, she's not like that. She's bad into you."

He pulled the deep-set spade out, took a bite, gave Willie's confidence some thought, smacked his lips, and frowned. "Is there fish oil in this?"

Willie lit up. "Oh no, salmon, Henry, raw salmon. I'm thinking maybe catch of the day, or bottom fishing. Come on Henry work with me. What do you think?"

He shook his head, put the cup on the table, then placed his arms on either side and stared at the slop. "Damn, the whole time I thought it was you, but now I know it's me. I couldn't outscore a potato right now."

Willie put his index finger on the table and tapped it as if he were trying to convince shareholders of his scheme. "Now Henry, I'm telling you it's the next big thing. Health is a killer right now." He looked around suspiciously before he continued. "All those health quacks are going to get pretty bored with frog licking, because they're always looking for the next big thing. I'm telling you."

Gwendolyn's appearance began to decline. Her nails were chipping and her hair a quick brush through. He worried and felt he should say something.

He loaded a small box with vials and digging tools. The

lab class filed out into the hallway and head outdoors for fieldwork, collecting soil samples for microbes. The hall was busy with other students. Gwendolyn stood a few paces ahead, while he tied his shoe.

As two young men walked passed her one remarked to the other. "Check those out."

His friend said, "Damn, there's blue, and there's that."

When she turned to face the wall, Henry flew at them, grabbed the one who made the last comment, slammed him up against the wall, put his forearm across his throat, and clenched his jaw. "She's not a that. What, you think she's fuck meat, something to plow, then roll over and light up afterwards."

He kept his glare on the startled young man who only wanted to make it to his next class. The big, pierced faced woman came up behind him, placed her large hand on his shoulder, which triggered his head to turn quickly, thinking he was about to be double teamed.

She winked. "Now, prince here has already intellectually emasculated a jock in the cafeteria several weeks ago."

The young man reached up removed his arm, headed towards his class, and said as he was leaving, "Dude relax, it's just a compliment, shit."

As Henry gazed upon Gwendolyn, he said sharply to the young man, who was double-timing it down the hall, "That's not how you compliment a woman. That's not how it's done. You don't eye fuck'um and call them this or that."

He was still huffing when Gwendolyn began to tear up. He turned to her, saw her pools, and said with soft reverence, "If you want to compliment a woman you look into her eyes."

He paused as he retraced the moment when he discovered a question through the heart of a frog. He thought, evolution has separated us eons ago and your heart hasn't changed. It seeks nothing and will never suffer. Yours was spared and will live out its life only as an organ. As he gazed deeply into her eyes, the poet felt the wind in the reeds blow in with a simple truth rooted.

The human heart can't go back, because the miracle of love can't let it go. He came out of his poetic muse and said, "You should say something that emanates from the kiln, only the kiln... so blue."

She hugged him. "Henry, you make me feel like a person." He put his arms around her, closed his eyes, while the scent and feel of her soft hair filled every sense his face had to offer.

The pierced faced girl watched with delight and thought about Barbie. She loved her as much as anyone could love, but when she witnessed the rapture of Henry's absolute commitment to Gwendolyn. She wanted to go home to Barbie and reaffirm theirs.

He released her, turned to the pierced faced woman, they fist bumped, and he said, "Damn, Patty, if you keep coming to my rescue, I'm going to think there's something between us."

She chuckled, and said, "Dude, the only thing between us is her and she's not my type."

They found soft soil under the bushes that lined the walkway by the Fine Arts building. He knelt down and began digging. She knelt right beside him, hip by shoulder. She put her hand on his wrist to stop his digging and kissed his cheek. "Thank you again, for making me feel like a person." Their eyes were inches from each other and he thought, oh how I want to kiss you, but after you would think I was just one of them.

"Gwendolyn, you're a person like no other, and I wish I could place you inside me just for a moment so I could show you."

She thought, Henry I would never leave, and said, "What would I find in your kiln?"

"A space," then he thought, that can only be filled by you.

She put her hand on his shoulder, looked up to the roof of the Fine Arts building. "Henry, have you ever been unsure?" She paused to squeeze her promise tight in her mind and said, "Then sure, but also confused by everything."

He sighed and squinted briefly as if to lock in on her statement for analysis. "Yeah." He studied her confused expression for a moment. "I don't think you should give confusion to the mind, though."

"Why?"

"Well, I don't think the mind tolerates confusion long.

It's too quick to give a decision. It's impatient and wants resolution quickly, because when things are confusing, the mind tends to be insincere and tries to throw an answer together, so it can move on to the next task. Important things can be overlooked, like a slight smile someone believes was created solely for them." He stopped abruptly and waited for his thoughts to recover from his explosive flight of feelings, precipitated by the glow of the woman next to him and simply stated. "But it's only polite."

The young poet felt flush with another flight. "A common hand that touches one far better, but knows it can't be better, because the world spins like a centrifuge keeping their castes forever segregated."

He paused; he was now back in her enchanting fields of lavender and blue iris. He watched as her fields were now fully flooded with her pupils and studied the only thing remaining, blue rings, and said, "But the heart is wise and sees everything. It will always take its time, turn confusion over and over, and may never resolve it, but the heart loves you and will never abandon you. It sometimes purposely blinds itself to hope, though." He poured into her eyes. "Gwendolyn, I don't think I'll ever forget you. You're like no other."

Two grad students, standing a few paces down, interrupted their gaze. One student was picking at a stain on the other's shirt with her thumbnail. She was of average height with authentic auburn hair and green eyes. He was slightly taller than Henry and of the same build with brown hair and eyes. The woman had a scowl on her face, and said, "Daniel, how am I supposed to get this out."

"The most beautiful hot dog spoke to me when I walked by the grease truck."

She chuckled, then said, "Shut up."

"She was the last one in the lard bin and she whispered, 'Daniel I was conceived only for you. I've been waiting all day for you my darling.' One dog, one stomach, one love.'"

She laughed, then said, "Shut up you idiot."

"Izzy, I'm telling you this was no ordinary dog. It was top dog, the dog to die for. The dog above all dogs, a born leader. The ruler of men, a dog I would willing go into battle for."

She crossed her arms still chuckling. "God, Daniel you are such an idiot."

Henry looked at Gwendolyn. "Damn he's funny."

"Like an old married couple."

"Dale and Marilyn in twenty."

She returned to the stain, staring at it and rubbing it lightly with her fingertips. She felt his eyes, hovering, while contemplating stain removal strategies. She kept her attention focused on the spot and said without looking up, "Daniel, stop looking at me like that."

"What's wrong with looking at a beautiful woman...You know it was a magical hot dog." She looked up and chuckled, then said, "Shut up and walk me to my car."

"You know the dog said something else."

"Daniel."

"What? It's true; I'm to meet a beautiful woman."

"Daniel, stop calling me that."
Gwendolyn cast her head down quickly and Henry asked,
"What's wrong?"

"I feel like I'm eavesdropping."

"Well she is beautiful."

She jerked her head up quickly, and he said, "You're
beautiful, too."

She blushed and cast her head down and he said,
"Why does that embarrass you? You've heard it all your life."
She avoided eye contact. "Henry, it's from you."

Patty sat heavily on her dorm bed staring at the floor
when a petite young woman with sandy blonde hair, hazel
eyes, and heavily pierced and jeweled about her face walked
in briskly, humming softly. She came to an abrupt stop.
"What's wrong?"

She looked up. "I don't know. I'm a little bummed,"
and cast her eyes back down. The petite woman jingled as
she crossed the room. She sat by her, kissed her cheek, and
said in a motherly tone, "Tell me what's wrong."

Patty sighed, kept her eyes fixed on the floor. "It's this
blue eyed woman." The petite one looked at her oddly. Patty
chuckled, then said, "Dolly, you're the only one for me. It's
this hetero couple in lab." She burst into tears.

The petite one rubbed her back until her crying spasm ceased, then said,"Do you want to hold my hand?"

She wiped her eyes on her blue denim work shirt, and already felt the peace. The petite one stroked her, placed her hand in hers, and said, "I remember the first time I saw you in that little grease jar of a bar where I was singing." She stopped stroking and searched the wall. "I sang you a song, but I don't remember the name, but I think it was a sweet little ballad-"

Patty broke in. "Only You."

"Softie, you would remember. You were so down."

Patty looked down at their hands. "I remember after your set you came over." She sighed and continued. "You didn't even introduce yourself. You sat down and said, 'Hold my hand.'"

Patty changed the subject abruptly when Henry's rapture consumed her mind. "Look down between us." The petite one furrowed her brow and looked down.

Patty said, "Barb, look at me."

Barbie looked up perplexed. "Patty, I don't understand." Barbie felt anxiety percolating in Patty and said, "Patty, what?"

Patty took a deep breath and sighed. "This space between us is the flame. Always keep the flame between us, and never press it, because when you press the flame you'll be lost. The flame is forbidden. You can't love long in the flame because you'll become ash. When you're inside the flame you're pressed inside one another, then love begins to consume itself, and when you see each other fading you begin to love as hard as you can, because you think you're losing their love, but you're not. You're blinded by love, and can't see each other any more, and you both perish."

"The flame is forbidden and this hetero couple is pressed inside one another. I saw it. The flame's now an aura around them, not between them where it should be. They love each other too much." She burst into tears. After a few minutes, she collected herself. "Their love is dying and they don't even realize it. God, all I want to do is cry."

Barbie wiped her eyes with a tissue and kissed her cheek. "Are you all right?"

"I don't know."

She kissed her cheek again. "You can't help them. Love is meant to perish if it's too much."

Patty sighed. "I think love should be like ours, strong, controlled, well managed, and sensible."

Barbie felt her past boiling up. "We should leave the hot blooded to songs, because that kind of love is brutal and boiling like the vapors of Jupiter. It's untamable and mean sometimes, because passion like that has the magnitude of stars and the heat it produces is unbearable. In the end you find yourself brutalized and alone. That's why I don't like to sing about love and passion."

Amy flashed into her mind and she trembled.

Patty, preoccupied, didn't notice, and said, "I know, but watching is so tragic. She's all over him and he seems to back up and she's totally unaware, she just wants to crawl inside him. I don't know why he backs up. Maybe he's aware they're in the flame, but I don't think so." She paused, glanced around, as if an answer would be merciful, pop through the door, and disclose. "He's always pouring into her eyes and calling her blue eyes."

Barbie was still wrestling for control with her tormenting passion, Amy. She closed her eyes briefly to slip away, then opened them quickly, freed, and said, "Maybe, he backs up because he doesn't think he's good enough." She kissed her cheek again, "Because you've thought that."

Patty blushed. "I'm so lucky."

Barbie glanced around the room when a lull popped in the room. She looked at the stack of books on her desk and smiled when she saw her western civ book. "Not good enough, huh." She readjusted herself and sat cross legged. "Want to hear a story? It was written by an old roman poet. He was on the beach early one morning before sunrise waiting for Venus to rise and wondered why she always appeared so white. He was inspired at that moment and thought perhaps that it was a veil. He knew of the gods' trickery and how they liked to torment mortals, so he was careful not to give her what he called 'too much eye', because the gods become suspicious if mortals pondered them too long."

"The veil began to eat at him and he became paranoid and thought that she was on to him and was tormenting him with obsession. He broke his daily ritual on the beach in an effort to throw her off and hopefully she would fall to boredom and leave. He turned to all night stargazing and planned to return to beach sunrises when her eyes traveled to a new torment. He felt better and the paranoia subsided."

"One time right before sunrise he noticed Mars was unusually red. He knew Venus was about to rise and decided to leave when she rose to avoid too much eye, but Mars' agitation held his curiosity. Venus rose and Mars appeared to be ablaze in a blush. He turned his attention to Venus, saw her shimmer, and left before she became aware of his presence. He was met on the path home by a goat."

Patty skeptically. "A goat?"

"What?"

"Oh hell. Now I know this is made up, you've always wanted a goat farm just like me."

"Let me finish."

"Please tell me the goat didn't speak to him."

Barbie giggled, then said, "Why yes it did. That's the beauty of a myth, no rules and facts are optional."

Patty pushed her. "Get out of here."

She continued. "Now, the goat..."

Patty burst into laughter.

"What?"

"You've got me tickled. Tell me it wasn't the god of goats."

Barbie playfully put her nose in the air, and said smugly, "No, it was Jupiter."

Patty chortled, "Must have been one gassy goat."

"I see you're feeling better already," and continued. "Now, Jupiter said, 'It's the veil of vanity.' Venus and Mars are madly in love and because her path around the sun is shorter, she passed him frequently. When the sun was at her back they gazed into each other's eyes for months, but when she started to pass around the sun, there was a glare in her eyes. She thought if she only had a veil to block the glare she could gaze into his eyes for a few extra moments, before she lost him totally. She thought better to get rid of the sun altogether and plotted. When she came around she told Mars of her brilliant plan. He was delighted, but Mercury overheard and told Jupiter."

"Jupiter disguised himself as Mercury, and said to both of them that he liked the idea. That way they could have each other and he could keep a permanent eye on all the gods he didn't trust. They all agreed and started planning. It was time for Mercury and her to pass around again, and they didn't have a plan yet. So he handed her a veil and told her it would keep the glare out for those few moments and they would all plot next season. She was delighted and put it on right as the glare became most intense and looked towards Mars for those last few moments. She saw Mars blush and thought that he must think I'm beautiful in my new veil."

"When she came into view the next season she applied her veil for the initial glare of the new season. Mars blushed again and thought she's embarrassed by me, thinks I'm hideous, and hides behind her veil in shame. When enough time had passed and the veil wasn't needed anymore she found she couldn't remove it. Jupiter whispered to her, 'You will be shrouded behind a cloudy veil as punishment for your vanity of love. The veil can never be removed and he will always think that you wear it because he's hideous to you and he blushes with embarrassment.'"

Patty chuckled, then said, "Veil or no veil there's a goat farm in my future after graduation."

"There should be."

Patty sighed, and thought about the campus Gay-Le festival coming up. "You think you and the band could write a song about them for the festival?"

She nodded. "I think I have enough time, but why? Even if they came to our festival it wouldn't help them."

"It'll help me."

"Big softy."

Saturday rolled up and she headed to the rooftop and planned to listen to the band at the festival. She didn't bother bathing, because Henry would not be in her day. A few students were milling around a small stage on the Fine Arts grounds. The cool air was held in check by the warmth of the sun, a welcomed gift that allowed her coat to take the day off. She observed a small woman walking the stage and repeating 'mic check' whenever she passed by her microphone. She had long sandy blonde dread locks that appeared as heavy jute.

A long queue had formed at the refreshment table as the band cranked out heavy tunes. She thought about joining them, but reminded herself. I'll just be this or that without my Henry by my side. She fantasized that Henry had found her and was right next to her, holding her hand, being incorrigible, and kissing her. She stopped abruptly as tears pooled and thought, poet find me before I disintegrate.

Barbie glanced side stage at softy, winked, turned to the band, and they all nodded. She stood at the mic clinching each fist rhythmically, and said, "So blue, and things we can't have." She didn't like ballads because most times they provoked thoughts of Amy. She closed her eyes and swayed. The songbird was listening for her lead in. She fluttered her wings and bounced on her perch, anticipating. Then that single note filled the air and brought lift:

"I know now why it rains.
To fill the river of shame,
So the ones above me
Can wash away people like me.

I know now why love can't be free,
Because it hangs with you and me.
The world frowns upon creeps like us,
And doubles the standard on every bus.

Gray skies above me.

There're skies so blue above you.
Where He sets every love free.
And whose love will always hang with you and me."

The crowd boiled over with exuberance clapping, hugging, and dancing. A small inebriated group chanted "Let my people go," which set the crowd off hooting and joining in.

When the crowd settled to a manageable level of energy, Barbie came back to the mic. "This is for love, only for love, **A**lways **M**issing **Y**ou." The Songbird was on the wing again:

"Come lay down by my side,
Take my hand and close your eyes.
I know I Love You is somewhere inside.

Lay me down and I won't cry.
I'll savor those tears, for our long good bye,
Now that I know you're leaving my side.

Now lay me down one last time,
Though my heart knows I'm left behind,
And I Love You is now impossible to find.

So much in love and always missing you."

Gwendolyn turned down the corners of her mouth down as her diaphragm began to spasm. She thought, Henry what can I do to make you love me. Henry, I'm going to write you a poem. It won't be a poem with frame or boarders, of rhyme and metre. No, Henry, it'll be all the words I've collected in my kiln and they belong only to you. Henry when I fly I'll repeat them over and over, because they're true and loyal and need no polish.

Tears flowed down Barbie's face. Big Patty smiled and thought they were for the hetero couple.

They weren't. She was crying because it happened. The flame ignited and Amy was standing right in front of her, ablaze with passion.

She was the young girl of her high school years who never left her heart. Sometimes late at night, while in Patty's arms, listening to her snore, she would ease out and sit at her desk, stare into the starry sky, and think about the short time with Amy.

It was in the middle of her sophomore year when they met. Amy was a new transfer. She had two classes with her, and would observe her intently until suspicion turned her eye.

Barbie didn't have close friends. The few she did have called her 'Knobs' because of her skinny frame and bony knees and elbows. She knew she was odd and the nickname wasn't meant to offend. She was stranded socially though, and orbited circles on the fringe.

She sat in the cafeteria alone most of the time and at

times someone would sit by her, but she knew it was only because the room was crowded.

She spoke with Amy on a few occasions and would find herself relocating her gaze whenever she felt Amy was looking too deeply into her eyes. She felt Amy was like her, but since she'd never been around anyone who was turned, she was unsure.

A few weeks later, she was alone at one of the back tables eating and reading when someone sat down right next her. She looked up startled because the room wasn't crowded. She blushed when Amy said unapologetically, "I'm going to kiss you before the day is out." She held her blush and shot her head down quickly. Amy discreetly reached down, squeezed her leg. "I know you're like me."

She looked up timidly. "I was unsure."

Amy put her hand back on the table. "You are now."

Amy was a little taller with pastel blue eyes and on the athletic side. She would push her down on the bed, jump on top of her, and not let her up, until after several kisses. It was their ritual every time they were alone in their bedrooms.

Her tears picked up as she held the microphone, because now she was holding her down and remembering the day she did it.

They were in Barbie's bedroom and Amy had just begun the ritual when Barbie said, "I'm going to change your name."

Amy gave a hearty laugh, and said, "To what?"

After several kisses, they stared into each other's eyes.

"But first I'm going to hold you down," Barbie said, and wrestled out.

Amy lay on her back. "Ok, Knobs I'll make it easy for you, because there's no way you could ever pin me." She jumped on top of her, straddled her belly, and put her hands on her shoulders.

"You know I could have you on your back in one move."

She kissed her hard and deep and poured into her eyes. She wouldn't say anything for a long time. Tears dripped in Amy's face, and the splashing released Amy's rivers. Neither spoke as they stared into each other's eyes, letting their rivers run to the end. When the flows ceased, Amy's hairline crusted like riverbanks during the dry season. They were still in a deep engagement as their riverbeds caked.

"I Love You."

Amy's rivers flowed back to the wet season and her tears turned her hairline back to mud as she said in a choked voice, "Knobs, I love you too."

Barbie shook her head. "No, that's your new name. When we're alone in our room, your new name will be 'I Love You'. Do you understand that I Love You?"

Barbie released the microphone when she realized she was crying in Patty's arms. Patty kissed her and grinned, then said, "Who's the softy now?"

The crowd clapped and a man turned to his partner. "The song was good enough without all the theatrics."

His partner rolled his eyes. "I'm so embarrassed for her. It'll be days before I can look her in the eye again. Why do women over paint?"

"I don't know. God, I've got to have another drink to wash that hideous image out of my mind. Would you be a doll?"

She sat at her desk in a bathrobe, with a towel around her head, staring at the wall. Patty was stretched out on the bed with her elbow buried in a pillow and her head propped in her hand, wearing boxers and the school T-shirt, studying. She looked up from her studies. The air was too still to concentrate. "Don't worry about it. Everybody thought it was sweet."

She snapped her head around. "No, they didn't. I saw that fat head Brian with his little toad rolling their eyes."

Patty chuckled at every high note of her rant. "Shit, that little worm. I'll probably run into him tomorrow and I can see him sniggering now."

"He won't."

"He can't help himself."

"He won't this time."

"It's in the worm's nature."

"You really can't stand him can you?"

She glared. "You have no idea."

Patty sat up adjusted her boxers. "He won't bother you."

"How do you know?"

"Because I told him if he did I would kick his ass."

She laugh, then said, "Do you think you can take him?"

"He does and that's all that matters." Patty closed her books and kissed her. "I'm going to bed."

She turned to the wall and snored lightly. Barbie turned the corners of her mouth down and cried quietly. She waited until the train was far from the station before she went to the closet to retrieve Amy's letter.

She unfolded it quietly while glancing at Patty occasionally. She laid it on the desk, brushed out the folds, and stared at the page. Amy had hand written the words 'I Love You, Too' on every line, filling the page, front to back, before she left this world. Amy was her aura. She glanced at Patty and thought, strong and sensible doesn't understand passion. Passion is hot blooded, quick tempered, and breaks things, but God, the way it holds me down and won't let me up until it has extracted every bit of love out of me. It tears at me, but I want it to. It says it wants to crawl inside me, and I try to tear my chest open to let it in. It sucks my mouth so hard my fingertips turn blue, but I don't care. It makes me scream out as if I'm going through birthing pains, but I welcome them, because I want to give birth to it over and over. Passion is the mother of all art and I'm holding a major work from one of its offspring in my hand.

It was late evening when he walked into the Fine Arts building. He noticed a young woman with her head cocked looking at a painting. His heart rate picked as he came up behind her. "Ma'am that's not for sale."

She whirled around and hugged him. "Henry, I've missed you."

As she hugged him, he thought, Gwendolyn you feel so good. I just want to press you inside, damn the slumming.

She released him quickly and blushed. "Sorry Henry, I didn't mean to hang on you."

He thought, I don't know anything about slumming, but she seems slow to make her move. Maybe Willie's right. Nah, he's an idiot, but what I do worry about is that she seems so sad sometimes and she doesn't polish. She's probably depressed. I think if I ease into it, maybe I can help.

"Remember, I was born without personal spaces, by the way, I think I forgot to feed my mother."

She laught, and he said, "It's good to hear you laugh." He held up a notebook. "Do you think you could help me appreciate some of this shit, gotta write an art appreciation essay."

They walked up to a painting titled *Love*. She looked up and observed his intent expression. "Henry, what is love?"

He turned, poured into her eyes, and stared. She cocked her head one way then the other, and thought, if I could empty my kiln as a poet who loathes the word, nothing would be lost in transfer, because it would be transferred in a kiss. A kiss loses nothing Henry. Kiss me now and empty me. Love is the emptying. It's that physical act Henry. It's the emptying that defines love. Empty me. Kiss me Henry and physically empty me like breasts.

He turned to the painting and then to her. "Hunger, Gwendolyn. Hunger that knows it'll spend all its life slowly starving, but can't die until the body expires." He paused and turned back to the painting. "I think perhaps we all starve to some degree." He turned back to her. "Hunger, Gwendolyn, sometimes I think it's the only way we feel alive, because if we weren't starving would we ever be aware of this incredible journey?" He paused, lowered his eyes when his father took his seat in his mind, and he said softly, "Not a journey, the experience of starvation."

He thought, may I kiss you, I'm starving. Gwendolyn, before you leave to float in the silver bowl of opulence, I think I will ask if I may kiss you, and if you won't that will be ok, because I'm perfectly pleased to hunger for your beautiful blue eyes, I'll never forget them, I love you.

The diffuse evening light had transitioned to pitch quickly and the interior lighting gave the windows a reflective quality. She circled a sculpture titled *Obsession*, while he was fixated on the live art walking around the dead, and noticed her reflection in a window. The lighting appeared to give her an eerie glow.

He dropped his fixation and pointed. "Hey blue eyes,

look, your glow." He chuckled, then said, "Hey, it's close to Halloween, why don't you rattle your chain?" As she stepped out from the glare, he said, "Damn, you're still beautiful even out of your glow and that chain is a wonderful accessory."

She clenched her fists, pursed her lips, flared her nostrils, and stomped towards the door.

He panicked and jumped in front of her, put his hands on her shoulders. "Gwendolyn I was joking, please."

"Leave me alone."

He unconsciously reached down, grabbed her hand, kissed her palm, and said, "Please, don't go." He released it quickly when he realized what he had done, and said, "You're obsessed by the book."

Her nostrils remained flared. "Yes, Henry, I am, it bothers me still, and I don't like to be reminded of it."

"Gwendolyn, it's just a book."

She released her agitation. "To you."

He was about to reach for her palm again but checked himself. "Obsession can be a good thing."

She cocked her head. "How so?"

They sat on the bench in front of the sculpture with obsession between them. She sat hip by shoulder, licking her lips, and rubbing her palm with her fingers unconsciously, as he said, "I don't think you should give it to the heart though."

Blue rings was now searching his eyes, and said, "Some hearts only want one thing. All their life, Henry, they've looked for it and when it appears they don't think they'll ever have it, because inside them lies an immoveable object placed by God and they begin to fade." He looked at her puzzled, and she said, "Henry, when the heart can't have what has appeared, it feels the need to fly." She looked down quickly as tears pooled.

"Gwendolyn, don't give it to your heart. Give it to the mind, because the mind knows obsession well and all its tricks." Now she was puzzled and he squeezed her hand. "The mind knows of its appetite and puts it away to pick up another day, because it knows obsession is like a scorned mistress consumed with revenge. You have to learn yours and know how to distract her eye. Find her buttonholes to work. If you can do that, then you'll have a peaceful rest of the day."

He almost picked her hand up again and thought, what the hell is wrong with me? I'm acting as if she's mine. The mistress of my house stirs.

She thought, Henry, if I can't have you, then I will at least kiss you before I leave. Surly one kiss, Henry, only one, because I believe that if God never allows you to find me, he will allow a goodbye kiss. Oh Henry, can I love you more than I should? Does God punish too much love? Henry, sitting here with you now, I feel like if I told you that I love you it would be an echo, and you can't be in love with an echo. If I can't have your kiss or kiln, then I will kiss you, glean mine, and fly.

A lull prodded them to stand and the quiet of the room

felt as soothing as an empty church. It was a large open room with a twenty-foot high ceiling. Along the back wall was a staircase running up to a large balcony that overlooked the entire gallery, with offices and studios buried down a hallway behind the balcony's back wall.

He came to the center of the gallery to a comical piece, admired the wit, then turned to Gwendolyn, who was a few feet from him, and pointed to it. "Gwen, check this out."

She exploded, drove up quickly, with nostrils flaring, gritted teeth, and red faced. She slapped him hard and shouted. "Goddamn it, don't ever call me that."

He exploded in equal force, and in a fit of rage grabbed her roughly by clinching her hair on the back of her head, with his left hand, and slamming her chin on his chest. He wrapped his right arm around her back and cinched her tight. Her right arm was free and dangled as if stroke flaccid, while her three bracelets appeared as a shackle on her wrist. She was like a doll in his arms and from a distance it appeared as if he were trying to revive her as a firefighter would a child.

A young woman emerged from the hallway in the back of the balcony and was about to descend the stairs. When she caught sight of the two, she fumbled for her camera. She turned pale and trembled, while trying to focus. She whispered in shock, "My God, an aura." She cursed under her breath as she fought the waves of trimmer assaults, and mumbled, "Damn it, get it together. You're a professional."

He clenched his jaw, while both were snorting hard, locked in a glare, eyes fixed, and unmovable. Pupils constricted in contempt. There was no searching the tender prominences of the face, no gaze, no smile, no Henry, no Gwendolyn. They were strangers now pressed against the hard edge of anger. The room was urban now, concrete, steel, and conduit. They felt the rumble of the subway under their feet.

He was drawn to the mint on her breath, and its gravity pulled him in, which forced his eyes to close. He loosened his grip slightly, and followed the anatomy of her lips with his nose. As he migrated to her chin, he still had her hair clinched and used it to crane her head towards her shoulder to accommodate his nose traveling down her jaw line. She encouraged his traveling by straining her neck as far as she could.

He stopped his nose at her hinge and nuzzled her ear lobe. Her perfume filled his sinuses and disseminated into his tissues, stimulating his receptors. They pushed to differentiate her scent, from the chaff of perfume, and submit her identification to his brain.

He blinked when he heard her murmur in a victim's raspy revived voice. "Oh, God, please empty me." Her bottom lip quivered as she said with tears pooling, "Henry, please, don't hate me."

He released her, put his arms around her quickly, and pressed her tight. "Gwendolyn, don't be angry. Let's not be angry."

She put her arms around him and pressed her nails lightly in his back. "I'm so sorry. I would never hurt you. It's just that I'm so tense inside."

He thought, maybe this tension is what's making her sad. I need to quit being such an ass and quit worrying about slumming and be a friend. I feel like even after the slumming we'll be friends. I like that. He was about to release her when she pressed her nails a little harder. "Henry please don't let me go," she hesitated, "yet, anyway." She thought, it'll happen soon enough, my poet.

He stroked her hair and knew at that moment, while fully immersed in the glow of the woman he loved that love had a simple definition.

She sighed. "God, it's so warm in here."

He thought, that the shortened version of her name comes with a great trauma and that mistake will never happen again.

As they walk the gallery, they found themselves by the comic sculpture in view of the piece *Obsession.* He chuckled, then said, "It's a damn minefield in here and it was supposed to be art." As her laughter echoed through the room, he purposely grabbed her hand, kissed her palm, and said, "See, that's my Gwendolyn. That's the Gwendolyn I know. Please don't be sad." He paused and searched her face. "Gwendolyn, if I could I would reach inside of you and pull your sadness out and lock it away inside of me." He thought, though it may paint my walls ill and draw my windows lightless, it'll never dim the light I feel for you.

She thought, no Henry. This sadness is not transient, but transcendent, and I am privileged, because before I saw the light in your eyes, I've always felt this or that was my life, and perhaps pick one, if the parapet allows and settle.

But now Henry, I've tasted the apple and I know now, I'd rather fly. You are the love of my life and now it's over and that's ok, because I've had the light in your eyes. I'm well satisfied to know that it was there, but not possible, it just wasn't meant for me. Goodbye Henry, my beautiful poet, I will love you always; I'm going to fly soon. Henry, the parapet has always whispered to me, but now the Sirens call. I hope I've given you something to write about.

Gwen dropped the book on the coffee table, jumped up, and thought, Aniel please, that hurts so much, please never think... Do I need to call you now to ease your mind?

She bit her nails and turned lamps on as the sun found its late afternoon seat, behind the other buildings.

The one behind her said, "He doesn't think that."

She thought, not me, him. Should I call Charles?

The one behind her chuckled then reassured her. "Gwendolyn, it's just a book. He has no intentions of jumping."

She thought oh, Frances, what do you think... oh, no, not the Irishman. I've already been through the confessional.

She remained at the dining room table after she finished her soup, and thought, I'm tired and enough of this book. I'm too old for this nonsense. I'm sure we'll live happily ever after, because books pander. Aniel, we in the working world don't have time for fairytales. She felt a little contemptuous towards him. I'm a businesswoman and my plans are to be still, now goodbye.

The one behind her was unusually reserved she thought as she left the table and pressed the window. She observed the malfunctioning streetlight, struggling for standing amongst its peers. Fatigued, she planned to bathe, go to bed early, wake to the real world, and go to work.

The one behind her said with a tone of wisdom in her voice, "Perhaps, it's not all about you and him. There're others. Have you not wondered who he is?" She paused to load an inflammatory question. "Who is Aniel Posey, besides the man you're in love with?"

She gritted her teeth and thought, leave me alone.

"Finish the book."

She looked towards the coffee table, satisfied, and thought, a schoolgirl with hearts in her eyes. That's all it is. I don't know this man. She sat on the couch, stared at the book, and felt a little irritable towards him, and thought, who are you? There are no feelings here. I don't even know you. Struck by her last thought, she did a search on the computer, but only found the bio from his book -single, born in the Midwest, parents still living, no siblings, debut novel.

She sighed and placed her hands in her lap.

The one behind her rested her chin on her shoulder,

and said reflectively, "Perhaps, you've inspired him somehow. I mean nobody knows why creativity happens or when. It just happens." The one behind her paused while extracting a bright spot out of the bayou, and said somewhat baffled, "You used to play the piano and write poetry." The one behind her beamed with pride. "Do you remember standing on the dock while the fishing boats cast off?" She bounced excitedly. "Remember, after you prayed for their safety and full nets, you wrote a poem that night and recited it to God."

Gwen smiled as she remembered the flowers floating upon the water and the prayerful rituals of all the families on the crowded dock before husbands and sons shoved off. She pulled her fisherman's poem from the place in her heart where all the others were carefully stored and committed to long-term memory. She hummed softly as she recited her poem in her mind.

Tis a fisher am I is you.
Petition Him for the timber and tides, do we.
Now blessed be our keel and the waves by He.
Lest we not forget the beasts we seek from the sea.
Tis priests me thinks fishers be.

She fawned over the few fond memories of childhood, content, while listening to the bayou sing spirituals from deep in the canes, until she heard her mother's instructions. She stood abruptly and fled to the sanctuary of his book.

"I need to be getting back."

"Let me walk you."

"It's ok."

"No, I insist. I've already screwed up twice, and its bad luck to screw up on an odd note. I've got a good chance to make an even three, if I walk you back."

She chuckled; feeling the night somewhat righted, then said, "Henry, it's not all your fault."

They were at her door when she turned to him and stroked the slapped cheek. "Henry, I'm so sorry."

He kissed her cheek, and placed his hands on her shoulders. "Gwendolyn I've already forgotten it. Please don't be sad. It worries me."

"Ok."

"Forget the nunnery and let's get you on the boxing circuit, because you have an amazing swing."

She gave a slight smile and went in. He stood at the door for a moment and thought, I'm so worried about her. Maybe she's an emotional slummer. That's it. She's bored with the body. It all makes perfect sense, but somehow I'm unsure. I hope it is, though. I think it's time to call her down and after she gets pissed maybe she'll give me a proper interview. God, how I love you blue eyes.

She looked towards Molly and heard her snoring lightly. She pulled her desk chair out, quietly, and found a sheet of paper. She thought, Henry, I'm going to compose my poem now and my pen will be like a paintbrush, it will be your favorite color, blue. Henry I will sweep my kiln and even check between the cracks of the bricks to make sure I haven't missed anything.

The corners of her mouth turned down as tears flowed. Her diaphragm gave a quick spasm. She glanced at Molly, sleeping, and looked up to the heavens, and thought, oh, God, I hear the far off cry of a violin and now my kiln is cracking, I love him so much.

A young woman climbed the stairs of the gallery balcony and headed down the hall to the offices buried in the back. She knocked on an office door. A voice said, "Come." She opened the door slowly. A middle aged man sitting behind a desk, said, "Now, what is it that you needed to see me so quickly, Bethany."

"Thank you for seeing me. I want to change my project."

He straightened up, frowned, and said puzzled, "Bethany, even if I granted it, I don't think you would have enough time, it's already November and graduation's next month."

"I've thought about it and I think it's doable."

She reached in to her satchel and handed him some photographs. "I think these will convince you."

He put his glasses on and studied the photographs. "Damn. Bethany, these are incredible, such tension." He stared at her for a moment, then said unequivocally, "You know you have it."

Puzzled, she cocked her head.

"Bethany, some think they have it, but don't. Some know they have it and do, and there are some who have it and don't know it, and that would be you."

He studied them for a while, and then looked at a photograph on his desk. "She has it too." He turned in his swivel chair and faced the wall, putting his back to her.

She coughed from the postnasal drip the tears precipitated, and said, "How is she doing?"

He didn't say anything for a moment, to allow his grieving feelings to finish their seizure. When they returned to their postictal, drowsy state, he admonished himself for his wife's sake. Strength, he thought, is worry's peace, and said, "She's responding to treatment and I can bring her home Saturday."

She fidgeted and he sensed it. "Bethany, I know you're uncomfortable and you want to say what anybody would want to say, but also know there's not a damn thing you can do, but I know you would if you could. You can have an extra week. May I keep these?"

She said in a chocked voice, "Yes, of course."

"That'll be all, Bethany."

She descended the stairs with her satchel in hand, while tears streamed down her face. She headed across campus and climbed the stairs of the freshman dorm to the third floor. She walked a few doors down and knocked. A young woman of her height and weight, but a few years younger, threw her arms around her and kissed her. She pulled the younger woman off. "Sit down, please."

"You're breaking up with me."

"Yes, Sweets, I am."

The young woman sobbed pitiably and Bethany said, "Come on Sweets, you're not that broken up. We haven't seen each other in weeks."

They both sat for a while as Bethany rummaged through her thoughts. She grabbed the young woman's jaw, as if she were a child and frowned. "You're a young freshman and you play too much. I'm not angry. Sleeping around and playing is part of it. I just want you to study."

She glared at her as an older sister. "I'm a loner, always have been. It was never going to work anyway and I think you knew that." She continued to hold her chin, then kissed her cheek and frowned again. "Now, study." She turned somber and said in a soft voice, "Don't squander."

She left and made her way back to the Fine Arts building. The afternoon sun was warm and the early morning snow had been sparse, which appeared as a light dusting of talc on the objects scattered across the landscape. She walked between yesterday's drifts on the walkway and brushed the light talc off the bench by the entrance. She sat with her hands in her lap, and laid her head on melancholy's shoulder, sighed, and gazed off.

Her gaze was interrupted when a young man with his backpack slung on one shoulder came up right in front of her. He put his hands in his pockets, rocked from his heels to the balls of his feet, and grinned, then said, "Well, well, well, if it isn't Izzy Lezzy."

She gazed up and said flatly, "Hey, Daniel."

"What's wrong?"

"I broke up with Sweets." As his grinned postulated, she rolled her eyes. "Alright, Daniel, I know you can't wait to say it so go ahead."

He sat beside her and kissed her hand. "How long have we been dating."

"Shut up you idiot, we've never dated."

"Oh, I don't know, I think we've been together what about eight months now."

"It's been ten and we're not together."

He stopped his kissing and interlaced her fingers. "Izzy, the light's wrong inside you. You're just confused. I don't believe it."

She furrowed her brow. "I know who I am."

"You're not hardcore and I can prove it."

He disengaged their fingers, kissed her hand, and scooted closer. "I've given Brian and Ziggy your signs and symptoms."

"What, we're conditions and diseases now."

"No, but for lack of a better term since you're not hardcore."

She watched him kiss her hand. "Stop kissing my hand like that."

He turned her hand over, and kissed her palm. "There, that's better."

She chuckled, then said, "I know I'm going to fall into the pot, but how's that better?"

He kissed her hand again. "Because you said not to kiss it like that, so I'll kiss it like this."

"God, you're an idiot."

She gazed off again and he stopped kissing. "Tell me what's wrong?"

She sighed. "It's not Sweets. That wasn't going anywhere anyway. I went to see professor Williams about changing my project..."

He cut her off. "Whoa, why would you do that? Your 'Campus Life' photographs are the best of the whole graduate class."

"I've got something better. I saw a couple of young undergrads in the gallery a few days ago, and I stalked them for a couple days." She was silent for a moment. "When I was asking him for an extension he said that I have it, but just didn't know it."

He nodded in concurrence. "You do, your stuff is better than any of ours."

She blushed. "He looked at his wife's picture and said she has it too. I felt so bad."

"Eww, how's she doing?"

"She's coming home Saturday, but what I feel so bad about, is that when I left the building all I could think about was how happy I was for the extension."

He put his arm around her and she leaned her head towards his shoulder. "Daniel, I know what art is to me. Art is just a brief distraction from the firestorm of life. The patron has a moment with a piece and for that moment he's at peace, but it's only a moment. The artist's distraction from her firestorm is her obsession."

He offered a soothing encouragement. "Sometimes I think God has banged the universe more times than we could ever comprehend. I think He stands in the middle wearing a smock, with brushes in his hands and thinks I know I can do it better next bang." He kissed her temple. "Don't feel bad, because there's no one more obsessed than God, and He's perfect. Williams would be happy as hell if he got an extension. It's just the nature of artist. Don't feel ashamed."

"Thanks." She sniffed from postnasal drip precipitated by a different emotion. "Damn, you always know what to say to make things better."

He sprang up, and danced around, singing. "Izzy's on the rebound, yeah. Daniel's got a shot, yeah."

She flashed a smile. "Sit down you idiot."

He sat down and came up close. "Yeah."

She furrowed her brow and pursed her lips. "I know who I am."

"Yeah."

She pushed him. "You are such a clown."

They sat perched for a moment with a lull between

them as their thoughts took different directions. When the undergrads came to her mind she bounced on their perch and said with exuberance, "Daniel, you have to see these." She reached into the satchel at her feet and looked around. "No, not here. They'd look like cheesy snap shots."

She closed her satchel. "They need to be in a proper frame and have proper lighting. I want you over at 8 o'clock. That will give me time to mat a few."

He furrowed his brow. "Are you going to feed me?"

She sighed heavily, rolled her eyes, gave him an irritated look. "Of course. When have I ever not fed you?"

He flashed a mischievous grin, then said, "I'll bring a little wine and we'll have us a little rebound party, yeah."

She frowned. "I know who I am. Bring the wine and leave the party in your mind. Now walk me to my car."

"Yeah."

She stood and chuckled, then said, "You idiot."

He stood, stretched, and put his hands in his pockets. She put her hands on her hips, looked at the satchel, then at him. "Really? Do you expect me to carry this heavy satchel all the way to the car?"

He chuckled and grabbed her satchel and his backpack. She put her arm through his, then laid her head on his arm. When they were a few paces down, she noticed her satchel brushing an occasional shrub. She came to a dead stop.

He looked at her puzzled. "What?"

She put her hands on her hips scowled. "Put the case

inboard. You're scratching the shit out of it."

"A few scratches won't hurt anything, besides when it has seen its last day, get another one."

"Good God, Daniel is that your solution to life, just buy your way out of it."

He laughed, then said, "No, but when something wears out I replace it."

She returned to his arm as they walked. He was still simmering from her antics as they were about to enter the parking lot. The sight of her car triggered a slight concern she had on her mind. All her concerns in the physical world were always slight, Daniel would always fix it.

"By the way my car is still making that funny sound."

"I'll take a look at it."

As they approached her car she reached into her purse and handed him her keys. He unlocked the door, and hit the door lock button. She slid in and he handed her the keys and closed the door. He opened the back door, placed the satchel on the back seat, walked around to the front. "Pop the hood."

She glanced around the dash nervously and stuck her head out the window. "You know I don't know where that is."

He shook his head, came around, and pointed to a lever. "Just don't pull it when you're driving."

She said with the wonder of a child, "I never knew it was there."

"Most women don't."

She crossed her arms. "What does that mean?"

He stared into her eyes. She blushed, shot her eyes down, and said softly, "Daniel, don't look at me like that."

"You're a beautiful woman Beth."

"Only to you, now please fix my car."

He raised the hood and gave the signal to start it. He waved to turn it off, closed the hood, and came back around. "Just the fan nipping the shroud. I'll fix it Saturday." He leaned over and rested his arms on the window opening. "How's the temperature been?"

She blushed again and elongated her neck. "My temperature's fine." He snickered and rested his forehead on his arms. She giggled and ran her fingers through his hair. "You mean the car." She pulled her hand back when she became conscious of what she had done.

He raised his head. "Damn, you're funny."

She pointed her finger. "Don't be late."

He nodded and headed back. When he was a few paces away she shouted his name, he turned around. She said playfully, "Just seeing if you're paying attention." He shook his head, and left.

He pulled up to her house, parked in the driveway, and grabbed the brown sack lying on the front seat. He and got out, and saw her through the kitchen window busy at the stove.

Daniel fell in love with Beth the first time she called him an idiot and always questioned her turn. He didn't believe it. The light wasn't right. His good friend Brian didn't believe it, either. Her behavior was incorrect. She didn't revolve around turned circles. Ziggy called her a poseur. Daniel would tease her and say, "You spend more time with me than Sweets." She would retort. "She can't fix a car."

He had been over to her house many times. They would drink into the night and discuss art. He knew her couch well and wasn't sure if this was a couch night. He felt something different again, but he's in love, and quickly disregarded it as he always did, because something different always whispered to him.

He knocked on the side door that opened to the carport. He heard her say, "Damn it, Daniel, why do you wait until I'm pouring something hot."

He cut her off and shouted, "Because you're hot." He heard her chuckle as she opened door. "What's the temperature?"

She laughed, then said, "Shut up and get your ass in here."

She grabbed his hand like an excited child. "Daniel, you've got to see these." He thought, it doesn't matter what it is, just take me by the hand and I'll follow. She pushed him back in the carport. "No, close your eyes first."

He chuckled, then said, "Damn, you're giddy."

He closed his eyes and she said, "Oh, Daniel, you're really going to love this," then suspicion stepped in with him when she saw the sack. She took it out of his hand. "Open your eyes."

"Is this what I'm going to love?"

She blushed, and thought, men frighten me, but not you, because you're Daniel. She applied her standard scowl. "Is that Crowley's wine?"

"God, you are so suspicious."

"He's a cheat."

"No, you were lit up last time we were in there, and you misread the price and argued to the point that he gave it to you at a discount, to get rid of you."

She pouted, but turned it off. Excitement was hanging on her wall. "Ooh, close your eyes."

She pulled him through the door which led directly into the living room. It had a couch with a coffee table to the left, and straight ahead was a hallway that led to the bedroom. To the right was a small kitchen which was one-step up. It had a four-chair breakfast table and behind the table was a large bay window with a view of the street and driveway.

She sat him on the couch and put the wine on the coffee table. "Ok, open."

His jaw dropped. He looked at her astonished and walked up to the wall directly in front of the couch. He turned to her. "Beth, the tension, my God."

She came up beside him reached down, slipped her hand in his and interlaced her fingers. It surprised him because she rarely initiated handholding. There were only two times she reached for his hand. Once when he had the flu, she insisted he stay in her bed while she slept on the couch. After class she would crawl up next to him, hold his hand, and go over what he missed. The other time was during their frequent walks around her neighborhood that started in September.

He wondered if it had any significance to their impending graduation. Maybe, it was her way of saying goodbye to a good friend. He often thought during those September walks about avoiding her, because to her, he was just another classmate who she had a few laughs with, and after graduation, she would turn the page and settle into her realigned life. There would be the awkward hug, and a few token emails, until she fatigued of the old school stories. He knew it would take a significant part of his life before he could reduce her to a simmer, and he started the day he fell in love.

She turned to him and looked into his eyes. He thought, why is she so affectionate? She picked nervously at the top button on his shirt with her free hand. He picked up the nervous hand and kissed it. "Beth, what's going on? You seem anxious."

She sighed. "When I took this picture..." She pointed to the urban press from the gallery, returned to his button, and looked away. "I know you'll think it's nonsense..."

He cut her off picked her chin up, which triggered her to wrap her free arm around his waist. He thought, is she having some sort of graduation anxiety. "Beth, this is Daniel.

I would never discount anything you feel as nonsense. I may not agree, but never discount."

She looked at the ceiling, felt slightly dizzy, and removed her arm from around his waist and let it dangle. He took it as a cue to disengage and released her chin. He didn't know what to do with his free hand, when she laid her head on his shoulder, it felt awkward. She had never moved towards intimacy. Touching for her was always well within friendship parameters. He moved his hands inside those parameters and patted her back. "What's this all about?" She was silent. He rubbed her back as friendly reassurance and thought, I'm so in love with you. The way your back feels. I've never explored it before. It's always just been pats, a few hand kisses, and your arm through mine for the last year. Oh, how I wish you were trying to find a way to me. He eyes glassed, as he speculated. I see this is the goodbye.

She looked back into his eyes. "Daniel, there was something spiritual between them that's beyond the ability of light to capture. I know it was only in my mind, because it can't exist in the physical world." He interlaced the fingers of her other hand, which brought her closer. She was pressed lightly to him. He felt her breast against his chest and thought, thank you for this intimacy. I never thought it would happen. I'll remember it always.

He furrowed his brow, puzzled. "Tell me." They were face to face. Her pupils were fully dilated and both bodies were flush. Her breathing labored and he felt she was about to flee.

She thought, why am I about to kiss you? I've thought about it ever since the first day of class when you sat down next to me, and said, 'A magical hot dog told me to sit here,' but I know who I am. I'm confused most of the time and even if I didn't know who I was, I don't think you would want this psycho baggage. I remember thinking you were about to hit on me, but somehow I knew you weren't, because you're Daniel. I can't explain it. And you always knew what to say to make me feel better. When I said I'm into women. You said me too, let's double date. Daniel, women are safe, but so are you and it's so confusing.

She laid her head on his shoulder again. "There was an aura around them." He thought, I feel one here too. She cried. He released her hands put his arms around her and pressed her tight. "Beth, what's wrong?"

She wiped her eyes on his shoulder and sniffed. "Love beyond measure."

They were silent for a moment, and then she said, "I don't want you to call me Izzy anymore. I feel like it's time for me to change."

He released her quickly, put his hands on her shoulders, and said with deep concern, "Beth, I would never hurt your feelings, you should have said something?"

"I know you were teasing me." She blushed. "I like it when you tease me, but I like this Daniel, too." She said sternly, "Daniel, I want both Daniels. I want you to tease me, but I want the serious one, too."

He chuckled, then said, "I'll agree if you can convince the other Daniel."

"Don't worry about that idiot." She froze briefly, acutely aware of the evening. "Ooh supper." She turned quickly and skipped to the kitchen.

He poured the wine, brought the two glasses up into the small kitchen, and placed hers on the table. He stepped back and leaned against the wood trim that separated the two rooms and watched her cook. She knew he was looking at her romantically by his silence and it always produced anxiety, but she was not uncomfortable. It was more of an elevated nervousness, an excitement, that she didn't understand and didn't know what to do with, so she would always decompress the tension slightly when she felt it too high.

She knew she could be harsh with him, but also knew she never would, because to be harsh would mean she didn't enjoy it. She knew this particular look meant he was chasing her and it always puzzled her, because it was moot, but welcomed. "Daniel, stop looking at me like that."

"What's wrong with looking at a beautiful woman?"

She blushed, put her spoon down, and turned around. "Stop calling me that."

"Hey, is this our rebound dinner?"

Hearty was her laugh, then she said, "You are incurable."

She admired his face for quite a while, and said, "Oh, God, you make me feel so good." She turned back, quickly, and thought, don't think the wrong thing. She turned back when she felt composed, and said in an attempt to cover up her unconscious mistakes of affection. "Why don't you sit down and quit being such a nuisance," He sat, then drummed his fingers on the table and she took the cue to chide again. "Stop thinking what you're thinking."

"You know I've always thought you were an attractive woman, but not drop dead." She whirled around, pursed her lips, and glared.

"Just doing an ego check. You're drop dead."

She blushed and turned back. "Only to you."

"Untrue, you're one of the very few who can fly."

She stopped stirring and turned to him. "What are you talking about?"

"People like you have anything they want. You're an absolute dream to look at. You're smart." He pointed to the photographs on the wall and continued. "And talented, so you fly. As I said you can do anything you want. You'll always be first in line and have the first pick of anything, whether it's a mate or a job. That's just the way it is, but people like me, which is most of the world we'll never fly. We'll always struggle for jobs and jockey for position."

She slid the skillet off the burner, wiped her hands on her apron, and sat next to him. "That's not true. I don't believe that and I never will. You're far more than me."

He kissed her hand, and gestured towards the photographs. "You've already edged me out."

She flared her nostrils. He saw her agitation and kissed her hand again. "Beth, you're misunderstanding me. I'm not insecure. I wouldn't feel emasculated or jealous, if my stuff was next to yours. My self-esteem is fully intact. Williams' is right, you have it." He looked deeply into her eyes. "But you also have everything else that goes with it. You want for nothing. You have it all. That's why you fly. You have the talent and you're beautiful. Having it all is rare."

She clinched her jaw and exploded. "How much shit is going to fall out of your mouth? Even if I had all those appointments, which I don't, what makes you think I would want that kind of life?"

"Because it's out of beauty's hands." He waited until she spent her last ordnance, then he said, "Beth, I don't think I would ever have known you if you knew you had it. I don't think you would notice me, because if you knew you had it, you would fly in those circles. Not knowing is the only thing holding you on the ground next to me."

She slammed her hand down on the table and reignited. "How much shit does a man hold? I thought you were through."

She huffed, flew out of her chair to the coffee table, quickly snatched a photo album, and marched back. She reclaimed her chair, pulled it close to him, and looked deeply into his eyes. The thought of kissing him reemerged and she blushed, which extinguished all her agitation. As she continued to stare, she said softly, "You're a beautiful man and I want to show you." She thumbed through the album to the chapter, titled, "My Daniel," and then she turned the page. "You see, these were taken when you were unaware and see, you're beautiful."

She paused briefly when she felt dizzy. When the room stopped rocking, she said, "I don't even have to focus the lens for it to emerge." She waved her hands around her head. "You mistake all this light reflecting off my face for beauty. My face is not beautiful. Beauty lies inside and is abundant. It's a gift. You don't need to sit in a blind for hours to capture it. It gives itself quickly and easily and is eager to keep giving itself. It's innate like the air. It's something I see all the time but don't possess. Most have it and you, Daniel, have a lot. She closed the album and looked down.

He narrowed his eyes, and said with the irritation of having to tolerate someone's complaint of their well-endowed appointments, "Well, what is beauty to you Beth?"

She clinched her jaw and narrowed her eyes to match his. "Closeness and no amount of reflective light can give me that."

He sighed, put his elbow on the table, and palmed his chin. They sat in silence long enough for supper to go cold. He looked at the cold stove and remained quiet. She watched him for a while. "Hungry?"

"Are we having alphabet soup?"

"Little old for kid soup."

"Not when you need to eat your words."

He interlaced her fingers with his free hand, and said somberly, "Beth, I'm sorry. None of us knows what's crawling around inside any of us." He paused and reflected on beauty and felt she added a dimension he had never thought about before. "You've always been perfect to me."

She chuckled softly, then said, "You just have something in your eye when it comes to me." Impishly, she added, "Crowley doesn't think I'm perfect."

"Well, he's an idiot."

She stood. "I need to finish supper." She looked down at his soulful countenance and squeezed his hand. "Pour us some more wine and let's start over." Acutely aware of the evening again, she said, "Oh, you haven't seen them all." She took him by the hand and sat him on the couch. She busied herself warming the meal while he poured wine.

As he thumbed through the photographs, his excitement escalated which sprang him to his feet. He paced as his eyes were fully engaged in the photographs. In the last, she captured Henry's eyes after Gwendolyn had left. He said reverently, "Damn, Beth, you really do have it."

She put her spoon down, turned towards him, scowled, and pointed her finger. "We just applied a band aide, now quit picking at it."

He tossed the photographs on the coffee table. "Damn you're funny."

"That wasn't meant to be funny, now leave the band aide alone."

He laughed, which triggered her to her chuckle. She

covered her mouth in an attempt to break the comedic cycle as she felt the matter serious.

He wiped his eyes, "Yes, Mother," and resumed studying the photographs. She turned back to the stove, and smile, which, quickly, vanished when the dizziness return. She grabbed the oven handle with both hands, and it felt as if the room was pressing in on her, then it stopped.

She shook her head briskly, blinked several times, and turned off the stove. Better, she stood at the table, while holding two plates to her chest like a schoolgirl holding books, and appeared to be in deep thought. He turned to comment about a photograph when he noticed her appearing to problem solve. "What are you doing?"

She looked up surprised. "I don't know where I'm supposed to put you."

"How about the back porch?"

"If I had one."

As he stepped into the kitchen, he said, "You've always been beautiful, but somehow you seem different now."

"I'm no different. This is just a nuance; we've never eaten together formally before. It's always been boxes and cartons on the couch."

"Nuisance or nuance, I like it."

"Where's the useful Daniel? I could use some help with this."

She nibbled her bottom lip, while lost in thought. He sighed and chuckled lightly under his breath, which caught her attention. He smiled warmly and it seemed as if it came from somewhere she'd never felt from him before. It felt as if it were from a place with deep reserves and would flow like a great river, if only asked.

He said in a very soft voice, "Beth, what feels natural?"

This type of warmth was one she couldn't articulate, and was deep inside him far beyond his soft tone. It was a type of warmth quickly returned, with the same proven reserve, and metabolized by love. A type of warmth she had lost long ago, intimacy. It passed through the room slowly and washed over her. As it passed, it purged a blush, provoking dilatation which her eyes eagerly released.

She penetrated his soft brown eyes with a gaze of proven reserve, which she thought had been scourged and banished after the brutal storm of her childhood, but the man in front of her was leading her out of her wilderness.

She thought, Daniel, this is not a nuance is it, because I want to kiss you. An aura flashed and surrounded them. Something different didn't whisper to him, it spoke to both.

After supper he squeezed her wrist. "Beth, that was wonderful, thank you."

She frowned. "Oh, Daniel that was just a skillet supper, nothing special."

He quipped, "Hey. Quit picking band aides. We're running out."

She carried a laugh and bright smile to the kitchen, and said as she entered, "Shut up and pour some wine while I clean the kitchen."

She dried her hands, hung up her apron, and turned towards the living room. She stopped at the threshold and watched him for a long time while he studied the photographs on the wall. She felt that pressing of the room again. He turned around as she stepped into the living room. She became very dizzy and held out her hands to steady herself.

He panicked, put his wine glass down, and ran quickly up to her and wrapped his arms around her. "God, Beth, are you ok?"

She looked up at the ceiling and it appeared very agitated and mean. He squeezed her tight and she felt it stop. She blinked several times. "Too much wine, maybe. I'm fine."

He released her, bent down, and scanned her eyes. "Are you sure?"

"I'm fine."

She sat on the couch and took a sip of wine. He sat beside her and looked at her oddly.

"I'm fine. It's gone."

He stood, upended his glass, and looked over at the photographs one last time. "Beth, they're great," and put his jacket on.

Acutely aware that the night was over, she stood. "Where're you going?"

"I've seen them. They're amazing and you're pressed for time now, and a week is cutting it close."

"No, stay."

"Don't you think you ought to get started?"

She snapped her fingers, scowled, and said, "Sit."

"Then do I roll over or give you a paw? I'm confused."

She lowered her eyes, and said sheepishly, "Please, stay for a little while."

He sat back down. "Ok, but no pony tricks my dogs are killing me."

She chuckled softly, then said, "Thank you."

She headed down the hall. "I'll be right back I'm going to change."

He perked up. "Ooh, rebound night."

She stomped back down the hall and refreshed her scowl. "Whatever is in your mind have it removed."

"Surgeons are expensive."

"Plumbers aren't."

She came back wearing well-worn flannel pajamas and slippers. She sat beside him and picked up her glass.

He snickered, then said, "Well, granny, I see you're ready for date night."

She spit her wine back into her glass and laughed. She cleared her throat from the near aspiration, and said, "Good, it spoke clearly and said exactly what I wanted it to say; besides I get cold at night." He thought, Beth, back into me and I'll keep you warm all night.

She took her slippers off and propped her feet on the coffee table. He sat his wine glass down and studied her feet. She felt his silence again and turned quickly. "Stop looking

241

at my feet."

"What? They're beautiful."

"Feet are feet."

He jumped up and she felt schoolgirl giddy. He was reaching for his antics, and was going to bring sparkles to her eyes. Her clown was about to perform.

"Beth, a woman's foot is a work of art and it's connected directly to the soul." He pushed the coffee table back, sat on it, and picked her left foot up. "Who needs a bunch of silly romantic prose or poetry, when I can prove it scientifically." He put his hand around her ankle and she furrowed her brow. "Stop at the ankle."

He patted the bottom of her foot. "See, it's connected directly to the sole."

Laughter was feverish that night, but it would turn.

"You incurable idiot." He kissed her foot, and she said, "Stop kissing my foot."

He put it down and picked the right one up. "Oh, I've got the right one now."

Bubble. "God, you're so incorrigible."

As she watched him kiss and caress her foot, she thought, his hands are so strong and beautiful, and studied their anatomy. She was conscious now of her heavy breathing. Her eyes widened when she felt a large volume of moisture flow. Moisture she'd never experienced with women. Her heavy breathing ceased when confusion entered her mind. "Daniel."

He looked up, expecting a standard scolding, but she didn't say anything just stared into his eyes. He blushed. "What?"

"Have you ever been really confused?"

"Not here in this room with you. I'm never confused when I'm with you." Playfully, unaware of the changes in the night, "I'm perfectly content to fondle your feet and listen to you bitch."

She crossed her arms and pouted, playfully as unaware. "Do I bitch too much?"

"Sometimes, but I like it."

He paused to consider a divulgence, now that the subject of confusion came up. "Have you ever wondered why I wear long sleeve shirts?"

"Yes, but I didn't think it was any of my business."

He narrowed his eyes, searching for the illusive starting point. She sat up, placed her hands on his knees, and said with deep concern, "Please tell me." He gave her a reassuring smile when he saw the concern on her face. He sat beside her on the couch and rolled up his sleeve.

She shook violently as an expression of horror spread across her face. She jumped in his lap, held his face, and cried. She wiped the snot from her postnasal drip precipitated by another emotion, the man she cared for.

"Please, Daniel, please tell me your soul doesn't worship her. If you think I'm perfect then listen to me. Please listen. I don't know what I'll do if she takes you from me. She's stronger than me, she's stronger than any of us. All I have is truth. Daniel, truth to her is just a simple debate of semantics, unimportant, and purely academic. She will rob you of your beliefs and convince you that they're just passing ideas."

He quickly reached around her arms, put his hands on her cheeks, and brushed her tears back with his thumbs.

"Shh, Beth, she's been gone for years." He pointed to his heart. "There's a spot right here where the lie dwelled, but now it's burned out, charred, and nothing can live there anymore. It can't support her anymore." He paused for saturation, then said confidently, "Beth, even a lie has to believe in something in order to keep its ruse alive. She's gone because she has to have someone to share her lie with, or she wouldn't believe. You see, she needs her host to believe with her, or she can't exist." He stroked her cheeks with his thumbs. "I've even forgiven myself for the ones I've hurt, no guilt. It's all gone."

Her feet felt icy as he massaged them in an attempt to soothe her. "Beth, it's all gone." She dropped her arms by her sides. They both appeared flaccid as if she suffered dual strokes. Her face paled and hardened to marble.

His heart rate and anxiety shot up. He trembled. "God, what's wrong? Why are your lips are turning blue?" He massaged harder as his tears welled up, and in a choked voice said, "Beth, what's wrong?" She turned catatonic and stiff. He squeezed her calves and thought, God, is she going through rigor mortis? Tears spilled over his lower lids, while panic suffocated his mind.

She now appeared waxy. He thought, she looks like a cadaver. He put his hands on her shoulders and pleaded. "Beth, please say something. God, I feel like you're dying in front of me." She wasn't aware of him. The small stone sculpture he held in his lap kept her marble eyes to the wall behind him, and the old familiar tears of home found their familiar cheeks, and soaked the soft marble.

As she continued to stare, she said in an angry voice, "I hate narcotics. My step father was a drug addict and would beat my mother." She turned the corners of her mouth down, her diaphragm gave a short spasm, and she said in a choked child's voice, "And when I was a little girl he would come into my room at night when Momma was asleep. My room always failed me. No matter how hard I tried to hide from him. He always found me."

A rigor shot through her and her mouth quivered, as she murmured, "Momma," and dove into his lap and balled up.

He was about to burst into tears, when a voice came up from deep inside, grabbed his throat, choked him, and said through gritted teeth, shut the fuck up and quit your blubbering, this woman has been crying for 20 years. Your tears are disingenuous and vulgar, now help her. He thought, but I don't know what to do. He laid his head back and stared at the ceiling, while tears soaked his hairline. The voice released its grip and grit and he found himself thinking about the album, especially the chapter 'My Daniel.'

He raised his head, stared into a blank space below urban press and lined up the photographs she showed him, in his mind. They were all from around her house. He thought, they weren't interesting not because they were of him, but because they were below her caliber. They were absent of serious composition, like the pictures his mother would take at holidays or birthdays, ordinary family pictures.

He thought about her confusion and trauma and suspended his confusion next to hers on the wall. His had end points, easy in and hard out, but hers, it's as if she were placed in the vacuum of space, no top, bottom, or sides, nothing to touch for reference. He realized all the pictures of him were her reference. He was a star in her cold vacuum and all she could do was orbit closeness. He reached back to when he first fell in love, turned that simmer up to a full flame, and thought, you'll never leave my heart.

She rubbed her feet together intermittently. He massaged them, and said in a soft voice, "Are your feet cold?" She didn't say anything, and only nodded as a child who was all cried out and refused to talk and could only answer questions that placed no demands on communication, beyond a simple nod or shake of the head.

As he stroked her hair and massaged her feet, he panned around the room and felt the closeness that had been emerging all evening, ever since she came up and reached for his hand. He felt something very different in her while she was pondering his plate, but now, with the revelation of their dark secrets, would that change the course of their closeness to intimacy?

He looked down and saw her blink several times, and said in a soothing voice, "Beth, are you back?" She didn't offer a response and he didn't press. He brushed her hair back, stroked her cheek with his fingers, and thought, I've never touched your face, Beth, thank you again for this intimacy.

She rose up, took his hand in both of hers, held it between her breasts, and said in a child's voice as she settled back in his lap, "Yeah."

He continued to massage her feet and said in the same soothing voice, "Is it hard to come back?" She was quiet and he checked his pressing.

After a long lull she said, "Sometimes."

He studied the soft features of her face, and thought, you're so beautiful, and perfect too.

He sighed and thought about their impending graduation, the sharing of their dark secrets, and didn't want to leave her. He fell somber and thought, surly this can't end in just a hug. Did we not share intimacies of the soul? Beth. I love you so much and if life refuses us, pulls us apart, and positions us so far from each other that our night sky's are punctuated with different constellations, then my hand in yours held between your breasts will be an act of tenderness never forgotten. I've held your hand, touched your cheek, gathered your scent and now your heart beats at my wrist.

Beth, my love has nowhere to go and knows it's trapped. A single love gathered in this storm of life is only hope, and knows it'll be blown apart by its winds, and eventually be laid waste like a shipwreck, shredded on the sea floor, never to be disturbed by the desire for intimacy, because its trail will always remain unattainable.

He thought about her turn, still didn't believe it, but understood the safety of women, and said softly, "Beth, I've changed my mind about a lot of things and I want you to be safe, so stay with women, and I promise I'll never bring up the light again."

While she remained quiet, anxicty prodded him to ask her about her plans post graduation, and he said softly, "What do you think you'll do after graduation?" She remained quiet. Her silence prodded his anxiety to fish, and he said softly, "I think I'll go to the coast where it's warm." He chuckled lightly, then said, "I know I sound like a pansy, but I'm tired of cold weather."

He paused for a potential bite. Nothing. He threw in another line. "But you should go to one of the big cities where your talent can thrive. God, you'll have such an amazing life."

She squeezed his hand tight and said, "I'm not going anywhere. I'm staying right here with you."

He closed his eyes as tears pooled. The desire for intimacy burst through, and he knew it couldn't be denied, it was too strong now, and affection filled the room. He thought about the way she felt to him in the kitchen, after he said what feels natural, and she poured into his eyes for the first time. He applied that same intimate voice that provoked that deep gaze and said, "Sweetheart, you have to go somewhere; we all have to get jobs and pay back loans."

She released his hand, sat up, and he took advantage to readjust his body from his cramped position, but was visibly surprised when she straddled his lap, and held his face in her hands.

She blushed and said, "Daniel," then looked away.

He reached around her arms took her face in his hands, brought it back, and said with that same intimate voice, "Sweetheart, tell me."

She released her proven reserve and moisture flowed as the gravity of intimacy pulled her orbit closer to her star. Her mouth was grazing his. She pulled back slightly and said with warmth he'd never heard from her, "Daniel, why I'm I about to kiss you?"

"Beth, what feels natural?"

She kissed all around his mouth gently and lay back down in his lap. He laid his head back, and thought, Beth thank you for the gift. I know now you'll always be seated in my heart and immovable. It will take a long time for you to settle back to a simmer. And I know I'll take a wife, but until you are reduced to manageable; I'll wait, because a wife should always have the first chair.

He took a deep breath and sighed forcefully. She

stiffened up and rose up slightly. She produced a scowl and said, "What was that?"

He chuckled loudly, because he knew she was bubbling back up. She straddled him, crossed her arms, and glared. He burst into laughter, then said, "What?"

"That sigh, what was that sigh?"

"God, you are so funny."

"I don't feel funny, not at all."

"Sweetheart, I sighed because I'm happy. I'm always happy when I'm with you."

"Daniel, I know sighs, and that was not a happy sigh, that was a put out sigh."

He burst into laughter again, then said, "It was not. Damn, you are so suspicious."

"You're lying."

He simmered to chuckling as he thought, I'm so glad you're back and it makes me happy when you're playful, and said, "God, you're so suspicious. I am not."

The kitchen was now back, when she took his face and kissed him deep. She continued to hold his face and stare into his eyes. She glanced towards the hallway and said, "I want to take you back there, but I'm frightened."

"Sweetheart, this is Daniel all you have to say is stop."

She thought, why does his affection feel so good and right, then she said, quickly, "Stop."

Playfulness had resurfaced. "You are so funny. I didn't do anything."

She scowled and put her hands on her hips. "You were thinking it."

"Well, yeah, I'm a man. I was already pouring your morning coffee."

"Good God, Daniel, really, is that how you live your life, just rush right through it to the other side, and just what do you think you're going to do once you get over there?"

He shook his head. "Sweetheart, only I could understand that... You could bring the world to a grinding halt with your Beth speak."

They got up and she led him down the hall by the hand. When she stopped abruptly he ran into her. She flipped the light on, whirled around, and said, "See, what happens when you rush to the other side. You wind up running people over."

"I didn't know you were going to come to a dead stop."

"Well, if you would stay on this side for any length of time you would understand how we walk."

He burst into laughter, then said, "More Beth speak." She giggled, grabbed his hand, and headed to her bedroom, but he didn't budge. She turned back and frowned and he grinned and said, "I'm confused, which side are we on?"

Playful were they in the uncertain night.

"Shut up you idiot and come on."

He was studying her photographs in the diffuse morning light, while sipping coffee. She slipped in quietly and stepped into the kitchen. He turned when he heard her coffee cup slide across the table, and said, "Just the way you like it." She took a sip and nodded. He turned back to the photographs. "These look even better in the morning light."

She cast her eyes down and said, "I'm sorry about last night."

Puzzled, he said, "Beth, it was wonderful."

She furrowed her brow. "Oh, come on, it was a disaster and you know it."

"It was wonderful. I wasn't looking to go over the top. I just wanted to lie next to you."

She kept her head down, and said softly, "Well, I did."

"Really, damn you never know with a woman... but I'm really glad."

She blushed and gave him her kitchen gaze. "Not like that, closeness."

He swallowed hard as tears pooled. "Beth, I'm in love with you."

She began shaking, splashing coffee as she set the cup down, and cried. He set his cup on the coffee table quickly, waved his hands franticly, and said in a choked voice, "Beth, please don't cry. I panic and don't know what to do... Don't feel bad. Please don't feel bad. I know you don't have any feelings for me. Please don't feel guilty. You've done nothing wrong."

She wiped her wet hand on her robe and her eyes on her sleeve. As composure settled over both, he said, "It's ok.

I'll get over it. It'll take a long time, but I'll get over it. Please, I don't ever want you to think that you led me, because you didn't. It was me. I led myself."

He gazed around the kitchen. "Beth, we'll all be blown around the globe chasing careers soon, and in years down the road when you look back, as we all will, I just want you to know that a man genuinely loved you. Beth, please don't hate men. There're a lot of good men out there."

He watched her wipe her eyes for a while. "Stay natural...I'll miss this kitchen," then turned and opened the door.

She stopped wiping her eyes and said in a choked voice, "Daniel, wait. When are you coming home?"

He closed the door, turned, and said puzzled, "Home?" She dropped her eyes and repeated herself.

Still puzzled he said, "Are you asking me to move in with you?"

She ran up, wrapped her arms around him, and said through crying spasms, "I can't say to you right now what you just said to me. I'm still too confused. Daniel, I would never say something now that I didn't mean down the road. You mean too much to me. I would never devastate you."

He held her face, and brushed the tears back with his thumbs. "I tell you what. I'll stay until you kick me out."

"Thank you." She searched his face while he still held hers. She said, "I know I'm psycho baggage. And I know that you'll leave me soon. I want to thank you for the closeness last night, though some of it was a disaster." She paused and he felt the kitchen. She smiled warmly, then said, "I was warm all night."

He kissed her hard and deep, then said, "Sweetheart, you know how I feel about you. I'm not going anywhere," He brought the playfulness back to reassure her that they were not fractured only their past, and added, "now quit picking at band aides."

"K."

He released her face and pressed her tight. She wrapped her arms tightly around him. "Oh, God, you feel so good and right." He closed his eyes when tears pooled and thought, if only, Beth come to me. She remained latched on and said, "When do you think you'll be home."

He sighed and thought for a moment. "Class is out at 4, traffic, about 5."

She released him. "Good. You can help me cut these mats."

"That's because you don't know how to use a mat knife." He chortled as she bubbled up. She put her hands on her hips, gave him her standard scowl that he cherished, and said, "I do too know how to use one. It hurts my hand."

He reached through her arms, held her tight, and kissed her deep, then said, "I'm going to be late." He mocked her by putting his hands on his hips. "I think you just want a free handyman."

She felt loved. "Don't go there if you don't want your feelings hurt."

He closed the door and she headed to the kitchen for coffee. She poured out the cold and poured fresh, and shook the carton of milk on the counter. She stomped her foot and thought, damn, out. She ran to the door, opened it quickly, and shouted as he was backing out. He put the car in park, and got out. "What?"

"Pick up some milk on your way home and don't get 2%, it's a cheat."

He blinked several times while processing Beth speak, and said, "What? Milk's a cheat?"

She rolled her eyes and said exasperated, "Good God, Daniel pay attention, 2% has always been a cheat."

He shook his head, got back into the car, and thought, I can't decipher this now. I'm going to be late.

It was late afternoon when he pulled into the driveway. She opened the door and met him in the carport. He kissed her, and handed her a bag. "I got it at Crowley's."

"No you didn't and I know you're tying to provoke me. Crowley's doesn't sell milk."

"Are you sure? I know I saw those little milk cartons in the back coolers."

She beamed, then said, "Game, set and match. Those are mixers and juice boxes. Daniel, when a man and woman walk into a store, the woman looks up and thinks, Mmm... how useful is this store going to be, but the man just eyes the woman, so how the hell would he know what's in the store."

He kissed her again. "Fair enough, now explain milk."

She put her hands on her hips and shook her head. "Just how remedial are you? They charge almost the same price as whole milk, while stealing your cream."

He had a renewed appreciation for absurdity. "Damn, you're so funny. Now how are they stealing your cream?"

She added a frown to her posture and said, "Good God, Daniel pay attention. They take your cream, put it into another container, sell it separate, and try to throw 2% percent at you at whole milk prices. That's why you should only buy whole milk it's all in one container, no cheating."

He rubbed his forehead now that Beth logic was in tandem with Beth speak, and said, "Well, maybe the process for making 2% is involved and expensive."

She threw her hands up. "Ok, Daniel, who's it going to be, me or the dairy board?" They shared laughs, but not as fellow students. They shared gazes, but not as fellow students. They were out of the wilderness sharing intimacy.

As they sat on the floor cutting mats, she looked deeply into his eyes again. He returned the deep penetration, expecting her to flinch. She kept staring into his eyes and said, "I need to tell you something." He became visibly surprised, when she grabbed his shirt with both hands at his shoulders and pulled him on top of her like a bed comforter. He rested on his elbows, stroked her hair, and kissed her face. She looked away and said, "I need to tell you something."

He became anxious and thought, please Beth I don't know if I can take any trauma tonight. I do want to absorb all of it, but in small amounts. Beth, I promise, I love you so much, but just not tonight. Spend you life with me and crush me a little at a time. I love you and I do want it all, but tonight let's just kiss. Remember when we first met. I sat down next to you and said a magical hot dog told me to sit here. I didn't know you, but somehow I knew you were down. Beth, lets laugh tonight. Let's go to the fair, eat hot dogs and cotton candy, get stuck on top of the Ferris wheel, and kiss all night. When it reengages and we come to the bottom, I'll lie down willingly and be crushed, just not tonight, let's rest to pick it up another day. Kiss me all night.

He pulled her head back gently and kissed her. "Sweetheart, tell me."

She appeared to be in deep thought and finally said, "I think I'm a bitch, just a whole milk drinking bitch."

He burst into laughter, rested his forehead on her chest, and said, "Sweetheart, you're not a bitch. You're a little bitchy sometimes, but not a bitch. There's a difference."

She ran her fingers through his hair and thought, I need to change. You're courting me. When you call me sweetheart I feel I'll never be cold at night. Daniel, I want to be so close to you. You've been chasing me for the last year and now I realize I'm behind. Court me and continue to chase me.

He picked his head up and she cocked her head one way then the other, turned the corners of her mouth down, and said, "Have you ever felt like it was time to change?"

Puzzled he said, "You've mentioned that before. What do you mean?"

"All my life, Daniel, I've had to change." She sighed, turned away, and continued. "When you were a child did you ever find yourself realizing you were too old for the toy?" He cocked his head. She turned back to him, sighed lightly, finished it with a sorely diminished chuckle, and said, "Didn't think so. All my life I was the slow kid, never got any of the jokes. Did well in school, but didn't have many friends. And when all the little girls became bigger girls and painted their toenails, had boyfriends, and talked on phones, I was still on my bike with a kitten in my basket holding a doll. I knew it was time to change."

As tears pooled, she said, "And now it's time to change again. Daniel, you're so strong and confident and always have been." Tears soaked her hairline. "You're the only man I've ever kissed and I don't even know if I'm doing it right... I'm on my bike again holding another doll."

Gwen checked the page number and put the book on the coffee table, grabbed a tissue off the computer desk, pressed the window and thought, what woman hasn't kissed in 12 years. It's so hard. Why did I not stay in my box and not fill in. She smirked as she her thought, I think all that happened was that I stood on my tiptoes and looked out of over my box, and we accidentally bumped noses, that's all.

Aniel, let's be honest, I did enjoy kissing you, and I know it's been awhile for me, but we both know it was just a schoolgirl crush, and lying with you was truly my first time and this pedestrian girl and her dream want to thank you for covering her mark during our incredible dream, which is all we'll ever have, because let's be honest, it was just a quick firework, and now it's fizzled and let's just leave it at that. I think I'll call you tomorrow and we'll both have a good laugh over this silliness.

I do want to be the very best of friends, though, and let's continue to not speak of love. You know, I have some single friends that I would be more than happy to set you up with, and maybe, well you never know, something might happen. Well, some are old like me.

She chuckled and thought, if you meet when the light's just right... She paused.

The one behind her drove up quickly. "What cha thinking about schoolgirl?"

She gritted her teeth and thought, leave me alone.

"Oh, good God, how much rationalizing can you vomit?"

Gwen poured some wine, sat on the couch, and steamed.

The one behind her splashed down beside her. "You know Charles is right. Why not love someone besides them?"

She thought, bitterly, I don't know, perhaps you could tell me since you know so much, but have failed at everything.

"That used to bother me, but not anymore." The one behind her paused to fish. "Now that we're being honest, what frightens you about love?"

She thought, what doesn't?

"Too vague, give me better."

She thought, I don't know how to hold them, but you know all about that.

"You already know that doesn't bother me anymore, so quit stalling, besides that was boy, girl nonsense. You're a grown woman now, so what gives?"

Gwen thought for a long time and looked at the clock, it was late evening. She thought, you don't understand what he's saying. It's not about romance. He's saying love doesn't exist, because all of the characters are being pulled apart past the point of tolerance and that's what frightens me. He's telling me we were just a firework of passion. Love doesn't exist, only passion.

"Poppycock, you haven't finished the book. Love always endures in the end and that's what he's saying. Love has to be tried and tested many times or else you wouldn't believe it. Put that in your pipe... now finish it."

She sighed heavily and thought no, I think I'll go to bed early and join the working world in the morning.

"He's never going to quit. He's madly in love and he won't stop until he has you. If you finish the book I think you'll see his intentions. He plans on holding you down and marrying you and that's what frightens you. Not love and romance, that's navigable. But a home is far more intimate, because a home is all about what's inside and sharing everything about one another, love is only the footing. You're afraid of intimacy of the home, which is a fully naked intimacy and it's full of flaws and failures." The one behind her proofed her philosophy ironclad with, "Remember Frances, 'Love is but a fairytale, until it is time to go home.'"

Gwen snatched the book and thought, I'd rather listen to him than you. She ran her fingers across his name and thought, damn you, Aniel.

The one behind her chuckled, then said, "See you're running a household already," the she turned somber. "You know I think he wrote it for both of you, to prove to you that he loves you and maybe, most importantly, to prove to himself that love does exist."

The pedestrian girl rubbed the love in her fairytale dreams, felt them lifeless now, and picked up her deliverance.

He brushed back her tears with his thumbs and kissed her. "You're perfect."

She furrowed her brow. "Band aides, Daniel."

"No, this is different." He kissed her hard and deep and lightly kissed her neck. She squeezed his shoulders, and thought, they're so strong and right, and welcomed the moisture flow.

He came back to her mouth, kissed her hard, and said with arousal in his voice, "Perfect, hot, and beautiful." He kissed her several times, returned to her neck, and repeated what he had just said several times.

She picked his head up and kissed him several times. She was flush and her pupils were fully dilated. She clenched her jaw. "Sit up."

He took it as a cue of fear and got up quickly. He was visibly surprised when she unbuttoned. He did the same. When both were bare from the waist up, he glanced at her breasts, and thought, damn she is perfect.

She grabbed her comforter again and kissed him deep, and whispered, "Oh, God, Daniel your skin. It feels so good and right." He kissed her several times, and traveled. He kissed her breasts, which provoked her back to arch, and now fully flush and hot, she said, "Stand up." He now understood her rhythm and knew where she was going. They stood disrobed and she pulled her comforter back on top of her.

She became fully wide-eyed and still but not stiff as before in the bedroom last night. He felt panic in her body and thought, Beth, please don't ball up. Let's get up and finish the mats. He said in a soft intimate voice, "Are you frightened?"

She released her shock, and said in a voice that appeared to be of an older adolescent, "No."

With the same soothing tone, he said, "Should I stop?"

She was quiet for a while, then said in her adult voice, "This sensation is so intense."

He kissed her, and said, "Ok."

She changed her countenance to melancholic and said, "I'm holding another doll."

He sighed and kissed her cheek. "Do you want to stop and talk?"

She grabbed his face and kissed him several times. "Oh, no, no I'm not sad." She kissed him again. "It's ok because it's with you" He felt the kitchen. She sighed, cocked her head, and said with a tone he had never heard from her before, "Daniel, this intensity is seeking something and I think I know what it wants. I can't explain it, but would you kiss me the whole way through." He kissed her hard and deep and his lips never left hers. He knew at that moment, his Beth had just pulled the kitchen forward and now every room in the house was filled with its intimacy.

He sat up with his chest sweaty and heaving. "I think somebody went over the top."

She sat up, beamed, and said, "Maybe, but you never know with a woman." She thought about dolls and performance, then blushed, and said softly, "Did I do it right?" He stood, helped her up, and pressed her tight and she said, "God, Daniel your skin feels so good." He picked her up, and cradled her. She became wide eyed and thought, he's so strong.

He kissed her cheek, gestured to the hallway, and said in a soft voice, "Let's get you caught up. Let's explore one another." She looked back at the mats and he said, "Don't worry, we'll get it done."

She put her arms around his neck, gently kissed him, and said, "Thank you."

They spent the rest November and the first part of December exploring one another.

It was now mid December and the Fine Arts gallery was crowded with alumni and guests viewing the graduates projects. Beth was wringing her hands and madly picking at his top button. He took the nervous hand, and kissed it. "Sweetheart, relax your project is the best here."

An older man came up, nodded at her photographs, and said, "Really nice."

"Oh, yes, my wifc has a finc cyc."
She turned pale and her jaw dropped. She collected herself, but could barely speak. She managed to say to the gentleman, "I'm not his wife." She whirled around to Daniel. "I'm not your wife." She nervously turned back to the gentleman. "Sir, I'm not his wife." She whirled back to a grinning Daniel as if he were inebriated. "What's wrong with you? I'm not your wife." The gentleman chuckled, shook his head, and left.

"Well, you're going to be."
She put her hands on her hips, gave him an augmented scowl with flared nostrils. "Good God, Daniel, is that how you live your life? You think you can just knuckle drag in here, like some Neanderthal, grunt at the first woman you see and drag her off?"

"Just you."

She shook her head, while chuckling, then said, "You're such an idiot."

She watched nervously as more alumni arrived, and said, "I'm so nervous. Would you get me some wine?"

He kissed her forehead. "I'll be right back."

The sun was pouring through the windows as he headed towards the refreshment table. He squinted through a sun soaked window, stopped, and waved to her. She skipped over and he put her in front of him. He placed his hands on her shoulders and pointed out the window. "Look. There're your subjects. Do you want to meet them?"

She whirled around, picked again, and said bluntly, "No, I don't."

He lifted her chin, and said suspiciously, "Why not?"

"Please, I just don't."

Agitated he said, "You don't think they're going to make it do you?"

"No, I don't."

He clinched his jaw, and said, "That begs a question now, does it not?"

The kitchen was back and she said, "Yes, Daniel, I know we're going to make it. And I emphasize the word know, so you'll know it comes from the bottom of my heart."

He sighed, relieved that his beautiful world, who picks at his buttons, talks in Beth speak, and drinks whole milk was committed. "Well, I'm satisfied, but what about the other Daniel?"

She scowled. "That Daniel is kind, considerate, and loves me very much," she paused and added, "and he's not remedial. Why don't you go find a sports bar and we'll pick you up later."

He laughed, then looked deeply into her eyes, held her face in his hands, and kissed the corner of her mouth. She blushed, pulled his hands down, glanced around furtively, and whispered, "Don't kiss me like that here."

Puzzled, he said, "Why are you whispering?" She frowned and whispered louder, "Because you don't know what a business kiss is. That kind of kiss is a home or stroll in the park kiss. Here, it should be only a business kiss."

He chuckled, loudly, then said, "What the hell is a business kiss?"

She frowned and tried to hide her conspicuous whispering, by lowering her volume further, "How could you not know what a business kiss is?" Bemused, he watched as she turned her head and said, "Here, kiss my cheek." He kissed her cheek and shook his head.

"Now, may I please have some wine?"

He rubbed his forehead and said, "Gladly, I need to decipher some Beth speak anyway." She was smiling as he left, when her dizziness returned. It started off as a mild swim, but rapidly turned into a violent pitching sea storm. Panic was incarcerated in her gut like a hernia. She thrust her hands out in front of her to steady herself, and followed the tall windows with her eyes up to the ceiling. She watched as black vapor boiled in the ceiling. It billowed out like the smoke in a burning high rise. The walls and ceiling popped and groaned as if the building plunged below crush depth.

She smiled as she looked towards Daniel. The movement and panic subsided, but the boiling black vapor was still present, angry, and inconsolable. She brightened as she watched the rolling, angry vapor, and thought, you can't get in. She kept her eyes fixed on Daniel and knew. He's my room now and this room will never fail me.

The little girl puffed her cheeks, blew towards the angry vapor, and thought, now blow away like the fuzz off a dandelion. The vapor condensed into a few small streaks and disappeared.

He came back with red wine and looked at her oddly. "Are you ok?" She reached around his neck, pulled his head down, and gave him a long deep kiss, and said, "I am now."

"Now I'm confused was that a business kiss or a park kiss?"

She beamed, and said softly, "Pay attention Daniel. The convention is over and we're in our room now... and stop all that whispering, it's rude."

It was Friday, the day after graduation as he walked briskly up the walkway to the Fine Arts building to remove their projects. Snow banked the sides of the walkway. The sky was clear and the air cool. The sun was very generous and would allow sweaters all day. He chuckled when he saw her with her standard scowl standing by their bench. When he was within hearing range, she said, "Get your ass up here, and look at what this little shit did."

When he was standing in front of her, he looked at her face oddly, and said, "I think you have something on your face."

She did a blind sweep. "Where?"

"Oh, never mind, it was only a scowl. It's gone now."

"Shut up." She grasped his hand, quickly, when she remembered her issue and stormed into the gallery. She dragged him up to a display of photographs. He said, "Wow, someone took photos of us at the reception."

"They're awful."

"Well, he's obviously a freshman."

"The lighting's awful."

"He'll learn proper lighting."

She smiled warmly, interlaced his fingers, and pointed to the kiss she gave him by the window, and said, "That's my favorite."

"Why is that?"

He watched as she engaged him like it was the first kitchen moment, purposely reenacted, and said, "Because that's the 'I love you' picture."

He wrapped his arms around her and whispered, "Beth, I love you so much." He kissed her. "I'll have to get a copy of it."

The standard scowl reappeared. "I've already taken care of it."

"Well, someone in this building has wet pants."

"Let's go home before I have to revisit the memory of that imp."

He grabbed the heavy satchel and put his arm around her as they headed towards the door. She stopped, and said, "Wait a minute." She reached into her purse, opened a plastic bag, and pulled out a cracker.

He looked at her oddly, and said, "You've been eating a lot of crackers."

She broke off a corner. "I've been sick to my stomach the last few days."

"Your not getting sick are you."

"No, it's probably a stomach virus."

"Maybe you should go to the doctor."

"Maybe. Monday, if it doesn't pass."

He opened the door and they headed down the walkway. She put her arm through his, laid her head on his arm, and sighed. He came to a dead stop. "That's not a put out sigh is it, because I know sighs."

She laughed, then said, after a long gaze, "God, Daniel you make me feel so good."

At that instant, he felt something spiritual around them. Something he couldn't articulate. "Are you ready for this afternoon?"

With full kitchen intimacy, she said, "Yes, I am, Mr. Taylor." She paused and said, "Why am I about to kiss you?"

It was Monday afternoon when he rolled up her street

pulling a small trailer. He had landed an assistant professor job at a large university in southern California and insisted that she not work in order for her to develop her talent. At first she was reluctant to go because she said there was no one normal in California.

He caught sight of her at the top of the driveway. She had her hands on her hips and a scowl on her face. He shook his head, and thought, well, there's my blushing bride. Would you look at all those expensive options? That scowl was a separate payment plan, but worth it, and those handle bars. I think I'll have her elbows chromed later. He pulled into the driveway, stepped out of the car and beamed. "How's my well equipped wife."

She glared for moment and snapped her fingers. Her arms appeared as handlebars by the way her hands rested on her hips. "Daniel, get your ass up here."

He stood in front of her amused. "Wait, I think there's something on your face."

"Yes there's something on my face. You have messed me up."

He put his arms through her handlebars and kissed her. "What did I do?"

"It's in there."

Puzzled by her Beth speak, he said, "What?"

She looked around and pointed to her abdomen. "It's in there."

He attempted to decipher. "Are you pregnant?" Glassy

eyed, she inched back. "Are you angry?"

He grabbed her quickly, pressed her tight, rocked her, and said, "Beth, I love you so much. I'm the happiest man in the world."

He released her, put his hands on her shoulders and with tears pooling said, "You've given me the woman I've always wanted and now this beautiful gift." He paused to reflect on his empty dower and felt inadequate. "Beth, I've given you nothing."

She looked at the wispy clouds and saw only a thin irrelevant haze, and said with full kitchen intimacy, "Yes, you have Mr. Taylor. You've given me my room."

He chuckled, refreshed, and said, "I don't know what that means, but I love you."

She visibly surprised him when she grabbed him quickly, put her arms around his waist, and squeezed him tight. "Daniel, I love you so much." He looked between the clouds and thought, thank you for her.

She picked nervously at his top button, acutely aware now of their uncertain future, and said, "Oh, God, what if we fail?"

"Sweetheart, with you, failure is not an option. I can sit back and ride coach, while you ride shotgun and shoot any hombre that tells you no." When she fell into a somber state, he held her chin. "Beth, the future belongs to those who live deliberately, and carry a check list, because they don't get it."

Her fear of their future naturally progressed to another

thought, and she said, "I'm thinking about dolls."

He chuckled the way he did in the kitchen, which caught her attention, and he said, "Sweetheart, you're all caught up, and from this point on we all hold dolls." He paused for a kiss. "Maybe there's a reason you held all those dolls." He kissed her again. "Now you're going to hold a real one and something tells me you'll be the best."

She beamed, flushing out her anxiety, and said, "I know I will, because this is something I've never had to catch up on. I've thought about it all my life." She grabbed him again. "I can't wait."

Mischievously. "Something's going to happen."

"What?"

He turned her around patted her ass and said, "This's going to get fat."

"Shut up. That's the least of my worries."

She peddled in place and said anxiously, "I'm so wound up." He kissed her hand, turned his back to her, and said, "Come on, let's go for a walk." She beamed, stepped back a few paces, and leapt onto his back.

"Where to?"

She put her arms around his neck, nuzzled his ear, and said, "I don't care. I'm in my room."

Patty closed the hood and wiped her hands on her jeans. She came around to the driver's side, and said, "I think your wreck will make it now."

Barbie started her car and gave her a nod of confidence. "I'll see you soon."

Puzzled, Patty said, "How about a kiss? I won't see you for a couple days."

Barbie pecked her on the lips. "I'm sorry. I'm distracted; it's just that going home always makes me sad."

"It's ok dolly. It's not the same for me, either." She paused as she always did when the subject of home came up, so she could go over her lines and recite her scripted feeling of home and said, "The same ones never stop loving you and the ones that never did still don't and tolerate you a little less every visit."

She gave Patty a polite smile and drove off. Barbie knew Patty was a mistake. Her stage collapse triggered her depression and going home seemed to prevent further slippage. She felt ashamed for letting it get this far. She knew that sometime before graduation she would have to let her go. Not because she didn't love her, she did, but only to a point, because to Barbie love and passion were inseparable. One can't exist without the other.

Strong and sensible love belongs to the mind and body only, she thought, hammered alloys, that clang deliberations as mill workers for the rest of their life. True love is natural, organic, and chemically complex, and it only understands passion. It's a thriving jungle growing through us and around us that we become part of indistinguishably.

Love for Patty was one of friendship only. She lies with Amy in their cold crucible. Patty was just unfortunate collateral damage now, and she knew it would be messy. When they met in the bar and she held her hand she felt Patty's currents, which were driven by storms. Patty found peace and couldn't let it go.

Barbie gave her hand freely to any one who wanted it. She didn't know why she did it, but it had consequences. Barbie was a sparer. She sacrificed herself to any extent to spare the feelings of others. But being a sparer had limitations, which she realized with Patty.

Amy was in her mind the whole trip sitting in the passenger seat. She glanced over occasionally to have a conversation. "How do you feel I Love You?"

Amy smiled at the smile that was only for her, unfastened her belt, slid right next to her, laid her head on her shoulder and rested her right arm across her belly, and Barbie felt her say, "Knobs, nothing is going to pull me away from you."

Sometimes with natural love, once committed, they place themselves into the crucible of consummation, and heat themselves to their melting points, which creates turbulence from passion's flashpoint. As their molten lavas begin to cool and amalgamate, they cure and set the foundation meant for a lifetime. Sometimes, though, one or both can't conform to the curing, because they have an insatiable craving for the turbulence created by passion's flashpoint. When that happens, the addiction drives them to cremation and they explode into ashes.

Tears streamed down Barbie's face and in a choked voice she said, "I know I Love You, I know." She wiped her tears on her sleeve, and said, "Why don't you lay your head in my lap, hold my hand, and I'll sing to you." She placed her right hand on the edge of the seat, massaged it, and hummed lightly.

She pulled into the driveway, unlocked the front door to her mother's house, and grimaced. She closed her eyes for a moment before she walked in. She waded through the cluttered living room to the open kitchen in the back. A heavyset, middle-aged, woman was seated at the kitchen table smoking pot and wearing a grimy back brace, dilapidated to the point that it was of very little support.

She stopped a few feet from her, glared in disgust, and said, "When was the last time you washed? I can smell your coochie from here."

The older woman pulled the joint from her mouth quickly. Her fingers yellowed from the pot stains and her fingernails packed with grime. She frowned and said, "You know I have a bad back. It hurts to raise my leg over the tub."

"Get really high and go for a pan of soapy water."

The older woman clinched her jaw. "Why is it every time you come home there's confrontation? I do the best I can with my disability and pain."

"Mother, you're not so disabled you can't at least wash, and keep house. And there are other methods of pain control besides narcotics and smoke inhalation." She paused, reflectively. "I do sincerely pity you. You're only 45, but look 60. If I could, I would reach inside of you and pull your addiction out, but even that wouldn't do any good. You would just go out into the street to search for her again." She pointed to her heart. "Mother, you have to burn her out of here."

The older woman cackled and pounced like a harsh schoolmarm. "You don't understand, because you've never had chronic pain. It has nothing to do with pain or narcotics. It's depression, because you finally realize, you're stuck in the room with it for the rest of your life."

She sat down beside her mother, sighed empathetically, and felt depression had given both of them too much eye, and said, "Mother, I'm sorry," as she held out her hand.

Her mother slipped hers in, and said, "You've been holding peoples' hands ever since you were a little girl." She studied her daughter's face intently, and after the exam, said, "Barbie, ever since you were little you've had this gift. I don't even know if you realize it or not. I can't explain it, but when someone holds your hand you take them to very quiet spot in their mind. It's a spot I think you made for them. Some place you can lay them down and sit with them," she paused, "and for no reason. All these years I could never figure you out. I now think it's some form of love that we who hold your hand will never fully understand. Barbie, it's like you came from somewhere else."

Barbie said, sarcastically, "So says the pot." She got up and said, "Do you have any food?"

"Barbie, I wasn't like this when you were little and what I've said is true. Ask anyone who's ever held your hand."

She dropped her sarcasm. "We still need to eat." She took some money from her mother's purse. "I'll stop by the store on my way back and make supper." She paused and said dead stoically, "Mother, please wash."

She stared at the huge stone building and thought, would these stones feel any colder if they housed something different? She climbed the long run of courthouse style minute riser steps slowly. She made her way to the second floor and went through an office door.

A woman's voice came from behind a desk, stacked high with file folders. "Hello Barbie. He'll see you in just a few minutes. He's on the phone. How have you been?"

As she searched through the high-rise landscape to find the voice's owner, she replied, "Good."

After a few minutes, the woman left her paper city and knocked on a door to the left of the desk. After a brief pause, she opened the door, looked in and nodded. She turned to Barbie and said, "You can go in now." She left the door cracked and returned to her desk.

Barbie came up, read the name on the door, as she had done many times before, which always triggered anxiety to percolate in her pit. There were only three males she was fond of and Dr. Tate was the second. She knocked softly and a middle-aged man with sandy hair and dark rimmed glasses opened the door. He smiled and hugged her, then said, "Come in." He closed the door and sat at his desk. She sat in one of the two chairs, close to the desk, of which both appeared to have a distinct personal bond to the desk. She looked down as if searching for hers.

He wrapped his knuckles lightly on his desk and said in a stern voice, "Barbie don't look down, we've been through this. I know I'm a trigger for you." She looked up, and he sat forward. "Do you hold your head down at school?"

She frowned and said confidently, "Of course not."

Proud. "Please don't here."

She fidgeted as tears pooled. "It's so hard."

"Give it time." His pride in her carried over to her academics. "I still want you to work here when you graduate, but only if you think you can take it."

She brightened a little. "I know I can."

"It's none of my business, but are you seeing any one yet?"

She said curtly, "No."

"You know as you continue to study psychology I feel confident you'll understand that what happened was not your fault. And with knowledge, time, and maturity, you'll release the guilt and find someone."

She said curtly again, "Only her."

He put his hand up as a calming gesture. "Ok, I won't

press."

He looked over her face piercing. "Now, when you enter in the professional world you'll have to leave the chain mail at home."

She chuckled, then said, "Yeah, I know."

"It's good to hear you laugh."

"So long as I don't have to look like Stacy Straightjacket."

He chuckled lightly, stood and walked to the window and put his hands into his pockets. Turning back toward her he sighed. "You know she's just like you."

She sat up puzzled. "She's straight."

"No, no, no." He paused and appeared to be following something with his eyes, and said while following, "She's just like you. She holds everybody's hand." He turned and searched her face. "Like you. You both came from similar homes except hers was abusive." He turned back to the window, and said, "Why do you hold people's hands?"

She thought for a moment. "They seem to need it."

He sighed and finished with a light chuckle, then said, "Yeah, just like her."

There was a knock at the door and the secretary popped her head in. "Meeting in fifteen."

He sighed heavily and clinched his jaw. "Thank you Erma." She frowned and popped back out. Barbie raised an eyebrow. Contrite he was not. "Psychiatrists get pissed, too. We just don't show it in front of the client. Hell, it's just a damn meeting. We'll just meet to plan the next meet." She laughed and he said, "Trust me, when you're staff you'll see the real side."

He came around the desk and she stood and took a deep breath. He put his hands on her shoulders. "Relax, it's ok. You've been coming for a long time."

She said deflated, "But it still feels like the first time, every time."

He looked at her sternly. "I don't need to reinforce, do I? You've had enough psychology at school to understand. It's not I Love You anymore. She's Amy. Don't be manipulated." Her eyes flew down. He squeezed her shoulders and lifted her chin. "Barbie, you know it's not your fault, and I'll keep reinforcing the truth until one of us is in the grave. Her mind was going to break anyway."

He put his arm around her as they headed down the hall to the recreation room. When they entered, he saw Stacy holding a client's hand and counseling.

He glanced at the clock. "I want you to meet her. I know you two didn't get along when you were in high school, but things are different now. You two will be colleagues." He spoke briefly to Stacy, came back, and said, "I've got to go to the meeting. After you meet with her, she'll take you to Amy."

Tate walked to the door and turned around. He used the meeting as a ruse. He didn't give a shit if he was late. He wanted to witness the two meet with quiet minds, on quiet ground, and without the distraction of Amy's presence. A young woman with dark hair and hazel eyes, average height and a few years older walked up and held out her hand.

As Barbie took her hand, she searched her face, and said, "You are like me. Ever since I was a child I always wondered if I would ever find someone like me."

Tears welled in Stacy's eyes as she said, "I've wished for you when I was little, then prayed for you growing up." As they held each other's hands Stacy blinked several times in a futile effort to dry the tears that were already soaking her lower lashes. She cleared her throat and gave her that rare kindred smile like two strangers exchange when passing because they both felt something more. She concluded. "But then I grew up."

Tate became astonished and gape mouthed when he saw what looked like the glow of an aura as they held hands. He squinted at the light fixture above them, and disregarded what he saw as nonsense. It triggered a boyhood memory, though. His mother was a devout woman and would read Bible stories to him nightly. He remembered the time he asked her how angels kiss. He chuckled under his breath when he remembered her fumbling for an answer, and said, 'Honey, they don't kiss like us. They kiss when their halo's touch.' He watched the aura for a moment and left.

Stacy took two tissues out of her coat pocket and handed one to Barbie, then said, "Are you ready?" Barbie nodded and Stacy said, "She's in the sun room." Stacy turned and walked through the doors of the recreation room with Barbie in tow. They headed down a wide hallway with windows to the left, covered with wire mesh, which gave the impression that the building was inside a cage. Stacy was slightly startled, but happy, when Barbie came around and put her arm through hers. Pleased to have a sister from the edge. "I'll stay as long as you need me."

"Oh I'm not nervous. I'm happy, my sister from the edge."

As they approached, Stacy felt her anxiety. She came to an abrupt stop, and said, "It's ok. I know you don't want to provoke her jealousy."

"I know you understand like me."

"I'll approach her first, like I do with all my clients who have visitors, and see how she feels." She paused when a memory surfaced. "She's not one of mine, but whenever I've held her hand, she always says 'you must know Knobs.'"

Barbie was grateful, like one mother to another who was kind enough to watch over her child, while she was away, and replied, "Thank you for holding her hand."

Amy was sitting cross legged on a small vinyl couch. Her chestnut hair cropped and brushed back. It saddened Barbie. Amy always kept her hair very long and model maintained. Amy was staring at the wall and listened to the music of their high school years.

She was still in high school and would be the rest of her life. Whenever Barbie visited it was always the same high school stories. It was as if she were frozen in amber, and resided high on a shelf unaware of the world outside the window. The amber suspended her memories before her and were continuously repeated in real time. Her mind followed the shoreline of an island.

Stacy stood in front of her line of sight and called her name softly. She uncrossed her legs, put her feet on the floor, placed her hands in her lap, and sat docile. Stacy smiled like a sparer. "You have a visitor. Do you wish to see her?"

She said with a blunted affect, "Who?"

"Barbie."

Her eyes brightened and she smiled a smile that belonged only to Barbie, and said, "Where is Knobs? I haven't seen her all day."

Stacy turned towards Barbie and nodded.

Barbie came up and Stacy backed out. She stood in front of her and Amy searched her face. Amy glanced at Stacy. "Where's Knobs?"

Barbie's eyes glassed. She knew they would. It was the first part of their new ritual now and the other part was Amy lying in her lap falling asleep. "Amy it's me, I'm just a little older."

Amy brightened when she heard her voice. "Kiss me Knobs and I'll make it easy for you." She giggled, while Barbie choked back tears.

She cleared her throat. "No Amy, but I would love to hold your hand."

Amy patted the couch. "Come sit."

Barbie glanced at Stacy and sat. Amy reached over to kiss her, but Barbie pushed her back by putting her hands on her shoulders and said in a stoic voice, "Hold my hand."

Amy furrowed her brow, sighed, dropped her hand by her side, and said, "Is it because she's here?"

"No, it's not appropriate anymore."

Amy flared her nostrils and escalated. "You have a thing for that bitch in gym class. I know you do."

Barbie squeezed her hand. "Amy high school's been over for 2 years. I'm in college now." Amy fumed as Barbie continued. "When I graduate I'm going to work here and take care of you."

Amy laid her head in her lap and held her hand with both of hers. "I'm sorry Knobs. I know you would never leave me. I just get so jealous sometimes."

Barbie stroked her hair. "I know. It's ok." She glanced up, nodded, and Stacy left.

They were silent for quite awhile as they held hands. Barbie's thigh felt warm in a small area where Amy's eyes were approximated. Amy said in a soft voice, "I know my mind is broken Knobs. Sometimes I feel that I'm in nothing but rooms, and every time I open a door it's just another room. I start to panic and shout your name and go from room to room. There's never any windows to climb out of, just rooms and doors."

"I sit down and cry because I can't get out and I can't find you. Then the nurses come from doors I've never seen before and pick me up. They wash me and feed me." She paused and concluded. "I feel like a child." Barbie tilted her head back and held her tears and spasms in check.

The new ritual was about to end. She knew Amy would forget she was there and the next visit when she removed her from the shelf, they would start over.

Amy fell asleep from the medications and this was where it started over for Barbie. Barbie placed a pillow under her head, kissed her cheek, and left. As she walked down the hall she burst into tears. She knew this moment was the turning point from which there was no hiding the fact that as she got older Amy would no longer be able to recognize her. As an unrecognizable older woman she couldn't answer her call in all those rooms. She would be alone the rest of her life and have only memories of high school Knobs to find her, then none at all. She knew in the end Amy would die as an old woman in high school. The thought of Amy's future forced her to bury her face in the wall and wail like a mad client.

She felt someone's hand on her shoulder. She turned and Stacy grabbed her quickly. Barbie pressed her face to her neck and cried uncontrollably. Stacy rocked her and reached for her hand, like either one of them would do for anybody in pain, but when Barbie slipped hers in, Stacy began to shake and whimper loudly. Stacy released her hand quickly and whispered in her ear, "I'm so sorry. I've never snatched my hand back from anyone before. Please forgive me. I'm so ashamed. I just couldn't take it. We were both out on the edge and my head was about to explode from all the turbulence. "

Barbie was back. She looked into Stacy's wet eyes, and said, "Thank you."

Stacy collected herself, reached in her pocket for a tissue. "Please, forgive me."

"Hold my hand," and reached for hers. Stacy, still distraught, was about to speak when Barbie cut her off and said, "Shh, listen."

Stacy thought for a moment, while scanning the edge, and said softly, "Storm is passing."

"You were with me in the violence, thank you."

"I should have stayed."

"That's all I needed to pull me back from falling into the chasm."

As they walked down the hallway a few paces, Stacy turned and looked out the window. They both stood gazing into a gray sky. Stacy took her hand and said, "Tell me a happy story." They held hands and both closed their eyes and sat hand in hand on the edge over looking the great chasm.

Barbie chuckled, then said, "She said the funniest things sometimes."

"Tell me."

"We were in her room making costumes for Halloween. She had this beige sheet and planned on going as a ghost, but when she slipped it on she said, 'Shit, I look like a damn turnip.'" Stacy cackled as Barbie went on. "I told her not to worry that I would go as a carrot and she said, 'Well shit, why don't we find a root vegetable festival, and see if we can win the cellar prize.'" The two laughed as their eyes remained closed. Barbie said, "I feel like I'm keeping you from something."

"No, no it's ok."

Barbie opened her eyes and released her hand. "No, go, it's ok."

"Are you sure?"

Barbie nodded. "I need to go anyway."

They walked to the end of the hall and before they split, Stacy hugged her and said, "I can't wait for you to join us."

"Me to."

She unlocked the door walked in and nodded to herself. Her mother was sitting at the table, freshened up, and rolling joints. Barbie looked around. "The place looks nice, thank you Mother," and put away groceries.

Her mother finished the last one and placed all but one in a cookie tin. She lit up. "How's she doing?" She took a deep puff, coughed, and said as she wiped her watery eyes, "You know, I did mean to visit but the ride hurts my back."

Barbie remained silent until the groceries were up to prevent her temper from boiling over. The sparer couldn't hold back any longer. "No, you didn't. Mother, you're tripping over your guilt again."

Her mother continued to puff and cough her health away. At the end of a long coughing fit, she said, "My back limits me."

"No, just you...You shouldn't have said anything, but because you did, now your guilt expects a statement and as usual you say something disingenuous."

She left her mother coughing soot and smoke and went to her old room. She lay on her old bed and thought about their vows. As tears streamed, she thought, oh I Love You, I always thought we would carry all our vows into our golden years, but our young lives are now golden and now I must archive all our vows, except two.

I will care for you always even though you'll never be aware. In a few years you'll forget who I am and only remember high school Knobs, then not at all. I Love You, I'm going to add a third, I promise to remember for the both of us, by writing everything down, though an untested vow will always remain upright and full. She wiped her eyes and scanned around the room. She stopped at the window when she saw all the scuff marks she made in early adolescence. She would climb out and dart across the street to the first male she was fond of, Todd.

She had little tolerance for boys at that age. She didn't understand the way they moved. Their eyes were always nervously flitting about and their knees were incessantly bouncing, and the fanatical fascination with a ball was intolerable. They seemed to be caged and restless most of the time.

Todd was quiet, methodical, and predictable. He was well satisfied for the answer he received, and didn't feel the pressure from doubt to dig deeper. She knew exactly where he would be regardless of the spin, roll, or tumble. His knees didn't bounce and balls seemed of no interest. He preferred video games and they would play for hours, especially "Dracula."

She remembered their first summer, sitting on his back porch steps, while Bear, his dog, sat in front of them panting and drooling. The sun was rolling over the house and about to heat the back yard, when Todd scooted close to her, which raised her suspicions and her brow when he said, "Barbie?"

She turned to him, craned her head back a little, and said, "Yeah, Todd."

He sighed, wrinkled his nose slightly, and said, "Barbie, will you be my girlfriend?"

She leaned back, furrowed her brow, and said in a calm but serious voice, "No, Todd. I won't be your girlfriend."

He furrowed his brow. "You don't like me?"

She held tightly to her serious demeanor. "Of course I like you. You're my best friend."

"Then be my girlfriend."

Exasperated, she thought with great deliberation. At the end, she blushed, diverted her eyes to the dog. "No, because I like girls too."

He sat up and began his thoughtful deliberation. She fidgeted, dropped her head in shame, and said in a somber voice, "Are you going to make fun of me?"

He sighed. "Well, do you have one yet?"

She looked up surprised. "No."

His persistence reignited. "Well, then be mine."

She turned quickly and said diplomatically, "I tell you what we're going to do. I'll be your pretend girlfriend and tell everybody at school that I'm your girlfriend until one of us finds a real girlfriend."

He beamed. "Sweet."

He leaned into her. "Can I kiss you?"

She glared, scooted back, and said irritability, "No, Todd you can't kiss me."

"Then what can we do?"

She released her irritation as she gazed into her friend's eyes and smiled, then said, "We can hold hands."

He beamed again. "Sweet." He reached for her hand and fell in love with the sparer.

The two sat hand in hand. One feeling the prestige of having a girlfriend and the other having the prestige of just being who she was. Both sat in a deep friendship as they slid down the birth canal of innocence towards the turbulent world of adolescence, with only confusion and uncertainty as their lamplights, while watching a drooling Bear.

They spent most of their first summer on his bedroom floor, playing "Dracula." When he was at a critical juncture, he said, "Barbie," and cursed when his character was killed.

She kept playing for a while, and said, "Todd, you talk at the wrong time. That's why you get killed."

He furrowed his brow confused. "What do you mean?"

She remained fixed on the screen, and said, "Watch."

She changed scenes to the dungeon. "Now watch" He watched her intently. She was silent for a moment. "See I can talk now because it's quiet, but I know in just a minute I won't be able to talk." She waited patiently, and said, "I can't talk now because it's kinda like my house. You have to know when to talk." She stopped talking abruptly, killed several gargoyles, and said, "See, I can talk now."

"That's so cool."

Barbie developed a rhythm around dysfunction. When she heard screaming in her house she knew not to talk. When things started breaking she knew to open her window and dart across the street.

Todd always left his window unlocked for her. She would run towards the backyard fence. The dog would growl until he caught her scent, or heard her voice, then whimper and give her an exaggerated tail wag. She would reach down, hug him and crawl through the window, take her shoes off, and sleep next to Todd.

Her rhythm watched over her and told her when not to talk, when to flee, and when to rise. She would rise just before sunrise, put her shoes back on, and slip out. Most times he never knew she was there. On some occasions her rhythm would let her sleep in, especially during the long summers.

He would wake her and ask if she wanted some cereal and they would sit, eat, and play video games. The disposable income in her house was always sacrificed for the love of alcohol. The cruelty in Barbie's house differed from Stacy's. Hers was the cruelty of neglect, an altogether different house, but just as potent in some ways.

Late summer, she was leaning back against his bed with the game paused watching the dog pant. He came back from the bathroom, noticed she was in deep thought, and said, "What are you thinking about?"

She sighed, blinked, and said, "I was wondering if I'll ever find someone like me." They both watched as the dog's tongue bounced in perfect rhythm to pant.

He said, "I think so."

She turned to him skeptically. "How do you know?"

"Because, when I was sick last year, Mom had to pick up Nicole at her high school and she wouldn't let me stay by myself." He wrinkled his nose and pinched his thumb and index finger together. "She's so nervy. I wanted to stay in bed. Anyway, when we got there..." He stopped abruptly, and said manically, "Barbie, there were more people there than at the mall."

Her eyes widened. "Are you sure?"

"It was scary." As she pondered, he said, "I know there'll be someone like you. Our school is too small."

As they both continued to stare at the dog, she furrowed her brow. "Todd?"

"Yeah, Barbie?"

"Bear stinks. He needs a bath."

"He won't let anybody wash him."

She turned to him puzzled. "Why not?"

"I don't know. Maybe he doesn't like water."

She stood, and said, "Come on, I'll help you."

Puckishly. "I'm telling you, he won't let you."

She opened the window and the three jumped out.

"I'll hold him, while you fill the tub," she said. He flashed a mischievous grin as he went through the gate to the garage. He came back through dragging a large galvanized tub. When the dog saw the tub, he bolted, dragging her across the yard like a spooked pack mule. She released his collar, and stumbled to her feet.

Red faced, she clenched her fists and jaw. "Damn you, Bear."

He burst into laughter, then said, "I told you."

She stomped up, still red faced, which triggered him to laugh again. She crossed her arms and kicked the tub, and said fuming, "Todd, we're going to have to trick him."

Reduced to a chuckle, he said, "How?"

She put her hands on her hips, walked around the tub in deep thought, then snapped her fingers, her plan superb. "I tell you what we're going to do. We'll fill the tub up, sit on the rim with our feet in the water, and pretend we like it. I bet he'll get in when he sees he's left out."

He nodded and filled the tub.

They sat on the rim, knees touching, with the soapy

foam clinging to their legs, and were pretending they liked it. The dog came up and put his two front paws in. "See, I told you. Nobody likes to be left out." He studied her anatomy as she washed. She looked up puzzled. "Help me wash." He turned his attention to her soft facial features. Still puzzled, she said, "What?"

He looked into her bright hazel eyes. "Barbie, do you ever feel left out?"

She stopped washing and pondered. "Sometimes. Why?"

He gazed deeply into her eyes. "How does it make you feel?" The sparer scooted closer when she felt his isolation and held out her hand. "Like holding hands."

He took her hand and stared at the soapy dog. "I hope you do find someone like you."

"Really?"

He sighed, while watching the soapy water drip off the dog. "Yeah, I don't want you to be left out."

They were several weeks into the school year and he was happy. She kept her word and told everybody that she was his girlfriend. They ate lunch together and when she didn't have a lunch he always shared his. He knew that on lunchless days there wasn't any food in her house. It didn't bother her though, but it did him. One day he watched her eating macaroni out of the box.

"I didn't have time to cook it," she said.

The next morning he sat at the breakfast table eating cereal and wondered if Barbie was eating breakfast. His eyes glassed over and he turned to his mother. "Mom?"

She had her back to him, packing his lunch, and said without turning, "What is it honey?"

He finished a fresh thought of Barbie. "Can I have doubles?"

She turned to him puzzled and he wrinkled his nose. He knew she was about to interrogate his request.

"Honey, now why do you want doubles?"

He held his wrinkle. "Nerves Mom. Can I just have them and not talk about it? Why do we always have to talk? I wish Dad was in charge of lunch. He doesn't ever ask questions."

She chuckled, then said, which agitated him further, "That's because some come attached with a problem and he doesn't open attachments. He leaves those to me. Now, honey, do you really think you can eat that much food?"

He didn't say any thing, and hoped she would just honor his request, and drop the interrogation.

"For Barbie?"

He went back to his cereal, and said, "She was eating macaroni yesterday."

She cocked her head, puzzled. "Macaroni is a very good lunch."

He said irritably, "It wasn't cooked."

She crossed her arms, confused. "It wasn't cooked?"

He wrinkled again and glared. "Nerves again Mom."

She fought for control as her eyes glassed over. She had a deep and very bitter animosity towards the Morgans, but she knew there was nothing she could do. When they played video games she would stand at his bedroom door, out of their peripheral vision, and check her over, but could never find any marks or bruising. She thought you can't force a parent to love their child.

She turned back and made doubles. When she finished she put the two sacks in front of him, sat close, and said, "Honey, do you know what subtlety is?" He frowned. A life lesson was about to come from his mother and it always required return demonstration.

She said, "It means I want you to find out what she likes without her knowing." She paused when she sensed confusion occupying his face. "Todd, I don't want her to feel embarrassed, so find out what she likes." She paused again when confusion appeared stubbornly imbedded. "You could say something like hey do you like apples and peanut butter?"

He cut her off. "Mom I'm almost 13 and I know what subtlety is."

A little irritated, she said, "Then why did you let me waste my breath."

"Because you're Mom."

"What does that mean?"

He said irritably, "It means even if I said I know what

it means, you would make me explain it, and then when you found a part you didn't like, you would explain it to me like you just did anyway."

She laugh which irritated him, and he said, "Can I go now?"

She collected herself and hugged him. "I still want you to be subtle."

"I'll just ask her."

"I don't want her to feel embarrassed."

"She won't be."

She sighed in exasperation. "Anybody would be. Now please do as I ask."

He gazed into her eyes. "Mom, you don't understand."

"Now what is it that I don't understand?"

He gazed into her eyes for a moment longer, and pierced them with the cool sensitive vision of a sage as he placed his hand over his head and waved it gently. "Barbie's up here."

She saw a deep sensitivity in her son's eyes, matched it, and said, "What does that mean, honey?"

"I can't explain it Mom." He put his hand down on the table and searched the wall. She watched him intently, and felt something almost spiritual emanating. "When I hold her hand she takes me far off and it's real quiet and she just sits with me and then it's there, that feeling I can't explain."

She felt a mother's pangs, a pang greater than birthing, and would be the greatest from here out until death, the reality of their child grown and gone. "Honey, you're discovering girls and Barbie's stirring feelings inside you that you don't quite understand yet, but you will."

He kept his eyes to the wall. "No, you still don't understand." He turned, and said confidently, "You've never held her hand, so you don't understand. It's like she lets you come to the edge with her. I watch her sometimes when we're far off on the edge. It's like she's listening to something even further off."

"You better go. I don't want you to miss the bus."

They sat together at the same lunch table since the beginning of school and he handed her a lunch, and said, "Mom is so nervy."

She thanked him, and said, "Your mom's nice."

He wrinkled his nose, pinched his thumb and index finger together. "She's still so nervy. You can't even ask her something without her having to know your whole life story." He sighed. "She wants me to ask you what you like, but don't tell her I said that." He went on exasperated. "Do you like mayonnaise?"

She smiled unconsciously at the thoughts of his mother, and said, "No, I like mustard, pickles, and grapes."

They ate for a while, and then he stopped and thought about the edge. She observed the expression he always settled into whenever they held hands. She moved her sandwich to her other hand. "Todd?"

"Yeah, Barbie?"

"Do you want to hold my hand?"

Surprised. "Here?"

She placed her hand on the bench between them.

He blushed. "This is so cool."

Their fifteenth year arrived and it was devastated by a damaging storm. He was sat down after supper and told that they were moving at the end of the school year. Adolescence sees its death too soon sometimes and was forced to stand in the ranks of the world from which it suckled. The thought of moving away from Barbie and starting high school without her was unbearable. He knew then in the fifteenth year of his life that holding hands, washing dogs, and playing video games would soon be memories and he realized he was holding their eggshells. The young sapling would grow thicker and harder rings from now on.

He didn't say anything about the move all spring. When she sensed sadness in him she would reach for his hand, but he would refuse and say he was ok. He wanted to wean himself from her hand. He wrote her a letter and handed it to her as they got off the bus towards the end of the school year. He told her to wait until she got home to read it.

She looked at him oddly, then at the letter, and said, "Todd is this about you being sad the last few weeks?" He didn't say anything and headed home. He closed the door to his room and buried his face in his pillow. The letter was his last eggshell and the adolescent stepped out of rank for a moment to cry.

Barbie's lower lids pooled, but she didn't cry, though she wanted to. She left adolescence long ago and knew what he was going through, hardening. At that moment she realized she was holding her eggshells, and tears rolled down her cheeks.

She waited until his household was settled in for the night and darted across the street. As she passed through the gate, the yard appeared hollow. Walking through the well established grass growing between the posts seemed to produce an echo, now that Bear was gone, she thought.

She tapped on his window and heard a low smothery voice. "Go away." She knew he was crying in his pillow. She ignored his demand, raised the window, and climbed in. He wouldn't face her. She came around to face him, but he turned his head. She sat on the bed. "Todd we'll always be together. I'm not going anywhere. We'll visit a lot and email."

She sighed, studied the stack of video games they knew intimately for the last three years, and said, "Todd neither one of us is dying. You'll be driving next year and you can come see me."

He muttered in his pillow. "I am."

After a long silence, she said in a stern voice, "Todd we're growing up and this is how you're going know."

He turned his head searched her face. "What do you mean?"

She looked deeply into his eyes, and said as a mother

giving a hard lesson that had no expectations of a return demonstration, only tears, "Because it hurts like Bear, and it's going to keep on hurting, because growing up never stops."

He turned his head back and she stared at the wall pondering. She stood and he turned his head quickly. "Don't go." The sparer stared into his eyes for several minutes and unbuttoned her shirt. He became wide eyed and blushed when he saw her small breasts, and said, "Barbie?"

She stripped down to her panties and lay next to him. She put his head on her shoulder and wrapped her arms around him. "Todd you're my best friend and I want to comfort you."

He fondled her breast and she flinched. "Todd let me show you." She took his hand, and said softly, "Girls want tenderness." She guided his hand as they explored her body well into the night. It was past midnight when he sat up. She dressed and sat back down, and said, "Hold my hand." As they sat holding hands for the last time, she said, "Now, when you get a real girlfriend you'll know what to do."

He did something that surprised her. He kissed her hand, and released it, never to see it again. She stood and headed to the window, but before she climbed out he said, "Barbie, I love you."

"I love you too, Todd."

Tears streamed down his face as he said, "Like a real girlfriend."

She climbed out, held the window for a moment, and

said, "I know you do Todd, you always have," then closed it.

That summer was long and lonely for both. They spent most of it passing emails. His mother drove him back to see her twice and they spent time in her room playing video games he brought, while she visited friends.

Well into their first high school year his emails trickled and by next semester they stopped. The sparer sat staring at an empty mailbox and smiled. She knew he had found a real girlfriend and knew what to do.

She sat up on the end of her bed and mused upon her childhood a while longer, then left it to the scuff marks and prepared supper. She planned to sit with her mother, but felt that their sparse conversations over the last semester coupled with her mother's insensitive behavior of smoking during dinner as confirmation that their growing distance was malignant.

She wasn't close to her mother, but now with their unbridgeable gap and Amy's spiral out of reality, she found herself seeking the solitude of the edge more so than ever and listening to the whispers from the chasm. She fixed her mother a plate, took hers, sat on the front porch, and gazed into Bear's old yard.

The porch, like the scuff marks, had its own memories. She remembered holding Amy's hand, frequently, late at night, as they waited for her parents to finish their assaults upon one another and pass out.

Her mind left the porch to the time when Amy's mind began to change. She didn't remember exactly when, but did remember one of the strongest outbursts that led to her institutionalization. She attacked her in gym class and accused her of sleeping around. The school district transferred her to another high school in her last semester of her senior year to protect her from ridicule.

After she finished the brief tour of her past, she set her plate down and thought about Todd and Bear for a while longer. The sparer burst into tears when the depression like her mother's wouldn't leave the room. She mumbled through soft sobs. "I wish someone would hold my hand." Her gift of resilience was her other hand and she picked herself up, went in and washed the dishes.

Her rhythm woke her before dawn. She cleaned up, ate, and planned to head back to school after spending the morning with Amy. She went to her mother's room, cracked the door, and listened to her snore for a moment and thought about whether or not to leave a note. Drunk and high didn't care, but courtesy did she thought as she wrote the note.

She met Stacy in the hallway; they exchanged smiles, and held hands as they walked. She sat with Amy on the same couch and waited for her turbulence to subside. When Amy drifted to her lap, Stacy left. Barbie stroked her cropped hair and hummed. "Always Missing You."

"Knobs what are you thinking about?"

She knew the complexity of reality was far out of her reach, and said, "You."

Amy chuckled which gave her great joy, then Amy said, "Knobs, when I'm in all those rooms and I can't take it any longer. I sit down and think about our poems." She rose up searched her face, frowned, and said, "Knobs you look different."

"Tell me about our poems."

She lay back down on her thigh. "I wrote this one right after I got here. I think." She began to escalate rapidly and in an agitated voice said, "God, was I here or was I there? I don't remember."

Barbie squeezed her hand. "Shh, Amy, recite."

She settled back into her lap, sighed, and said, "Sorry Babbs."

Barbie never met Babbs. She was the maternal grandmother who raised her. Amy told her many stories about her grandmother, but she questioned many of them, because of her inconsistencies. Barbie discovered early on that as time went by, reality and imagination in Amy's mind became very fluid, and would slosh back and forth.

There's a place in the mind that houses the physiology of distinction, but Amy's was an empty space. Her interpretation of reality was a guess, which makes all things plausible.

She rose up again, agitated. "Why did I write it Babbs?

I don't know why I wrote it. I can't remember."

She squeezed her hand a little tighter, and whispered, "Shh, it doesn't matter why. Poetry isn't words. That's for books, recite."

Amy nuzzled the top of her thigh, sniffed and scratched her nose, and said with exuberance, "Babbs, I remember now. I call it 'Apology' for breaking Knob's things when we were little, now this is how it goes.

Me damp and fermenting, brooding in my deepest bark.
You, dry and fragrant, nuzzling the blades of your fatted grasses.
I admire your perfumed serenity, as I decay in my bark.
And pray my compost might nourish some of your nuzzled grasses.

My passion reached for your love, but swallowed insatiable.
I thought it read inseparable and now it's unbearable.
And I know there's no ipecac available.
Now lying in your blades I plead for anything forgivable."

Barbie continued to hum and stroke, while tears streamed without spasms. The sparer never planned on a degree in psychology. She always wanted to be an elementary schoolteacher. The reason for the career change fell asleep, starting the cycle over, but meeting Stacy made the change tolerable.

She pulled into the dorm parking lot and headed towards the door. She looked out over the student parking lot, saw the poet's car. He was the third male she was fond of. They were in same western civ class and she sat next to him in the back, enjoying the entertainment from his clever tongue. He was always bubbly and had a twinkle in his eye. She called him Twinkles, and over the semester she observed a slow decline in his mood. Sadness blotted out the twinkle leaving his eye opaque.

The second to last class before finals she pushed her desk right up to his, raising his brow. "What? Are you turning back?"

She chuckled, then said, "No, just recruiting." Her expression became intense as she gazed deeply into his eyes. "You've been following sadness all semester."

He returned her deep gaze, but angrily. "Have you ever wanted something, but knew it isn't for you, but still can't let it go?"

Amy flashed in her mind, but the sparer did something she'd never done before. She pushed her aside, and said, "Hold my hand."

He looked at her oddly. "Which way are you turning?"

She took his hand. He felt as if he were at the edge of a great chasm. The vista was as vast as the universe itself, and was filled entirely with an aurora, even around them. It didn't make any sense to him, because every direction that he turned was the same view. He thought he was somewhere out in the universe, but where? And she appeared to be listening to something far off.

After the last regular class was over, he came up, and kissed her temple. "I think I know who you are."

Puzzled, she cocked her head as a gesture for clarification. He slipped a folded paper between the pages of her book and left.

She waited until Patty was asleep before reading the poet's letter. When she held his hand she sensed him undressing her deep emotions. She felt a little embarrassed and now sought privacy. His was the only hand that didn't lie down and feel the peace. He walked around her and observed her, and examined her feelings. It didn't bother her. She just felt naked in front of him. She had never held a poet's hand and didn't know that poets are never at peace, they only rest. She opened and read:

Placed by grace 'neath an angel's sole.
Lies the one just above us.
Charged by heaven to sit below.
To give her hand, a mystery from far above us.
Slip yours through and she'll gently draw it in.
And you'll travel her birthing grounds lying just above us.
Then will you realize she was born half way to heaven.

She smiled as tears pooled, and thought silly poet. She looked over at Patty, folded it quietly, and thought, you're the second male that has explored me, then she placed the poem with Amy's letter.

It was towards the end of December and the bitter cold had reduced the sun light to the warmth of a desk lamp. He wore a heavy coat unzipped as he walked towards her dorm on the main walkway. He saw her emerge from the door with her head down walking towards him. He stepped behind a tree quickly. When she arrived parallel to the tree he stepped out, and said, "Ma'am I've been approved for a federal grant to study the habits of stalkers. Do you know any?"

She beamed, dropped her books, ran her arms under his coat, and hugged him tight. "Oh, God, Henry I've missed you."

He wrapped his arms around her. "Gwendolyn I'm worried about you. I think about you all the time."

She thought, Henry, I don't even sleep.

He said, "Why don't we skip class and spend the day together. I want to try and cheer you up, besides we're just going over stuff we already know. We can study in this little diner where I used to eat lunch when I worked at the hardware store during the summer."

She nuzzled his chest with her cheek. "Oh Henry, I would love to."

He took her nuzzling cue and nuzzled the top of her head with his cheek. He closed his eyes because he was now back under the fully dressed sycamore of August, but this time peace sequestered tension to the far periphery. He didn't know how long it would last and didn't care. The poet was at rest.

A young woman looked out a third floor window and observed their aura for a while, and thought, silly poet. I can only give you my hand, then left for finals.

He sighed heavily and she whispered, "Henry, shh." He chuckled, then said, "Why are we in whisper mode?"

"I'm listening to your kiln."

He turned somber and felt peace under the sycamore being questioned by tension over property rights and thought, all you're going to hear is I love you. He whispered, "What's it saying?"

She didn't say anything for a while, pulled her head off his chest under protest from her kiln, and said with sadness in her eyes, "I couldn't hear it over mine."

He searched the sadness in her eyes and said, "Hold my hand." She gave him a grand smile and interlaced his fingers. He picked up her books and they walked slowly towards the parking lot. He thought, I'm not the One above us, but Gwendolyn if I could I would take both of us to the edge and propose. I know it would be futile, but when you refuse me on the edge, it will be as close as we can be to the One far above us all. And when He hears your rejection, I pray He'll pity me and give me a new heart, because this one has been crushed by the glow of the only woman I'll ever love.

She pulled him, and said, "Come on Henry let's run, like we're running away." When they arrived at his car slightly winded, she searched his eyes. "Henry, listen to my kiln." She pushed his shoulders down. He rested on one knee, and thought, marry me. She pressed his head to her chest. A he listened to her rapid rate, he could only close his eyes and wonder about the soul behind the soft breast of women. She held him there for a while. She was in rapture with the only man she would ever love. "What did you hear?"

He stood and looked deeply into her eyes. "A lot of love." The poet paused to allow her rings time to form. "Gwendolyn, I think you possess more love than your heart can possibly hold and would fill a man many lifetimes. I think at your creation you were given a great capacity to love and a loyalty like no other, and when you pass, it will remain in the ones you leave behind. Your children will talk of it often and pass it down like a maternal wedding band. I think your glow of beauty is love. And I think that you prove that inside the glow of a woman lies a great vessel chosen by God to house love's spirit. And the glow of a woman's beauty is merely the reflection of that vessel."

Blue rings didn't say anything for quite a while. She wrapped her arms around him, nuzzled his chest again, and thought, Henry I know you will find me. She nuzzled his thick flannel shirt pocket with her nose and applied an almost imperceptible quick kiss. She thought, Henry if you don't find me and you won't allow a goodbye kiss, I'm well satisfied now that I've kissed your kiln.

He pulled into the side parking lot of the diner and opened her door. A heavyset middle-aged woman, dressed in standard waitress uniform and standard white hose and white shoes, with the heels well worn on the outer edges due to her thick thighs pitching her ankles, watched them intently through full-length standard glass business door.

She scowled when she saw them coming closer, turned to the narrow rectangular order window, and said to a slim middle-aged man in the kitchen, standing over a grill, "Well, shit, here comes more college trash to waste my time."

The slim man drew taught, jerked his head up, gave her a stern look, and said, "Now, Effie, be nice. Remember college trash today, paying customers tomorrow."

She glared at him. "Shit, its still 2 dollars worth of food and 10 dollars of my time." She paused abruptly in her rant. "Well, at least he opened the car door for her."

"See, you're sweet on him already."

When they were close to the door she smiled and the slim man, said, "Real sweet, must be a looker."

She turned to him, her day refreshed. "Teddy, it's Henry, remember he worked at the hardware store during the summers, damn hard worker."

He nodded. "Remember grilled cheese and fries every lunch."

She sighed heavily. "Yeah."

They walked in and he tossed his backpack in one of the benches of a booth by the door and sat, while she sat opposite him. He began digging through the pack, while she placed her knees in the seat and propped her elbows on the table. She cocked her head, and smiled unconsciously, while observing him.

The waitress's smile warmed significantly. She turned back to the narrow window and whispered, "Teddy look."

He poked his head out. "Damn. I thought PDA was a contact sport." He continued to observe Gwendolyn and whispered, "Shit, she's all over him." He thought he saw a slight flash, fell somber, and retracted his head quickly.

Puzzled by his odd behavior, she said, "What is it?"

He kept his head down. "Nothing."

She narrowed her eyes, and said sternly, "Theodore nothing with you means something. Now what is it?"

He flipped a grilled cheese, turned back with a deep sadness in his eyes. Her countenance changed to a puzzled concern when she saw the expression he always produced when he was troubled.

"Effie, they're in the storm and they're going to get hurt real bad."

She dropped her concern quickly, and said patronizingly, "Oh, Teddy, it's just Henry and his girlfriend. He'll have a new one by summer."

He glared at her patronage. "What do you see different?"

She glanced over quickly, and patronized again, "Oh, Teddy, you've always been fond of Henry, now if you take him out of the boil, it's just a couple of kids on a date."

He shook his head. "You remember last Saturday night when that group of trash came through?"

Puzzled by the apparent irrelevance, she said flatly, "Yeah."

"What was the first thing they did when they sat down?"

She pondered for a moment to piece and stitch, then lit up when she stepped back. "Phones." He nodded when he saw his point unfurling in her mind and gaining his perspective.

He watched her through the window as she observed them, and said, "Eff, the couple in the group that were engaged to be married, they weren't in love, only the idea through their phones. They never even looked at each other." He paused when she appeared distracted. "What are they doing?"

She turned to him glassy eyed. "Being in love." She grabbed a napkin from the counter, wiped her eyes, while flipping through the pages of her life with her husband, and added, "They look just like us 20 years ago."

He grinned, revealing missing bottom teeth. She adjusted her small moderately stained apron, grabbed two menus from under the counter, and brushed back her home dyed fallen perm.

She came up, planted her balding shoe heels firmly, and grinned, revealing a large gap between her two front teeth. Gwendolyn sat back down as the waitress approached. "How've you been Henry?"

He looked up from his pack and smiled, then said, "Good Effie."

He introduced her to Gwendolyn, and said, "You don't mind if we spread out and study for a while?"

She smiled at them both, and said, "Not at all if you think you can." She paused and pointed her pen at him. "Grilled cheese, right?" He nodded, and then turned to Gwendolyn, and she nodded. After the waitress took their order, she commented. "You two are the only young people without a phone glued to your fingers."

Gwendolyn looked at her intently, while Henry returned to digging, and said, "Phones take from you something you can never get back. It's something that's only going to be there, briefly, then it's gone. It doesn't allow for the creation of little things, like a smile you know is given just for you, and will always belong only to you." She glanced at Henry, momentarily, and continued. "Even when they're not with you that smile remains with you, comforting you and it will never leave you. Phones rob you of their gaze and the beautiful tactile joy of their hand."

She nodded, headed back to the window, placed their order, and rested her elbow on the window. When he came for the order she said, "Teddy, give them extra cheese and fries."

"Looks like Henry's got you in his back pocket."

She sighed, then said, "The girl, too."

She glanced around the room for customers in need of

service. Most of her customers were regulars and uncomplicated. Well satisfied, she turned back to the young couple. She was in deep thought as she observed them, but was interrupted when a plate was placed in front of her. She frowned, while looking over the plate. He tapped a small bell at the other end of the window, and said, "Order up."

She flared her nostrils and glared. "Damn it, Teddy. I'm standing right in front of you, stop ringing that damn bell." He rang it again to fan the flames of her irritation. She fumed. "I swear to God, Theodore, I'll be on the ten o'clock news, cuffed, while the police are digging your body parts out of the walk in, if you ring that damn bell again." She looked the plate over, glanced at the grill, and saw the young couple's food. "Who the hell is this for? Everybody's been served except those two?"

Ding. "Roy," Ding.

She glowered flat out. "There's still the 5 o'clock news."

She turned towards the end of the counter, frowned at a grizzled older man, who had been listening to their entire conversation, while admiring the young couple, and said, "Well, damn. It's about time you ordered something besides three dollars worth of coffee, and head to my bathroom and flush ten dollars worth of my water."

He shouted through the order window. "Hey Ted, it says a smile with every order on the front door." He chuckled, then added, "Does the customer have to pay extra for that?"

She stared at the old man long enough to gather her

retort and said, "Meet me in the walk in and you'll get your smile." Teddy shouted back. "That's only for take out. She doesn't' have to wait your table." She took the plate and set in front of him. "Walk in dining is still available," then she grinned, fondly, and went back to her post. She had just perched her elbow back on the window ledge when the old man said, "Hey Eff, I need silverware."

She craned her head around and rolled her eyes. "Damn it, Roy, can you not see I'm busy? Get it yourself."

Henry was rearranging books on the table like an idle store clerk, bored with the slow counter traffic, while she put her knees back in her seat and placed her elbows on the table. She placed her chin in both her hands and curled her fingers down resting along her jaw line. She watched his clerking for a while then blew.

He felt a slight breeze, and his sinuses filled with a mint fragrance, swelling his receptors. They fired one potent impulse into his brain, which climbed to a euphoric state, during the rapture of feeling all things known about his Gwendolyn for that mint moment.

He looked up quickly and saw her smile in full bloom. He returned the smile with a bright bouquet, and said, "What?" She blew again.

"What's that for?"

"No reason."

"Are you happy?"

Blue rings nodded. "You've made me happy, Henry."

He blew back. "I'm so glad."

She sat back down when their lunch arrived and gazed out the window. He watched her for a while, and then pushed their books away. "What's wrong blue eyes?"

She cast her eyes down reverently and felt as if she were dressed in all black, and said, "Henry, would you do something for me."

He tenderly lifted her chin, gazed into her eyes, and said with that same serious demeanor of cafeteria catch up, "Anything." She took his hand in both of hers and rubbed her thumbs nervously across his knuckles. He watched her nervous rubbing for a while and thought, please, be my wife.

She looked into his eyes and said with the sadness she had been carrying for so long, "Henry, would you read the book again and find a way. I won't believe in hopelessness, there has to be a way. Surly she doesn't give up on love, and accepts this or that for the rest of her life."

"This book really bothers you." She nodded and turned her attention back to knuckle massaging.

"I tell you what," he said, "Christmas break is coming up." He paused to admire the sun lamp streaming through the window, striking the soft features of her face. Mesmerized, the poet thought, though the season has emasculated the sun of its warmth, it can't belittle the radiant energy it gives to beautiful things, and she now appears more beautiful than she ever has before.

She looked up when she felt his pause was of an inordinate amount of time, and said, "Henry, what?"

The poet rendered his thoughts, aloud, "I know you've heard this all your life, but Gwendolyn you're a beautiful woman and I don't just mean your incredible eyes. I mean all of you. If I were a poet I would write reams and never allow them to leave my kiln. I don't think I could bear the transfer."

She blushed, cast her eyes down, and stared at his hand in hers.

"Why would that embarrass you? You've heard it all your life."

She raised her head, still blushing, and said, "Henry, when you say it I know it's not from this or that." She paused to gather a perspective that he might grasp. "All my life it has come from this or that. Henry you're the only one who has said it through your kiln, and I've never experienced that before, and like any girl who's told for the first time that she's pretty, blushes."

She looked down and felt dressed in all black again, and said, "Henry, will you give serious thought to the book, it means a lot to me."

"Let's both read it. We might find something, because sometimes little things can be over looked. I believe like you. I think her love is stronger than her glow even though they both come from God. I don't believe she would abandon her faith in love so easily."

As he paused for her radiance she blushed, which drew a warm smile and a chuckle from him. She quickly mimicked the frown Beth gave to Daniel, and said, "Daniel, stop looking at me like that." They both burst into laughter. She released his hand, covered her mouth, and was thankful for the comic relief.

When the chuckling simmered, he said, "I'll be going into the city for the holidays and I'll read it and text you if I find anything."

She brightened. "The city, ooh Henry, I'll be close to the city at my parents." She paused, when she felt in black, and said, "Henry, text me even if you don't find anything."

He picked her chin up. "I'll call often."

She beamed. "Henry, I'm so happy."

Mid afternoon and the lunch crowd was long gone and preparations for supper started. The only customer left was Roy. Effie had cleaned and restocked all the tables, and returned to her window perch when Roy came from the kitchen and reclaimed his seat. She turned, and said, "Thanks, brother, for dish washing." He nodded and she poured him fresh coffee. She sighed heavily as she returned the carafe.

He looked up. "You seem blue."

She looked out the standard door by the side parking lot, and said, "I hope they make it."

"I do too, Eff."

The storm rumbled in his heart as he stared into his cup. The rain was coming. "God, I miss Bobby so much."

She turned slowly, gave him a nervous look, and said,

"Roy, now don't go off." He grabbed a napkin out of the dispenser, quickly.

He had a permanent soggy watershed in his heart, created by loss.

"Eff, I miss him so bad sometimes. I start to cry and it feels like I can't stop. Its like one wave finishes then another one starts. The only time I know I'm going to stop is when I walk it out." He stood abruptly, and said, "I gotta go."

She raised her voice as he walked, briskly, towards the door. "Damn it Roy don't go off and start breaking things. I swear to God. I won't bail you out this time."

Teddy stuck his head out the window quickly. "Effie, leave him alone. He won't go off." When she started after him he grabbed the bell and banged it on the window ledge like a gavel. He raised his voice to match hers. "Goddamn it Effie leave him alone." She whirled around, and fumed as he slipped out the door.

He released the bell, and said softly, "Eff, he won't go off. I've had long talks with him. I know where he's going, so relax." She was still fuming as he continued. "Eff, I got him to stop drinking and to just walk when those feelings come." She stood down and listened to her husband. "He's headed to Gibson's field. He'll walk until he's all cried out. That's their spot"

He paused to divulge a personal effect from their marriage. "Eff, you know where our spot is for me?"

"Teddy, I didn't know we had a spot."

He put his elbows on the window ledge. "Yeah, it's our back porch."

Confused she said, "The porch?"

He looked deeply into her eyes. "Remember, how down I was all those years ago when we didn't have a pot to piss in and I didn't think we would get the loan for the diner?" She nodded and he continued. "We were sitting on the bottom step of the porch and you laid you head on my shoulder and said, 'Theodore, whether we get the loan or not won't matter, we'll still be together in this spot.'" Her damp eyes gave credence to her husband's wisdom and devotion to her, and she listened intently.

"Right then and there I didn't care about the loan, because you were right. Nothing matters when you're lucky enough to have a spot with someone. Now don't worry about Roy." She nodded, confident in her husband's wisdom, and kissed him though the window.

"Do you know why Gibson's field is their spot?"

She knew the exact reason was out of reach and only had a hypothesis to offer, and said, "I know Bobby liked to pick wild flowers."

"Gibson's field was their first kiss. You know how quiet Roy is. He keeps his feelings all locked up. Well they had been dating for a while and Bobby was ready to move things along, so he took him on a picnic to the field. When they sat down to eat, Bobby looked at him and gave him a love sigh, and Roy cried, thinking he was going to break up with him."

"That damn little Bobby stood straight up put his

hands on his hips and chewed his ass out, and said, 'Damn it, Roy. I think when a man sits real close to another man I don't think he's trying to break up. I think he's tying to tell you something,' then he crawled into his lap and kissed him."

He grabbed a dishtowel wiped his eyes, while she laughed, then said, "When did he tell you that?"

"He didn't, Bobby did years ago. I just now remembered. He told me after they were solidly hooked up."

Late afternoon and the sun lamp was of little value. He walked her to her door and she turned, put her arms through his coat hugged him, and said, "Henry, you've made this day so happy."

The poet was back in the glow of the woman he loved and sequestered from tension. Intimacy was allowed to brood in its absence. He put his arms around her, and they rocked. There was now peace in the aura, freeing their minds from its turbulence, which gave their private thoughts of the other a feast.

When they released, the poet held her face and said, "Gwendolyn, I sometimes think God created Eve to ease his own loneliness and to give Adam a great joy. I believe her glow has been passed down through all women, and when I'm immersed in yours I somehow feel a remnant of her creation. Eve was anointed with the first glow and now it travels through her descendents, endlessly, like starlight through space and will never end, because the glow of a woman comes from God and can only be removed by him.

"I think when a woman passes from this sojourn, a remnant of her glow is placed inside the ones she loves, as a reminder that the mother of us all watches over her children, and the rest is returned to the heavens as she completes her journey to the Creator."

He searched her face for a long time and felt gravity pulling him in. He stopped himself when his private thoughts told him to kiss her deep. He kissed her cheek, gave her another hug, and said, "I'll call often," and left.

As he left her dorm the poet felt compelled to stand under their sycamore. The lamp was nearly gone when he arrived and the air became the sole possession of the cold and appeared to petition the wind for assistance in dropping the temperature, forcing him to button up.

He visited all the spots on their journey around the sycamore, especially spacing. After many conversations with her, he turned to the tree and thought, you're deciduous, your tears then? Oh grieving, wind battered sycamore. As the goose flies, to fetch despair for our spring, how does it feel to wake to your buds and never know what became of the faces you've grown to love? Do you long to be evergreen, as I long to be a mountaintop above?

Tears pooled and his diaphragm gave a short spasm. He wiped his eyes quickly on his coat cuff, cleared his throat, and looked around suspiciously. He returned to the tree and thought, there's a corridor that connects the mind to the heart and it's dimly lit now that they're angry with one another, an almost inconsolable anger from being deeply hurt. The mind feels the other has committed an infidelity, because it knows the other had no intentions of honoring the vows of the project. And the heart just can't let her go, so I'm a liaison now, residing in that dimly lit corridor, consoling the two.

There was a loud obnoxious knock, one of those startling knocks, which was unnecessary in the quiet evening. She sat straight up in her bed with her heart pounding. She knew it wasn't Henry, but didn't rush, because no one was shouting in distress. She assumed it was a wrong door food delivery.
She frowned, and clinched her jaw slightly. She turned the knob quickly and jerked the door open. A young man on crutches and a cast on his right foot, said, "What up, Gwenie?" Then corrected himself and said sarcastically, "Excuse me, Gwendolyn."
"What do you want Jordan?"
Oblivious to her uninterested demeanor, he said while tapping his cast with a crutch, "Out for the season and I've got the room to myself."
Her demeanor now added irritation to its rank. "So?"
He grinned which agitated the newly formed rank. He said, "Well, I thought we'd get a little beer and go back to my dorm and help each other over the top."

"What?"

He thrust his hips slightly. "You know."

"Is that what it's called now or did you just make that up."

"Damn, that's the best part."

She was now visibly impatient. "Jordan, I wouldn't know about that. I think we're done here."

Shocked he said, "Damn, you've never been over the top, shit you don't know what you're missing."

She was about to slam the door in the rube's face, but paused, and said, "Even if I were looking for that it wouldn't be with you. You've already sufficiently eye humped me when you asked me out the first time, and physically tried the second. I think you've humped me enough."

His subconscious quickly stuck the iron of exasperation back into the fire, heated it red hot, and placed it on the anvil of anger and with one swift blow, he banged aggressively, "Why the fuck do you bother dating if you're not going to have a little fun?"

Glassy eyed, she replied somberly, "Because I was shopping for this or that, and settled into it." She paused to slip into her black dress. Henry was passing away, and said, "But something happened and now it's passing me by."

Puzzled, he furrowed his brow. "What the hell are you talking about?"

She sighed impatiently. "Ok sport, let me minimize the syllables, and reduce the discourse to an insipid sports analogy." She paused as the rube stood bewildered.

"Sport, you won't be in the red zone with me." She snickered, then said, "Did you catch the one syllable words or did you drop the ball?" She smirked, then said, "I could punt this all day."

He clinched his jaw. "You are so weird. Witty Book Boy is in for one sorry ride."

"We're done." She closed and locked the door, quickly, and thought, no telling what they're giving you in the locker room. She relaxed when she heard him hobbling down the hall.

The sun lamp had been down for quite a while when he rolled off of her and came to a sitting position in the middle of the kitchen floor. She stood, put her panties on, and slipped into her stained, standard waitress dress. She wadded up her white panty hose, socked them into her pocket, slipped her large feet into her shoes, and wore them like slippers for the short trip to the car. She turned, and said, "Damn, Teddy you still have some moves." He grinned and grabbed his pants.

He was about to put them on when he noticed her staring through the narrow window. He watched her for a while, and said, "What's wrong Eff?"

She turned back, and said with sadness in her eyes, "I was thinking about the young couple." She paused to divulge a personal effect from middle age. "Teddy, when we were young it seemed like we only had a small serving of worry on our plates and sometimes we could just flick it off with one finger." She sighed, turned back to the window, and continued. "Now it seems like that's all that's on our plates and no amount of flicking is going to get rid of it. It just comes back the next day and brings friends." She turned back to him glassy eyed. "And I worry about you."

"Ahh, Eff, now don't worry about me. I take my medicine," then added, "and I don't drink or smoke or carouse anymore."

She glared at his anatomy, and grimaced on the bitter memories that caused her lip canker to flare and ooze as a result from his shenanigans transmitted long ago. "That's because things don't work so well now."

He retorted with useless homespun wisdom. "Eff, when the wood goes soft, that's when a man knows it's time to row the boat home."

"That's the only thing keeping you out of the clubs."

He dropped his pants, danced around the kitchen, snapping his fingers to an imaginary beat, and said, "Damn, I could tear that floor up. I mean tear it up."

"Everybody called you Slink."

They chuckled, and then she said, "Damn, we all thought you were made out of rubber."

His mood turned somber abruptly. "I miss it, Eff." He put his pants on, stared out the narrow window, and said, "You know when you would come in early to stock and leave me at home." She felt her husbands growing sadness that had been brooding over the last few years, waking.

He sighed. "Well, I would get on the computer and read a little news." He paused and studied the narrow window frame. "I read this article about how to maintain your vigor in middle age." He frowned in disgust. "It was worthless, Eff. It didn't say anything. It just talked about vitamins and exercise." He looked through the window, and said, "I don't know why I read it, desperate I guess."

"What do you mean desperate?"

His eyes lost their brightness for the dance as he continued to gaze through the window. He said irritably, "Effie, I looked up the writer." He frowned in disgust again and turned to her. "That punk was only 28 years old."

He returned to the window. "Then I would look at my ladies."

She narrowed her eyes, as her canker oozed, and said disappointed, "Why are you looking at that nasty shit?"

He turned to her, sighed, and said as his spirit diminished, "I don't look at them for that." He went back to the window and stared into the dark abyss forming in the black lifeless dining room that compelled his spirit. "I used to look fine like them." He remained fixed on the abyss, as he said ruefully, "Effie, I miss my vigor. I miss it bad."

He finished dressing, and said, "Do you remember Uncle Leo?"

She curled her upper lip in disgust. "I hated that nasty bastard. He had the filthiest mouth. You couldn't even walk past him on the porch at the holidays without him calling every woman that passed the 'c' word." She quickly segued to exuberance. "The happiest Thanksgiving we all had was when Cletus beat the shit out of him." She glared at her husband. "You know it wouldn't have hurt you to defend me like that."

"Effie, what would you really think of me if I beat the shit out of a 78 year old man?" He paused to collect the wisdom that he acquired through his observance of his pitiful uncle and perhaps some sympathy might infer. "Eff, the reason he was so bitter and sour was that he had lost everything."

She frowned, unacceptably. "He had enough to get by."

He picked up a mop and placed it in its bucket, rung it out, and said, "No, he lost his vigor and his nature and that's what made him so mean." He began mopping the grill area by the window, stopped, and said, "A woman will never understand what a man goes through when he loses his nature and then his vigor."

"Teddy, a woman doesn't care about that. She can do without it."

He glared, clinching his jaw, and said with contempt, "When a woman says that, what she's telling a man is that she doesn't care, because she'll have her nature until the day she dies and doesn't care whether yours is there or not. She takes hers for granted, and knows hers isn't going anywhere."

She said heatedly, "Women don't care. That part isn't important, only being together."

He continued to glare, and said, "Like I said, a woman will never understand, because she doesn't lose hers half way through her life, then spend the other half crying because she knows it's never coming back. It's easy for a woman to give a token pat on the back and say it'll be all right, it doesn't matter to me, because I'll have mine to the end. Hell, all a woman has to do is just lay back and wait for a drive by when she's in the mood."

He continued his mopping. "Most women probably don't care, but they'll never understand what it's like to cry inside all the time. That's what Uncle Leo was doing. You just didn't understand."

He stopped mopping, addressed the abyss, and offered a homily on understanding. "Middle-aged men cry inside all the time, they just don't let anybody know. Middle-aged women are content to sit on the porch or visit with their neighbor across the fence, or bury themselves in their children's lives, or live at the church all day."

"A woman busies herself throughout the day and she's content, because she just stays in the day, but a man has already reckoned the day before he even gets out of bed. He spends his day in tomorrow and wonders when more is going to be taken away and if death intends to put him on the short list." He sighed through the abyss and concluded his homily. "So, you can either sit in the rain or become a Leo."

Itching with anxiety, she said nervously, "Teddy, are you getting depressed? Do you need to see a doctor and get on some medicine?"

He shook his and turned to her. "Oh, Doc Jones would get a kick out of this."

She looked at him irritably at the mention of his name. "You need to find a young doctor that keeps up and knows the latest and get rid of that old quack. Hell, he should of retired years ago."

"Damn smart man," then mopped with delight. "Effie, he's not that much older than us. He just doesn't dye his hair or do what he calls 'pasting up young.'" He shook his head. "Everybody has a prejudice of older people even older people. Doc's right, you better not have too much wisdom or show too much experience, because you'll look old."

He stopped mopping. "We talked a long time last time I was there." He turned back to address the abyss. "I sat in the chair and told him it feels like it's raining inside of me all the time." He paused, searched futility, and continued. "He rolled his stool right up to me, and said, 'Ted if you want me to write for something I'll write for anything appropriate.' I asked him if he thought any of that shit they advertise does any good."

"He looked at me very seriously, and said, 'Many years ago there was a small pool of drugs from which we could dip into, but now there are hundreds of puddles around the pool. Ted, all that shit you see advertised is just the splashing out of the pool, forming small puddles of mimic products of the ones already in the pool. And they all claim distinction and, of course, higher efficacy.'"

"'People see an apparent new medicine and think it will do what they want it to do in their mind, regardless of what the drug company actually claims. It's not all the drug company's fault, but they don't help either. I can give you a drug to keep the pressure down in the ticker. I can give you a drug for your rusty joints and even a drug to help keep the pressure up in the ole hydraulic pump, but in the end, all drugs do for aging is give you a hell of a lot of side effects.'"

He paused as Doc's wisdom rang its bell and continued. "Doc's right, Effie. There's nothing you can do about anything. He said towards the end of our talk, 'Ted you and I are on the shady side of the mountain. We're not going to see the sun anymore, that's for the young. When I look down the sunny side at all those young well-intentioned providers who have all these amazing ideas, I'm jealous, not because I don't have ideas. I don't have the necessary enthusiasm anymore and that's aging, not depression, which is what the young assume.'"

"'Ted, all that those well-intentioned, enthusiastic young providers have is just another puddle to splash in. They design all these health programs around their puddles and are real proud of them. The public gets excited and thinks if they follow it; it's going to enhance their life. It may help some, but you're still going to age and all those programs aren't going to add a minute to your life, other than a good diet, exercise, and routine check ups. Shit, you can meditate until you pass out, or polypharmacy vitamins until your urine smells like the bottle they came in, but nothing's going to change. '"

Teddy paused, but remained fixed on the abyss, and said, "He looked at me with tears in his eyes, and said, 'Ted I've lost some patients because they didn't like my opinion about all those mushroom programs. A lot of them thought that as I got older I didn't want to keep up. All providers keep up, it's part of the oath, but more importantly, we genuinely care for our patients. They just didn't like me calling it what it is, a pitch, and thought me a quack, and then look for younger.'"

"'Wisdom doesn't hold a seat of respect anymore, because the newest study contradicts it. Ted I'm 10 years older than you and I've managed to reduce the rain to a drizzle, and I'll be happy as hell if the rest of my life is filled with just cloudy days. We're both on the shady side now, and all I can do now that I'm a few years farther down, is say watch your step.'" He placed his elbows on the window ledge and remained quiet.

She came up behind him, put her chubby arms around his spindly waist, rested her heavy head on his back, and said, "Oh, Teddy, is middle age going to be nothing but shadows and darkness. Teddy, women do just live in the day because we don't know what else to do and it makes us crazy if we think past it." Tears began to roll down her cheeks. She pulled her arm back, wiped her eyes on her cuff, and said, "You know, maybe it's time for a new spot." He chuckled lightly, and she said, "Maybe, here at this window is our middle aged spot."

They were silent for moment. She nuzzled his back. "Teddy, maybe as we grow older our spots change, and depending on how lucky we are, the fewer the better. Maybe life kicks some of us around a lot more than others and won't let them just rest in a spot or two. Maybe the more spots we have the less fortunate we are. We've only had two spots so far and I don't know if that's good or bad."

She paused to settle into a new spot. "I don't know about you and I know this is coming from a woman, but I'm happy in our new spot at the moment and I know it may not last, but you're all I got and that's the only spot I need."

He was quiet for a while. "You know Doc Jones divorced his wife?" She picked her head up quickly.

"Eff, never, I love you." She laid her head back down, and squeezed him tight. "I love you, too."

"Doc told me, 'When a man first enters middle age, the sun is still in his face. But the time will come when he's fully immersed in the shade and all he sees is black below. And no amount of jumping up to try and catch the last rays of youth is going to do any good. And all that last minute futile body shaping or hair dying and flirting, which he hasn't done since he was young is going to help. He just looks foolish.'"

"He looked me square in the eye, and said, 'Ted I was one of them. I panicked when my head sunk into the shadows. I looked down the mountain and all I saw was black. I left Annie for a young nurse we'd just hired. I knew it was stupid going in, but the fear of the blackness below told me there was nothing left.'"

"Eff, he got real quiet, then said, 'Ted it can pull your whole belief system apart. So, I shacked up with her and gutted my whole family.' Doc didn't say anything for a long time, then he said, 'The whole time all I thought about was Annie. Is she all right, what is she doing? God, she's alone in the house. What if there's a break in, or a violent storm.' Doc didn't say anything again, and he got tearful, and said, 'Ted, I panicked again, but this time it was a greater panic, because I realized I was losing my life as I was living it. Taking my beliefs was death's brutal beating for looking into its blackness for no reason. I prayed and flew back to Annie and told her that even if she didn't take me back I was going to watch over her.'"

"'She looked at me oddly, and said, "That won't be necessary, but if you feel compelled, mow the lawn." I thought it was her way of punishing me, because she knows how much I loathe mowing grass. I figured she would punish me for a while and rightfully so. When I had finished the front she brought me a glass of tea, and said, "When you're finished with the back, be sure you lock the garage. I have a date tonight and I don't want to worry if it's locked when I get back."

"'I began to cry and she said real coolly, "Don, I've moved on as you should." I broke down bad and realized she didn't need anyone watching over her. She had been running a household for the last 25 years, while I spent my time in the clinic. She didn't need me, but I needed her. Tears ran down her face, while she brushed mine away, and said, "It's time we both move on." She stared into my eyes for quite a while, then rubbed my stubbly cheek with the back of her hand, and said, "I'm going to Corners restaurant tonight, and I want my date clean shaven." I grabbed her held her tight, sobbed, and begged forgiveness. I held her for a long time. Before she headed back inside, she said, "Don, forgiveness is a lot easier than forgiving yourself." I didn't know what she meant a first, but as time began to settle things, I knew she meant that the affair was meaningless. She didn't care about that, what hurt was not coming to her, and confiding in my best friend of the last 25 years. She was right. I still haven't forgiven myself completely. I told her that I didn't think I would ever forgive myself and would always push this regret out in front of me like the mower. She gave me a grand smile, and said, "I purposely put my regrets up on a shelf right next to happiness, so when I walk by and look up, they can't over state their stature."'

"Eff, he said it wasn't easy, but they finally buried the whole matter, permanently, and their lives went back to normal."

She raised her head up. "What did it?"

"Doc's a funny man. He said that she was still angry and when it welled up, she would make him mow the lawn." He chuckled through the abyss, which triggered her to chuckle, and he said, "Doc looked at me and laughed like hell. Ted I knew she was over it when she hired a lawn service.' He gave me the wisdom I always pull out whenever I'm blueing. 'Ted our youth and all our joys are gone, and the enthusiasm for all the wonders in the world have been severely blunted, or like most perished post youth. There is happiness in the shade, though. It doesn't have the punch or drive of youth, but it'll stick with you as long as you want it to.'"

"When I left his office, and went through the waiting room, and saw all those blue, middle-aged men, I knew right then that all his stories were for us." He paused, turned to her, put his arm around her, and said, "All the experience and wisdom coming out of his office may not hold a seat for some, but it sits at the head of my table."

He finished up mopping, and as they were about to leave, he looked at the stove, and said, "You know when I make Wednesday's soup and cut up all those fresh vegetables and put them on to boil. I'm always having to watch it for boil over, or having to work the temperature or adjust the lid, but when it's finally done and seasoned to a nice soup, I push it to the back to simmer, and I don't worry anymore, because I know it will stay warm and unchanged until I decide to do something. He paused to reflect on his wisdom. "There's happiness even though getting older shoves us to the back burner. Sometimes it just takes longer realize it."

"Come on my little licorice whip. Let's go home."

The young woman descended the stairs and headed to the kitchen. A middle-aged woman of her height and weight, with blonde highlighted hair and deep blue eyes, smiled as she entered, and greeted her. "Hey, sweetie, did you sleep well? I made your favorite, oatmeal, and bananas."

"Thanks Mom."

Her mother placed the oatmeal on the table in front of her as she sat down, and then she sat close to her. The younger one blew and ate slowly.

Her mother, placed her elbow on the table, palmed her chin, and cocked her head slightly, admiring her daughter. "Sweetie, I haven't heard much from you this semester," then assumed. "Well, I guess you and the ball player must be hitting it off."

Her daughter dropped her spoon in her bowl and curled her lip. "Mom, some people ought not to be allowed to breed."

Her mother popped her chin out of her palm, quickly, chuckled, and said, "I see college is honing you a clever tongue."

The young woman grinned, then said, "You know it's quite embarrassing when the head of the psychology department says 'ma'am I'm sorry, but you're not allowed to date the primates. You'll have to return him.'"

Her mother chortled, her joy was home from collage and appeared genuinely happy. "Where in the world did you get that clever tongue?" The young woman beamed at her quip, turned her gaze over to the fluffed napkins, pinched tightly in their dispenser, and held a buoyant smile.

Her mother palmed her chin again and observed her daughter. She watched her for a while, then concentrated on the glow in her face, of which she had not seen before and thought, she's never been this bright. She had always been a brooding child. She watched for a while longer, then said, "What's his name?"

She continued to stare over the napkins, sighed heavily, and at the end said, "Henry."

Her mother nodded. "Nice name. I like it."

Campus tension seeped into her mind, extinguishing her warm thoughts. "Momma, I'm unsure if he sees me." She pulled her chin out of her palm quickly and felt the anxiety all parents feel when their adult children regress to their child voice, because that far of a regression was a sign of being very troubled. And at this age there's not much a parent can do.

"Momma, I want him to see me so bad."

Her mother, moved quickly to the window, stared over the porch at the back fence to her flowerbeds, and said pensively, "I've been unsure for 20 years, but now..." Shocked, her daughter said, "Dad sees you."

She remained quiet and kept her eyes to the fence, and then turned to her daughter and stared with a stern cold expression.

"Mom?"

She stared her down the way she used to do during a

childhood scolding, drawing anxiety in her daughter from all the memories.

"Gwen, we don't have to seek out every truth. We just need to know enough to keep our world from flying apart." She paused, while remembering the last twenty years. "There's nothing wrong with oblivion. If it's applied right, no one gets hurt." She closed. "A bargain can be had with contentment."

She turned back to the window and worked her flowerbeds. "Gwen, you're in love with Henry."

Gwen shot across the room, burst into tears, buried her face in her mother's chest, and said through crying spasms, "Momma, I love him so much."

Her mother rocked her for quite a while and when her spasms ceased, she said, "Gwen, pursue him even if he doesn't see you."

As she lay on her mother's shoulder, she said, "Momma, he has to see me."

"Sweetie, you've brooded all your life, especially in adolescence. When you were a child on the play ground you used to sit under the slide and remain still as a stone whenever boys came around."

"I felt like a freak."

"Sweetie, it's all a fairytale. Men will never see women like us and if one does..." She hesitated, looked over her daughter's head to the fence post past her flowerbeds, and said, "It will be a blessing from above."

"Mom, have you ever felt like you were fading away?"

Her mother, sighed, kissed her, and said, "Not anymore."

She raised her head up, and said, "What stopped it?"

"You."

"What do you mean?"

Her mother held her hands. "I know exactly what you're going through." She searched her daughter's anxious face, and said, "Gwen, marry Henry and have children, even if he doesn't see you." She chuckled, then said, "You know what a bitch I can be."

Her daughter snickered, then said, "Oh yeah."

Her mother squeezed her hands and imparted. "You see, no fading, no doubts of identity. Your children will always know exactly who you are. Give him time. After children and many years he might see pieces of you." She stared her down again. "That's a bargain no woman should pass up."

She felt the throws of joy her daughter brought home to her, and said, "Gwen, there's a light in your face that I know Henry's put there. You see there's your contentment. Mine comes to me every morning by my flowerbeds."

The corners of Gwen's mouth turned downward. "Oh, Momma, I don't know if he wants me."

"Sweetie, who's he dating?"

She cocked her head, thought for a moment. "I don't think any one. I don't know. The last few weeks he's been walking me to my classes. I've never thought about it. All I've thought about was him." A false revelation pushed her to tears. "Oh, God, Momma he probably already has a girlfriend. What am I going to do?"

"He does... you."

They sat back down at the table and her mother grabbed a napkin and handed it to her. "Looks like you two are blind dating." She watched her daughter dry her eyes, and asked, "Has he kissed you?"

"Mmmm... Mother we were so close."

Her mother laughed, and said as she stroked her daughter, "Sweetie, you've gone from Momma to Mother in the short course of breakfast and now that you're all grown up." She winked. "For the moment anyway. It's time for a throw down."

She looked at her mother oddly. "Throw down?"

"You two have been seeing each other exclusively the whole semester," she winked again, "and, of course, not dating. So, its time to find a quiet place and sit him down, and stand in front of him, then throw your purse down, and say are we an item or not?"

They both chuckled and then her phone rang. She jumped up, put both hands on her cheeks, beamed, and said, "Oh, Momma, it's Henry."

"Well, when it's Mother again, we'll have to move fast and set the wedding date before Momma comes back." Gwen frowned, grabbed her phone, and said as she bolted towards the stairs, "Gotta go."

Her mother went back to the window, stared at the house past her fence, and thought about the day she met her neighbor.

It was late last spring while grocery shopping. When she arrived in the pasta section, she squatted to compare brands, while her abandoned basket blocked the aisle. A man of her age with average looks and height, but well toned, stopped a few paces before her cart, glared at her, and said, "Seriously, I know damn well you can see me in your peripheral vision, now move the damn cart."

She jumped up, shocked, pulled her cart to the side, quickly, and said genuinely, "I am so sorry."

"No you're not." His thoughts collapsed when he saw her eyes. He quickly recovered, and said, "With those eyes, attractive is always entitled." He shook his head, looked over his readers, noted her crisp pressed skirt, and said, "Skirts, I've seen you all my life. You walk up to an establishment, read entrance on the door, then make one, and throw towels to all the foolish drooling men." He paused to enjoy her red face, and flaring nostrils. "You know it doesn't matter whether you step off a curb, or a plane, there's always a puddle of drool to navigate. I feel sorry for you." He pointed his finger, and said, "Minus the sensitivity of course. It must be hard."

He pushed his basket along side hers and noted her well jeweled bracelet. "But you're well compensated." Well satisfied, he added, "Have a nice day Skirts and don't worry about a towel. I don't drool."

She pursed her lips, and pushed her cart briskly to the next aisle, beet red. Delighted by his antics, he thought, damn, that was so fun... just desserts.

They were dismissed by his indignation when it called in regards to the world's blind acceptance.

A few days later she was surveying her fallow flowerbeds by her backyard fence and contemplating spring planting. She flinched and let out a loud, but short girl scream when startled by a man's voice coming from the other side of the fence. He had his hands on his hips with furrowed brows, and said, "Shit, seriously?"

When she recognized him, their store encounter was reignited and now it was her turn. She drove up quickly, grasping the fence firmly as a territorial show, and said hotly, "You asshole."

He chuckled loudly, then said, "Entitled bitch." As she punctuated her contempt with a glare, he said, "I think one of us needs to move."

She stiffened, and said steadfastly, "I'm not going anywhere. I've lived here for years."

He sensed something encroaching on the fringes of his thoughts. He felt nudged from behind as images of Allison flooded his mind, and then it was over. He found himself pondering her perspective and felt that his sarcastic remark about his new neighbor, navigating drool, truly might be difficult. He thought, the best way I can apologize is to be a jovial neighbor. "As new kid on the block, I'm guessing you're the neighborhood bully."

"Why, yes I am," then she added, passionately, "and I ought to beat the shit out of you for the way you treated me in the store."

He chuckled, then said, "I think you just did."

"I'm still punching."

"Damn, you have a temper."

She chuckled softly, and thought, wrong foot.

"Well, Skirts, it looks like we're stuck with each other." He stuck his hand over the fence. "Harry Bedford."

She smiled, shook his hand, and said, "Silvia Dupree."

She had a great appreciation for his handshake. He didn't drool. Most of the handshakes she received from men, even married, always flirted at the end with either a light squeeze or a thumb rub and a deep look attached. His was a straight business agreement without anything attached.

He looked over her fallow beds, and said, "From the looks of your soil, you over fertilize." She furrowed her brow, and said, "I think I know how to garden."

"Well. You'll need to stop. It's ugly all over there. The thinking part I mean." She turned quickly and stomped off. He felt bad and thought, damn she's too sensitive, won't be any fun. "Skirts, wait. I'm sorry." She didn't respond and he raised his voice. "Silvia, please, I'm sorry." She came back with a scowl on her face and stared at him. He put his hands up, and said in a soft voice, "Silvia, I'm sorry. I didn't realize you were such a sensitive woman."

She curled her lip in disgust. He huffed, and said contemptuously, "Shit, I just gave you a genuine apology and if that's not good enough, piss on you." As his ranting turned him into knots, she grinned. When he saw her expression, he stopped dead in his rant. "You just played me."

She smirked, triumphant. "Yes I did, Mr. Bedford."

He pointed his finger at her, and said, "I like you, Skirts."

They talked of gardening and she found that he was as mad about it as she was. They exchanged tips and advice. She was pleased with her new neighbor and especially his love of gardening. They talked well into dusk and both felt it was getting late. They exchanged waves and started their departures.

She turned back quickly, scowled again, and said, "You owe me another apology for the grocery store."

When he saw an emerging smile she couldn't suppress, he said, "Nice try Skirts."

"Damn, I was going for a double header."

"You only get a door prize."

She cocked her head. "What's the door prize Mr. Bedford?"

"A good neighbor."

"I'll take it."

They met at the fence early mornings before he left for work and in the evenings to talk all things gardening. As summer began pushing spring aside their conversations naturally moved to personal ground. He talked extensively about his consulting business and the deep pride he had in his stepson.

She knew he was alone and speculated that he was one of those middle-aged panics, who erroneously felt old age approaching quickly. They marry younger women they can't possibly keep up with, or have any meaningful communication or conversation with over the gap. And when they're both in the ski lodge, she wants to hit fresh powder, and all he wants to do is sit by the fire, with his middle-aged peers, sip warm toddies, and chat. And that's when disparity meets parody, one blushes, and the other grins sheepishly, and divorce drives them home after the honeymoon.

He listened intently as she talked about her daughter. Pride, he thought, but not prideful. Between family conversations she versed him well on all the neighbors, especially Wilson. He chuckled, then said, "I've already had the pleasure," he said, "now he's a real asshole."

"I should have warned you before now," she said playfully, "You know those times when you're feeling too good and life couldn't get any better and you feel it's just not right to feel that good? Go pay him a visit."

"Damn. Skirts you are a funny."

He found it very odd, though, that she never talked of her husband. Even strained, a spouse would get an occasional mention, especially if a topic needed to draw reference from their well-established expertise.

With spring well routed, summer turned its full attention to its duties and he needed to move quickly to establish beds. The previous owners were not gardeners and the planting window was closing, quickly. He worked hard in the evenings and on the weekends.

She would stand in her well-established beds by the fence and offer help. He would help her over the fence occasionally and she would rake while he plowed. After his beds were completed she said playfully, "Now, I'll tell you what you need to plant." He enjoyed his jovial companion.

Summer was now well defined and their conversations were still expanding. She thought about his handshake and felt him genuine. Even during the lulls and kneeling close by the fence she felt comfortable. He stuck to his duties and she felt that he wasn't struggling with arousal. His body movements weren't agitated and his mind appeared peaceful.

She sat down close to him on her side of the fence one late afternoon, watching him dig out a few remnant roots, and expressed to him how his handshake felt, and how wonderful it was to sit next to a man and just be liked.

Puzzled, he said, "Liked?"

She put her hand through the pickets, and said, "Harry, shake my hand." Struggling with her puzzling behavior, he nodded. They shook hands while their eyes were locked in a deep engagement. She released his hand.

"Thank you for liking me."

Grappling for clarity, he said, "Silvia, I don't understand."

"Harry, most of the men that have shook my hand and looked into my eyes, only wanted one thing afterward. They neither bothered to like me nor get to know me. Silvia has always been the wall flower at the office party... thank you."

Saturday morning brought welcomed clouds, which allowed the air to remain cool as he brought bags of top soil around and stacked them by the back fence. She had her hands clasped, resting on the fence, and watching intently. He would look up occasionally and smile and she would reciprocate. As he continued to stack, he noticed she appeared to be in deep thought. He continued to stack and smile and she continued to reciprocate and ponder.

She moved to a post, and rested her elbow, palmed her chin, and nibbled her bottom lip. She gazed down to the sacks and tapped her index finger on her cheek.

His curiosity wasn't going to leave him alone and neither was she. He watched her for a while longer and chuckled, which drew her attention. "Ok, Skirts, what's on your mind?"

"Harry, I want to ask you something, but you're not allowed to say no."

He laughed, then shook his head. "Ok, what is it that I'm not allowed to say no to?"

She took her chin out of her palm and crossed her

arms. "Harry, say the word yes."

"God, you're so funny."

She narrowed her eyes slightly. "Now say the word yes."

He put his hands on the fence. "Seriously, you think I'm going to fall into that?"

She brought her eyes to a glare and stomped her foot. "Say yes."

"Damn, you've got a temper."

"You have to meet me at the flower and garden show next Saturday." He laughed with joy at the antics of his playful companion.

"Harry, I'm going to ask you a few simple yes / no questions."

"Ok, shoot."

"Now is Wilson a sweet man?"

He wiped his eyes on his cuff. "You are so fun. Ok no."

"Ok now if a flower and garden show came to town next week would you go?"

"Only if I can bring Wilson."

She snickered, then her excitement flipped her serious, and she said, "Oh, Harry, you'll love it. Now, I want you there at 8."

He looked at her skeptically. "When does it open?" She felt his suspicion circling and offered him a qualifier that she hoped would appeal to his reason. "10, but we have to be there early to get in line..."

Dashed, he cut her off. "Whoa, what do you mean line?"

"You can't just sashay up, read entrance on the door, and make one, because everything will be picked over."

"What the hell are we supposed to do in line for two hours?"

She put her hands on her hips as her jaw dropped. "Well I suppose you could talk to me."

"Who the hell is Wilson suppose to talk to?"

She pointed her finger. "Now, don't be late."

She waved, while bouncing on the balls of her feet as he pulled in. She gave him a grand smile as he walked up, and said, "Good, you're on time. Now, let's get a cart." They came up to several rows of flatbed nursery carts and he reached out and grabbed the closest one. She waved her hands. "Harry, you never go for the most convenient one."

"What?"

"They always place the ones that have been ridden hard first and hope you'll be too far advanced in your shopping before you realize it and complain."

"You are so damn funny."

"Now pull it around and let me check it." When she was satisfied they stood in line.

She pulled a brochure from a rack next to them and gasped. "I've always wanted a greenhouse."

He looked over skeptically. "I don't know, Silvia. When you sit at the table and go over the cost, and weigh it against maintenance and value it might be a loser."

She frowned. "Harry, do you know what kind of joy it would bring? You can't think of cost before joy. Joy always comes first."

He shook his head. "Let me get this straight. In your mind you always load the joy on the front end and toss the cost on the table and deal with it later."

Disappointed, she said, "You spend too much time at the table, while joy passes you by. Now get out and exercise."

As he was laughing the doors opened and the queue lurched forward. When they passed through the door she turned quickly, and said, "Now you have to move aggressively or they will take advantage of you."

"I'm not going to plow people over."

She looked at him disappointed, again, then winked full of playfulness. "This is not a hockey or football game where a little assertiveness may be required. These are aggressive flower and garden people. You can't take any crap." He laughed and she took the handle. "Let me show you."

The line moved a little faster as shoppers filled the peripheral aisles, taking pressure off the center. They were still in the center aisle when she became excited, dropped the handle, and rushed to a display. He stood studying the snoozing handle on the floor, and shook his head. He heard a man's voice. "Dude." He looked up and a man a little older than he, said, "Dude, your wife is causing a major pile up."

He shook his head, picked up the handle, and said, "I'm not her husband. I'm her neighbor."

"Well, she pulls you around like one."

He curbed the cart next to her. "Silvia, you're being attractive again."

"What?"

Distracted, she placed her open palms on her cheeks, beamed with the wonder of a child. "Harry, I've always wanted one of these."

"You are something else. It's Christmas for you."

She held a bulb up for inspection. He squinted at the name tag, and said, "Oh, hell no, that's a Voodoo Lily."

"I think I'll name her Susan after a sorority sister I couldn't stand. Besides, it only stinks when it blooms," she felt bubbly and added, "but Susan stunk all the time."

"Where the hell are you going to put it?"

She winked. "Your yard." He was enjoying his playful companion. "Alright Harry, we'll split the difference and put it by the fence."

"Somehow, I feel it in my yard."

"That's because you're a gracious neighbor and I wish I could be more like you."

Both enchanted by the other. A lull appeared, followed by a faint flash above them. The safety of their fence was gone. He searched her blue rings, and she encouraged it for the first time in her life. They both broke off quickly and looked nervously between rows of flower bulbs. Confused by this lull for removing their fence, she now felt betrayed by it.

He found his feet and brought them out of the closeness. "Hey, you know what we can do?"

Relieved the uncomfortable ride was over. "What?"

"When it blooms we'll extract the essential oils and make soap and give it to all the assholes on our Christmas list." She pushed him. "Harry, you ought to be ashamed."

"Hey, I get Wilson."

She pushed him again. "Come on."

They bought each other's lunch and shopped until mid afternoon. When they finished, he pulled their full cart up to her car. As he loaded, she picked up the lily bulb, sniffed, and grimaced. "Harry, can you do me a favor and give Susan a ride? I think she prefers the company a man."

He chuckled as he studied her broad smile she just gave him, then said "Silvia, you know how to make a man feel good."

She felt their fence move again. He felt it, too, and found footing quickly, and closed the hatch. "Well, Skirts, it's been pleasure, but I gotta go. Susan wants to freshen up before our date."

She laughed, and thought, as she drove off that perhaps the lull was just some sort of unfamiliar social language outside their flowerbeds, one she needed to learn. The fence was compelled to move from the obvious fact of a location change and she needed to be mindful of fence movement when it happens and lockstep with it accordingly.

Early morning he stood at the glass door of his kitchen, peering into his backyard, sipping coffee and contemplating his beds. His face lit up when he saw her enter her beds and hack at something with a shovel, then thought, Skirts, what are you up to? He changed out of his suit, put on work cloths, and made a quick call.

He came up to the fence, put his elbow on a post, palmed his chin, and watched her hack a very large root. "I think you'll pass a few birthdays before you get that out." She looked up and gave him her traditional morning smile she had been giving him all season. She wrapped both hands around the handle, and said, "It's a work in progress."

"Well how long has this work been going on?"

"I started last spring."

"When can we expect your debut?"

She put a hand on her hip, and said mischievously, "You know, Mr. Bedford..." She took her hand off her hip, and panned it all around to the adjacent houses. "All our neighbors, excluding Wilson of course, are watching this poor woman-" He cut her off. "You're not poor, Skirts."

"Helpless-"

He cut her off again. "You're not helpless."

"Ok, struggling, then."

He nodded. "I'll give you that one."

She cocked her head as she said, "Now, they're all watching this poor, helpless, struggling woman," she propped her chin on top of her shovel handle and said, "while a strong, well conditioned man just stands there watching."

"You are so fun. I know you're trying to pin me."

"Why, Mr. Bedford, I'm sorry to inform you, but its check mate."

"How so?"

"Well, if you don't dig this root out for me, all our neighbors will gossip and believe you're lower than an asshole. And everybody knows the only thing lower than an asshole is Wilson." Hearty was his laugh as she pinned him. "Now, when the gossip works its way around to me I don't think I'll discourage it."

She pulled her chin off the handle, narrowed her eyes slightly, and pursed her lips. "Harry, you have to remove this root."

"Well, gossip needs fertilizer. Wilson and I are proud to provide such an essential service."

She narrowed her eyes farther, frowned like a child, and stomped her foot. "Damn it, Harry, you have to remove this root. It's been irritating me all year."

His companion cast him into the throws of joy. "God, you're so fun." He hopped over the fence and she handed him the shovel. "Thank you Mr. Bedford," and rolled him in happiness. "Now when the gossip works its way around to me, I'll discourage it," she held up her index finger and added, "depending on the quality of the work of course."

He shook his head, and plunged the shovel at its base, looked up surprised. "Damn, Silvia, you didn't fully disclose.

Shit, this is a 6 inch anaconda."

"Mean as hell, too."

"Would it not be easier to pay it off to leave?"

"I tried that, but it's prideful."

He hacked it out in just a few minutes, and as he pulled it out, she said playfully, "Impressive, you hack with such passion. How do you feel about stumps?"

He chuckled as he tossed the 6-inch section of root aside. "All it takes is a good man which would be any man above Wilson."

"God quit making good men after Adam."

"What?"

"Oh yeah, he's still sore about the snake incident with Eve and we haven't had one since."

He shook his head, looked at the anaconda's hole, and saw a small garter snake struggling to get out. He picked it up. "Well, it looks like your incident is back." She went pale, stumbled back a few paces, and trembled as it coiled around his wrist.

She shouted. "Please kill it, kill it."

He quickly put it behind his back, dropped the shovel, and said calmly, "Silvia shh, I'll relocate it, but I won't kill it."

He walked briskly to the corner post and tossed it in Wilson's yard. She was still trembling when he returned. He put his hands on her shoulders, looked deeply into her eyes. "Are you all right?" He released her when she nodded.

"Harry, doesn't anything frighten you?"

He turned from her and stared at the corner post. "I

was frightened for a long time after my wife died."

She felt ashamed for thinking him a middle age panic. "I'm so sorry."

He remained fixed on the post. "It's ok; she's been gone nearly 5 years," he paused when he realized their magical moment left, "but, God, I miss her sometimes though."

She placed her hand on his shoulder, and with deep affection said, "Harry, what's her name."

He cleared his throat. "You mean what was."

"No, she's still alive inside you, so she's still with us."

He was silent and she waited. He collected himself, and said, "Allison."

She wiped her eyes quickly on the other sleeve and swallowed hard. "Beautiful."

He sighed. "She was beautiful."

He turned to her and gazed into her deep blue eyes. "But not like those." He turned back to the post and mused upon the mystery of beauty. "She had so many beautiful things inside."

She removed her hand, bowed her head. "Harry, I can't help the way I am."

He placed his fingertips under her chin, met her eyes, and said, "Silvia, you have beautiful things inside of you, too." He cocked his head and studied her rings. "You're not a bitch, just a little pissy." She turned the corners of her mouth up, slightly, as he released her chin, but he remained fixed on her eyes, and for the second time in her life she encouraged it.

The flash above them returned and as an aura shrouded them he felt compelled to express to her his inner most feelings about women. "You know there's a quiet place in a man's mind where he goes to think about women." She raised her eyebrows.

"Not that, there's no thinking involved with that."

"True."

He turned back to the corner post, put his hand out as if he were blind, trying to feel his way through. "It's a place that can never be articulated. Silvia, when I look at you, sometimes this place comes to me. I don't see you as Silvia, the person, or even try and trace the almost endless seam of your identity and wonder how vast it might be inside." He turned back and studied her rings again. "It's silly I know. I can't articulate it."

She searched his face and felt anxious when the lull whispered this time in their personal environment. She felt betrayed by the fence for letting it intrude. "It's not silly, please tell me."

"I sometimes ask God why a woman?" As she cocked her head, puzzled. He did his best to articulate. "I know it's hard to describe, because the essence of a woman is so far removed from words. It's as if words are just crude animal vocals when compared to your essence. Silvia, there's something about a woman and that's why I ask God."

"What do you ask God?"

"Why such a gift?"

He turned and looked deeply into her eyes. "Maybe its God's way of saying I love you to man."

It was at that moment she realized there never was a fence. She was the betrayer and now the winds picked up in her mind.

As he gazed deeply into her eyes, he was hearing the lull's whispers also. He blushed. "Well, I need to go. I've got something in the oven." He hopped back over the fence and headed briskly towards his back door.

She called to him and he turned around. "Have nice day Harry."

"You too, Skirts."

She knelt down and began to fill in thc holc with surrounding soil, while tears pooled. She looked quickly towards his porch, saw that he was already inside, and burst into tears. She wiped her eyes quickly and stared at her flowerbeds.

Her quiet place was a little lagoon between the rows of flowers where she had traveled for years. There were tall crowned palms which had long feathery fronds hanging like stately boughs that shaded the beach below.

She knelt in the warm sand and placed her feet in the water and felt the tiny warm waves of the well-protected lagoon lap rhythmically at her feet, which reminded her of her contentment that she kept loosely tethered to her by a cotton string that had countless knots from repairs that she had made over the years from breaks.

She occasionally caressed it and checked it for the tautness of discontent. She knew from experience that contentment can't be permanent and would always be rift with knots. But now, the winds of change had picked up and her string was drawn taught again.

The corners of her mouth turned down sharply. She knew now that her little lagoon was about to feel a storm surge. As she looked out over the ocean, into the deep blue sky she had depended on all these years to remain cloudless, her discontentment was gathering into a storm. Next to it was a figure forming, holding a bridle. And that figure was Harry Bedford.

She dropped the spade in the hole, moved briskly across the yard, and kicked her gardening shoes off when she landed on the porch. She rushed through the door, grabbed a dishtowel off the oven handle, and pressed it to her face, to hide from the spasm. The spasm sat her on the kitchen floor and handed the betrayer her tears.

A few days later their fence conversations appeared to have halted their advancement into personal ground. She felt that perhaps they had reached their fullness and are now well established, and in no need of further amending. She believed that over the years they would slowly mature like healthy flowerbeds and the comfortable lull of their initial spring planting would soon permanently displace the recent uncomfortable turbulent lulls and her good neighbor past her back fence would return.

She reached for her purse on the kitchen table as she was about to leave, and went to the window over the sink, as she always did before leaving her house to gaze at the fence for a moment. She saw him wandering around his yard and knew something was wrong. She knew his outdoor movements intimately.

She kicked her heels off quickly, slipped into her old gardening shoes, and skipped across the yard. He didn't realize she was there until she called his name. He stiffened up, turned his back to her, and said, "Silvia, please go away."

She turned down the corners of her mouth, and in a choked voice said, "I'm sorry, Harry." She turned quickly and skipped back briskly while wiping her eyes.

He rushed to the fence and shouted her name. She turned, and said, "Harry, I'm so sorry. I didn't realize you wanted to be alone," and continued across her yard.

He shouted her name again. She stopped, and he said, "Silvia, I'm sorry this is just a bad time for me."

She felt anxiety welling up, and returned to the fence quickly. She noticed his eyes were red and swollen. Her anxiety escalated and she cried. "Oh, God, Harry what's wrong?"

He turned from her and cleared his throat. "Silvia I thought you were at your ladies club meeting. I would have never come out if I knew you were home. I was trying to avoid you." She burst into tears and he turned back quickly, and said, "Silvia no, no, nothing like that."

She stopped crying, wiped her eyes on her sleeve, which left large make up stains, and said, "Harry, I'm so worried about you."

He turned his back to her again. "Silvia, this is the date of my wife's death." He paused and cleared his throat. "I'm sorry. I know you don't want to hear your neighbor blubber about his problems. I know it's uncomfortable and if you want to put your toes on your heels and ease back I won't think anything of it. We'll always be friends, no hurt feelings. That's why I avoided you. I just need a day or two." He turned to her composed. "I'm sorry I threw that out there. I know you don't want to hear all that."

She turned beet red, clinched her jaw, flared her nostrils, and said, "Damn it, Harry, you're not me."

They stared at each other caressing the other's raw feelings. She released her anger, lowered her eyes, deflated. "Harry, I haven't slept with my husband in years. We sleep in separate bedrooms." She looked up, blushed with embarrassment, and said, "He's a good man. We're just a poor match. We live separate lives." She smiled stiffly. "Now we're both out there."

"Thank you, Silvia, you're a good friend."

He turned and headed back in. "Harry, please don't go. Stay and let's talk." He felt a deep desire in her for the type of intimacy that only a best friend could have. She gestured. "Sit over here with me."

He climbed over and they sat with their backs against the fence in view of her house. They talked for hours about their personal lives and knew every intimate detail of the other. She felt the lulls of the fence would not be uncomfortable anymore now that they were filled with the genuine love for a good friend.

Late afternoon arrived and the sun was well over his house. There was a long lull and he chuckled. She looked up. "What?"

"You remember back in the spring when you stomped off." She nodded, unaffected, and he said, "You know, Allison was like you in that way. She would stomp off when she was pissed." As happiness brightened his face, a type of which she'd never seen before, it made her happy, and her face lit up. He looked down into her bright face. "You seem very happy."

Her eyes dilated. "I am Harry, very."

"Shit, we need to get you over to Wilson's before it too late." She rolled in laughter and pushed him.

When she settled, he continued. "Over the years her stomping became more dynamic and sometimes she meant it as a cue for me to chase her." He shook his head. "Why do women love to be chased?"

Excitedly, she said, "Oh, Harry, we love it." He looked at her oddly, because he meant it rhetorically. He dropped his expression and listened.

"When you're chased and caught that's when the light

groping and kissing begins." She paused, when her back door shamed her. "And then they say I love you." She cast her eyes down slowly, fully deflated from her shameful fairytale.

He lifted her chin with his fingertips, but she refused to make eye contact, and he said, "You've never been chased?"

She pulled away and blushed. "I'm embarrassed. I've only heard my friends giggle about it." He cupped the palm of his hand under her chin, but she resisted eye contact. "Silvia, look at me. There's no shame between good friends. We've shared everything." He paused, pulled light traction against her resistance, and said, "You know you have it right, except for one thing."

She ceased her resistance and engaged his eyes, while he still held her chin.

She said with bright curiosity at having been close to the complete answer, "What?"

He rubbed her cheek lightly with his thumb, and said, "The light groping and kissing is the courtship. It's only when you hold them down and press them tight, and kiss their giggling face all over." He paused, to listen to the lull's whispers, and said, "Do you say..." He paused to listen again, but too long, and said, "I love you," inadvertently changing the context. He blushed immediately after the error. He gazed deeply into her eyes and her encouragement was petitioning hard.

He released her, still blushing, as they stood. "Silvia,

I'll never forget this day. Thank you for sitting through this storm with me." He searched her face with unconscious intensity, as the aura shrouded them, and he said quickly, "I need to go. I've got something in the oven." He hopped the fence and walked briskly towards the door. She shouted his name, and he turned around, still full of intensity. "Harry, you're my best friend."

"You're mine too, Skirts."

She watched him closed his door, and she skipped back briskly, trying to make it inside before bursting into tears. She made it to her kitchen, cried, then blew her nose into a dishtowel, and burst into tears again.

She headed upstairs to clean up. As she made it around the banister by the front door, Gwen opened the front door, startling her. She didn't realize how late it was. She always lost track of time when she was with him. Gwen cried when she saw her mothers wet face, smeared make up, and said, "Mom, are you all right? What happened?"

She collected herself, and said, "I'm ok, Sweetie." She paused when she heard the lull's whispers. "Don't worry. I just fell hard in the garden," and added after the whispers ceased, "and got stung."

Gwen looked her over frantically. "Where?"

"I'm ok, Sweetie. I'm going to clean up, then start supper."

"I'll start supper."

"Thank you, Sweetie."

She undressed and placed her stained blouse and dirty skirt in the hamper in her bathroom, sat on the edge of the tub, and cleaned up. She gazed into her lagoon and saw the storm pushing her warm waters and then driving them hard across her sands. Her palms were laid over and the contentment she'd been repairing for years had now drowned. Her cotton string was now just a few useless threads and her contrived world was now coming to a close. Sometimes beautiful blue lagoons attract the attention of storms and then encourage them.

The next week she kept her fence conversations restricted to gardening. He obliged because he felt his preoccupation with her was moving Allison around too much. He knew that as soon as the season was over and their beds became still and fallow, Silvia would recluse, and he could resume his chase of Allison, because the love for a woman was always in bloom.

Late afternoon and she was about to start supper when she gazed through the kitchen window over the sink. Since his only time to tend to his garden was after work he would be out later in the day. She was now preparing most of the meals at the sink and watching him.

She watched him disappear between his and his neighbor's house and return with pruning shears. She became anxious as he headed to the corner of his yard by Wilson's fence. Tears pooled as he began cutting down a wild rose. She wiped her hands quickly and rushed through the door shouting his name. She ran up to the fence pleading. "Oh, God, please Harry, don't cut it down. Please don't cut it down."

Distraught over her anguish, he said excitedly, "Silvia, shh, it stays. I can't stand to see you this upset. It stays."

"Harry, I want to tell you about this wild rose."

He gazed deeply into her eyes. "Tell me."

She turned the corners of her mouth down slightly. "Before Gwen was born I was really down." She lowered her eyes. "Harry, I had thoughts of hurting myself."

Visibly shocked he dropped his shears, and came closer. "God, Silvia you're frightening me."

She snapped her head up quickly, and squeezed his hand, reassuringly. "Harry, it's ok. It's all gone." She added with a reserved exuberance, "It all went away when Gwen was born. I knew I would never do something like that, especially while carrying her. Harry, those thoughts were momentary. I would never do that."

She looked towards the rose bush and produced a faint smile. He smiled and felt back in the throws of joy as her smile was now in full bloom. She turned back, and said, "It bloomed out of season, right before she was born, and I always felt it bloomed for me, as a comfort, saying hang on because something wonderful is coming," she wiped her eyes, "and it did."

She searched his face for a long time. "All my life I've just wanted to be liked. I want to thank you for liking me and not just drooling like all the others."

He cocked his head. "Silvia, I see your beauty like all the others." Her jaw dropped slightly, and she lowered her head, disappointed. He lifted her chin with his fingertips, and said, "But I wait for it to pass, because pretty is coming." He released her chin.

Puzzled, she said, "What do you mean?"

"You know when the sun just begins to rise how it's just a glare at first." She nodded and he continued. "The glare is just light and isn't warm, because warmth always follows the glare." He paused, pointed at the post at his elbow. "Towards the end of spring I was standing here waiting for the sun to rise and there was a honey bee on that post. We were both patiently waiting for our warmth, but different warmth."

"As it rose we both felt its glare and became excited, because we both knew our warmth was coming. The bee flapped excitedly and danced because he knew it was almost there. The sun peaked over your house and its warmth struck us. The bee's excitement escalated and when he was toasty, he flew off." He looked deeply into her eyes. "My warmth hadn't emerged yet." She blushed as her pupils dilated.

"When you appeared on your porch that was when I saw your glare of beauty. When you began to cross your yard I squinted, because your glare of beauty was your mistress and you, her entourage. After she passed and you were still in the yard, I waited for my warmth. You came closer, but it still hadn't emerged yet."

She cocked her head puzzled. "What is it?"

"That."

"A smile?" He shook his head.

"A wave then?" He didn't say anything.

"Harry what?"

"That."

"I don't understand."

He remained fixed on her eyes. "The sound of your voice." He paused, while they both listened to the lull's whispers. "My warmth is the voice of my pretty little pissy chambermaid."

She looked deeply into his eyes and at that moment her lagoon passed away.

"Harry, could you do me a favor?"

He picked her chin up, and said, "Anything."

She took his hand and held it. "I promised Gwen I would take her and her friends to beach. Would you watch over my flowers while I'm gone?"

"Always."

She squeezed his hand. "A week's a long time."

"It can be a short time, too. Email me and tell me how you're feeling."

"I will Harry, every evening."

He picked up the rose canes he cut, looked deeply into her eyes again, and rolled one of the buds between his thumb and index finger. "You know there's an old gardener's poem about the wild rose."

"Tell me."

"If you groom her before she blooms.
By combing her canes, then cinching them round your post.
When she wakes and finds her canes caressed and groomed.
She'll lay her muzzle along your fence and claim you as host.
If she offers a stirrup, don't claim her canes or possess her blooms.
'Tis a wild one you gave it to, now bare is your fence and post."

She reached between the pickets and held his hand, as her little lagoon released a few bubbles and sank. She looked deeply into the eyes of her storm. "I'll miss you Harry," and walked back slowly. After a few paces he called to her.

She turned. "Can I prune it back a little?"

She raised her hand and held her thumb and index finger about an inch apart. "Just a little," then the gardener, penchant for her wild rose, added, "mind the buds."

She turned back and moved quickly. When she reached her porch, she burst into tears. She was now standing in the hot sands of a wild beach, listening to its pounding surf, while staring into the eyes of a man holding a bridle. An average man with a beautiful mind and spirit had just handed her his heart and she knew she couldn't return it. Silvia Dupree was deeply in love with Harry Bedford.

She emailed him long letters of regression. He was surprised to see her talk extensively about her childhood. He reciprocated and all week were long tales of childhood. He found himself rushing home from work, tending to their gardens quickly, and sharing their childhood. She always signed her emails 'pissy chambermaid' and he, 'warm honey bee'. He asked her at the end of one of his tales why she chose the topic of delightful childhood stories. She wrote back. "I feel liked my whole life now."

Late afternoon she rushed through the front door and turned to her bronzed daughter. "I need to check my flowerbeds, will you unload and go next door to get the mail."

Gwen nodded. "Then I'll go get us something to eat. What cha want?"

"You pick, but make mine light. I'm not real hungry."

Gwen frowned. "Mom, you've hardly eaten all week."

"Sweetie, I'm all right. Summertime heat wilts my appetite. Now I need to check my flowerbeds."

When they parted, she walked briskly through the kitchen and out on the porch. She tapped her garden shoes on the railing and checked for insects. After her shoes were on, she looked towards her flowerbeds. Tears pooled as she saw her wild rose neatly woven onto an elaborate trellis.

She ran up to it with a throbbing heart, and out of the corner of her eye she saw him walking down the fence line. She turned quickly with tears in her eyes. "Oh, God, Harry it's so beautiful."

When he was in front of her he took his gloves off and

placed his hand between the pickets. "You look good Silvia."

She snatched his hand quickly, squeezed it, and said, "Harry, I feel so good."

"I was wrong."

"About what?"

He looked deeply into her eyes. "A week is a long time." He pointed to the base of the trellis. "It bloomed while you were gone." He reengaged her eyes. "I thought maybe if I groomed it, perhaps I might have it." She blushed as her eyes fully dilated to match his, then an aura shrouded them. Gravity took control and pulled him in. She matched it with equal attraction. They were inches from a kiss when he disengaged, straightened up, and blushed. "Sorry," he attempted a recovery, "well, it's good to have you back Skirts. I need to go. I've got something in the oven."

He turned quickly and walked briskly towards his house. Tears streamed down her face as she called out. "Harry, please stop. Please, Harry." She paused briefly, and said in a stern voice, "Harry stop, I have the same thing in my oven." He turned slowly. The corners of her mouth turned down. "Harry I'm in love with you, as I know you are with me. I don't ever want you to feel bad and think this is some sort of cheesy extra marital throw down."

One of Allison's last conversations flashed in his mind. As she wiped her eyes on her sleeve, she said, "Harry, it's not, because it would be running from that." She gestured to her house, and said, "To this," and pointed to him.

"When you run from that to this, it's nothing but

escape from that, and when you're down the road and your bruises have had time to go from purple to yellow, you realize it was just escape from that, and you never really wanted this. All you really wanted was away from that."

"Harry, I could have left long ago and it wouldn't have been escape, but now I want to leave." She paused to collect her thoughts. "I know it's not escape because I never planned escape. The last two seasons have brought me some of the greatest joys of my life and the whole time I never thought about escape, only being with you."

He cleared his throat. "When the treatments stopped working, I brought her home and laid her 80 pound body on our bcd. All shc wanted to talk about was me finding someone else when she was gone and I would stomp off." He wiped his eyes. "Silvia, she grabbed my jaw one afternoon, and put her thumb under my tongue and buried it so I couldn't leave, and said, 'Don't ever feel bad for falling in love again because I want you to."

He paused when he felt the periphery of his mind breeched. The nudge came up from behind him, wrapped her arms around him, squeezed him tight, and whispered in his ear, "Nor disease, nor death, nor the love for another will ever take our moment." She shoved him away. He wiped his eyes and collected himself. "Silvia, I feel like she's looking down from above, nudging me towards you, and giving us her blessing."

She gazed into to the hazy summer sky, and

whispered, "Thank you Allison."

She turned back to his wet face and found her previous stern voice. "Harry, we all get something in this life and it may not be what we want or even what we need. It may be something we never thought about but we all get something." She released her stern voice, and said somberly, "You and Gwen are my something."

She looked down at the wild rose in full bloom. "Harry, my marriage makes me appear as unattainable as a wild rose, but I'll be on your fence always and my canes and blooms are yours and my stirrups are settled."

The lull's whispers spoke to them both when he said, "I love you."

Her tears picked up. "Harry, please wait for me. Don't leave me."

"Silvia, we've been given a blessing from above and our moment is just beginning."

"The season is about over. How am I supposed to see you?"

"The library. There's nothing more public than the library." He paused and thought, truly the love for a woman will always be in bloom. "I leave the office at one o'clock for lunch and spend it on the second floor in the back. Where it's quiet, so I can think about you."

"I'll be there everyday."

She pulled herself away from the window, carried her smile across the kitchen, and warmed her coffee. She listened to her daughter's chatter for a while, then turned back to the fence, and thought about being in the library last week.

They had been meeting for lunch all fall and well into winter. They would take a dimly lit stairwell that led to the parking lot when it was time to leave. When they landed on the ground floor, he would hold her tight, and they would kiss for several minutes before separating.

She smiled as she remembered last week's kiss. He held her tight and kissed her several times, then lightly groped her.

She pulled his hand down. "Harry, not here."

He kissed her nose, released her, and said, "That's the light groping and now I'm going to count to five, so you better take off."

She giggled and put her hands up in a futile protest. "Harry, now stop."

"One..."

Her giggling picked up. "Now stop. This is silly."

"Two..."

She rolled into a fit of giggling, stopped abruptly, and pointed her finger. "Harry, now stop. I'm in heels and this is silly."

"Three..."

Her giggling escalate again as she backed up, and said, "Now stop. We're too old for this. You're embarrassing me. I'm giggling like a silly schoolgirl."

"Four," then he made a sudden lunge. She girl screamed and ran up the stairs. She made it up three treads before he snatched her. She screamed again, and her face went up in flames, as she giggled out of control. He pressed her to the wall, kissed her warm giggling face all over, and said in a soft voice, "Now how does it feel to be chased?"

She settled down to an occasional light chuckle, looked deeply into his eyes for a long time, without speaking.

He cocked his head. "What?"

She kissed him deep several times. "I'll let you know after you hold me down."

She pulled away from the window, sat on the bottom step of the staircase, and listened to her daughter's exuberance, then looked up the stairs and thought, oh Sweetie, Momma's going to be held down this spring. You see, a chambermaid has found a honeybee and she's going to join him in his private place.

The sun lamp was denied access by the persistence of thick gray clouds. He buttoned up as he made his way through the amusement park. Their smiles brightened significantly in direct proportion to his advance. He was a few paces from her when she ran up and hugged him. "Oh, Henry, I've missed you."

He matched her exuberant hug, and said, "It may not be much, but I think it's a start."

"Henry, I knew you'd find something."

As they sat, her sycamore spacing moved quickly to his hip and shoulder. "Tell me." He smiled broadly, and then teasing pushed through and winked at him. She cocked her head, puzzled. "What?"

He blew gently in her face. "Nothing."

She bounced in her seat excitedly. "Henry, tell me."

He blew again. "Tell you what?"

She pursed her lips, whipped her index finger up quickly, and pointed it at him. "You're getting into trouble mister."

The tease went lifeless now that he was looking deeply into her eyes. "Like I said it may not be much, but in the end when her clan humiliates her, she does something that I missed during the first read."

She beamed and put her arm through his. "Tell me." He grinned broadly, but held back, teasing was up for another round when he saw her excited state. She extinguished her excitation when she caught his mischievousness off the chain, again, and frowned. "Henry, you're twinkling and it's going to get you into trouble. Now tell me."

He blew again. "Tell you what?"

She jumped up, put her hands on her hips, and stomped her foot. "Henry, your life's headed in the wrong direction, now don't cross me."

"Damn, you have a temper."

"And I'll be more than happy to share it with you,"

and added, "now tell me before you get into trouble and things go very badly for you."

The giddy tease danced. "What sort of things?"

She crossed her arms and chuckled from the joy of their warm banter. "I don't know. I haven't gotten that far."

"Damn, you're so funny."

He stood when their campus gaze returned. The poet held her face, as tension culled the banter and teasing. "Gwendolyn, there's a happiness you've placed inside of me. It's spiritual not secular. That happiness can only suckle when mood's breasts are full. This is unmovable and I'll carry it all my life." She placed her hands on his wrists and listened to her poet. "Sometimes I wish I could lie in your fields and just listen to the wind and ask how does a woman transcend happiness into joy in a man's heart?"

He listened for that wind and continued. "Happiness, like faith, is trusted to be there always. It's a covenant. Right before she leaves, jaded and humiliated, and before she steps into the circle of her clan, she turns back because her faith compels her. She hasn't lost her faith. She doesn't just give up. She just can't touch her love yet but it's inside her, unmovable, like the happiness you placed inside of me."

He released her and placed his hands on her shoulders. "The author didn't believe in hopelessness either and I think that's why she had her turn to let the reader know that love never quits and will find a way." He was mindful of the shortened version of her name and the author's.

She hugged him. "Thank you Henry. I needed that hope."

When she released him, he kept staring into her eyes and cocking his head from one side to the other, but remained silent.

"Ok Henry I know you're trying to make me blush." He shook his head.

"What?"

He felt gravity pulling him in, she sensed it and moved closer. The poet recaptured her face. "Gwendolyn deep inside the core of a man's heart he has defined a woman with only one thought, well constructed and as familiar as his own name. He will carry it all his life and it will remain as incorruptible as scripture... My definition is the thought of you."

He released her and put his hands in his coat pockets. She put one hand in her pocket, the other in his and held his hand. They strolled through the dormant park with its summer amusements cocooned in colorful tarps while he held the single thought of the only woman he would ever love and she clutched a refreshed hope.

They found a bench by a lively ice skating rink and sat until an occasional annoying shiver turned to a persistent pest. They scanned the gray clouds for sun lamp redemption, but conceded to the stubborn pest, and gave up their bench and he drove her home.

They pulled up to her house and walked into the

saffron ring of her porch light. She reached for both his hands, and held them. "Henry, you've made me so happy today." She kissed the corner of his mouth, and slipped in.

She sat on the bottom step and listened as he left. She panned around the house and found it sleeping, and burst into tears. She leaned back against the wall, craned her head up to the ceiling, and whispered, "Henry, I can't go any farther. I've given you the kiss that says I love you so much. Please find me." She did as she had done so many times before. She craned her head up to the heavens and whispered, "Oh, God, please help him find a way, I love him so much."

He wiped his eyes on his coat sleeve as another spasm erupted, contorting his gut as he drove. His belly muscles burst into a fit of clonus tremors as he wailed from his bereft, berated, and beaten soul. "Oh, God, Gwendolyn how could you. I'll never understand the rich. I thought we had a wonderful day and you were my rich friend. I see now you're an emotional slummer. You are so cruel. I could understand if you kissed me hard and deep and started you're slumming. Or better yet, a friendly peck on the cheek, and a hug, which is what I expected, but the corner of the mouth. How could you? That's the kiss that speaks I love you so much."

He wiped his eyes again, and thought, that's it, I'm done. His anger flared as he thought, I'm finished with her. I'll meet her one last time, under our sycamore, and call her down. He fell stoic and hoped it was seated permanently and thought, I have enough now.

Her crying spasms ceased and she thought I'll fly tomorrow, but thought, oh no I can't tomorrow, I haven't had my good bye kiss yet. I'll have to register for school one last time. She looked up the staircase and whispered, "I love you Momma."

Dale sat in the front seat drumming his thumbs on the steering wheel while Henry sat in the back. He caught his son's eyes in the rearview mirror and craned his head around. "It's your turn for a life lesson." They both turned their gaze to Marilyn as she continued to talk with her mother on her mother's front porch.

"Ok, Son, explain to me how they could possibly have anything else to say. Shit, we've been here for nearly a damn week and all they've done is talk their mouths dry and swell their tongues." He turned to an interesting thought. "Perhaps I'm being a bit hasty. All that swelling might be good for the trip home."

Henry chuckled, then said, "Damn, Dad do you really think a woman's tongue swells for any length of time?"

"No, Son, it was just a pleasant thought."

A somber thought popped into his mind. "What about the girl?"

Henry sat up eye level with his father, and said confidently, "You know the rich do think differently and in a way I feel sorry for them. I think they've been conditioned all their lives to think of us as just playthings."

His father nodded. "I guess it's man to man from now on. I'm proud of you, Son. I know it was hard, but I think you're beginning to understand wisdom now that it has pierced your flesh." He paused for what he knew was to come, and said, "But you're still in love with her." Henry cast his eyes down, quickly. Dale put his hand on his shoulder. "I'm glad, Son," then turned back around and thought, you won't understand until you're crushed.

She found a window to climb out of while wandering through all those rooms. A massive hemorrhage displaced the sloshing fluids in the 20th year of her life.

Social services chased leads to find next of kin, but with Babbs gone they had little to work with. They found a half sister and a distant cousin, but neither came to the funeral. It seemed a genetic match was without standing with blood if gain was absent and a state funeral knows granite had no standing in budget.

Tate, Stacy and some staff stood in the state's Paupers cemetery staring at an acrylic plaque, while Barbie read a poem reconstructed from all the incoherencies sloshing in Amy Lloyd's last writings. The sparer smiled and read the dried stanza:

"Though the grove afar appears as one,
A tree stands alone.
Though branches intimate as the weft and warp,

Still, a tree stands alone.
Though what lies inside is all heartwood,
Remember always, never lonely was this tree alone.
Though now felled, wood... weep not,
For you hold the space of this tree alone."

Tears pooled but her smile was sturdy. The sparer took great comfort in knowing though lost in all those rooms and the point had been reached when high school Knobs could not be found, Amy Lloyd never felt alone because Knobs always held her down in verse.

The poet became the sparer to Barbie many times. It was he who gave her peace by deciphering most of Amy's incoherencies. She engaged him many times out on the edge, and he learned many intimacies about the two women, while she was impaled by truth about a poet.

An icy wind whipped up from the east as the mourners slowly disengaged from long hugs which forced them to draw their heavy coats tighter around their chilled torsos. Barbie slipped away from the group, stared out over the cemetery, and closed her eyes. Stacy came up quietly, slipped her hand in hers, closed her eyes, and joined her out on the edge.

Stacy was astonished as they both stood several paces from the edge. "My God, Barb, how long have you had that? It wasn't there last time we were here."

Barbie turned to her, still wearing her sturdy smile, and said, "Just now." Stacy cocked her head, perplexed but intrigued and then they both turned back to admire it.

When Stacy felt the winds in her mind pick up, she turned to Barbie, and said, "I'm must leave you now."

Barbie turned quickly. "No, stay."

"I can't," she said consumed.

"Why?"

Trembling, Stacy said, "I've been told to," and looked deeply into her eyes. "A gift is coming," and she released.

The sparer turned to the chasm and heard her gift say "Come, sit." Her heart swelled when she heard the sound of her voice. She walked under the large boughs of a tree alone on the edge of the great chasm that she and Stacy had been admiring.

She sat in its fatted grasses, nuzzled her cheek against its warm healthy bark and chuckled when the gift said, "I'm going to change your name."

Still chuckling she said, "To what?"

The gift remained silent until her chuckling settled to a sigh, and waited as instructed while joy filled the space under the tree alone.

"Angel."

Her eyes flew open as she stood overlooking the grounds of perpetual loss, then her gift whispered for the last time, "Now you know what to do." The sparer walked up to a novice widow, kneeling in a fresh mound of grief, sat, smiled warmly, and held out her hand.

She skipped across campus from the registrar's office

under gray skies to meet him under their sycamore. She was anxious, he hadn't called in days, then an abrupt text appeared without any rhythm to it, to meet. When the tree was in sight she beamed. Sycamore memories were flooding her mind. Her beam dimmed to a dismal basement light when she saw the field meat conversing with him. He snickered and hobbled off when he saw her coming.

She drove up fast with nostrils flaring and a red face. "What did he say?" Shocked by her aggression he attempted to put his hands on her shoulders to calm her. She drew back quickly, and said with venomous anger, "Don't touch me." He drew his hands back. Her face remained in flames, as she shook. "Tell me, damn it."

He stumbled over his words. He'd never seen her so consumed. After collecting himself, he felt his anger demand the podium. "I'm not obligated to tell you anything."

They locked themselves into an angry glare. He felt the gallery sympathy well up and he said softly, "Gwendolyn, he said something about you've never been over the top and thought it was weird. I don't care what he thinks because he doesn't. He's bred for collision."

She gritted her teeth as tears rolled down her cheeks. "Do you know how humiliating this is?" She felt the book spilling out of her heart and emptying her spirit.

She turned briskly and walked away. He shouted. "Wait."

She stopped, and said with her back to him, "Henry,

you know I'm supposed to turn around."

His jaw dropped from his pale face. "The whole time you've thought your life has paralleled the book?"

She turned with tears streaming. "You just haven't figured it out." She paused while the book closed her life. "Henry, I so hoped you would. I feel so far away and now it's too late." The corners of her mouth turned down as she closed the book. "Good bye Henry."

She turned and walked briskly towards disintegration.

He shouted again. "Gwendolyn, I won't quit. I promise. I'll find a way."

She turned back. "You're all I have Henry."

Volleys of spasms erupted in his diaphragm as he drove home. It was just a book he thought, a minor read. Why is she so obsessed? Why is this so upsetting to her and now to me? I feel something in my pit now and it's percolating.

He parked, walked across his front yard that had 4 inches of new snow, and thought, she doesn't remotely parallel this book. She has more love...

He stopped himself cold. He climbed the front steps slowly, dropped his backpack on the porch, fell to his knees, and burst into tears.

He knew at that moment Gwendolyn Dupree was the book. She knew it better than he did. She didn't need to read it. She had been the book all her life. As he continued to sob he realized that she was losing her identity inside the glow of a woman and it had nothing to do with love. She was fading away and loosing faith in who she was and now Gwendolyn Dupree held only pieces of herself and those pieces disintegrated a little each day. Even with the pieces that remained, she was unsure of who she was.

This and that had robbed her of her birthright of identity. There was nothing he could do, because faith and love, like the glow of a woman's beauty, were immovable creations of God and you can't beat God.

He picked himself and his backpack up and went upstairs to his room. He tossed his pack, found the book, and headed out the door. He met his father at the bottom step of the porch. Dale surprised that his son didn't speak said, "What's wrong?" He ignored him and continued to walk across the yard. He chased after him and grabbed his arm.

He jerked it away, and said in a choked voice, "Leave me alone."

He knew, and said in a calm voice, "Son I'll leave you alone, just tell me where you're going."

He cleared his throat. "To the lake."

Dale grimaced, held out his keys, and said nervously, "Please take my car, yours won't make it. Please, Son, it'll worry me."

He turned but didn't make eye contact. "Thanks Dad."

Dale nodded. "Take your time." He paused as the storm of life pulled his son apart, and ran tears down his own cheeks. He raised his voice. "This is loneliness Son, because something inside will be cut off and remain stranded. It will stay alive the rest of your life and always call out to you."

He paused as the winds whipped. "You'll never be able to reach it. I think you'll realize that some experiences gain nothing. And that, in and of itself, is an experience. This wasn't meant to make you wiser because there's no such thing as wisdom. Only a collection of experiences to benefit from and it takes being crushed to realize this and move into the adult world as an experienced man." As the stormed raged, he shouted. "Write her, Son."

He watched as he drove off, went inside and took an immediate right to the living room, reached into the cabinet and grabbed a bottle of whisky and wiped his eyes on the cuffs of his winter shirt. He sat at the kitchen table, poured a glass full, and sipped. He sat for several minutes sipping when the front door opened. He heard his wife call out to her son. He didn't say anything.

She was startled when she saw her husband in the kitchen. When she saw the liquor, she frowned, and said in a stern voice, "What on earth are you doing and where is Henry?" He didn't say anything. Anxiety squeezed her tight in its fist convincing her of the worst. A talent anxiety wields proudly against all mothers.

Plangent were the sounds from her grieved womb. "Where is my baby?"

He sniffed, cleared his throat, and placated her stricken womb. "At the lake."

"Why is he at the lake?"

"She's crushing him."

Plangent was sound of her purse as it hit the floor and the psalm sung from her broken heart. She burst into tears, sat on the floor, and laid her head in her husband's lap.

As she sat on her dorm bed and waited for Molly, she thought I must have my good-bye kiss before I go. She stood when she heard her cackling in the hall. When Molly entered, she asked if she would drive her to Henry's house. Molly put her arm around her and they left.

They heard a soft knock at the door. Marilyn stood quickly and scanned for a tissue. He put his hand up in a calming gesture. "I've got this." As he stood, he searched the glow around his wife's crushed face, and thought, truly the cord stretches to the grave.

He opened the door and prayed it wasn't a solicitor; patience was at a premium right now. He'd never met her, but knew it was her by her deep blue eyes and forced a smile. Dale never hated anyone until today, but thanked her in his mind for helping his son. He left her at the door for a moment, and came back with directions to the cabin, forced another smile, and closed the door. He headed back to the kitchen feeling the sting of assumption.

It was early afternoon, cold and cloudy with no hope of

lamp redemption when they found his father's car in front of cabin number 5. She hugged Molly and thanked her. She knocked softly which startled him. He jumped up, wiped his eyes, and opened the door. Molly drove off, while they stared at one another. "Gwendolyn, I'm so sorry."

"It's ok Henry. It just wasn't meant to be." She came in, sat on the bottom bunk, and thumbed through the buildings on her phone. He sat at the table and hung his head. When she finished, she doubled checked her purse for her poem that was already stamped and addressed to him.

While she contemplated her good-bye kiss, he looked up. "I'm so sorry. I thought I could do it."

She turned the corners of her mouth down. "It just wasn't meant to be."

He stood, left the book on the table, and headed towards the door. She thought I'll get my good-bye kiss at the train station. As he opened the door she checked the train schedule. He stood on the small porch and craned his head up to the sky while she was standing in the threshold, scrolling. He squinted at the clouds breaking for redemption, and said, "Well, at least we'll have blue..."

The wind in the reeds blew in. The young poet plucked what was rooted and picked up the young man sitting in the dimly lit corridor. The young man looked up towards his mind and nodded to the poet. The young man took what the poet handed to him, and made his way briskly to his heart and gathered all things known about his beloved Gwendolyn, except hope, which he purposely left behind.

He rushed to his mind and delivered everything known and watched as it turned everything over and over, analyzing. The mind uses truth as a point of reference but the discovery that the poet plucked had taught him to extract the truth immediately, before it had a chance to cloud it with torrents of idle speculation.

He returned to his heart, reinstalled all of it, dove into the deep pool of wistfulness, and swam down a fathom. He stood on the sandy bottom between the gerbil wheel and ladder rungs, found hope, grabbed it by the throat, and swam back up.

He dragged it to the warmest blood of all, core blood. He found a stream and drowned it. He watched as it kicked weakly, and then it went lifeless. The stream became angry and began to boil and churn violently. This blood hates hopelessness as if it were Satan. It doesn't stop for anything when it's hungry and wants to ravish. It doesn't understand no, nor does it tolerate it. This blood takes what it wants, because it's the warmest blood of all, core blood, and core blood is passion.

He turned slowly, and his lip quivered like a dog about to bite. She became wide-eyed and pale, as he gritted his teeth, flared his nostrils, and narrowed his eyes. His chest heaved like a boxer after many bouts. He shoved her hard. Her phone flew across the room, hit the wall under the bottom bunk, and landed on the bed.

She tumbled, but sprang up quickly and slowly

backed away, while groping blindly for the edge of the table. He slammed the door, rattling the window, and it sounded like the aftershock of a huge lightening strike. He stood there red faced and chest heaving. He waited, because this passion was at its critical level and its boiler was well past tolerance. It needed saddling by love.

He waited, and felt love slip it on, foot the stirrups, and when he heard the warm creaking rub of leather, he felt love deep inside him. The pressure was now well below critical. Passion was balanced by love.

He stepped closer, and said through gritted teeth, "I am blue. I've worked hard and never quit, so it will be me. Like love, faith, and the glow of a woman, I am a creation of God and just as strong." He took another step, and said, "I have worked hard to have you and I won't be denied, because I am blue."

She trembled. "Henry, please don't hurt me."

He grabbed her roughly and urban press was back. He pulled hair and slammed her chin into his chest. She was flaccid in his arms with bent knees. He closed his eyes when her panting ventilated in his sinuses. The mint disseminated into his tissues and was immediately separated by his receptors.

His brain received a firestorm of signals and his mind was a battlefield of sensation of his Gwendolyn. Volleys of all the memories, images, scents, and sensation raged. He opened his eyes and relaxed which eased her panting. Gravity pulled him in and he followed the anatomy of her lips with his nose as before. He traveled to her chin. He craned her head and she took the cue to strain. He ran her jaw line with his nose, but when he came to her hinge, he didn't hesitate or flinch, no apology.

Passion took what it wanted and he nuzzled her ear lobe and whispered, "Mine," and began kissing her neck.

She whispered in a victim's revived raspy voice, "Please empty me."

He did what he had longed to do the first time he saw her deep blue eyes. He kissed the corner of her mouth, and the other. Her panting ceased as the kissing began. The sycamore was evergreen and he a mountaintop above.

He kissed her mouth lightly but maintained his grip.

"I'm going to kiss you deep, and when I do little blue will guide me across your glow of beauty and I will pick you up. But before my journey begins, I'm going to reveal your identity."

She tensed up and her pupils constricted. She flared her nostrils. "Let me go. This or that is my identity."

He shook his head, and said stoically, "No, no, your glow is this or that, not you" She narrowed her eyes as a sign of credibility.

The stoic smiled, clutching his insight. "I can identify you and I will." She flared and constricted in contempt again and squirmed. The stoic maintained his solid lock, and said while he kissing her face, "I know you don't like green. I know you count all the frogs in the terrarium every Thursday and are sad when some come up missing. I know you have a favorite and he has an odd spot on his head. I know you're sentimental about animals and dissection upsets you. I know you wrinkle your nose right before a test when you're not confident."

He paused, confident with what the poet had plucked. "I know all your fidgets." He kissed her lips lightly, but maintained his grip on his agitated filly, and said stone cold, "And especially the fidget when it's not warm."

Her eyes widened and her pupils dilated. The stoic smiled when he saw the dilatation. "And I know why the pupils in your beautiful fields of lavender and blue iris dilate whenever I'm around." She blushed as he continued. "You think you appoint your identity." He cocked his head, kissed her blushing face all over several times, and said, "You don't." She furrowed her brow, puzzled, and he said, "Your personality is chosen by you, but not your identity." He kissed her mouth again.

"Your identity is given to you by the ones who love you." He kissed her flushed cheek, and said, "The ones who love you know what colors you like. The ones who love you know you get upset when frogs are missing. The ones who love you ask every one in the lab to please leave the spotted one alone because the ones who love you don't want you upset. You see the ones who love you identify everything there is about you," he paused, nuzzled her lips with his nose, and said, "and place all of it in their heart and love everything about you."

Her pupils were fully dilated and tears were soaking her hairline. He released her, and said somberly, "I've seen those blue rings since August and never thought they were for me." The poet held her face, and said, "Beauty is a beast when the one that loves her foolishly believes in the glow of a woman."

Tears pooled in the poet's eyes as he released her face and said, "I know who you are." As tears ran their rivers down his cheeks, he said, "You are the love of my life." He held her face again as he had done many times, and said, "I love you Gwen and I'll never let you go." He kissed her hard and deep, and traveled across the glow of Gwen Dupree's soul and picked her up.

When he released her, she burst into tears, and said through crying spasms, "Henry, you've found me. All my life I just wanted to be Gwen, the girl next door." Her prince slew the dragon. "Henry you've beaten the book."

"That's a book like no other. I just fell in love with a home town girl." He searched her face, intently as he had done many times in lab. She for the first time stroked his cheek, deliberately, unapologetically, and with great joy, and said, "What, Henry?"

"When Gwen turned the protagonist around and she gazed upon the world one last time, Gwen was telling us that the glow of a woman has nothing to do with beauty, but the spirit of a woman. That's her glow. When the protagonist smiles as she turns to her clan, she realizes all women are beautiful and all have a beautiful spirit."

She kissed the corner of his mouth. "I want to listen to your kiln." He wrapped his arms around her, and she said, "No, not like that." She took off his coat, unbuttoned his shirt, and pressed her cheek to his chest. "Henry all my life I've been this or that," she looked up to her prince, "and I've felt like I've been fading away a little every day." Remnants of her disintegration briefly choked her thoughts. "Henry you don't know how bad I wanted to tell you who I am..."

He cut her off, pressed his fingertips to her lips, and said, "Gwen, shh, you couldn't. If you did that, it would just be you reaching back and grabbing a fabricated identity to hand to me, and then I would to hand it back to you. I had to discover you. How else would you truly believe that I know who you are?"

Her prince handed her the dragon's heart. "No more fading, no more disintegrating, no madness. You're home."

She searched his eyes, and removed his shirt, kissed his chest, and nuzzled his kiln. "What's it saying now?"

"What it has been saying since August. I love you." She kissed him deep and undressed him. He lay on the bottom bunk and watched her undress. She came to him, and kissed him hard and deep. When they engaged, he began to move his hips. She panicked, and said, "Henry please stop."

Startled, he said, "Oh, God, Gwen do you want me to just lie next to you?"

"No, no, please let's just be still. Please no movement."

The poet cocked his head, blew gently, and kissed her

face all over, while saying, "When both become forever still, don't believe in love's last light." He kissed her hard and deep, pulled off, and with both mouths soaked said, "Because after ever is their love fulfilled." He kissed her deep several times, and said, "You are the love of my life and I will never let you go." He repeated it several times while kissing her deep and hard.

Her lower back arched, her eyes flew open wide, and she shouted, "Henry something's pushing, and I don't know what it is, and I can't stop it." Her eyes rolled back, she took a deep breath and shouted, "Oh, God, Henry I love you so much," and shivered. When she opened her eyes she felt him stiffen and rigor violently. She smiled and caressed his face when she felt his warmth.

As he remained on his elbows and their positions unchanged she ran her fingers through his hair. She held his face, and poured into his eyes. "I love you so much. My beautiful poet of word and lightness of soul. You would still truly fly, even if you were mute and made of lead. Some just have that gift from life, an easy stroke. Life, Henry, even a poet doesn't know, and after that who knows?"

Though her prince slew the dragon, she was unaware the shrike was circling above and would change her black dress.

She said somberly, "Henry, most of the world can't fly. We just have the one world and leave prints."

As they dressed, she found her phone. She took the

phone and her poem, buried it in the bottom of her purse, and thought, I'll burn you later and buy a new one of you. She dropped her purse on the table, and groomed her hair with her fingers. The poet eyes twinkled as he took note of the whole procedure, though she was unaware. When she looked up and caught his eye, she said puzzled, "What?"

"You forgot to hold your head back and shake." He ran his fingers through her hair, pulled it all back with one hand, and held it in place like a clip. "You always shake before you groom." He released her and held her face. "I know every detail about you." He put his arm around her and she grabbed her purse as they left.

Gwen realized at that moment when she tumbled over the top for the first time with the only man she would ever love that she had just crossed over the threshold to experience. She knew that it was now time to shed the whiny, self absorbed, adolescent girl. She knew that door was now permanently walled off by an experienced woman, who may or may not possess her true love, and her planned suicide of the last few years a mere nightmare now that death was paid its ransom by the only man she would ever love.

She had no doubt that Henry loved her, but the woman inside of her also had no doubt that he would always view love poetically, which could propagate reams without a single devotion and she needed to know how her promise, which she was about to give would ring with this poet.

She stopped at the door, looked back at the table, and

thought for a moment. "Henry, wait." She stared into his eyes with deep concern.

He matched her concern. "What's wrong?"

She went back to the table and turned a chair around. "We need to have a throw down."

"What the hell is a throw down?"

She took him by the hand. "Please sit."

He shook his head, and sat. "Damn, you're funny."

She faced him and threw her purse on the floor. "A throw down is when you find a private place and sit a man down." She paused as anxiety griped her tight in its fist.

He knew that anxiety well, which he learned from his first love, his mother. He culled all his playfulness and said in a soft reverent tone, "Gwen, what's wrong?"

Her tears dripped. "Henry, you're the only man I'll ever love and I know the goose will be turning back his path soon and I need to know something."

She lamented over their long semester together. She crossed her arms and narrowed her eyes as the woman inside of her felt irritable and a little hostile towards him. "Are we an item?" The woman inside, searched his face, and said, "For a while anyway?"

Anxious by her behavior, he reassured. "Why of course."

She did something very cold. Something he'd never seen her do before. She unconsciously gave him that polite smile, stabbing him through the heart. She rubbed her index finger under her nose quickly, sniffed, and said cold polite, "Thank you."

At that moment it was as if she was a POW and he was her captor and he was sitting at his desk. Pathos began to burn in his pit, and, 'for a while,' rang in his mind. He thought, is humiliation at the core of love? She's at my desk humiliated, asking to share rations.

He felt as if they were the only survivors of a prison camp from a great war, and all she wanted was to share until one eventually perished, or the war was over. The captor watched as his POW knelt down and began to pick up the meager rations he had thrown off his desk. He watched her run her finger under her nose again and curl her hair around her ear.

He thought, why am I hurting her? He felt they were on common ground now and the horrors of war were coming to an end. The captor felt a deep pity for all the humiliation he ran her through. He was only doing his job and now it was coming to an end.

He felt he was as much a victim of this war as she, and like the end of all wars, all parties remained bewildered by their brutality. On common ground now, he wanted to pick her up, shake her hand, and walk through the prison gate, and part, not friends, that would be asking far too much, but merely two souls trapped by forces neither understood and agree to leave the camp as a bygone, a memorial. He wanted to go home as much as she, never meaning to hurt or humiliate. It was just his job. It was like they were from completely different walks of life, and if it wasn't for this great war, they would have never met, and he now felt a deep respect for the one he had been tormenting for so long.

She picked up her purse and was about to get up. He reached over, and put his hand on her wrist.

The POW looked up, gave her captor another polite smile, and he said, "My throw down now."

Puzzled, she stood. He stood, took her purse, tossed it on the floor, sat his prisoner down, and towered over her.

He didn't say anything as his eyes glassed and tears pooled. The prisoner sat submissively, with her hands in her lap, spinning her promise ring, while waiting for instructions. She studied his tears and now that they were on common ground, she matched her captor. These were cool tears absent of emotion, no frowning, no spasm; they were stoic, because both were now on common ground, coolly asking one another, what next now that this great war was over.

The aura disappeared, causing the crucible to fracture and turn cold. The amalgamated lavas were rapidly cooling and setting the foundations meant for a lifetime. The captor's tears began to spill over and the prisoner matched again. "Gwen Dupree will you?"

The captor just released his prisoner to her husband.

She burst into tears, jumped up, clung to him, and said, "Yes, yes." He rocked his wife until her spasms settled.

She looked up with her wet face, took off her promise ring, handed it to him, and said, "I've had this ring since I was thirteen, and that's when I made a promise to myself." She paused, to allow joy to fill the space under their sycamore. "As I give you this ring." She paused again, and said with her face set sternly, "Henry, with this ring I give you the promise of a woman, my loyalty. I will always love you and never leave you and nothing will ever get in the way. I give it unconditionally and with great joy."

He kissed her deep. "Always."

Her tone became somber as before when she spoke of him as a poet. "Poet, come home occasionally. I know your flights will be long."

He put his hands on her shoulders as reassurance. "Gwen, it doesn't work like that. Stuff just pops into my head and I write it down that's all." He kissed her cheek, and said with confidence, "I'm not going anywhere."

She smiled wryly. "You are gone everywhere poet. You just don't know it." She thought, love and devotion but a stanza and a wife but the mistress. Somehow, I feel now that I've stepped with this poet all semester, my promise ring will be handed to her, and now I know.

"Henry even when you look at me sometimes you fly off to wander the world of wonder and it all starts with a twinkle," she thought, this young girl was too busy with love and a promise to notice, "and it got me into trouble once and I feel it will again." She kissed the corner of his mouth. "You have both now, poet, love's flesh and you've always had its heart, but only one kiln, which we both will compete for."

The poet shook his head patronizingly, squeezed her shoulders. "Gwen, poetry's bullshit, it's just a bunch of words." He squeezed a little harder to emphasize his point. "This is all I want." He gave her a reassuring smile and inspected the ring. He read the inscription inside the band, and said with surprise, "Wow this is old." He squinted and read the inscription out loud. "Wake to me."

She kissed his cheek, and said as his eyes twinkled from the inscription, "I want to tell you about a promise."

She told a story when she was thirteen. She and her mother were in an antique store when she came across a couple dozen rings in a glass case that had a small label titled promise rings fixed to the glass. She asked her mother what it meant.

"Sweetie, those are old promise rings. I haven't thought about those in years." Her daughter stared puzzled.

"They're rings given to young girls, like you, as a symbol. It's a promise to always love them, but they're both too young to hold such a commitment."

Her daughter reached for a stray in the upper left corner of the group which appeared as if it were trying to flee and search for its promise. Her mother took the gold band with its etched stars all around, read the inscription, and said, "This one was given the year I was born." She chuckled, then said, "Now that was a time when bell bottom jeans were king, hot pants were queen, and everybody was smoking something." She rolled her eyes. "God, the clothes were hideous."

Her daughter looked at her intently. "Mom, do you think they're still in love?"

"Sweetie, that's called a rhetorical question. You're rummaging through a graveyard. They were just like you at thirteen and felt love emerging, but too young." She held her daughter's chin. "Sweetie, they were too young to date and explore one another."

"At thirteen all they can do is sit at the end of her porch, sneak kisses..." Her daughter shot her eyes down quickly and blushed. Her mother punctuated her point. "See, too young. All they can do is kiss, tell each other how much they love the other, and make unrealistic plans to meet at the top of her street and elope when they're old enough," she felt somewhat rueful, "but life gets in the way between thirteen and twenty one."

Her daughter took the gold band. "I think they're still in love, but just not together anymore."

"They're middle aged and probably have grandchildren by now." She took the ring, back, ran her finger across the stars. "You're too young to understand, but even if they were the love of other's life, they've already forgotten each other by now."

He daughter set her chin like stone and stated unequivocally. "No, Mother. They're still in love. They just can't get to each other, because things have gotten in the way and they're always thinking about the other."

"Such faith in love." She touched each star as if conducting a head count. "Do you know what the stars mean?"

The fresh faced adolescent said with unwavering confidence, "Stars mean forever, and stars on a ring are a promise to love forever."

She gave the ring back, and said, "But a ring of stars is faith to love beyond forever."

She searched his face and said with an unwavering stern tone in her voice, "Beyond forever Henry." She grabbed his chin firmly and said stone cold with an expression that he'd never seen before. He listened, intently, while his pen flowed.

"I want you to understand our vow Henry that we will love each other beyond forever, a promise that will ring forever, no one else, ever. And when we pass, it will be our faith in our promise that will take us beyond forever."

He kissed her, and repeated their vow. As ink flowed, he said, "All those promises in the graveyard, do you think they are being kept in the heart?"

She sighed, and gestured to him and the ring. "I don't know. I just know this one and that one is."

She grabbed her purse and they headed to the car. He opened the car door for his wife. She tossed her purse on the front seat and turned to embrace her husband. The experienced woman felt the wind pick up in her mind and was impaled through her chest by the shrike's thorn and as she dangled, he perched and waited for truth.

She obliged as she thought, I'm emptied for more, but what's in the next experience? I fear will always be less. All this woman naively thought about was her world of thirteen. My wide road of innocence has ended in a narrow footpath of experience where my foot will certainly be dashed. And though I'm free from the black dress, I now wear the one for a mistress that the poet handed me.

Irony, you've enclosed me in a case of stubborn rings who only knew love through the poetry of a wide road. The shrike gathered the wind under its wings and was gone.

He looked over the bygone camp for a moment and walked around to the driver's side. The aura that surrounded them as they fell in love was gone and the young romantic poet believed that their journey was complete and they possessed love's spirit and that spirit was an eternal sacrament. When they both pass that spirit will gather their spirits and possess them beyond forever. He gazed up at the icy blue sky, and thought, so blue, while his pen bled reams.

THREE

She placed the book on the coffee table and stared at the black windows.

The one behind her drove up quickly and plopped down. "What cha thinking Mrs. Posey?"

She flared her nostrils slightly, but too tired to fight and was quiet.

The one behind her felt especially provocative at the moment. "I told you love always endures to the end and wins. Now you better start practicing writing your new name."

She ignored her, laid her head on a couch cushion, and fell asleep.

She woke to a sunny room. She jumped up quickly, because she knew she overslept and Charles had probably left several texts. She grabbed her phone and saw she was late, but no text, which surprised her because the grunt's never late. She texted she would be ready in an hour and received an immediate response, and thought well that's more like it.

She was waiting on the curb when he pulled up. As he got out to open her door, they exchanged strained smiles, and he noticed she hadn't polished. The ride was quiet and tense. He would glance over on occasion and she knew he was following up.

When they arrived at the office, she put her purse in the bottom drawer as she always did to convince herself it was business as usual. She pulled out her manicure bag and frowned. As he pulled up a chair as he always did, she said, "See? Polishing."

He glared. "Did you read the book?"

The teakettle exploded. She stood quickly which caused the chair to slam against the repaired bruise. She glared back; open palmed the desk, which caused her last bracelet to break into pieces. "Goddamn it. I'm not in love with him."

"All I asked is if you had read it."

He thought bullshit you've been madly in love since you stopped polishing and I'll bet even before then.

She broke from the hostility, walked briskly to the window, and bit her nails. He watched the biting and thought, I'll be goddamned you fell in love the minute you laid eyes on him. Oh, buddy. I don't know what I can do. Even if I brought you here and locked you two in, it wouldn't do any good. She has to want to see you, but I don't know how to help you or her.

He strained his thoughts, come on grunt, military time. You have the objective now I want the plan. He thought about the wisdom of Colonel Sky. How do you take their spirit and kill their will. What's their life about? What's the only thing they care about, then have them watch you take it away. He glanced furtively around her desk while searching his mind for answers. He noticed the shambles her desk was in, her last broken bracelet, the ledger.

He smiled and thought move out. He cleared his throat. "Winnie, please sit down. There's something you need to know." She turned and furrowed her brow suspiciously. He waved his hand gently. "No, it's not about him." She was hesitant, and he said firmly, "Please sit." She kept her suspicion and sat. He put his hands out. "Please, hold my hands."

She cocked her head, and said with steadfast suspicion, "What's this all about?"

"Please."

She slipped hers in, and he said, "I want to tell you something, but I want you to listen and not go off." She narrowed her eyes, and he said, "I think you ought to see him."

She resisted and pulled against him. "I thought we were best friends."

He squeezed her hands as she tried to escape, and said quickly, "Winnie, you're hurting the business."

She turned pale. "Never."

When she scooted closer to give reassurance, he released her. "When was the last time you balanced the books?"

"I'll do it now."

"Before or after you polish, which you said you would do yesterday." He sighed like a fatigued, but unwavering father with a deep love for his daughter. "Winnie, I think you need to see him one last time, straighten everything out, and get back to work."
She jumped up and headed back to the window.

"The girls and I depend on you. Don't let us down." She pressed her hands to the glass, while he thought; come on Winnie the business is your weakness. Come on you can do it. Aniel, buddy, I gave it my best shot. I don't know. God, she's stubborn.

As he observed her demure frame he was struck as to why she resisted loving him. He thought, two people can know and work together for many years and somehow can only know so much about the other until a third walks in. I always assumed we'd grow old together and take care of each other. He paused in his thoughts, and thought, she has always kept her back to the wall when it comes to men.

He thought, somberly about the age disparity between the two of them, and concluded, but she still has juices flowing; it just took the right man. He cleared his throat. "I know you're ashamed of your past." Her diaphragm tightened as she covered her mouth quickly with her hand. He continued. "We all carry shame and if we all throw it in a barrel, it all looks the same." He went very quiet for a moment. "When we were in deep desert we captured a group of raggedy men." He paused to clear his throat. "We tortured them." The thought of violence visibly tensed her up as if to brace for another Louisiana blow.

"Torture is part of war, but what shamed me..." He paused as if to allow her to brace again. "I enjoyed it." He paused longer, to allow her frame to settle, and offered wisdom given by loving father. "All you did was scratch out a living on your back, so you wouldn't starve. Where's the shame in that?"

She flicked a tear, pressed her hands to the glass, and started to speak. She stopped abruptly when the image of the Irishman cleaving the menu flooded her mind. The winds of next time began to pick up, pushing the response, "Charles, would you please take me home?"

There was a soft knock at the door which startled her, though she had buzzed him in. She was in the same blue dress, fully polished, and felt beautiful. Her hand shook as she turned the knob. She crouched and opened it enough for just a peek. Her face was greeted with a forest of white carnations. Her eyes traveled up to his face, and she captured the light in his eyes. She murmured, "Oh, God, Aniel."

His smile grew rapidly, then he said, "Gwen, I've missed you." He looked at the narrow opening. "I'm a thin man, but I think I'll need more than a mail slot to pass through."

She chuckled, then covered her mouth, briefly, and said, "I'm so sorry. Please come in."

He handed her the bouquet, she put her nose to it and then placed it on her computer desk. She gazed into his eyes and felt the winds of next time blowing her back towards the post behind the desk that separated the kitchen and the dining room. She bumped it softly like a yacht's rub rail against its piling. After the passing of wind and wave she slipped back into still, steady, waters and was contemplative. He chuckled when she appeared in deep thought, then said, "Gwen you're scripting. Just say what you feel."

She looked up, and he poured into her eyes, and said, "So blue."

She blushed and put her hands up in a calming gesture. "We have to talk."

He looked around the room and noticed a pearl white modern gas log fireplace, a white couch and chairs, even a white rug under a white coffee table. He gazed upon the white carnations she hadn't noticed, and said in a soft voice, "Bride's white, the sacred white, a gift from heaven that only women understand."

Her eyes widened slightly when she saw the flowers. She picked them up and caressed them. "How did you know?"

"A patriot who is in love with his country and loves you very much." He turned to the flowers. "The white carnation isn't a stand alone," he cocked his head, "Is it? The florist uses her as a highlight or to enhance the local color of the arrangement, but would never pick her as the centerpiece. She is merely meant to fill a gap or perhaps... to fill an empty space."

He watched her tears pool, and said, "Do you know what she symbolizes?"

She turned down the corners of her mouth slightly. Her diaphragm gave a quick spasm. "Love."

"Love is colorless and her only gift is capacity. The rose is beautiful, but pompous. The iris is engaging, but bends to the weight of conceit, but the white carnation stands alone and waits to be picked to fill the needs of the arrangement, the arrangement in all of us."

He felt the captor in him while watching her tears run their rivers. The POW wanted to go home to her husband. Her captor gazed deeply into his prisoner's eyes, and returned her to her husband. "Do you want blue?"

She cried, and crushed the bouquet against her chest. "Aniel, please. I'm not the one. There is no blue. It doesn't exist. It's just imagination."

The stoic, said, "I didn't ask if it was real or imaginary. Do you want it?"

"Please, it's just fantasy. That's what writers do. They live in a world of fantasy and bring wonderful stories to the weary working world to enjoy and give us a brief distraction from our tedious day that's all. You're just a vendor in the market."

He stepped towards her and she bumped her piling again. He said, in the same soft voice when they were in the hotel room, "Gwen, am I frightening you?"

Tears streamed as she said, "Please don't call my name like that." He came up, further crushing the flowers between them, held her face, and gazed deeply into her eyes. With her pupils fully dilated and her face flushed, she said as her diaphragm fell into full spasm, "Aniel, I beg you. Please don't kiss me. I get so dizzy."

Tears pooled in the poet's eyes. "I love you, Gwen."

He kissed her hard and deep. She dropped the carnations which piled like snow around their feet and wrapped her arms around him.

The one behind her came up from behind, rested her chin on her shoulder, and whispered, softly, "He wasn't meant to fill your empty spaces. I am. And you didn't awaken me, he did."

She thought yes he woke you.

The one behind said, "I know your secret. It was you who opened my door and let him in."

Gwen thought yes, I fell in love with him the first time I captured the light in his eyes and now I'm frightened because I have abandoned love long ago and put you away like winter bedding. Love is just for a select few. It chooses who it graces. I wasn't meant to be one and I understand. It's not an indictment or judgment. Some of us were meant to spend our lives in boxes. One that we adorn with a few chosen comforts and let our lives slow down and become as still as the bayou. But now that I have the light in his eyes, I don't fit in my box anymore. And because I've never used you, I'm inadequate now that it has come along, and I feel it's cruel that it waited this late. And now that I don't know what to do, I'm scared it'll become impatient and abandon me.

The one behind her chuckled lightly, then said, "Silly schoolgirl. Love is the most patient in all creation and will never abandon you. Look, there is love in front of you. There is love piled at your feet like snow. There is love far above us all and I'm behind you." The one behind her wrapped her arms around her. "Gwendolyn I've neither left you nor have I been asleep. You've turned your back on something that has been missing you for years, but has never left, and never will because it was given at your birth." She paused, and pressed her, tighter. "Do you feel that?"

She thought, my faith.

"Yes, your faith in yourself has never abandoned you and never will. So, rekindle your self esteem and be the woman of standing you've always been. Gwendolyn, all your adult life you've hesitated when next time blew in. Don't let the bayou freeze you this time. Free yourself from it. Now step the door is open. And remember always love yourself. You have to love yourself before you can love another. Love of yourself is the essential element needed to love another." The one behind her added with the scathing rebuke of a mother, "Never let me hear you talk of yourself as trash ever again... birthmark, pedestrian girl next door, pishposh."

She thought sternly, oh next time, this time and turned to the one behind her, and thought, why did you push me from behind last summer when I saw his name on the schedule?

"Because I was pushed. Do you remember that odd little woman that sat by you in the park before he arrived, and said, 'Hold my hand'."

Gwen thought as the memory unfolded in her mind, I remember. She flashed in my mind when you pushed me, and I thought her smile was like that of a mother's and I knew I could trust her.

She felt warmth in her chest, as she let the one behind her in, and now she and her heart were fully integrated sharing the essential element.

He continued to hold her face. "Gwen, I will always love you and never leave you."

Her tears picked up, and she said through crying spasm, "Oh, please let this time be."

He unzipped her dress and she raised her arms. He took the dress, looked it over, and gazed into her eyes. He wadded it up and hurled it across the room. She watched as it streaked across like a meteor and hit the window. When the zipper hit the pane it sounded like the last drop of rain from the ending storm in her bayou. He picked her up and she nuzzled her cheek against his shoulder. He came around the couch, pushed the coffee table back with his foot, and laid her down gently.

He kissed her cheek, and repeated, "Gwen, I will always love you and never leave you." He kissed her hard and deep several times.

Her eyes widened fully as her lower back came to a full arch. She panicked and shouted. "I'm so sorry, but it's stronger than me. It's pushing me out of the way. Forgive me." She closed her eyes and murmured in a low husky voice "Oh, God."

Her eyes remained closed as she tried to hide from her shame, then she flushed and was set ablaze. This heat came from deep inside, something she'd never experienced before. She felt the winds of next time blow through like an unforgiving storm. All she could do was watch as next time routed shame out of existence and heated her chest as if it were a kiln and her heart's edges were now softening and preparing for transfer. She glanced around her mind to see what possible damage the storm might have done to the past of her frozen peace but only saw all her burning buds abloom in mid spring and ready to fruit her future in forever summer.

The pedestrian girl had unmitigated confirmation that the only man she had ever climaxed with was in love with her and she was about to be free from the shrike, by a more potent and inescapable opponent, the storm of life.

She felt a slight movement as if she were lying in a small boat in a tiny cove and a powerboat had just roared passed in the main channel, releasing its potent wake, which charged across the wide channel. It broke up into several platoons of smaller waves as it drove into the isolated cove towards her small boat. But the distance, all too punishing, could only muster a few soft laps from the diminished platoons as they tried to elicit a response from the placid hull.

Her eyes flew open when she felt him rigor. He rose up and brought her with him. As he sat on his heels she locked her ankles, scissoring his waist with her legs. As she observed the light in his eyes dance, she said, "I'll never let you go."

She leaned back with one hand behind his neck, while her ankles remained locked. She caressed his face with her free hand, and said in a soft voice, "You offered me tenderness. I found that illicit, and a link broke. And as you kissed me I said this is illicit, another link broke. You laid me down and said I love you. Now all my illicit responses are in pieces."

She put both her hands behind his neck and kissed his him deep several times. The woman with standing gave her husband a smile that belonged only to him. "If the love in your heart ever wanted another, I will always love you Aniel Posey."

She paused while observing the light in his eyes. "You have a flicker in your eyes, and I think it's going to get me into trouble."

The poet held her face with both hands and tenderly

kissed the corner of her mouth and thought, though the goose migrates to another, its promise does not, but my mind is teeming once again and you, my apology, bear my pen, and I pray that it will only leave when I and my works are but corpus this time.

She laid her head on his shoulder, sighed, and nuzzled his neck with her nose. He turned his gaze slightly upward, towards the ceiling, and thought, Silvia Dupree you are wise indeed. I have my beloved's image and that's a bargain with contentment I will not turn down.

An odd little woman with hazel eyes stood by a malfunctioning lamppost across the street and gazed up to Gwen's window. She smiled and craned her head up to the heavens, towards a field of resplendent solitary stars, and whispered, "Sleep mistress. All are at peace now. Our poet has found his pen."

Epilogue

A wise woman once said we don't need to seek out every truth. We just need to know enough to keep our world from flying apart. If you are one who seeks out every truth, finish the book. If not be well satisfied with a sweet love story and close it.

Though they married, Aniel was not in love with Gwen. He was passionately in love with Gwendolyn, the young woman from his college years, but he lost her. He honored her wishes and took her ashes to the bygone camp, but decided to burn the book and mix their ashes and spread them on the cabin grounds. He took the promise ring back to the antique store. The clerk became puzzled when he wouldn't take any money and asked him why. He said, "Only the kiln can keep a promise."

We all have a double in this life. No one doubts it. Who hasn't been accused of being someone else, sometimes adamantly by an accuser, almost to the point of blows? Gwen saw Aniel's double on the beach.

You see, Gwen had many of Gwendolyn's traits from her blonde hair and those distinctive deep blue eyes with flecks of lavender, to the way she put her heels together and cocked her head, even some of her temperament, the sound of her voice, and that unmistakable laugh, bloodless twins. The only thing she couldn't reproduce was her scent and soul.

When a poet can't write he lists like an abandoned

ship, isolated, far out on blue water, and heels greatly to one side, appearing to cradle a deep wound. Down below, the silence from his empty space was maddening. He concluded that perhaps the absence of everything is truly the absence of nothing because an empty space is all we'll ever be.

His ship in irons, he was nudged towards the service, subconsciously, by the Sparer, while they were emotionally engaged out on the edge which they did many times after the loss of Gwendolyn. As a poet he felt it harbored something only the service could provide, the absence of love, and he felt compelled to dwell and examine it, though he lost his will to write, the poet hadn't lost his curiosity. He believed his miserable terrestrial life would be a bat of an eye, and then he and his beloved Gwendolyn would be bound together beyond forever, but he never expected to see his pen again.

He always felt God had unjustly punished him for reaching to the top tier which created a long-standing battle over conscience. But on that warm June evening when she walked into his hotel room with those deep blue eyes, that nudge he felt he believed was God's apology, which to him was far more than a blessing, the return of his pen, brought by the glow of a woman.

Henry Aniel Posey was now perfectly pleased to lay in his new field of lavender and blue iris and fragrance his thoughts with poetry again while keeping his promise. His ship now free from irons of the last twelve years was underway with the image of his Gwendolyn as the figurehead on his bow and well ballasted. He set sail on his inky sea.

As a man though, he gasped through a chokehold of guilt for his ruse until he saw the unfathomable joy she carried after the birth of their child. It was reduced to a mild constrictive band and manageable.

But as a poet, he witnessed a tragic woman who loved two men, but neither loved her. It crushed his kiln, but the idea impassioned his pen and he planned to leave behind reams for the world.

He was content with his duplicitous life but it wasn't until the birth of their child that the shrike returned for his deliverance. As he stared into little Henry's eyes, the wind in the reeds blew through his mind and with it a simple truth was rooted.

The poet had held him under an illusion. Love is a spirit he thought that resides in no one and cannot be possessed or promised to anyone beyond the grave.

His life now reckoned, he turned to a field of resplendent solitary stars, kissed Gwendolyn Marie Dupree goodbye, and found the courage to appear before the shrike he had fled since youth, and pluck that simple truth from its talon.

For love can be etched round a star.
So placed beyond the heavens can its spirit be.
But temporal do these things ring.
And yet, so still, a promise also rings.
Nor a promise or its eternity shall achieve the moment.

The man felt at peace. He conquered the self-absorbed poet and fell passionately in love with Gwendolyn Deja Dubois who felt her life with her family was si bon.